Cover Painting

"WHERE IT'S ALWAYS 1895"
Pencil sketch by Albert Earl Gilbert

Albert Earl Gilbert did this freehand copy at age 15. It is based on Robert Fawcett's color painting in Collier's Magazine in the 1950's on *The Exploits of Sherlock Holmes* by Adrian Conan Doyle and John Dickson Carr. Gilbert dedicates his pencil drawing to the memory of the great American illustrator, Robert Fawcett, who studied art at the Slade School in London.

Praise for the DD McGil Literati Mystery Series

The Conan Doyle Notes: The Secret of Jack theRipper

Honorable Mention, London Book Fair

"Diane Gilbert Madsen's "The Conan Doyle Notes: The Secret of Jack the Ripper" was the best book I've read in a long, long time. I was hooked by page six and couldn't stop reading. Spellbinding, intriguing and with a beguiling wit, Ms. Madsen delighted me to no end." - ***Catherine Lanigan, author, Romancing the Stone & The Jewel of the Nile & Love Shadows***

"Who was Jack the Ripper? Was Sir Arthur Conan Doyle protecting his identity? Conspiracies abound in this intelligent thriller that will make you think twice the next time you read a Sherlock Holmes' mystery." ***--Steve Alten, best-selling author of MEG & THE OMEGA PROJECT***

"The Conan Doyle Notes: The Secret of Jack the Ripper" should be considered a 'must read' by the legions of Conan Doyle fans and would be an enduringly popular addition to community library collections. ***–Midwest Book Review Volume 13, Number 7***

Hunting for Hemingway

Honorable Mention, New York Festival of Books

"Crime follows DD McGil almost as closely as eligible bachelors do. DD's dry wit and internal monologue go far... Another fast read with quirky characters and due reverence for the Second City." **—*Kirkus Reviews***

"The story is sexy and fun, a combination of not-too-gritty, hard-boiled detective novel and cozy mystery infused with neat little bits of Hemingway lore." **—*Booklist***

"Madsen includes local Chicago points of interest, technical details on crime scene investigation and copyright law, exciting chase scenes, and a cinematic climax." **- *Mystery Scene Magazine***

A Cadger's Curse

"Madsen's promising debut, the first in a new cozy series set in Chicago, introduces DD McGil, a 38-year-old freelance insurance investigator and former English professor who's a whiz at breaking and entering. Well-drawn characters and a suspenseful plot will leave readers looking forward to the next installment." **–*Publishers Weekly***

"Madsen's debut introduces enough mystery, enjoyable characters and literary tidbits (DD's a former English prof) to attract a wide audience for her planned series."
—*Kirkus Reviews*

Cracking the Code of the Canon:

How Sherlock Holmes Made His Decisions

OTHER WORKS BY DIANE GILBERT MADSEN

THE DD MCGIL LITERATI MYSTERY SERIES

A Cadger's Curse

Hunting for Hemingway

The Conan Doyle Notes: The Secret of Jack the Ripper

FORTHCOMING IN THE DD MCGIL LITERATI MYSTERY SERIES

A Cardboard Palace

Dark as Shadows

Restless Bones

SCREEN PLAY

Young Hemingway

STAGE PLAY

Sherlock Holmes and the Queen of Hearts

DIANE GILBERT MADSEN

CRACKING THE CODE OF THE CANON:

HOW SHERLOCK HOLMES MADE HIS DECISIONS

Paperback ISBN 978-1-78092-971-2
ePub ISBN 978-1-78092-972-9
PDF ISBN 978-1-78092-973-6

Published in the UK by MX Publishing
335 Princess Park Manor, Royal Drive, London, N11 3GX.
UK. www.mxpublishing.co.uk

Cover design by Brian Belanger, MX Publishing
Editing by: Simon Hetherington

Dedication

To the wonderful Tom, husband extraordinaire, the inspiration for this statistical analysis of the Holmes stories. Doing this was one of the really fun things in my life.

Acknowledgements

Heartfelt thanks to my friend across the pond, Sheriff Valerie Johnston, member of the Scottish Judiciary, for sharing her knowledge of British and Scottish law. Her kind assistance was invaluable in every chapter, and she never failed to extricate me from terminology dilemmas.

Special thanks to Mr. Simon Hetherington, Publisher of *Halsbury's Laws of England* from *2002-13*, and a Member of the Sherlock Holmes Society of London, for reviewing the chapter on the crimes of Holmes and Watson and providing valuable advice and editing.

Thanks to Mr. Martin Wishnatsky for sharing his interesting article entitled, *The Theology of Sherlock Holmes*, at http://goodmorals.org/doyle

"Lang may yer lum reek"
Olde Scottish Saying

"Live long and prosper"
Translation by Mr. Spock
of Star Trek

CRACKING THE CODE OF THE CANON: HOW SHERLOCK HOLMES MADE HIS DECISIONS

Table of Contents Page

Table of Contents — Page

FOREWORD

The genesis of this book came from research I did for my novel, *The Conan Doyle Notes: The Secret of Jack the Ripper.* The thesis of that book is that Sir Arthur Conan Doyle, together with Dr. Joseph Bell, discovered the identity of Jack the Ripper and having done so, decided not to reveal the identity to the public. Early on, I discussed the thesis of that book with a friend who strongly objected. His view was that Conan Doyle would never have kept this identity a secret. He cited Conan Doyle's well-known probity, using the example of Doyle's tombstone inscription, "Blade straight, steel true," to dispute that Doyle would have kept the identity a secret.

This was a serious objection, and I set out to resolve it. I used the theory that a novelist's core values and fundamental beliefs were inevitably revealed when examining the plots and protagonists of the novel. This theory seemed especially applicable since the Holmes adventures were written over a span of 40 years and the Canon itself is a substantial volume of work.

I reread the entire Canon – I have been a lifelong Sherlockian – and found many surprises. All of my previous readings had been for enjoyment or to analyze a single story. When I began to consider the entire Canon as a whole, I was struck by the diverse nature of the outcomes of the cases and how they were affected by Sherlock Holmes himself as he implemented his own brand of justice, and certain themes began to emerge.

- First, that Holmes let many criminals, including murderers, escape legal justice.
- Second, that Holmes considered himself to be outside of the law when investigating. He and Watson committed many criminal acts themselves and also felt free not to advise the authorities of their findings.
- And third, that discretion was one of the hallmarks of Holmes and Watson and that a problem was often far better resolved privately.

With my concerns on this matter resolved, I wrote my novel, *The Conan Doyle Notes*, which I hope you will enjoy along with the others in my DD McGil Literati Series of murder mysteries. As for all the research I did on the Canon, I've compiled it into this book you are now reading, and I want to thank my publisher, MX Publishing, for the early interest and encouragement in this project. I hope you will enjoy reading it as much as I did writing it. I think some of the conclusions may be eye-opening.

INTRODUCTION

My analysis led me to find that the outcomes of the 56 Sherlock Holmes short stories could be organized into five categories, as follows:

1. Category 1 – Cases with no legal crime

2. Category 2 – Cases wherein the Villian IS Brought to the Law

3. Category 3 – Cases wherein Villain is NOT Brought to the Law

4. Category 4 - Cases in which Holmes and/or Watson take the law into their own hands and commit crimes

5. Category 5 – Cases in which Sherlock Holmes is wrong

Chapters 1 through 3 examine what we really know about Sherlock Holmes, including his ideas of justice and how his personal ideas are firmly embedded in the Victorian and Edwardian eras with all of their complex spoken and unspoken rules.

Chapter 4 details which stories fit into each of the five categories and provides a brief statistical analysis of each category.

Chapters 5 through 9 review Category 1 through Category 5 stories in detail with discussions on various cases, villains, types of justice, and statistical analyses.

Chapter 10 profiles the crimes and the victims. Chapter 11 profiles the Holmesian villain and also compares both psychologically and physically the villains Holmes sends to the law to those he does not.

These chapters all provide an analysis of some Holmesian decisions on justice and consider questions such as whether revenge can ever be justified and the question of whether it is morally right to avenge past crimes.

Chapter 12 profiles victims. Chapter 13 looks at impersonations, aliases and disguises in the Canon, and Chapter 14 examines Watson as the fixed point in the Canon. An Afterword reveals Doyle's own favorite stories and what they have in common.

I hope you will be as interested in the information about Sherlock Holmes and his decision-making process as I was, and that you, too, will enjoy looking at an overview of cases in the 56 stories by category and see how each category of justice fits into the Canon.

Chapter 1

Who is Sherlock Holmes?

Sherlock Holmes is the "most portrayed literary human character in film & TV," according to the award given by the *Guinness Book of World Records*. When his name is mentioned, we picture him calling "the game is afoot," and urging Dr. Watson to bring his revolver along as they hail a hansom cab on the foggy streets of London, ready to right a wrong and catch a criminal.

Sherlock Holmes, consulting detective, fascinated the world when Conan Doyle's stories appeared. The "great brain" [i] of Sherlock Holmes amazed readers. They loved his idiosyncratic traits -- smart and quirky – and he knew God-knows-what about you before you ever opened your mouth. He was a man "whose knowledge was not that of other mortals." [ii] His remarkable attention to detail and analytical reasoning were far superior to those of the everyday man. His keen intelligence, superior powers of observation, incisive analytical prowess, wide ranging knowledge of ephemera and minutiae, and his love and pursuit of justice formed the basis of his famous "Method" -- the technique he employed to unravel a mystery, unmask a villain and solve a case. Dr. Watson notes, "There was something in his masterly grasp of a situation, and his keen, incisive reasoning, which made it a pleasure to me to study his system of work, and to follow the quick, subtle methods by which he disentangled the most inextricable mysteries." [iii]

Above all, he was a man of science – "an automaton" [iv] – a man who seemed more like a machine than a man -- a machine that considers logic, fact and cold hearted analysis instead of empathy, sympathy and accommodation. "I am a brain, Watson. The rest of me is a mere appendix." [v]

Holmes was the epitome of scientific rationalization. "He was ... the most perfect reasoning and observing machine the world has ever seen ... .[vi] He was a machine that never failed, according to Watson. "So accustomed was I to his invariable success that the very possibility of his failing had ceased to enter into my head." [vii]

Holmes the scientific man is someone special, someone unlike the average man. Holmes makes it clear to Watson and the reader that his rational, scientific approach doesn't approve of emotions, and his nature doesn't contain the stuff of romance nor does it invite casual friendship. He is highly self-disciplined, but his asceticism is not strictly austere or self-denying. The closest counterpart of a well-known character reflecting Holmes' austere, highly intelligent and aloof nature is perhaps Mr. Spock, the Vulcan alien in Star Trek played by Leonard Nimoy. Mr. Spock is the most famous character in that series, and he is loved and admired for his uniquely logical and unemotional take on everything in the universe.

In many ways Holmes is a man's man. In sports, Watson tells us that Holmes is "an expert singlestick player, boxer, and swordsman. [viii] But in *The Yellow Face,* we hear Watson clarify that, "Sherlock Holmes was a man who seldom took exercise for exercise's sake. Few men were capable of greater muscular effort, and he was undoubtedly one of the finest boxers of his weight that I have ever seen; but he looked upon aimless bodily exertion as a waste of energy, and he seldom bestirred himself save when there was some professional object to be served. Then he was absolutely untiring and indefatigable." We see him manifest his strength and exertion for professional reasons in *Black Peter* when, in Allardyce's back shop, he furiously tried to stab a dead pig with one blow of a harpoon.

Of women, Holmes is wary, and he makes no secret of it. "I am not a whole-souled admirer of womankind," he admits in *The Valley of Fear*. In *Sign of the Four*, he suggests, "Women are never to be entirely trusted – not the best of them." He tells Watson in *The Second Stain* that, "the motives of women are inscrutable;" and "Watson, the fair sex is your department." The closest Holmes comes to having a romantic relationship with someone of the opposite sex is in *Charles Augustus Milverton,* when he becomes engaged to Agatha, Milverton's housemaid. He admits to Watson that the engagement is not for romantic reasons but rather to obtain information to burgle Milverton's house. We tend to think of Holmes as celibate, so the nature of their courtship provides interest for our speculation.

The Holmes we get to know in the Canon seems dispassionate and cold - arrogant and dominated by his extraordinary logic and reasoning powers. While he may have keen emotions, readers get only rare glimpses of his affections, empathy and sympathy, such as in *The Three Garridebs* when he reacts emotionally to Watson getting shot. Watson tells us, "It was worth a wound; it was worth many wounds; to know the depth of loyalty and love which lay behind that cold mask."

Throughout the Canon, Sherlock Holmes carries one true passion– a deep love of justice. It is this pursuit of justice that impels Holmes in his profession as consulting detective and makes him a hero. In *The Three Garridebs,* he asserts, "I am not the law, but I represent justice so far as my feeble powers go." And in *The Crooked Man,* he says, "It is every man's business to see justice done."

To most people, bringing a criminal to justice involves the law. The wrongdoer is arrested by the police, brought to trial, and subsequently suffers the punishment in consequence of the criminal act. For Holmes, sometimes justice could be something different from the law. He notes in *The Adventure of the Red Circle*: "The law is what we live with. Justice is sometimes harder to achieve." He does indeed bring criminals to justice, but it is through his own brand of justice which, in a surprising number of cases, does not involve handing over the criminal to the law. As such, if justice is not simply turning a malefactor over to the law, how does Holmes define and decide justice? What is his moral code? What are his ethical principles? Further, does Sherlock Holmes follow his own precepts? Is he consistent in the application of his principles of justice? What, if any, extenuating circumstances does he take into consideration?

Holmes is always confident in his own abilities to mete out justice, just as he is confident in his own intelligence. He tells us in *The Five Orange Pips*: "I shall be my own police," and "I am the last court of appeal." Readers accept the Sherlock Holmes brand of justice in the stories. An examination of the 56 short stories in the Canon will help us uncover what constitutes that brand of justice. What are the underlying principles Sherlock Holmes uses as the foundation for his idea of justice? What is the underlying decision-making process that Holmes uses to mete out justice to wrong-doers in the canon?

Chapter 2

The Sherlock Holmes Brand of Justice

"But there was something in the ice-cold reasoning of Holmes which made it impossible to shrink from any adventure which he might recommend. One knew that thus, and only thus, could a solution be found. I clasped his hand in silence, and the die was cast."
-Watson, *Wisteria Lodge*

English law has its roots in Common Law, a generally agreed upon set of crimes and torts and the penalties incurred for violating these rules. As the justice system evolved, these laws were codified and written procedures for enforcing and judging crimes were enacted. The Holmesian perception of justice seems to owe a great deal more to the flexibility of Common Law than it does to the codified procedures which, if followed without reason, can result in grave injustice. The central foundation on which Holmes bases his brand of individual justice is the Victorian code of ethics. This code is a complicated, sometimes contradictory and complex set of governing principles based upon many unwritten and unspoken rules reflecting behavioral standards and ideals that evolved over time and constitute the fabric of correct social interactions. The application of these rules is distinctly English in character. Unwritten, they depend on their acceptance and enforcement by society in general. They have the effect and force of law in Victorian society, even though the government never formally enacted them.

The Code reflected the class system in Britain. The rules were slightly different for each class – lower, middle and aristocrat – and they were the strictest and the most codified for the upper class aristocrats. By the time Sherlock Holmes came on the scene, the middle class was growing in size and influence, and the Code of Honor was applying more rigorously to them as well. Throughout the Canon, there's a mix of all classes. Sometimes aristocrats are the criminals and sometimes the lower classes help to solve the crimes. Royalty and illustrious clients ask Holmes to take their cases. But he's also approached by many middle class persons, such as Violet Hunter in *The Copper Beeches*; Violet Smith in *The Solitary Cyclist*; Mary Sutherland in *A Case of Identity*; the landlady Mrs. Merrilow, in *The Veiled Lodger*; and Victor Hatherley in *The Engineer's Thumb*, to name a few.
For Holmes - as for most Victorians - living by this Code meant strictly obeying the unspoken, unwritten laws that governed not only society, but also governed business, politics, sports, and indeed all activities of daily life. The Code set down the ground rules of Fair Play. It was the Code – a complex evolution of common law - that defined what was cricket and what wasn't.

The unwritten rules expected women to be respectable, moral and virtuous. The Code dictated almost everything from how a woman should look, what she should wear, how she should behave, and what she could and couldn't say. Women were considered fragile, and the Code dictated that a gentleman must exercise sexual restraint and treat women with the chivalry of the medieval knight. A gentleman must maintain self-control, be responsible, have integrity and be discreet. The code dictated that the Captain is the last to leave a sinking ship; women and children first; never talk about money; and above all, a gentleman must not cheat. With prostitution, gentlemen's clubs, gambling and other crime flourishing in Victorian England, it is obvious people were hypocritical.

Sherlock Holmes himself, however, is always perceived as a straight shooter – one who acknowledges and follows this Victorian code of conduct – one who is in fact an embodiment of it. "My business is that of every other good citizen -- to uphold the law," he tells us in *Shoscombe Old Place*. Readers believe he is a good citizen and take his character to be honorable, upright and correct. Readers rely upon the "rightness" of his moral compass and worldview. "Watson, you are a British jury, and I never met a man who was more eminently fitted to represent one," Holmes remarks in *Abbey Grange*. He and Watson are painted as true Victorians, and we need to examine the Victorian code of ethics and honor closely to understand it clearly and to see how it is embodied in Holmes' decision making process.

In the Canon there are times when Holmes assumes the role of judge and pronounces his own brand of justice on the criminal. Even in these cases, the Unwritten Laws and the Victorian Code of Ethics play a prominent role.

Chapter 3

Holmes and Watson and the Written and Unwritten Victorian Codes

"They have, for example, their insular conventions which simply MUST be observed."
- Baron Von Herling, His Last Bow

When we think of Sherlock Holmes and Dr. Watson, they are living perpetually in the Victorian England of 1895. They reflect that particular time and place, its culture and its sensibilities. It's important for modern readers to keep this in mind because, as we read the Canon, our own 21st century sensibilities must be suspended.

The Sherlock Holmes stories spanned 40 years beginning with a novel, *A Study in Scarlet*, published in 1887 and ending with *Shoscombe Old Place*, published in 1927. More than half of this 40 years – 27 to be exact - are in the new century, but all the later stories except one remain set in the midst of the late Victorian and the Edwardian Age through 1910. The one that is set later is *His Last Bow*, which was published in 1917 and set in 1914 on the eve of the Great War. In this tale, Holmes is 60 years old. In *The Creeping Man*, published in 1923 and set in 1903, we are told that this is "one of the very last cases handled by Holmes before his retirement from practice."

All the stories are so firmly rooted in this time period because they employ heroes, villains, women, crimes, beliefs, newspapers, scenes, modes of transport, language and characteristic customs of the late Victorian way of life. Victorians lived, worked and thought in a world very different from that of the early 1920's and still more different from the 21st century. Their social, religious and political loyalties might seem alien to us today. During the Victorian era, everyone belonged to a certain class, and everyone was sensitive to certain manners and mores. In order to understand the essence of the era, we must be sensitive to these differences in attitudes, behaviors and beliefs and realize that the norms of today did not apply in 1895.

It was 1837 when Queen Victoria ascended the throne at age 18. The first British stamp was issued for Victoria's coronation. She reigned over a country that, like America, was still in the age of the horse and buggy, largely illiterate and mainly agricultural. It was a very class driven society where you were in one of several classes and there you stayed for the rest of your life.

In America in 1837, Martin Van Buren had just become the 8th President; the government was still fighting Indian tribes; Michigan had just become the 26th state; Chicago was newly incorporated as a city; and the American Civil War was still almost a quarter century in the future.

During Victoria's 63 year reign, the scientific revolution grew and fostered incredibly rapid changes with telegraphs, railroads, electric lights, sewers, compulsory elementary schooling, industrialization, printing, typewriters, cameras, automobiles, and the explosive growth of the middle class. By the time of her Diamond Jubilee in 1897, crowds celebrated the success and expansion of the Empire. With the huge population shift from agricultural to industrial, now over 81% of the population lived in towns and cities instead of the country. These massive transformations required new rules for proper behavior, and those new rules made up the Victorian Code of Ethics and the many Unspoken Rules that derived from accepted custom and habit.

The Victorian code of new rules was stricter, according to Brett and Kate McKay in their essay, "Manly Honor: Part III – The Victorian Era and the Development of the Stoic-Christian Code of Honor." [ix] This "reformation of manners," stressed "the importance of morality, particularly chastity, piety, and charity towards others. Nostalgia for the idealized chivalry of medieval knights inspired respect for women, while adherence to ancient Stoic philosophy put a premium on self-sufficiency, self-control, and unflappable reserve – the famous British 'stiff upper lip.'"

The Victorian code of honor for the upper class was based on heritage, lineage and what they held as a divine right to rule and maintain their wealth. Above all, they abhorred scandal and the consequent disgrace for themselves and their families. They viewed themselves as father figures in society, with their first born sons carrying on their rights of inheritance.

As for the burgeoning middle class, it prized "sincerity and earnestness," and spurned "vanity, frivolity and foppishness." It emphasized heavily the "virtues connected with economic success – those that could help working and middle class men rise in the world: initiative, pluck, ingenuity, independence and personal responsibility (going into debt was shameful), ambition, thrift, punctuality, orderliness, cleanliness, patience, dependability, and most of all hard work." [x] A common thread in all classes was the fear of scandal and disgrace, and people would do anything to avoid it. In T*he Musgrave Ritual,* Brunton is horrified at losing his position as butler, much as James Ryder is in *The Blue Carbuncle* at the prospect of being exposed as a thief, and Neville St. Clair at the revelation of his double life as a beggar in *The Man with the Twisted Lip*, and Gilchrist at being uncovered for trying to cheat in *The Three Students*. Sometimes people became criminals when faced with a scandal and shame.

However, English gentlemen or gentlewomen must never involve themselves in crime. When it does happen, it surprises and shocks Sherlock Holmes. In *The Bruce Partington Plans,* when Colonel Valentine Walter, a perfect English gentleman on the outside, is exposed for his part in stealing secret documents, Holmes remarks: "How an English gentleman could behave in such a manner is beyond my comprehension." Holmes says much the same to young Gilchrist in *The Three Students*: "We want to know, Mr. Gilchrist, how you, an honourable man, ever came to commit such an action as that of yesterday?"

Although Holmes and Watson themselves embody many of these Victorian virtues, Holmes has his behavioral peccadilloes. He isn't always neat and tidy – except for the furniture in his attic - and he never throws away anything. He isn't patient, especially with stupidity. But he is never crass – he doesn't like to talk about money and frequently chooses his cases for other reasons. Watson tells us in *Black Peter* that, "I have seldom known him claim any large reward for his inestimable services. So unworldly was he – or so capricious – that he frequently refused his help to the powerful and wealthy where the problem made no appeal to his sympathies." Holmes managed to avoid the public eye for much of his career. "Notoriety (was) hateful to him." [xi]

Holmes and Watson are also very patriotic. Like most Victorians, they are royalists, proud of their Queen and realm. In *The Musgrave Ritual,* Watson informs us that "Holmes, in one of his queer humors," sat in an armchair and proceeded "to adorn the opposite wall with a patriotic V.R. done in bullet-pocks." And in *The Bruce Partington Plans* we learn how Holmes cherishes an emerald tie-pin, a gift from the Queen.

Queen Victoria took pains to ensure her children and grandchildren married other European rulers, closely linking British royalty to the continent. Being a royalist, it is not surprising that Holmes was also involved in cases in which he assisted foreign royal families and was presented with exotic rewards. In *A Case of Identity*, he uses "a snuff-box of old gold with an amethyst in the center of the lid," a gift from the King of Bohemia, and he also wears a "remarkable brilliant" ring that "sparkled upon his finger," a gift from the reigning family of Holland for actions in a case too sensitive for Holmes to mention, even to Watson. Other royal households he served were the King of Sardinia, mentioned in *Noble Bachelor*; and the Sultan of Turkey, mentioned in *Blanched Soldier*. Holmes also served the Pope in "the famous investigation of the sudden death of Cardinal Tosca," mentioned in *Black Peter*.

One other important aspect of the Code was that scandal must be avoided at all costs. Like all good Victorians, Holmes and Watson hated scandal. "A day which has saved England from a great public scandal," said banker Alexander Holder approvingly in *The Beryl Coronet*. In *The Creeping Man*, Trevor Bennett warns Holmes and Watson that Professor Presbury must be protected from scandal, even above consideration of the Professor's health. Bennett says, "At present the scandal is confined to our own household. It is safe with us. If it gets beyond these walls it will never stop. Consider his position at the university, his European reputation, the feelings of his daughter." "Quite so, said Holmes." And in *The Three Students*, Soames, the University tutor, tells Holmes, "When once the law is evoked it cannot be stayed again, and this is just one of those cases where, for the credit of the college, it is most essential to avoid scandal. Your discretion is as well known as your powers, and you are the one man in the world who can help me."

At the beginning of *The Adventure of the Veiled Lodger*, Watson explains the important part discretion plays in all the adventures and how much significance Holmes attaches to being discreet. "There is the long row of year-books which fill a shelf and there are the dispatch-cases filled with documents, a perfect quarry for the student not only of crime but of the social and official scandals of the late Victorian era. Concerning these latter, I may say that the writers of agonized letters, who beg that the honour of their families or the reputation of famous forebears may not be touched, have nothing to fear. The discretion and high sense of professional honour which have always distinguished my friend are still at work in the choice of these memoirs, and no confidence will be abused." In *The Adventure of the Noble Bachelor*, Lord Robert St. Simon writes to Holmes, "Lord Backwater tells me that I may place implicit reliance upon your judgement and discretion." And Watson reveals in *The Naval Treaty* that: "To my certain knowledge (Holmes) has acted on behalf of three of the reigning houses of Europe in very vital matters." Holmes surely wouldn't have gotten many of his cases were it not for his reputation for being discreet.

Watson, too, must ever be discreet. In *The Devil's Foot*, Watson says, "My participation in some of his adventures was always a privilege which entailed discretion and reticence upon me." In *The Creeping Man* when Trevor Bennett questions Watson's presence, Holmes says: "Have no fear, Mr. Bennett. Dr. Watson is the very soul of discretion." And Watson himself assures us in *Thor Bridge*, that among the notes in his tin dispatch box, "there are some which involve the secrets of private families to an extent which would mean consternation in many exalted quarters if it were thought possible that they might find their way into print. I need not say that such a breach of confidence is unthinkable ... ."

Discretion is one paramount factor Holmes uses in his evaluation of justice, and it often makes him willing to bend the strict application of British law to accommodate the Victorian requirement to keep secrets he's learned in the course of his detection. It is why he sometimes withholds information from the police in a case – information that might create a scandal and compromise or ruin individuals, families or governments. It explains many of the actions he takes independently of the police and the courts.

Holmes values his privacy in equal measure. Watson explains in *The Devil's Foot* how much Holmes hates publicity: "In recording from time to time some of the curious experiences and interesting recollections which I associate with my long and intimate friendship with Mr. Sherlock Holmes, I have continually been faced by difficulties caused by his own aversion to publicity." This is in conformance with the rule that no good Victorian gentleman would seek to have his name in the papers. Women were supposed to have their names mentioned in the paper only with their birth, marriage and death announcements. This Victorian respect for privacy is one more touchstone that Holmes regularly includes in his tool kit to evaluate his brand of justice in a given circumstance.

There were good reasons why so many rules for proper behavior in the Victorian world existed and were strictly enforced. If you knew and followed all these rules, you were virtually guaranteed acceptance by your peers. If you stepped outside the rules and got caught, you risked being snubbed by your peers. Discretion was one of the unwritten laws that made it possible for a Victorian to maintain respectability and keep a place in one's class. The very fact that many of the rules governing propriety of behavior were unwritten and possibly contradictory served as an obstacle to keep members of a lower social class from entering into a class above their own. There were rules of behavior and manners in abundance that one had to follow to lay claim to respectability, and the rules you followed identified you as part of the class. Deviations, even if inadvertent, were punished by ostracism from the class. Extensive manuals on etiquette were written to codify what one needed to know about any situation that could arise -- from table manners, to dinner parties, calling cards and visiting, conversation, shopping, mourning and traveling. If one knew them all, and if one also had an opportunity for economic upward mobility, then one could aspire to be a gentleman - even if not by birth. However, nonconformance with the rules and their nuances meant being an outcast. Despite the widespread pretense and hypocrisy over these Victorian rules, the appearance of being a gentleman – the appearance of respectability - was everything.

The code of behavior and the nuanced unwritten laws were frequently anathema to foreign characters in the canon who found it difficult to conform to proper behavior. In the canon, a number of foreigners are directly or by inference mentioned as different because they don't conform or behave like the British. One example is Mrs. Ferguson, the Peruvian wife in *The Sussex Vampire*. Her husband tells Holmes: "...the fact of her foreign birth and of her alien religion always caused a separation of interests and of feelings between husband and wife, so that after a time (I) may have cooled towards her.... there were sides of her character which (I) could never explore or understand."

Another example is Maria Pinto Gibson in *Thor Bridge* who is "a creature of the tropics a Brazilian by birth." Her husband describes her as having "a deep rich nature ... passionate, whole hearted, tropical, ill balanced, very different from the American women whom I had known." And in *The Second Stain*, Mme. Fournaye, who stabs her husband to death, is described as being of Creole origin and of an extremely excitable nature who has suffered in the past from attacks of jealousy which have amounted to frenzy. These non-British foreigners have fundamentally different natures that are volatile and connected to the hot climates of their birth, and Sherlock Holmes is quick to recognize these differences.

In *Wisteria Lodge*, there are two tenants who are foreigners. One is Don Murillo, known as the Tiger of San Pedro, described as "a fierce, masterful man, with a red-hot spirit behind his parchment face. He is either a foreigner or has lived long in the tropics, for he is yellow and sapless, but tough as a whipcord. His friend and secretary, Mr. Lucas, is undoubtedly a foreigner, chocolate brown, wily, suave and cat-like with a poisonous gentleness of speech." They are both given foreign traits - "red-hot spirit" and "wily, suave and cat-like." These descriptions do not fit the mould of Victorian Englishmen, and therefore in the stories we cannot expect them to act like Victorian Englishmen. They don't follow the code.

One foreigner in the stories is not from a hot clime but is an American. The California heiress, Miss Hatty Doran, only daughter of the wealthy Aloysius Doran, Esq., also behaves in a most un-British fashion in *The Noble Bachelor*. She deserts her bridegroom, Lord St. Simon, immediately following the wedding ceremony and before the wedding breakfast. She also, according to her new husband, has a maid who takes great liberties in her behavior. Lord St. Simon doesn't want a scandal, but he acknowledges to Holmes, "Still, of course, in America they look upon these things in a different way." In this story, it isn't the hot climate but rather the general tenor of Americans – their notions of freedom – freedom from the Victorian class system and its strict rules and regulations – that make them different from the British.

Foreign characters in the stories also have difficulty in understanding or predicting the behavior of an English gentleman. For example, Baron Von Herling and Mr. Von Bork, two German agents for the Kaiser who appear in *His Last Bow,* have this revealing conversation about their preconceptions of the English:

"They are not very hard to deceive," (Von Bork) remarked. "A more docile, simple folk could not be imagined."

"I don't know about that," said (Baron Von Herling) thoughtfully. "They have strange limits and one must learn to observe them. It is that surface simplicity of theirs which makes a trap for the stranger. One's first impression is that they are entirely soft. Then one comes suddenly upon something very hard, and you know that you have reached the limit and must adapt yourself to the fact. They have, for example, their insular conventions which simply MUST be observed."

"Meaning 'good form' and that sort of thing?" Von Bork sighed as one who had suffered much.

"Meaning British prejudice in all its queer manifestations. As an example I may quote one of my own worst blunders--I can afford to talk of my blunders, for you know my work well enough to be aware of my successes. It was on my first arrival. I was invited to a week-end gathering at the country house of a cabinet minister. The conversation was amazingly indiscreet."

Von Bork nodded. "I've been there," said he dryly.

"Exactly. Well, I naturally sent a resume of the information to Berlin. Unfortunately our good chancellor is a little heavy-handed in these matters, and he transmitted a remark which showed that he was aware of what had been said. This, of course, took the trail straight up to me. You've no idea the harm that it did me. There was nothing soft about our British hosts on that occasion, I can assure you. I was two years living it down."

Within their strict code of ethics, Victorians lived in a tightly controlled circle behind closed doors. Their solutions to problems were not the ones we might endorse today. The Sherlock Holmes truth was a Victorian truth. Sherlock Holmes, Dr. Watson and the average Victorian would tolerate an action outside the code if it was done by a gentleman in the service of a noble cause, such as avoiding scandal, protecting the realm, or preserving a woman's safety or reputation. The danger in such an action was trying to predict whether it would be perceived as such a noble cause or simply as unacceptable. With one you were forgiven and even received accolades, but with the other you were ruined. With such a high and unpredictable bar, the tendency was to not get involved or, if involved, to conceal such involvement to lessen the possibility of uncertain consequences. Both of these outcomes fostered the need and desirability of discretion – keeping your business and actions private. If it is judged that you should have taken action, but did not, you could be ruined. However, if you did take action which was judged unacceptable, you were also ruined. Best to avoid judgement and publicity.

Our current culture is completely different, and our century is the opposite of the Victorian era. Today, nobody is discreet. Our culture views Victorian mores as old-fashioned and outdated. Today we demand total transparency. Everybody must know everything. We thrive on the 24/7 news cycle. People want to know it ALL; and they want to know it NOW. The 21st century man desires publicity and will seek the status of victimhood to achieve notoriety. Our culture embraces Facebook, Twitter, Instagram, Snap Chat, Selfies and Reality TV where intimate revelations about one's personal life are freely shared for the public to peruse. Everybody wants to be famous – or at least be in the news and in the know.

The Victorians embodied the antithesis of this view. They valued order, tradition, privacy, stability and discretion over transparency. They feared public scandal. In *The Priory School,* the Duke of Holdernesse "was extremely desirous to avoid all public scandal. He was afraid of his family unhappiness being dragged before the world. He has a deep horror of anything of the kind." In the end, he begs Holmes to consider "how far we can minimize this hideous scandal." This view is reflected again and again in the stories. It is this attitude and the entire Victorian Code of Ethics – the fair playing field – that constitute Sherlock Holmes' underlying decision-making process in all facets of life – but especially so in rendering Sherlockian "justice."

Although there are sixteen (29%) of the 56 Sherlock Holmes stories that were published after 1910, the end of the Edwardian era, they are all set in the earlier Victorian and Edwardian eras except for one, *His Last Bow,* which is set in 1914 at the beginning of World War I. These stories include:

The Adventure of the Red Circle - 1911
The Disappearance of Lady Frances Carfax - 1911
The Adventure of the Dying Detective - 1913
His Last Bow - 1917
The Adventure of the Mazarin Stone - 1921
The Problem of Thor Bridge - 1922
The Adventure of the Creeping Man - 1923
The Adventure of the Illustrious Client - 1924
The Adventure of the Sussex Vampire - 1924
The Adventure of the Three Garridebs - 1924
The Adventure of the Blanched Soldier - 1926
The Adventure of the Three Gables - 1926
The Adventure of the Retired Colourman - 1926
The Adventure of the Lion's Mane - 1926
The Adventure of the Veiled Lodger - 1927
The Adventure of Shoscombe Old Place - 1927

Twelve of these stories (22%) were written in the 1920's, but not one is set in the twenties. These later stories contain no references to flappers or to the gangs that developed in the twenties after the war. There are no women working in factories during the war years or soldiers in the trenches during WW I either. All these elements were signals of the vast changes and the upheaval in society and in the unwritten laws that were taking place during the twenties. None of these elements could play a part in the hansom cab, fog laden, gas lamp world in which Sherlock Holmes operated and which had become iconic and which readers had come to expect. We firmly remain in the Victorian and Edwardian eras to the last, except for *His Last Bow*.

The pioneering spirit of the Victorian age gave rise to many new scientific discoveries, and Sherlock Holmes employs many of them to help solve cases. In fact, he often utilizes some of these new techniques before they have been formally adopted by Scotland Yard. He makes use of fingerprints in *The Sign of the Four*, published in 1890; yet it wasn't until 10 years later in 1901 that Scotland Yard began using them. Fingerprints are also used in another six stories throughout the Canon, including *The Man with the Twisted Lip* (1891), *The Cardboard Box* (1893), *The Norwood Builder* (1903), *The Three Students* (1904), *The Red Circle* (1911), and *The Three Gables* (1926).

Other new forensic tools Holmes uses include typewriters, handwriting analysis, a test for bloodstains, phrenology and atavism, the use of bloodhounds, and the telegraph. Holmes is truly a forensic crime scene pioneer. In *A Case of Identity* he remarks, "It is a curious thing that a typewriter has really quite as much individuality as a man's handwriting." Then he reveals he is thinking of writing a monograph on the typewriter and its relation to crime. In *The Missing Three-Quarter*, he tells us he's going to write one about the use of dogs in detective work.

He brings his keen observations and vast knowledge to every crime scene to examine footprints, wineglasses, bicycle tires, rope bell pulls, bloodstains, spectacles, cigar ash, and horse and cattle tracks, and he uses this vast array of knowledge to outwit the criminals and best Scotland Yard.

Both Holmes and Watson also deal with various poisons throughout the canon, from strychnine in the first two novels - *A Study in Scarlet* and *The Sign of the Four* - down to later works including curare in *The Sussex Vampire* and Cyanea in *The Lion's Mane.* Several murder cases of the time, especially the sensational Palmer case, involved poisons, and undoubtedly Holmes and Dr. Watson were familiar with these cases that had fueled great interest in the Victorian populace.

Religion was also a fundamental underpinning of the Victorian era, and the 56 stories contain many references that reflect the Victorian worldview on religion. Although Holmes is the great rationalist throughout the Canon, he manages to use religious references to support his overall philosophy of right and wrong and good and evil. Religious touchstones such as heaven and hell, evil, confession, forgiveness and redemption connect him to the other characters. Holmes is never a very demonstrative person, and in the instances where religion is referenced, he becomes more emotional and sympathetic, and we feel he is capable of feeling sorrow, regret, and joy. There is a dichotomy Holmes exhibits between religion and rationalism in the Canon. Yes, Holmes investigates and solves cases based on rationalism, but because religion played such a fundamental part in the Victorian concepts of order, behavior and justice as underpinnings of society, Holmes also includes it as a touchstone to evaluate both victims and wrongdoers and to mete out punishment or redemption.

Holmes himself makes many references to God, and he believes in sin. In *The Illustrious Client*, Homes refers to both: "The wages of sin, Watson -- the wages of sin! ... Sooner or later it will always come. God knows, there was sin enough." And in *The Beryl Coronet,* when Mary Sullivan escapes, Holmes tells Watson, "whatever her sins are, they will soon receive a more than sufficient punishment."

The religious element of life and of crime detection appears significantly in the very first short story, *A Scandal in Bohemia*. Here Holmes is disguised as a groom and witnesses Irene Adler's marriage at the Church of St. Monica in the Edgeware Road. This is a religious wedding performed by a clergyman, and it changes Irene Adler's status from mistress of the King of Bohemia – a sinner – to wife of Godfrey Norton – an honest, respectable woman. In this story, justice for Irene comes not from the law, but from the heavens when she is married, with Holmes as witness, and she then drops her blackmail attempt. Irene's act of religious marriage is her redemption, and it gives Holmes the right to call her "The Woman." Irene Adler's religious wedding stands in stark contrast to the attempt by Williamson, an unfrocked clergyman, to marry an unwilling Violet Smith to Woodley in *The Solitary Cyclist.*

Throughout the Canon references to religion frequently appear, illustrating Holmes' sense of right and wrong and his search for true justice, a justice that is not necessarily the same as legal justice. In *The Blue Carbuncle*, significantly set at Christmas time, Holmes talks about "saving a soul." In this story, the jewel thief, James Ryder, gets down on his knees, begs for mercy, and invokes Christ, as a penitent does in church. “Ryder threw himself down suddenly upon the rug and clutched at my companion's knees. "For God's sake, have mercy! ... Think of my father! of my mother! It would break their hearts. I never went wrong before! I never will again. I swear it. I'll swear it on a Bible. Oh, don't bring it into court! For Christ's sake, don't.” And the story ends with Holmes forgiving Ryder after he confesses and expresses remorse, just as Christians hope Christ will forgive them, especially at Christmastime, which, Holmes reminds us, is “the season of forgiveness.”

Holmes mentions the soul again in *The Sussex Vampire* when he talks about the boy Jacky: “His very soul is consumed with hatred for this splendid child.” And Watson mentions the soul in *The Retired Colourman*: “In a flash we got a glimpse of the real Josiah Amberley, a misshapen demon with a soul as distorted as his body.” Holmes refers again to the soul when he twice borrows from Luke 21:19, “Let us possess our souls in patience,” in *The Valley of Fear*, and “Well, we can only possess our souls in patience,” in *Wisteria Lodge*.

Holmes even believes in miracles. He mentions one in connection with his escape from Reichenbach Falls *in The Final Problem*: “I slipped, but by the blessing of God I landed, torn and bleeding, upon the path.”

The murderer in *The Boscombe Valley Mystery* was being blackmailed, and he tells Holmes, “God keep you out of the clutches of such a man as he.” Holmes sympathizes, and after the murderer confesses, he agrees to let him die peacefully, saying: “God help us! Why does Fate play such tricks with poor helpless worms? I never hear of such a case as this that I do not think of Baxter's words, and say, 'There, but for the grace of God, goes Sherlock Holmes.' "

At the conclusion of *The Crooked Man*, Watson asks Holmes about the word 'David" - a clue that refers to a Bible verse. In *The Three Gables,* he references Isaiah, 36:6 "Thou trustest in the staff of this broken reed," when he feels that Mrs. Maberley's attorney, Sutro, has failed to take care of her. He says to Watson: 'This fellow has clearly proved a broken reed."

And in one of the last stories, *The Veiled Lodger,* Eugenia Ronder sends for Holmes, much like she might send for a clergyman, to confess her old sins before she dies. She tells Holmes and Watson that after her marriage to her brutish husband, she "was in hell, and he the devil who tormented me." She describes her lover, Leonardo as "like the angel Gabriel." Holmes is moved by her story and cites heaven as her consolation: "The ways of fate are indeed hard to understand. If there is not some compensation hereafter, then the world is a cruel jest." He also ponders religion and the afterlife in *The Cardboard Box.* After catching the man responsible for a double murder, Holmes hears his confession and questions the meaning of life and death. "What object is served by this circle of misery and violence and fear? It must tend to some end, or else our universe is ruled by chance, which is unthinkable."

Many different religions and church figures are referenced in the stories, and in *The Veiled Lodger,* Watson describes Holmes as "some strange Buddha, with crossed legs."

Throughout the Canon, Holmes offers forgiveness or redemption to wrongdoers as if he himself was a clergyman. It is requisite that his villains confess and feel remorse for their misdeeds, just as in church a penitent must confess and repent to find forgiveness and redemption. When a wrongdoer refuses to cooperate, like Count Sylvius in *The Mazarin Stone*, Holmes turns him over to the law for punishment. In the cases of James Wilder in *The Priory School* and young Jacky Ferguson in *The Sussex Vampire*, the confessions don't come to Holmes first hand and may be somewhat questionable, so Holmes relies on the parents to provide a path for redemption for the wrongdoers.

Holmes' view of religion however has no room for the supernatural, as in *The Devil's Foot* and *The Sussex Vampire*. In *Sussex*, he exclaims: "Rubbish, Watson, rubbish," and he equates the supernatural with a belief only a child might hold: "we seem to have been switched on to a Grimms' fairy tale." He also rejects the voodoo practices in *Wisteria Lodge*.

In *The Three Garridebs*, Sherlock Holmes demonstrates directly how religion influences his precepts on justice. After Killer Evans fires two shots and hits Watson in the thigh, Holmes tells Evans: "By the Lord, it is as well for you. If you had killed Watson, you would not have got out of this room alive." His remarks touch on two separate elements in the Holmesian concept of justice. The first is that Holmes is ready to avenge Watson's death by committing the crime of murder. Holmes clearly believes in revenge and vengeance. This is important because in the Christian concept, the Bible says otherwise. Romans 12:19 states: "Vengeance is mine;

I will repay, saith the Lord;" and in Deuteronomy 32:35: "To me belongeth vengeance, and recompense; their foot shall slide in due time: for the day of their calamity is at hand, and the things that shall come upon them make haste." But in his overall scheme of justice, Holmes takes this prerogative onto himself and acts here as *locus standi* for God. Secondly, as in many cases of revenge, the second crime done for revenge is often worse than the first crime, as in *The Boscombe Valley Mystery* where a murder is committed to revenge blackmail. Murder - the worst of all crimes - is done in this case to stop blackmail, a far lesser crime. The murderer is already dying, and Holmes takes pity and lets him die outside of prison. Why? It is worth remembering that in Victorian times, blackmail was regarded as a particularly nasty crime. It's no accident that Charles Augustus Milverton is referred to as 'the worst man in London' and described in such a way as to cause repulsion. So in this case, Holmes plays judge and jury and agrees to keep family secrets – secrets that could shatter the future for his client, the murderer's daughter, if they are revealed. Discretion and privacy are always factors in his judgments.

In assuming the prerogative of judge and jury, Sherlock Holmes believes his judgement is the best because his method "is founded upon the observation of trifles." Unlike the law, which does not bother with the small, trivial things - *de minimis non-curat lex* - his detection and analysis of the crimes and the criminal take into account the smallest details. It is these details, as opposed to the sole application of the law, that affect real justice. And Holmes always seeks to render real justice.

Holmes evaluates each crime by considering not only the Victorian Code, but also by considering the character of both the criminal and the victim. The following chapters examine what constitutes Holmesian justice in the stories along with what Holmes considers to be extenuating circumstances in the nature of the wrongdoers or the nature of the crimes or the victims, and even perhaps in the nature of the seasons.

Chapter 4

Overview of Categories of the 56 Stories Based on Holmesian Justice

In the categorical analyses, only the 56 short stories are being used. The novels, with their longer and more complex plot lines, can also be fitted into these categories, but comparing the short stories to each other, apple to apple, provides a more straight line relationship to the categories. Even in the short stories, there may be more than one crime and more than one wrongdoer in the plot line. Therefore a story may fall into more than one category based on how the villains are treated.

The events within the 56 short stories can be classified into 5 categories of Holmesian justice as follows:

1. Cases in which no crime is committed
2. Cases in which the villain IS turned over to the law for justice
3. Cases in which Holmes does NOT turn the villain to the law for justice

3 A. Cases in which Holmes dispenses his own brand of justice

3 B. Cases in which the villain escapes

3 B 1 – Escapes and is never again heard from

3 B 2 – Escapes and later meets justice from above

3 C. Cases in which the fates deal justice from the heavens

4. Cases in which Sherlock Holmes and/or Dr. Watson take the law into their own hands and commit crimes; and Cases in which Sherlock Holmes was wrong.

A brief statistical analysis of the cases in each of these five categories and a listing of the stories included by category will be provided. Each category will then be analyzed more extensively in a later chapter. Again, it should be noted that a story may appear in more than one category in order to cover how Holmes deals with wrongdoers when he has more than one in a given story.

CATEGORY 1 – CASES IN WHICH NO CRIME IS COMMITTED

There are four cases in the 56 stories in which Holmes and Watson solve a mystery in which no crime is committed. These 4 cases constitute 7% of the 56 stories.

The Adventure of the Blanched Soldier (BLAN)
The Adventure of the Lion's Mane (LION)
The Adventure of the Missing Three Quarter ((MISS)
The Yellow Face (YELL)

Chapter 5 contains a discussion of further details on the particulars of each case.

It should be noted that there are other cases in which Holmes believes no crime has been committed, and these cases will be explained in the next chapter.

CATEGORY 2 – CASES IN WHICH A VILLAIN IS TURNED OVER TO THE LAW FOR JUSTICE

A wrongdoer/villain is turned over to the law for punishment in 21 cases, constituting 38% of the 56 short stories. They are:

The Adventure of Black Peter (BLAC)
The Bruce Partington Plans (BRUC)
The Cardboard Box (CARD)
The Adventure of the Dancing Men (DANC)
The Adventure of the Dying Detective (DYIN)
The Adventure of the Empty House (EMPT)
The Adventure of the Illustrious Client (ILLU)
His Last Bow (LAST)
The Mazarin Stone (MAZA)
The Norwood Builder (NORW)
The Priory School (PRIO)
The Red Circle (REDC)
The Red-Headed League (REDH)
The Reigate Squires (REGI)
The Adventure of the Retired Colourman (RETI)
The Adventure of Shoscombe Old Place (SHOS)
The Adventure of the Six Napoleons (SIXN)
The Adventure of the Solitary Cyclist (SOLI)
The Stock-Broker's Clerk (STOC)
The Adventure of the Three Gables (3GAB)
The Adventure of the Three Garridebs (3GAR)

In some of these cases, it is not the primary villain who is turned over to the law. Chapter 6 contains a more detailed breakdown of each case, the villains, crimes and other particulars.

CATEGORY 3 – CASES IN WHICH HOLMES DOES NOT TURN A VILLAIN TO THE LAW FOR JUSTICE

There are 37 cases in which the wrongdoer is not brought to the law for prosecution, amounting to 66% of the 56 stories. In some cases, the wrongdoer escapes. In some, Holmes lets the wrongdoer go free. In others, the wrongdoer dies or fate is an instrument of justice. The 37 cases in this category are:

The Adventure of the Abbey Grange (ABBE)
The Adventure of the Beryl Coronet (BERY)
The Adventure of the Blue Carbuncle (BLUE)
The Boscombe Valley Mystery (BOSC)
The Adventure of the Cardboard Box (CARD)
The Adventure of Charles Augustus Milverton (CHAS)
The Adventure of the Copper Beeches (COPP)
The Creeping Man (CREE)
The Crooked Man (CROO)
The Devil's Foot (DEVI)
The Adventure of the Engineer's Thumb (ENGI)
The Final Problem (FINA)
The Five Orange Pips (FIVE)
The Gloria Scott (GLOR)
The Adventure of the Golden Pince-Nez (GOLD)
The Greek Interpreter (GREE)
A Case of Identity (IDEN)
The Adventure of the Illustrious Client (ILLU)
The Disappearance of Lady Frances Carfax (LADY)
The Musgrave Ritual (MUSG)
The Naval Treaty (NAVA)
The Adventure of the Noble Bachelor (NOBL)
The Adventure of the Priory School (PRIO)
The Adventure of the Red Circle (REDC)

The Resident Patient (RESI)
A Scandal in Bohemia (SCAN)
The Adventure of the Second Stain (SECO)
Silver Blaze (SILV)
The Adventure of the Six Napoleons (SIX)
The Adventure of the Speckled Band (SPEC)
The Adventure of the Sussex Vampire (SUSS)
The Problem of Thor Bridge (THOR)
The Man with the Twisted Lip (TWIS)
The Adventure of the Three Gables (3GAB)
The Adventure of the Three Students (3STU)
The Adventure of the Veiled Lodger (VEIL)
The Adventure of Wisteria Lodge (WIST)

Chapter 7 contains a detailed compendium of these cases, the types of crimes, whether the villain is primary or secondary, what happens to the villains, and the reasons why Sherlock Holmes in many cases elects not to send the perpetrators to the law for justice.

CATEGORY 4 - CASES IN WHICH SHERLOCK HOLMES AND/OR DR. WATSON TAKE THE LAW INTO THEIR OWN HANDS AND COMMIT CRIMES.

In 23 cases in the 56 stories, Holmes and /or Watson, the two arch-enemies of crime, take the law into their own hands and commit crimes themselves. This constitutes 41% of the 56 stories in which they act outside the law. The cases are:

The Adventure of the Abbey Grange (ABBE)
The Adventure of the Blue Carbuncle (BLUE)
The Boscombe Valley Mystery (BOSC)

The Adventure of the Bruce Partington Plans (BRUC)
The Adventure of Charles Augustus Milverton (CHAS)
The Adventure of the Copper Beaches (COPP)
The Devil's Foot (DEVI)
The Final Problem (FINA)
The Adventure of the Illustrious Client (ILLU)
The Disappearance of Lady Frances Carfax (LADY)
His Last Bow (LAST)
The Adventure of the Missing Three-Quarter (MISS)
The Naval Treaty (NAVA)
The Adventure of the Noble Bachelor (NOBL)
The Norwood Builder (NORW)
The Adventure of the Retired Colourman (RETI)
A Scandal in Bohemia (SCAN)
The Adventure of the Second Stain (SECO)
Silver Blaze (SILV)
The Adventure of the Solitary Cyclist (SOLI)
The Adventure of the Three Gables (3GAB)
The Adventure of the Veiled Lodger (VEIL)
The Yellow Face (YELL)

Chapter 8 explores these 23 cases, examining the details of the crimes, the persons involved, and how Holmes justifies his illegal actions in each case.

CATEGORY 5 – CASES IN WHICH SHERLOCK HOLMES WAS WRONG

Holmes himself admits in *The Five Orange Pips* that he was wrong four times-- three with men and once with a woman.

The four cases in the Canon which fit these criteria are:

A Scandal in Bohemia (SCAN)
The Five Orange Pips (FIVE)
The Yellow Face (YELL)
The Man with the Twisted Lip (TWIS)

Chapter 9 explores these four cases and the reasons why Holmes says he was wrong. It also examines six additional cases in which the great detective admits he made some wrong decisions before finding the right solution. These include:

The Adventure of the Abbey Grange (ABBE)
The Adventure of the Dancing Men (DANC)
The Disappearance of Lady Frances Carfax (LADY)
Silver Blaze (SILV)
The Adventure of the Three Gables (3GAB)
The Adventure of the Creeping Man (CREE)

Chapter 5

Category 1: Cases in which No Crime is Committed

There are 4 cases in the Canon with mysteries but no legal crimes.

The Adventure of the Blanched Soldier (BLAN)
The Adventure of the Lion's Mane (LION)
The Adventure of the Missing Three Quarter ((MISS)
The Yellow Face (YELL)

Two of these four stories - *The Adventure of the Blanched Soldier* and *The Lion's Mane* – were both written in 1926 and both are told by Sherlock Holmes instead of Dr. Watson. Both stories use medical components as the basis of their mystery.

Some readers may recall that in *The Blue Carbuncle* and *The Copper Beeches,* Holmes discusses with Watson four other cases which he believes "have been entirely free of any legal crime." The four cases he mentions are *A Scandal in Bohemia, A Case of Identity, The Man with the Twisted Lip, and The Noble Bachelor.* At the heart of each of these four cases is someone who commits a crime either by intent or by accident. The important factor is that crimes were committed. All four cases involve scandal and a breach of the unwritten code. So despite Holmes saying there are no legal crimes in these four cases, we have named the crime and the wrongdoer and have included them in the statistics for the 56 stories. In *A Scandal in Bohemia*, Irene Adler attempts blackmail, although she did not succeed thanks to intervention by Holmes. *A Case of Identity* contains the crime of Fraud/embezzlement, and this crime will be included. In *The Man with the Twisted Lip*, we have included the crime of Begging. In *The Noble Bachelor*, the bride clearly sees her first husband before she takes her vows, so we have included bigamy as the crime in that case. These four cases are included in Category 3, those cases that do not go to the law, because none of the wrongdoers was legally tried and punished.

<u>4 Cases in which no crime is committed</u>

1. <u>*The Adventure of the Blanched Soldier,*</u> written in 1926, is one of the medical-based mysteries in the canon. The case presents a mystery, but no crime. Holmes himself writes this account because Watson had no notes on it. Holmes takes pains to show us how his "method" works: "It is my habit to sit with my back to the window and to place my visitors in the opposite chair, where the light falls full upon them. ...I have found it wise to impress clients with a sense of power, and so I gave him some of my conclusions." And the client, Mr. James M. Dodd, is duly impressed. "Mr. Holmes, you are a wizard." "You see everything." Holmes cracks the case – all except for one detail - by sitting in his armchair listening to Mr. Dodd, much like his sedentary brother Mycroft might do. Holmes then confirms that one final detail after arriving at the Emsworth house. He crows: "Alas that I should have to show my hand so when I tell my own story! It was by concealing such links in the chain that Watson was

enabled to produce his meretricious finales." Some say this tale isn't written well, but it is arguable that its style is a deliberate way of making it seem as if Holmes is struggling to tell the story in a manner that will interest the reader without including any of Watson's sensational style. In other stories Holmes berates Watson for making the cases too sensational. In *The Abbey Grange*, for example, Holmes tells Watson, "Your fatal habit of looking at everything from the point of view of a story instead of as a scientific exercise has ruined what might have been an instructive and even classical series of demonstrations. You slur over work of the utmost finesse and delicacy, in order to dwell upon sensational details which may excite, but cannot possibly instruct, the reader." "Why do you not write them yourself?" (Watson) said, with some bitterness." "I will, my dear Watson, I will." In the end, readers may speculate that perhaps if Watson, the medical man, had been involved in this case, not only would he have foreseen the conclusion of a misdiagnosis of leprosy and corrected it well before Sherlock Holmes did, but also the story might have been written with more panache.

2. *The Lion's Mane*. Published in 1926 and set in 1907, this story is a medical mystery without a legal crime. Like *The Blanched Soldier*, this case is also *sans* Watson and is written by Holmes, now retired and living in a "little Sussex home." Holmes has made at least one good friend there, his neighbor, Harold Stackhurst of the Gables, a "large place which contains some score of young fellows preparing for various professions, with a staff of several masters." Holmes

tells us that Stackhurst "was the one man who was on such terms with me that we could drop in on each other in the evenings without an invitation." However it's interesting to note that Stackhurst addresses Holmes as "Mr. Holmes," the more formal manner of address implying the high regard and respect Stackhurst holds for Holmes. In this tale, suspects and motives abound in the deaths of Fitzroy McPherson and his faithful Airedale terrier, and an attack upon Ian Murdoch. Murdoch and McPherson were two parts of a love triangle, the third being a Miss Maud Bellamy, "the beauty of the neighbourhood." Without Watson as a filter, we get Holmes' first-hand reaction to Maud Bellamy when Holmes writes, "Who could have imagined that so rare a flower would grow from such a root and in such an atmosphere? Women have seldom been an attraction to me, for my brain has always governed my heart, but I could not look upon her perfect clear-cut face, with all the soft freshness of the downlands in her delicate colouring, without realizing that no young man would cross her path unscathed." His description is perhaps even more poetic than Watson's might be – and yet it is Watson, not Holmes, who is considered the ladies' man. The retired Holmes ranks Maud somewhere near Irene Adler: "Maud Bellamy will always remain in my memory as a most complete and remarkable woman." Perhaps Holmes developed this more polished literary style after penning the duller story, *The Blanched Soldier*. Eventually Holmes learns from a book in his library that the culprit who killed McPherson and his dog was a murderous jellyfish -- *Cyanea capillata* -- also known as the Lion's Mane – the last words McPherson whispered. Inspector

Bardle of the Sussex Constabulary is sure the jellyfish-killer isn't English. He says, "I never saw such a thing. It don't belong to Sussex." This story is unique because Sherlock Holmes himself kills the murderer by throwing a rock onto the jellyfish and smashing it to death. This is a pure example of Holmesian justice -- and Holmes never gets arrested for this murder. Holmes admits he's been as dull witted as Scotland Yard in this case. Had Dr. Watson been involved, as a medical man he might have solved the mystery much sooner, but we will never know. Had it been set today, a quick Google search would have put Holmes immediately onto McPherson's dying words, the lion's mane.

3. *The Adventure of the Missing Three Quarter,* published in 1904, concerns the disappearance of sportsman Godfrey Staunton, star three-quarter for the Cambridge rugby team. Suspects abound for a kidnapping, but it isn't a kidnapping. Instead, Holmes solves the mystery using an ink blot on a telegraph form, aniseed on carriage wheels, and Pompey the drag hound, to track the carriage. Holmes unearths Staunton's marriage, kept secret from his wealthy uncle, Lord Mount-James. He finds that Staunton disappeared from his team in order to visit his wife who is dying of consumption. Holmes is criticized for prying "into the secrets of private individuals" and raking up "family matters which are better hidden;" but Holmes insists that, "... so long as there is nothing criminal I am much more anxious to hush up private scandals than to give them publicity. If, as I imagine, there is no breach of the law in this matter, you can absolutely depend upon my discretion and my

cooperation in keeping the facts out of the papers." "We are endeavouring to prevent anything like public exposure of private matters which must necessarily follow when once the case is fairly in the hands of the official police."

4. *The Yellow Face* is an earlier case published in 1893. It has no crime and no criminal and revolves around a wife's secret. Grant Munro tells Homes that three years ago he married his wife, Effie, a widow who'd lived in America for some years. They've been happy but are now suddenly estranged due to some secret Effie won't share. Munro thinks it must be another man, and he watches his wife visit a house where he sees a strange yellowish face in the window. He employs Holmes as a consulting detective, but also he wants Holmes' "opinion as a judicious man—as a man of the world" - on what he ought to do next. Although he loves his wife, he is afraid she may be involved in a love triangle. Munro, Holmes and Watson break into the house his wife entered and find that Effie has kept secret the existence of her black daughter from her first marriage to a black lawyer in Atlanta. After hearing the explanation, Grant Munro accepts the daughter, and the family walks into the sunset. This case, like *The Blanched Soldier, The Man with the Twisted Lip* and *The Veiled Lodger*, is based on a facial deformity, although in this case it is only perceived and not real. Holmes admits he had not solved the mystery. He says famously, "Watson, if I should ever strike you that I am getting a little overconfident in my powers, or giving less pains to a case than it deserves, kindly whisper 'Norbury' in my ear and I shall be infinitely obliged to you."

Statistical Overview

These 4 cases constitute 7% of the 56 stories. The initially perceived crimes center around mysteries involving Missing Persons/Kidnapping; Murder / Attempted Murder; and Infidelity. Suspicion of the crime constitutes the basis of the mystery. In all four cases, the individuals under suspicion are exonerated. In one case, the real killer – a jellyfish – is murdered by Sherlock Holmes.

Missing Person/Kidnapping – 2 - (50%)
The Adventure of the Blanched Soldier (BLAN)
The Adventure of the Missing Three Quarter (MISS)

Murder/Attempted Murder – 1 (25%)
The Lion's Mane (LION)

Infidelity - 1 – (25%)
The Yellow Face (YELL)

Four individuals are involved in these 4 stories - one female and two males. The real villain in *The Lion's Mane* is an animal. Two of the individuals are of British origin, one is Non-British. The Lion's Mane itself may or may not be British.

Female – 1 (25%)
The Yellow Face

Male – 2 (50%)
The Adventure of the Blanched Soldier
The Adventure of the Missing Three Quarter

Animal – 1 - (25 %)
The Lion's Mane

British – 2 – (50%)
The Adventure of the Blanched Soldier
The Adventure of the Missing Three Quarter

Non-British - 1 – (25%)
The Yellow Face (American)

Chapter 6

Category 2: Cases in which the Villain is Turned Over to the Law

"My business is that of every other good citizen -- to uphold the law."
- Sherlock Holmes, Shoscombe Old Place

Sherlock Holmes isn't averse to working with the police to catch a criminal; but he always insists on detecting the criminal in his own manner and is always several steps ahead of the police. In *The Five Orange Pips,* he says, "I shall be my own police. When I have spun the web they may take the flies, but not before." Holmes frequently turns the criminal over to the police as the best option for justice and punishment. He tells us in *The Devil's Foot,* "It is not for me, my dear Watson, to stand in the way of the official police force. I leave them all the evidence which I found."

In 21 of the 56 stories (38%), Sherlock Holmes sends the wrongdoer/villain to the law for punishment and justice. And in four of these 21 stories, namely *Shoscombe Old Place, The Red Circle, The Illustrious Client*, and *The Solitary Cyclist,* the villain receives only a censure in one and possible short sentences and "nothing to worry about" in the others. Compare these statistics to the 37 cases in Category 3, or 66%, in which the "villain" is not brought to the law for prosecution in Chapter 7. Surprisingly, only about half as many villains go to the law as do not.

To understand these criminals and the crimes, it's essential to understand the Victorian justice system, which was different from our justice system today. According to Carolyn Conley in *The Unwritten Law: Criminal Justice in Victorian Kent,* "The Victorian criminal justice system was run exclusively by men. All judges, jurors, police and legislators were men. Women were only involved as victims, witnesses or suspects." [xii] She adds: "Violence had a legitimate place in Victorian society, and few people would have favored its complete eradication. The criminal justice system, if not the law itself was geared to regulating interpersonal violence, not abolishing it. Criminality in interpersonal violence hinged more on motive and victim than on degree of injury. ... The limits on violence were established with considerable clarity. Occasional bursts of violence among equals in a pub or among relatives in private were understandable; public assaults on inoffensive, respectable persons and any violence directed towards social superiors were not. In Victorian Kent, the judicial system was concerned with allowing respectable people to walk the streets safely. To a large extent, they succeeded."

For the most part, the violence and crimes in the Canon center on respectable, even aristocratic and royal persons. There are burglaries with added violence, there are murders, there are blackmailers and there are love triangles that end in violence – almost all among respectable persons. Many of the villains are not respectable – consider Abe Slaney and other gang member types as well as some foreign gangs (KKK) and gangsters (Mafia). But when a respectable person such as Neville St. Clair, alias Hugo Boone in *The Man with the Twisted Lip*, steps out of a gentleman's role to make a living as a beggar, then, if revealed, his fraud is such a deep breach of the Unwritten Laws that he could never again be able to take his place in Victorian society. He tells Holmes that he would rather die than admit he was a beggar, and he demands discretion from Holmes and Watson.

We know that Sherlock Holmes makes discretion an essential part of his job description. When a case goes to the law, justice indeed may follow, and it may be the Sherlock Holmes idea of justice. However, it also means that the crime, the criminal, the victim and everything and everybody involved in the case are on public display. There is no privacy once a case is given over to the law, and privacy is of ultimate importance to the Victorians, who want to keep family secrets in the family. In many cases, Holmes' clients insist upon discretion, and this is certainly one reason why there are fewer cases in which Sherlock Holmes hands the wrongdoer over to the law for punishment.

The 21 stories in which Holmes sends villains to the law for justice are:

The Adventure of Black Peter (BLAC)
The Adventure of the Bruce Partington Plans (BRUC)
The Adventure of the Cardboard Box (CARD)
The Adventure of the Dancing Men (DANC)
The Adventure of the Dying Detective (DYIN)
The Adventure of the Empty House (EMPT)
The Adventure of the Illustrious Client (ILLU)
His Last Bow (LAST)
The Adventure of the Mazarin Stone (MAZA)
The Adventure of the Norwood Builder (NORW)
The Adventure of the Priory School (PRIO)

The Adventure of the Red Circle (REDC)
The Red-Headed League (REDH)
The Reigate Squires (REGI)
The Adventure of the Retired Colorman (RETI)
The Adventure of Shoscombe Old Place (SHOS)
The Adventure of the Six Napoleons (SIXN)
The Adventure of the Solitary Cyclist (SOLI)
The Stock-Broker's Clerk (STOC)
The Adventure of the Three Gables (3GAB)
The Adventure of the Three Garridebs (3GAR)

In some of these 21 stories, Holmes turns over to the law either the chief criminal, a secondary criminal, or both. In one case, although Holmes gives the criminals to the police, they escape (*The Disappearance of Lady Francis Carfax*). In some stories, one villain may not be given over to the police but another one is. Where this happens, stories are listed in multiple categories.

<u>21 Stories in which Holmes gives the villain over to the law</u>

1. <u>*The Adventure of Black Peter*</u>, published in 1904 and set in 1895, is a clear-cut case where Holmes turns a murderer, Patrick Cairns, over to the police because he's harpooned "Black" Peter Carey. Holmes not only has to deal with sins of the past and sins of the present, but also with a case in which both the murderer and his victim were criminals. In the past, the victim had committed murder, and in the present, blackmail leads to the victim's murder. No one is sorry to see Black Peter Carey die, and although Patrick Cairns claims it was self-defense, Sherlock

Holmes sends him off to jail for trial by jury, trusting the British jury to get it right.

2. In *The Adventure of the Bruce Partington Plans,* published in 1908, we again meet Mycroft Holmes who tells his brother Sherlock, "You are the one man who can clear the matter up." Holmes solves the mysterious death of Arthur Cadogan West, a clerk at Woolwich Arsenal, and he catches one criminal, Colonel Valentine Walter, who's stolen secret plans for monetary gain to pay off his debts. Holmes persuades Walter to confess and adds: "How an English gentleman could behave in such a manner is beyond my comprehension. Let me advise you to gain at least the small credit for repentance and confession, since there are still some details which we can only learn from your lips." Colonel Walter agrees to help devise a trap to catch the master spy, Oberstein, and the scheme works. The plans are recovered and Oberstein is sentenced to 15 years in a British prison. Colonel Walter pays severely for his transgression. He's convicted and dies ignominiously in prison, having been the proximate cause of his brother's death.

3. *The Adventure of the Cardboard Box,* published in 1893, is a case in which Holmes deals with a double love triangle. Holmes tracks down James Browner, who has murdered his wife and her lover, and turns him over to the police. Browner, haunted by his crime, implicates Sarah, his wife's sister, claiming she instigated everything out of jealousy and, "... she had some hand in bringing about the events which led to the tragedy." Browner curses Sarah who wanted his affections and who, jealous of her own sister,

instigated the double murder. Although Holmes cannot extract legal justice from Sarah, she does pay a price. "Miss Sarah Cushing is extremely ill." "She has been suffering since yesterday from brain symptoms of great severity."

4. *The Adventure of the Dancing Men* is another case in which Holmes nets the murderer, Abe Slaney, a crook from Chicago, and gives him straight over to the constabulary. Slaney is part of a love triangle with Elsie, a girl from Chicago he'd planned to marry, and her new husband, Hilton Cubitt, of Ridling Thorpe Manor. Hilton Cubitt is described as "a fine creature, this man of the old English soil, simple, straight, and gentle, with his great, earnest blue eyes and broad, comely face." Hilton is "a tall, ruddy, clean-shaven gentleman, whose clear eyes and florid cheeks told of a life led far from the fogs of Baker Street. He seemed to bring a whiff of his strong, fresh, bracing, east-coast air with him as he entered." In contrast to this, we find that Hilton's wife of one year, Elsie Patrick, is the daughter of the head of the Chicago gang that Slaney works for. She unfortunately withholds information about the stick figure drawings that have appeared at the Manor, with awful consequences. Holmes tells Hilton to beg her to share what she knows, but she won't, thus making her husband Hilton a target for murder. Slaney, the other end of the love triangle, is "a tall, handsome, swarthy fellow, clad in a suit of grey flannel, with a Panama hat, a bristling black beard, and a great, aggressive hooked nose, and flourishing a cane." Holmes saves Elsie from being charged with her husband's murder, and Watson admits that Hilton Cubitt is "the client whom (Holmes) had failed to

save." His wife Elsie tries to commit suicide but recovers and devotes her life to the poor. Slaney is convicted and gets penal servitude instead of the gallows.

5. *The Adventure of the Dying Detective*, published in 1913, opens with a dramatic scene with Watson and Mrs. Hudson terrified that Sherlock Holmes may be dying of a rare and fatal tropical disease that he has contracted on the docks of London. In reality, Holmes is faking his illness in order to trap the evil villain, Culverton Smith, a planter from Sumatra. Smith is guilty not only of the crime of murdering his nephew, Victor Savage, which he did for monetary gain, but also of the attempted murder of Sherlock Holmes in order to keep his secret. One other crime, though not prosecutable, is Smith's sin of hubris. Smith crows, "You are proud of your brains, Holmes, are you not? Think yourself smart, don't you? You came across someone who was smarter this time." But Holmes defeats Smith and gets him to confess to Victor Savage's murder while Watson is hiding in the sickroom. Smith is then summarily arrested by Inspector Morton and charged with murder.

6. In *The Adventure of the Empty House*, published in 1903 and set in 1894, we find Sherlock Holmes, in disguise as a bibliophile, returning from the dead three years after he was supposedly killed at Reichenbach falls. Watson faints as Holmes reveals himself, and then they set a trap to successfully capture Colonel Sebastian Moran, the second most dangerous man in London and now in command of what is left of Moriarty's gang. Colonel Moran,

described as a tiger hunter, hates Sherlock Holmes, and calls him a clever fiend. Holmes says Moran "must have started with great capacities for good or for evil. But one could not look upon his cruel blue eyes, with their drooping, cynical lids, or upon the fierce, aggressive nose and the threatening, deep-lined brow, without reading Nature's plainest danger-signals." Lestrade and his men arrest Moran for the murder of the Hon. Ronald Adair, the motive ostensibly being that Moran cheated at cards and Adair was going to have him black balled. The reader wonders why, with access to the spoils from the criminal gang, Colonel Moran has to cheat at cards to win money to live on. Holmes would probably say it is in his nature. At Holmes' request, Moran is not charged with the attempted murder of Sherlock Holmes. "... Come what may, Colonel Moran will trouble us no more. The famous air-gun of Von Herder will embellish the Scotland Yard Museum, and once again Mr. Sherlock Holmes is free to devote his life to examining those interesting little problems which the complex life of London so plentifully presents," Holmes says, speaking about himself in the third person.

7. *The Adventure of the Illustrious Client* was published in November 1924 and set in 1902. In this case, as Holmes anticipates and tries to prevent a crime – possibly murder - he goes head to head with the dangerous Austrian murderer, Baron Adelbert Gruner and gets assaulted by Gruner's thugs. Kitty Winter, an earlier victim of the Baron, acts as the instrument of justice when she takes her private revenge and throws vitriol in his face. This is another

case in the Canon with a marred face, but Baron Gruner's disfigurement comes at the end of the story and isn't part of the mystery as in *The Yellow Face, The Veiled Lodger, The Blanched Soldier* and *The Man with the Twisted Lip*. Kitty is arrested and goes to court, but in consideration of extenuating circumstances she is given the lowest possible sentence. Thanks to Watson's impersonation of an expert in Chinese pottery and some breaking and entering, Holmes steals the Baron's beastly book of ruined souls and thus successfully prevents the marriage between the Baron and Colonel de Merville's daughter Violet. Gruner, possibly an aristocrat but certainly not a gentleman, threatens Holmes with prosecution for burglary. However, the Illustrious Client, probably King Edward VII, ensures that does not happen. The Baron himself never gets arrested for his prior crimes, including the alleged murder of his wife and a witness, because they cannot be proven, so he escapes legal justice. But the wages of his sin turn him into a badly scarred, disfigured man - the objectification of his soul.

8. *His Last Bow,* published in 1917 and set in August 1914, concerns espionage and spying at the outbreak of World War I. Holmes very successfully disguises himself in this story as Altamont, an Irish American spy. He has gotten himself trusted by handling a wide breadth of information and is now carrying material on naval signals. This is another case in which Holmes and Watson commit kidnapping and burglary, helping them to deliver the criminals, Mr. Von Bork, an agent of the Kaiser, and Baron Von Herling, Chief Secretary to the German Legation, to Scotland Yard.

9. *The Mazarin Stone*, published in 1921, begins with Holmes confiding to Watson that he expects to be killed that evening. He even tells Watson the name of his murderer. "You can give it to Scotland Yard, with my love and a parting blessing. Sylvius is the name—Count Negretto Sylvius. Write it down, man, write it down! 136 Moorside Gardens, N. W. Got it?" Holmes is hired by the Prime Minister, the Home Secretary and Lord Cantlemere, to retrieve the missing Crown jewel, the great yellow Mazarin stone. Holmes disguises himself twice in this case and also uses the newly invented gramophone to trick information out of Sylvius and his confederate in crime, Sam Merton. He even promises to "compound a felony" and let Sylvius and Merton go free if they will return the stone to him. They won't, so Holmes grabs the stone and with an "inrush of police, the handcuffs clicked and the criminals were led to the waiting cab." Holmes then summarily plants the Mazarin stone in Lord Cantlemere's coat pocket to show him up for doubting Holmes's ability to solve the crime.

10. *The Adventure of the Norwood Builder* was published in 1903 and set in 1894. Its plot is similar to *Thor Bridge* wherein a supposed victim attempts to frame someone else for murder. A young solicitor, John Hector McFarlane, bursts into 221B begging for help because a warrant has been issued to arrest him "Upon the charge of murdering Mr. Jonas Oldacre, of Lower Norwood." Holmes delivers one of his greatest deductive observations when he says, "You mentioned your name, as if I should recognize it, but I assure you that, beyond the obvious facts that you are a bachelor,

a solicitor, a Freemason, and an asthmatic, I know nothing whatever about you." McFarlane then explains that although Oldacre had been a friend of his parents many years ago, he'd never seen him until the previous day when Oldacre hired him to write his will. McFarlane complies but is surprised to find that he is named heir to all Oldacre's property. That night, McFarlane visits Oldacre's Norwood house, and after he leaves, Oldacre disappears. The police think McFarlane has murdered him because they found some charred remains in the ashes of the burnt wood-pile in Oldacre's timber-yard, and they also have McFarlane's bloody walking stick for the murder weapon. Holmes employs fingerprint evidence and cleverly exposes Oldacre's hiding place in a secret room in the house and turns him over to the police. Holmes then reveals Oldacre's treacherous scheme to fake his own death and have young McFarlane hang for his murder as an act of revenge against McFarlane's mother, who'd rejected him as a suitor many years ago. Oldacre's revenge has lain simmering for many many years. He has expended a great deal of planning, thought and energy into this scheme, putting this attempted murder into a wicked sphere all by itself. He has nurtured his revenge and reveled in what he was doing to young McFarlane and how he was getting back at Mrs. McFarlane. One could almost hear his evil laugh coming from the secret room wherein he hid himself. This is one criminal Holmes and the reader are delighted to see handed over to the law. Oldacre couldn't have hidden without help from his housekeeper, Mrs. Lexington. She is clearly a party to this convoluted conspiracy as well. She's an interesting female villain because we wonder about her motive and whether Oldacre coerced her into being an accomplice or if she did it of her own free will.

11. *The Adventure of the Priory School*, published in 1904 and set in 1901, is the third longest of the 56 Holmes stories at 11,507 words. In it, ten-year old Lord Saltire, son of the Duke of Holdernesse, has disappeared from the Priory School. Holmes is disappointed in getting a three-day old case, but the headmaster explains, "I am not to blame, Mr. Holmes. His Grace was extremely desirous to avoid all public scandal. He was afraid of his family unhappiness being dragged before the world. He has a deep horror of anything of the kind." "Well, now, Watson, how many cows did you see on the moor?" Holmes asks, and then he solves the mystery and identifies the kidnappers using clues from cow tracks, bicycle tracks, the dead body of the German master, and the absence of any ransom request. Only one wrongdoer, the murdering innkeeper, Reuben Hayes, will go to the gallows, and Holmes says: "I would do nothing to save him from it." The Duke's secretary and illegitimate son, James Wilder, who is the brains behind the abduction, is motivated by jealousy and a hatred as strong as that of Cain for Abel. His involvement is hushed up because he repents to the Duke and emigrates to Australia. Holmes also overlooks the Duke's "condoning a felony" and abetting a murderer. The case has, ultimately, a happy ending. Young Lord Saltire is found unharmed, and the Duke and his Duchess reunite. Who can foretell what becomes of James Wilder.

12. *The Adventure of the Red Circle*, published in 1911, concerns a mysterious tenant and a secret society of Italian criminals called the Red Circle. Their leader, Giuseppe Gorgiano, tracks down another member, Gennaro Lucca and his wife Emilia, who've come from Italy to London. Gorgiano plans to murder the husband and get hold of Emilia, who is the mysterious tenant. Holmes makes use of the agony column of the Daily Gazette, a substitution cipher, and his knowledge of Italian in order to help, but Gennaro kills Gorgiano in self-defense and is arrested by Gregson of Scotland Yard. "The Law is what we live with. Justice is sometimes harder to achieve," Holmes remarks, and Gregson adds, "I do not think she or her husband has much to fear," signaling that their punishment through legal channels will be slight.

13. *The Red-Headed League*, published in 1891, concerns a clever attempt by criminals to trick Jabez Wilson, a red-headed pawnbroker, to stay out of his shop so that they can dig a tunnel from the shop's basement under the street to a near by bank vault. But Vincent Spaulding - really John Clay, along with red haired Duncan Ross – alias Archie alias William Morris, cannot fool Holmes with the spurious Red-Headed League's ploy of having Wilson copy out the Encyclopedia Britannica. Holmes finds clues in the cheap wages Wilson paid his assistant Spaulding, in the hollow sound under the street in Saxe-Coburg Square, and in the dirty knees of Spaulding's trousers. These clues allow Holmes and Jones of Scotland Yard to catch the two criminals red-handed, as it were, in the act of burgling the vault. In this case, the law fully

handles the criminals who are summarily handcuffed and taken into custody.

14. In *The Reigate Squires,* published in 1893 and set in 1887, Holmes tackles a "little country crime," while taking a rest cure with Watson and friend Colonel Hayter at Hayter's home near Reigate in Surrey. When a neighbor's coachman is shot to death, Holmes is drawn into a mystery involving not only the murder, but also some local burglaries and a long-standing legal battle between two of the Colonel's neighbors, the Actons and the Cunninghams. An attempt on Holmes' life is made, but he unearths the clues, including the new science of handwriting analysis, that prove the Cunninghams - father and son together - were not only responsible for the burglary at the Acton estate but also for the murder of their own coachman, William, who'd seen them burgling the estate and was blackmailing them. Acton was pressing a claim for half the Cunningham estate, and the Cunninghams were determined to steal papers that could prove Acton's claim. Holmes happily turns his would-be murderers over to the Inspector for trial.

15. *The Adventure of the Retired Colourman* was published in 1926 and is set in 1898. This is another case of a love triangle in which Holmes has to untangle the truth from a layer of lies. Holmes takes the law into his own hands and enters Josiah Amberley's house, the Haven, illegally. He deduces from some paint, an unused theatre ticket, and a secure strong room, that Josiah Amberley, the awful and hubristic husband, has murdered his wife and her lover and buried them in a disused well. If miserliness

was a crime, Josiah Amberley could have been sent away for life on that charge alone. Holmes likens Amberley's unusual mentality to "the sort of mind which one associates with the mediaeval Italian nature rather than with the modern Briton." Holmes refuses to take any credit for solving the double murder and gladly turns Amberley over to Inspector MacKinnon to be tried and sent either to a scaffold or to Broadmoor. Watson has the taxing job of traveling with Amberley and suffering Amberley's horrid personality. Holmes shows less sympathy for Josiah Amberley than for James Browner, another double murderer in *The Cardboard Box.*

16. *The Adventure of Shoscombe Old Place*, published in 1927 and set in 1902, puts Sherlock Holmes' famous method to the test. When a woman goes missing, Holmes discovers there was no murder involved but that Sir Robert Norberton had moved the dead body of his sister and did not immediately notify the coroner of her death by natural causes. Holmes refers the case to the police and the coroner for investigation in order to provide the proof and verify that Sir Robert's story is true. This proof is the third element of the Sherlockian method – verify. We are told, however, that "beyond a mild censure for the delay in registering the lady's decease, the lucky owner got away scatheless from this strange incident." Sir Robert has two confederates helping him keep his sister's death secret – his sister's maid who knows about the death, and her husband Norlett, who impersonates Sir Robert's sister. However, although they are accomplices to keeping the death secret, technically they commit no crime and are not included as villains.

This tale has a happy ending with Sir Robert's horse winning the Derby and providing enough money to pay his debtors and maintain his lifestyle, emphasizing that Sir Robert was no murderer.

17. In *The Adventure of the Six Napoleons*, published in 1904, Holmes helps out Inspector Lestrade in "the singular adventure of the Napoleonic busts." Lestrade is stumped when four identical busts of Napoleon are smashed, the last coincident with a murder. Holmes finds clues in a photograph and in light posts, and he deflects attention from the true nature of the crime by using the press to propound the theory that the crimes are the work of a lunatic. Next he plants a false clue in a newspaper to smoke out the villain. It works, and Watson reports that "with the bound of a tiger, Holmes was on his back, and an instant later Lestrade and I had him by either wrist, and the handcuffs had been fastened." Beppo is captured and given to the law, but as often happens in life, he never finds what he's been searching for in the smashed Napoleon busts because it was in the last of the six. In a tour de force, Holmes tracks it down, purchases it from the owner, then dramatically smashes it to bits in order to uncover "the famous black pearl of the Borgias," stolen earlier by Beppo and his confederates.

18. *The Adventure of the Solitary Cyclist* was published in 1903 and is set in 1895. Following a visit from Miss Violet Smith, Holmes and Watson separately visit the country estate of Charlington Hall to investigate the strange goings on. Violet has reported she accepted a too-well-paying job of music tutor from Carruthers, who, along with his partner

Woodley, had been acquainted with her Uncle Ralph in South Africa. In what turns out to be another strange love triangle, Violet then refuses marriage proposals from both of them and gives notice she'll be leaving her job. Holmes and Watson are perfect Victorian gentlemen as they confirm Violet's story and watch out for her wellbeing. They bring a revolver along on their next trip to the Hall to ensure Violet has an unmolested trip to the train station on her last day. But they are too late, and fear she's been abducted or murdered. Instead they find she's been forced into a marriage ceremony performed by Williamson, an ex-priest. Carruthers shoots Woodley, the bridegroom, and Holmes detains them all under his personal custody, representing the official police until the county constabulary arrives. In trying to force a marriage, Woodley and Williamson face serious felony charges and prison terms of ten years. Carruthers faces assault charges; but Holmes, believing Carruthers was trying to protect Violet, offers to testify on his behalf at his trial, suggesting a reduced sentence. In the text of this story, both Holmes' client, Violet Smith and one of the villains, Bob Carruthers, are each named as the figure of the Solitary Cyclist.

19. *The Stock-Broker's Clerk*, published in 1893, has a plot similar to *The Copper Beeches, The Red Headed League* and *The Three Garridebs* in which trickery and money are used to entice an innocent person to do something that will allow the villain to accomplish a crime. In this story, Holmes' client, Hall Pycroft, puts his "head in a basin of cold water" to help him think through a problem he's having with two brothers, Arthur and Harry Pinner. Both brothers have the

same figure and voice, but one was clean-shaven with lighter hair than the other, and it's all connected with Pinner's new job with great pay. Pycroft recognizes that the brothers sport the exact same tooth stuffed with gold in the same way, and he realizes that they are the same person. He calls on Holmes to help him find the truth. Holmes believes that the person playing both brothers is scheming to keep Pycroft from showing up at his new London brokerage job. Holmes and Watson pose as Mr. Harris and Mr. Price to investigate, but the real hero of the case is Sergeant Tuson, of the City Police. Tuson captures Pinner's brother, Beddington, the famous forger and cracksman who has committed murder while pulling off a gigantic robbery at Mawson's brokerage house where Pycroft had obtained then rejected employment. Holmes foils Arthur Harry Pinner's attempt to commit suicide and tells Watson: "You see that even a villain and murderer can inspire such affection that his brother turns to suicide when he learns that his neck is forfeited. However, we have no choice as to our action. The doctor and I will remain on guard, Mr. Pycroft, if you will have the kindness to step out for the police." Both brothers are duly arrested.

20. *The Adventure of the Three Gables* is a case in which four villains are treated very differently. The major villainess is Isadora Klein, yet Holmes decides to let her go unpunished in exchange for a five thousand pound check to send Mrs. Maberley on a round the world trip (Category 3 A). Sherlock Holmes tells us that the other three villains, Susan and Barney Stockdale and the boxer, Steve Dixie, have been

arrested for burglary by Scotland Yard and will face the full measure of the law. These members of the Spencer John gang were involved not only in burgling Mrs. Maberley's home, The Three Gables, but also in beating up Sherlock Holmes. They HAD to do some prison time -- if not for the beating, for which there was no evidence, then for the burglary.

21. *The Adventure of the Three Garridebs*, published in 1924 and set in June 1902, has a plot similar to *The Red Headed League and The Stock-Broker's Clerk*, in which a client is hoodwinked into a bizarre scheme in an attempt to get him out of the way on a "wild goose chase" so the villain can use the client's premises to commit a crime. Holmes immediately deduces that the proposal from American John Garrideb to locate a third male Garrideb in order to inherit a fortune is "a rigmarole of lies." This time the villain's crime is counterfeiting, and the many clues include John Garrideb's clothing, the absence of advertisements in the agony columns, a fictitious person from Topeka, and misspelled words in an advertisement. The "rogues' portrait gallery" at the Yard identifies John Garrideb as the Chicago murderer, "James Winter, alias Morecroft, alias Killer Evans." One of his victims was "Rodger Prescott, famous as forger and coiner in Chicago," and Holmes finds the connection that Prescott was the previous tenant at Nathan Garrideb's establishment. In their efforts to capture him, Killer Evans shoots Watson in the thigh. Holmes, relieved to find it is only a superficial wound, tells Evans, ""By the Lord, it is as well for you. If you had killed Watson, you would not have got out of this room alive." Evans tries first to make a deal with Holmes for his freedom

in exchange for the printing press and counterfeit bills, and then he claims he's a hero for breaking up the counterfeiting gang. Finally he tells Holmes that he's done nothing for which he could be arrested. Holmes disagrees, Watson phones the Yard, and Evans is arrested for attempted murder and sent back to prison.

Statistical Overview

In these 21 stories, 23 crimes are committed in 6 categories including: 12 Murders; 3 Attempted Murders; 2 Assaults; 2 cases of Espionage; 3 Thefts/ Burglaries; and 1 case of Concealing a Death. Following is a listing of the stories in which each crime is committed and the motive for each crime.

MURDER – 12 – 52% of the 23 crimes

- Motive - Self Defense - 1 - 8% of 12 murders
The Adventure of Black Peter (BLAC)

- Motive - Love Triangle – 4 – 34% of 12 murders
The Adventure of the Cardboard Box (CARD)
The Adventure of the Dancing Men (DANC)
The Adventure of the Red Circle (REDC)
The Adventure of the Retired Colorman (RETI)

- Motive - Monetary Gain - 5 – 42 % of 12 murders
The Adventure of the Dying Detective (DYIN)
The Adventure of the Empty House (EMPT)
The Reigate Squires (REGI)
The Adventure of the Six Napoleons (SIXN)
The Stock-Broker's Clerk (STOC)

- Motive - Kidnapping / Revenge –1 – 8% of 12 murders
The Adventure of the Priory School (PRIO)

- Motive - Espionage – 1 – 8% of 12 murders
The Adventure of the Bruce Partington Plans (BRUC)

ATTEMPTED MURDER – 3 – 13% of the 23 crimes

- Motive - For Monetary Gain
The Adventure of the Three Garridebs (3GAR)

-Motive - To Avoid Detection
The Adventure of the Dying Detective (DYIN)

- Motive – Revenge
The Norwood Builder (NORW)

ASSAULT – 2 – 9% of the 23 crimes

- Motive - Revenge - 1
The Adventure of the Illustrious Client (ILLU)

- Motive - a forced marriage - 1
The Adventure of the Solitary Cyclist (SOLI)

ESPIONAGE – 2 – 9%

The Bruce Partington Plans (BRUC)
His Last Bow (LAST)

THEFT & BURGLARY – 3 – 13% of the 23 crimes

The Adventure of the Mazarin Stone (MAZA)
The Red-Headed League (REDH)
The Adventure of the Three Gables (3GAB)

CONCEALING A DEATH – 1 – 4%

The Adventure of Shoscombe Old Place (SHOS)

In these 21 cases in which Holmes turns the villains over to the law, three cases have female villains. One is Kitty Winter, a secondary character who takes her revenge by throwing vitriol at Baron Gruner, the main villain in *The Illustrious Client.* She faces the law, but Holmes makes sure her sentence is mitigated. The second female villain is Mrs. Lexington, the housekeeper who aids and abets Jonas Oldacre in his scheme of attempted murder in *The Norwood Builder*. The third female villain who gets arrested is Susan Stockdale, a member of the Spencer John gang in *The Three Gables.* Male villains in 20 of the cases are arrested and go to jail, with two of the cases as mentioned (*The Norwood Builder* and *The Three Gables*) sending both male and female wrongdoers to jail.

Within the 21 cases, two cases have more than one villain. So in 14 cases, there are British villains, and in 9 cases, the villains are Non-British. In *The Bruce-Partington Plans,* there are two villains – one British and one German; and in *The Solitary Cyclist,* both British and South African villains are arrested. More Male villains than Female and more British villains than foreigners were arrested in these 21 cases.

FEMALE VILLAINS – 3 Cases (14% of the 21 cases)

The Illustrious Client – Kitty Winter
The Norwood Builder – Mrs. Lexington
The Three Gables – Susan Stockdale

MALE VILLAINS – 20 cases (95% of the 21 cases)

The Adventure of Black Peter
The Bruce-Partington Plans
The Cardboard Box
The Dancing Men
The Dying Detective
The Empty House
His Last Bow
The Mazarin Stone
The Norwood Builder
The Priory School
The Red Circle
The Red-Headed League
The Reigate Squires
The Retired Colourman
Shoscombe Old Place
The Six Napoleons
The Solitary Cyclist
The Stock-Broker's Clerk
The Three Gables
The Three Garridebs

BRITISH – 14 (66% of the cases)

- Black Peter
- The Bruce-Partington Plans (Colonel Walter)
- The Cardboard Box
- The Empty House
- The Illustrious Client (Kitty Winter)
- The Norwood Builder
- The Priory School
- The Red-Headed League
- The Reigate Squires
- The Retired Colourman
- The Shoscombe Old Place
- The Solitary Cyclist
- The Stock-Brokers Clerk
- The Three Gables

NON-BRITISH - 9 (43% of the cases)

- The Bruce-Partington Plans (German)
- The Dancing Men (American)
- The Dying Detective (Sumatran)
- His Last Bow (German)
- The Mazarin Stone (Italy)
- The Red Circle (Italy)
- The Six Napoleons (Italy)
- The Solitary Cyclist (South Africa-2)
- The Three Garridebs – (American)

Of these 21 stories, only four are early cases, published through 1893. The other 17 are later stories. Seven cases were published from 1903 and 1904, and ten published from 1908 through 1927. Clearly Holmes trended more toward turning wrongdoers over to the law in the later cases than in the early ones.

Early Published Cases through 1893 – 4 - 19% of the 21 stories

The Red-Headed League - 1891
The Cardboard Box – 1893
The Reigate Squires – 1893
The Stock-Broker's Clerk - 1893

Middle Cases 1903-1904 – 7 – 33% of the 21 stories

The Dancing Men – 1903
The Empty House - 1903
The Norwood Builder – 1903
The Solitary Cyclist - 1903
Black Peter - 1904
The Priory School – 1904
The Six Napoleons - 1904

Later Cases – 1908-1927 – 10 – 48% of the 21 stories

The Bruce Partington Plans – 1908
The Red Circle – 1911
The Dying Detective – 1913
His Last Bow - 1917
The Mazarin Stone - 1921
The Illustrious Client – 1924
The Three Garridebs - 1924
The Retired Colourman – 1926
The Three Gables - 1926
Shoscombe Old Place - 1927

This statistical analysis was done by case. A detailed profile and analysis of the crimes and the victims is contained in Chapter 10, and an analysis of the Holmesian villain is contained in Chapter 11.

Chapter 7

Category 3 - Cases where the Villain Is Not Taken to the Law for Justice

"The Law is what we live with. Justice is sometimes harder to achieve."
- Sherlock Holmes, The Adventure of the Red Circle

"Once or twice in my career I feel that I have done more real harm by my discovery of the criminal than ever he had done by his crime. I have learned caution now, and I had rather play tricks with the Law of England than with my own conscience," Holmes says in *The Adventure of the Abbey Grange*.

And indeed Holmes often does act outside the law and metes out his own brand of justice. In *The Five Orange Pips*, Holmes says, "I shall be my own police," and "I am the last court of appeal." In *The Norwood Builder* Holmes says, "All my instincts are one way, and all the facts are the other, and I much fear that British juries have not yet attained that pitch of intelligence when they will give the preference to my theories over Lestrade's facts." And in *The Musgrave Ritual*, Holmes tells Watson, "... I am generally recognized both by the public and by the official force as being a final court of appeal in doubtful cases."

Based on these statements, it is no surprise that in so many cases Holmes acts not as an agent for the police but as a neutral judge and jury to render his own verdict. He tells us in *The Sign of the Four* that as the "only unofficial consulting detective, I am the last and highest court of appeal in detection." As readers, we are ready to believe that Holmes, in the capacity of the highest court of appeal, has the capability to render fair decisions and bring criminals to justice. We like the fact that Holmes is a hands-on detective – he knows not just the person but also the soul of the wrongdoers he encounters. Thus Sherlock Holmes, in acting as the final court of appeal, is not simply a slave to objective laws, but he applies those laws and their precepts with individuality and humanity. He prefers the spirit of the law to its letter. In *The Five Orange Pips,* Holmes explains how a reasoning and knowledgeable observer can describe a whole animal by looking at one single bone utilizing all his intellect as well as the facts he can assemble. Holmes notes that, "a man should possess all knowledge which is likely to be useful to him in his work, and this I have endeavoured in my case to do." Thus we have every confidence that Holmes is smart enough to analyze a crime, affix blame, and, taking into consideration the character of the villain, set out a course of fitting punishment.

Sherlock Holmes in his role as judge and jury wants – demands – that wrongdoers confess their crimes. In these cases, Holmes gathers the facts and carefully crafts a scenario – often dramatic – in which the villain is faced with the implacable truth of his act. Later this would be known as the Perry Mason Moment - the moment in which the villain repents and makes a confession. Bringing these wrongdoers to the point of confession is due to Holmes' great powers of observation, analysis and deduction – what he calls his method. It's also due to his careful study of the villains.

In the following 37 cases or 66 % of the stories, wrongdoers are not brought to the law for prosecution:

The Adventure of the Abbey Grange (ABBE)
The Adventure of the Beryl Coronet (BERY)
The Adventure of the Blue Carbuncle (BLUE)
The Boscombe Valley Mystery (BOSC)
The Adventure of the Cardboard Box (CARD)
The Adventure of Charles Augustus Milverton (CHAS)
The Adventure of the Copper Beeches (COPP)
The Adventure of the Creeping Man (CREE)
The Adventure of the Crooked Man (CROO)
The Adventure of the Devil's Foot (DEVI)
The Adventure of the Engineer's Thumb (ENGR
The Final Problem (FINA)
The Five Orange Pips (FIVE)
The Gloria Scott (GLOR)
The Adventure of the Golden Pince-Nez (GOLD)
The Greek Interpreter (GREE)
A Case of Identity (IDEN)
The Adventure of the Illustrious Client (ILLU)
The Disappearance of Lady Frances Carfax (LADY)
The Musgrave Ritual (MUSG)
The Naval Treaty (NAVA)
The Adventure of the Noble Bachelor (NOBL)
The Adventure of the Priory School (PRIO)
The Red Circle (REDC)
The Resident Patient (RESI)
A Scandal in Bohemia (SCAN)
The Adventure of the Second Stain (SECO)
Silver Blaze (SILV)

The Adventure of the Six Napoleons (SIXN)
The Adventure of the Speckled Band (SPEC)
The Adventure of the Sussex Vampire (SUSS)
The Problem of Thor Bridge (THOR)
The Adventure of the Three Gables (3GAB)
The Adventure of the Three Students (3STU)
The Man with the Twisted Lip (TWIS)
The Adventure of the Veiled Lodger (VEIL)
The Adventure of Wisteria Lodge (WIST)

These 37 cases can be subdivided into three categories:

A. Cases in which Holmes decides justice for the wrongdoer (18);

B. Cases in which the Villain escapes (11); and

C. Cases in which the wrongdoers get justice from above (13).

Where a story has more than one wrongdoer, it will appear in multiple categories, as in *Charles Augustus Milverton, The Devil's Foot, The Musgrave Ritual, The Second Stain,* and *Silver Blaze.*

<u>Cases where Holmes decides justice for the villain – 18</u>

The Adventure of the Abbey Grange (ABBE)
The Adventure of the Blue Carbuncle (BLUE)
The Boscombe Valley Mystery (BOSC)
The Adventure of Charles Augustus Milverton (CHAS)
The Crooked Man (CROO)
The Devil's Foot (DEVI)
A Case of Identity (IDEN)
The Naval Treaty (NAVA)
The Adventure of the Noble Bachelor (NOBL)

The Adventure of the Priory School (PRIO)
The Adventure of the Second Stain (SECO)
Silver Blaze (SILV)
The Adventure of the Sussex Vampire (SUSS)
The Problem of Thor Bridge (THOR)
The Adventure of the Three Gables (3GAB)
The Adventure of the Three Students (3STU)
The Man with the Twisted Lip (TWIS)
The Adventure of the Veiled Lodger (VEIL)

In the Holmesian Code of Justice, Holmes has his reasons when he does not turn the wrongdoers over to the law. Whenever Holmes lets a wrongdoer go free, he finds forgiveness for the criminal in a variety of reasons, all connected to the Victorian code of honor and the unwritten laws.

Importantly, Holmes also takes the character of the victim into consideration when he decides to forgive a villain. If the victim of the crime was leading a double life, for example, or was not an honorable or respectable person, Holmes places some blame on the victim and is much more inclined to forgive the wrongdoer or at least mitigate the punishment.

In the Canon, Holmes acknowledges that a villain has a right to revenge or to avenge a wrong. And this power to right a wrong is part of the Victorian code and the unwritten rules, as long as the end justifies the means. We find that often Holmes and Watson break the laws for these same reasons (See Chapter 8). In *The Abbey Grange*, the victim is Sir Eustace Brackenstall, a horrid man who not only mistreats his wife but also sets his wife's little spaniel dog on fire. By letting Brackenstall's killer go free, Holmes is tacitly admitting that Sir Eustace got what was coming to him because in the Victorian code, women are fragile, should be treated gently, and it is justifiable to defend them. Moreover, as we see later, the killing was probably committed in self-defense.

While Holmes sometimes feels sympathy for the wrongdoers, he does not always forgive them. In some instances he lets the wrongdoer go free because he finds it necessary to cover the crime itself for the sake of the government or to avoid scandal to a family or a business, as in *The Naval Treaty*.

A. Holmes decides justice for the wrongdoer – 18

1. *The Adventure of the Abbey Grange*, published in 1904 and set in 1897, finds Sherlock Holmes mixed up in another love triangle that ends in murder. The beautiful, golden haired and blue eyed Lady Brackenstall had recently emigrated from Australia and married Sir Eustace Brackenstall, who turned out to be a drunken brute. Now he is dead, killed by a blow to the head. In a series of deductions based on the discrepancies between the crime scene and the testimony of Lady Brackenstall, Holmes concludes that Captain Croker killed Sir Eustace. Croker is no common criminal. Instead he's an officer with an impeccable record who serves on the Adelaide-Southampton line. Holmes warns Croker, "Be frank with me and we may do some good. Play tricks with me, and I'll crush you." Croker explains that the incident took place during an "honorable" fight in self-defense, one on one, in which Croker tried to save Lady Brackenstall from further harm. After testing Croker, Holmes is convinced his intent was self-preservation, and he shakes Croker's hand. "Once or

twice in my career I feel that I have done more real harm by my discovery of the criminal than ever he had done by his crime. I have learned caution now, and I had rather play tricks with the Law of England than with my own conscience." Although Hopkins of the Yard had summoned Holmes to the case, Holmes decides to circumvent the police and convene his own court to decide whether Captain Croker is guilty of murder. Holmes tells Croker, "Well, it is a great responsibility that I take upon myself, but I have given Hopkins an excellent hint and if he can't avail himself of it I can do no more. See here, Captain Croker, we'll do this in due form of law. You are the prisoner. Watson, you are a British jury, and I never met a man who was more eminently fitted to represent one. I am the judge. Now, gentleman of the jury, you have heard the evidence. Do you find the prisoner guilty or not guilty?" "Not guilty, my lord," says Watson. "VOX POPULI, VOX DEI. You are acquitted, Captain Croker." Holmes' decision takes into account Croker's service record and overall good character compared to Sir Eustace's brutal temperament and the fact it was a fair fight. Self-defense is, in itself, a defense for murder. Holmes strikes a bargain with Croker: "So long as the law does not find some other victim you are safe from me. Come back to this lady in a year, and may her future and yours justify us in the judgement which we have pronounced this night!" Because Holmes concludes that Croker's act was not wonton murder, Holmes feels that he himself is committing no felony or withholding evidence by letting Croker go. He also overlooks the fact that Lady Brackenstall and her maid, Theresa Wright, were accessories and withheld evidence. Instead Holmes accepts the mitigating circumstances in the case and feels confident that his judgement is ultimately more fair and just than that of the law. The very British Sir Eustace Brackenstall is cast as the real villain, while Lady Brackenstall and Captain Croker are given the moral high ground. This case is a clear example of the Holmesian Code of Justice based on the Victorian code of honor, and Holmes keeps Croker and Lady Brackenstall free from a scandal which would ruin forever their chance of future happiness.

2. *The Adventure of the Blue Carbuncle*, published in 1892, is a case involving a stolen jewel, a goose, and some forgiveness – all a paean to the English Christmas holiday season of peace and goodwill towards men. As Holmes is in the midst of a literal goose chase to trace where some geese were raised, he runs into James Ryder, the hotel attendant at the Cosmopolitan Hotel from which the Countess of Morcar's blue carbuncle jewel has been stolen. He suspects that Ryder is the thief, not Horner, the person already arrested by the police. Holmes encourages Ryder to confess and repent: "And now let us hear a true account of the next act. How came the stone into the goose, and how came the goose into the open market? Tell us the truth, for there lies your only hope of safety." Ryder, who has no criminal record, is penitent about the crime, freely confesses all the details, and asks Holmes for mercy: "I never went wrong before! I never will again. I swear it. I'll swear it on a Bible. Oh, don't bring it into court! For Christ's sake, don't!" Holmes decides not to send him to prison and make him a "jail-bird." Instead, in a rush of Christmas spirit, Holmes lets Ryder go free and

predicts he will sin no more. Holmes is confident that the case against Horner, who is innocent, will collapse. He tells Watson, “I am not retained by the police to supply their deficiencies. Maybe I am committing a felony, but I am saving a soul.” Holmes played Santa on a grand scale.

3. *The Boscombe Valley Mystery*, published in 1891, is a convoluted tale of blackmail and murder beginning in Australia and ending up in a little town in Herefordshire England. John Turner murders Charles McCarthy who was blackmailing him, but McCarthy’s son James is wrongly charged with the murder, even though Turner’s daughter Alice believes James to be innocent. Holmes listens to the account of the murder, examines the crime scene, and puts together clues pointing to the murderer as “... a tall man, left-handed, limps with the right leg, wears thick-soled shooting-boots and a gray cloak, smokes Indian cigars, uses a cigar-holder, and carries a blunt pen-knife in his pocket.” Using the victim’s last words, Holmes makes the Australian connection between the victim and John Turner and deduces that Turner is the probable suspect and James McCarthy is innocent. Turner, dying of diabetes with only a short time to live, tells Holmes he’d rather die under his own roof than in jail. Importantly, Turner then gives Holmes a full, signed confession and assures him that he would have intervened if innocent young McCarthy went to trial. "Well, it is not for me to judge you," Holmes says. "I am no official agent. I understand that it was your daughter who required my presence here, and I am acting in her interests.” On this basis, Holmes decides not to expose Turner as long as James

McCarthy gets off the murder charge. Holmes treats old Turner gently, agreeing to let Turner die at home with his daughter. This decision is based on Holmes' belief in a higher power. "You are yourself aware that you will soon have to answer for your deed at a higher court than the Assizes. I will keep your confession, and if McCarthy is condemned I shall be forced to use it. If not, it shall never be seen by mortal eye; and your secret, whether you be alive or dead, shall be safe with us." James McCarthy was acquitted, and seven months later, John Turner died a natural death, his secret kept by Holmes and Watson, allowing James and Alice, the son and daughter of the murderer and the victim, "to live happily ... in ignorance of the black cloud which rests upon their past."

4. *The Adventure of Charles Augustus Milverton.* Holmes deals with Milverton, "the king of blackmailers," but he can't arrest him and bring him to the law for justice. Though Milverton's blackmail schemes have ruined many lives, his victims want to avoid scandal and refuse to go to the police, so he succeeds in operating outside the grasp of the law. But one of his female victims, a noblewoman whose life he ruined, murders him by pumping six shots from a little gleaming revolver into him at close range while Holmes and Watson, in hiding, watch from behind a window curtain. Holmes tells Lestrade, "I think there are certain crimes which the law cannot touch, and which therefore, to some extent, justify private revenge. No, it's no use arguing. I have made up my mind. My sympathies are with the criminals rather than with the victim, and I will not handle this case." Holmes finds out her true identity and decides

her fate by never revealing it, thus allowing her to elude the law. Holmes clearly believes she has suffered enough and that her crime will never be repeated. We include this under villains Holmes sets free rather than escapees because Holmes does know her identity and could pursue her for the crime but does not.

5. *The Adventure of the Crooked Man*, published in 1893, is another tale of a love triangle and long-ago crime and betrayal. Holmes solves a locked room murder where the body of Colonel James Barclay of the Royal Munsters is found in a locked room in his own home. Although Barclay is the murder victim, he is also the real villain in the case. Many years ago Barclay betrayed Henry Wood, a fellow soldier in his regiment and a rival for the woman Barclay later marries, by dispatching him into certain death. But Henry Wood managed to survive, though crippled and bent and forced to make his living performing conjuring tricks. The Colonel's old sins come back to haunt him, and he drops dead on the spot when he catches sight of Henry Wood after 30 years. Because the servants heard the Colonel and his wife arguing loudly, his wife Nancy is the prime suspect in his death. Holmes immediately deduces that Barclay many not have been murdered when he tells Watson about the "supposed murder of Colonel Barclay." Later, visiting the crime scene, other clues contribute to that theory, including a club, a missing door key, the name David, the word coward, and an animal that ran up a curtain. "It's every man's business to see justice done," Holmes announces as he locates Henry Wood, who reveals that although he had murder in his

heart, it was "Providence that killed" the Colonel. "He was dead before he fell. I read death on his face as plain as I can read that text over the fire. The bare sight of me was like a bullet through his guilty heart." Medical evidence does prove that the Colonel's death was due to apoplexy, and many would say he got his just desserts. With Nancy exonerated, Holmes elects to avoid scandal by not bringing the Colonel's cruelty to light. He tells Henry Wood, "There is no object in raking up this scandal against a dead man, foully as he has acted. You have at least the satisfaction of knowing that for thirty years of his life his conscience bitterly reproached him for his wicked deed."

The basic plot of this story is related to the David and Bathsheba story in the Bible, and it's worth noting that Holmes didn't pick up the Biblical reference clue, "David," until later when he tells Watson, "My Biblical knowledge is a trifle rusty, I fear, but you will find the story in the first or second of Samuel."

6. *The Adventure of the Devil's Foot*, published in 1910 and set in 1897, the fifth longest of the 56 stories, is an interesting locked room and revenge case that's known throughout the West of England as "the Cornish Horror." It begins with hints of "supernatural forces" when Brenda Tregennis is found dead and her two brothers found apparently insane, but Holmes quickly eliminates the supernatural when he tells Watson that "neither of us is prepared to admit diabolical intrusions into the affairs of men." Instead they must "exhaust all natural explanations." Sherlock Holmes quickly deduces that the Devil's Foot root was the poison used in the crime, thus bringing the case

back from supernatural to murder committed by person or persons unknown. Holmes suspects the third brother, Mortimer Tregennis, of murder and attempted murder for poisoning them all with Devil's Foot root in revenge for their taking some monies from an inheritance due him. Mortimer Tregennis is subsequently found dead, killed by the same poison. Dr. Leon Sterndale, the great African explorer and lover of Brenda, confesses to Mortimer's murder. After his confession, Holmes lets Sterndale go free because he feels that Sterndale was morally right in avenging the murder of the woman he loved, Brenda Tregennis. During this case, Holmes came to the secluded Cornish area on a sick leave ordered by his physician, Dr. Moore Agar of Harley Street, who told Holmes to "lay aside all his cases and surrender himself to complete rest if he wished to avert an absolute breakdown." Perhaps a lapse of judgement on Holmes part, due to his exhaustion, contributed to the ill-conceived, "unjustifiable" experiment Holmes performs with Devil's Foot root, nearly killing himself and Watson. Perhaps that same exhaustion kept Holmes from fully investigating the relationship between Brenda and Dr. Sterndale. Holmes surely should have talked to the Tregennis solicitors about their wills, as we expected him to do. In the end, Holmes approves Sterndale's avenge killing, and he allows Sterndale to return to Africa to finish his work. Holmes believes Sterndale committed a crime, but he finds it morally excusable. Holmes says, "I think you must agree, Watson, that it is not a case in which we are called upon to interfere." "I have never loved, Watson, but if I did and if the woman I loved had met such an end, I might act even as our lawless lion-hunter has done." Holmes definitely shielded a confessed murderer on the basis that he believed Sterndale killed Mortimer Tregennis in self-defense. Holmes, whether wrong or right, is guilty of conspiracy to aid and abet a murderer, but he's never brought to the law for this crime.

7. *A Case of Identity*, an early case published in 1891, is one in which the Victorian code and the Unwritten Laws are broken, yet Holmes feels there is no legal crime committed by the villain, James Windibank, Mary Sutherland's stepfather. He and his wife develop what Holmes calls, "a cruel and selfish and heartless a trick in a petty way as ever came before me." Mary Sutherland, at her wits' end because her fiancé disappears on their wedding day, asks Holmes to find him. Holmes uncovers another *affaire de coeur* – a bizarre love triangle in which Mary's stepfather, James Windibank, disguises himself and invents the character of Hosmer Angel who becomes Mary's suitor. He and his wife concoct the scheme hoping to hold Mary's love to prevent her from marrying anyone else so they can continue to control her money. James Windibank plays a dual role of husband and suitor in this love triangle with his older wife and his young, moneyed stepdaughter, Mary. Holmes uses the new science of typewriter forensics to compare typewritten letters to solve the case, and he confronts Windibank, telling him he knows about the impersonation scheme. However, Windibank is confident he can't be arrested. "There is no law, I fear, that can touch the scoundrel," Holmes says. By trying to obtain money under false pretenses, Windibank and his wife are guilty of the crime of Fraud-

Swindling. Strangely, Sherlock Holmes never reveals Windibank's dastardly impersonation to Mary, his client, who is paying him and to whom he owes an explanation. "If I tell her she will not believe me," he says cynically, and we're left with Mary waiting for her real-but-not-real suitor, Hosmer Angel, to return to her. Windibank and his wife escape completely, and we speculate that they will try this dastardly impersonation again unless the wife comes to realize the sexual implications and forbids him to do so.

8. *The Naval Treaty*, published in 1893, is the longest of the 56 stories and is a case that highlights Sherlock Holmes' powers of observation, analysis and deductive reasoning. It's also a case in which Holmes surprises us when he lets the criminal go free after committing theft of a government document, attempted murder, lying to the police and concealing evidence. Holmes hears the details concerning the theft "of the original of a secret treaty between England and Italy," stolen from the offices of Percy Phelps, an old school friend of Watson who's now working for the Foreign Office under his uncle, Lord Holdhurst, the foreign minister. Next Holmes and Watson visit Percy's home where his fiancée, Annie Harrison, is staying to nurse him as he recovers from a nine-week bout of brain fever, brought on by Percy's horror over the theft. Holmes considers a series of clues including the absence of wet footprints and the ringing bell at the crime scene, as well as the fact that no one other than Percy knew of the treaty. He rapidly deduces that the criminal is Joseph Harrison, his fiancée's brother, and immediately makes inquiries to confirm his theory. When Holmes hears that an attempt was made to

enter Percy's room at 2 a.m., he sets a trap in which Joseph Harrison reveals where he hid the treaty. Harrison attacks Holmes with a knife, but Holmes gets the better of him and secures the precious papers. Holmes then dramatically presents the papers to Phelps, and he tells Watson and Percy that he let Harrison go, but that he has wired the information to the police. He expects Harrison will escape capture, which, he believes, is a better outcome in the long run for the government since the whole affair can be kept secret. The papers are returned, and no treason is committed. Once again Holmes uses discretion as one of his touchstones for justice in this case. He ensures the story is kept out of the courts and the newspapers so that Percy Phelps can hopefully return to his former high position at the Foreign Office. We can't consider Harrison as an escapee because Holmes purposely allows him to fly the coop.

9. *The Adventure of the Noble Bachelor*, published in 1892, presents Holmes with a mystery concerning Lord St. Simon's bride who vanishes from the wedding breakfast. This piques Holmes interest, and he remarks to Watson, "They often vanish before the ceremony, and occasionally during the honeymoon; but I cannot call to mind anything quite so prompt as this." This case revolves around two different love triangles. One concerns Lord St. Simon, his bride Miss Hatty Doran, and his former mistress, Flora Miller of the Allegra. The other love triangle is one that Holmes reveals linking Miss Hattie Doran, Lord St. Simon, and Frank Moulton, Hattie's former husband whom she believed dead. The police arrest Flora Miller in Hattie Doran's disappearance, but

Holmes disagrees. He figures out the mystery immediately and tells St Simon: "I have solved it." He remarks to Watson, "I had formed my conclusions as to the case before our client came into the room." "Circumstantial evidence is occasionally very convincing, as when you find a trout in the milk, to quote Thoreau's example." The mystery of the missing bride hinged on Hatty seeing her former husband at the wedding ceremony. He'd been declared dead but had escaped from captivity among the Apaches and followed her to England. The crime in this case was bigamy. Hatty allowed the wedding ceremony to go forward after she saw her first husband sitting in the church pew. Since Hatty didn't consummate her marriage to Lord St. Simon, perhaps an annulment would suffice to correct the bigamy. However, Holmes glosses over the illegalities of the bigamy and prepares a wedding feast for Hatty and Frank and Lord St. Simon. Lord St. Simon, predictably, leaves. Holmes does not report the bigamy to Lestrade, and it's questionable whether Lord St. Simon, who values his privacy, will do so. Holmes never mentions how Hatty will legally rectify her bigamous position. He does mention that Lord St. Simon lost both a wife and a fortune, but we are left to wonder if Hatty's wealthy father – "the richest man on the Pacific slope" – will make some accommodation to St. Simon for the humiliation he and his family endured. With all the pre-wedding and wedding day publicity, it's hard to imagine the press not finding out the facts and making a sensation of this case of bigamy, even though Holmes and St. Simon try to suppress it.

This is the only case of Bigamy in the Canon. Bigamy had become a frequent crime in Great Britain, with 2,555 cases tried between 1815 and 1861, according to Anthony Camp in his article 'The English church courts and their records." [xiii]

10. In The Adventure of the Priory School there is one guilty criminal whose crime was murder, and he goes to the gallows (see Category 2). However, there are two other guilty men involved in this case. One is James Wilder, the illegitimate son of Lord Holdernesse, who is guilty of masterminding the kidnapping of Lord Saltire, the Duke's legitimate son. The second is the Duke himself. Holmes cites English legal principle when he informs the Duke that he is a co-conspirator in the crime because he aided the escape of a murderer and was culpable in putting Lord Saltire into a dangerous situation. He points out that the Duke has condoned a felony, and Holmes tells him: "I must take the view, your Grace, that when a man embarks upon a crime, he is morally guilty of any other crime which may spring from it." The Duke agrees to be frank about everything and admits his complicity. He pleads for mercy for James, who confessed that he was behind the kidnapping of his half-brother, but that he had no hand in the murder of Heidegger, the German master. The Duke begs Holmes to help "minimize this hideous scandal." It is then that the Duke finally reveals that James Wilder is his illegitimate son. Although Holmes seems shocked, we suspect he already knew this fact, and he tells the Duke that "having secured the future, we can afford to be more lenient with the past. I am not in an official position, and there is no reason, so long as the ends of

justice are served, why I should disclose all that I know." Thus Holmes agrees not to bring the illegitimate James to the law, but to let him go free to "seek his fortune in Australia." Holmes perhaps concludes that Wilder might have a harder time in Australia away from the protection of the Duke rather than in a British prison. The ending of this adventure can be viewed through two separate prisims, one of which embodies the Victorian code completely while the other illustrates a more current point of view. Holmes neither justifies the Duke's behavior nor does he forgive the Duke his crimes. Nonetheless he follows the Unwritten Law and uses his discretion to repress the Duke's complicity and to avoid scandal for the Duke and his family. Holmes mitigates his judgment by forcing the Duke to write a large reward check. A more modern view may well be that Holmes bowed to the prerogatives of class distinction by making such a lenient judgment. However readers must remember it is the Victorian code Holmes follows and not the code of liberty and equality for all that we moderns have since adopted. In another story, *The Three Gables*, we find a similar situation in which Holmes agrees not to report Isadora Klein to Scotland Yard and extracts a five thousand pound payment from her for his client. Isadora confesses all and says she is sorry. She must avoid scandal because of her engagement to the Duke of Lomond, and Holmes agrees. Common threads in both stories are that each one involves a Duke, each one involves a monetary payment, and in each, the wrongdoer confesses and repents.

11. *The Adventure of the Second Stain,* published in 1904 and set in the late 1881's, is, according to Watson, "the most important international case which (Holmes) has ever been called upon to handle." It combines a tale about spies and treason with a love triangle, blackmail, a wife's betrayal, and murder and madness. It is also a fascinating example of the Holmesian brand of justice. One wrongdoer is murdered, one is pardoned by Holmes, and one escapes, only to go mad. Lady Hilda Trelawney Hope, wife of the European Secretary, steals a secret paper from her husband's dispatch box, a paper which, if made public, would lead to war. She breaks one of the most sacred rules of Victorian life – she betrays her husband. Then she commits treason when she gives the sensitive document to Eduardo Lucas, an international spy and secret agent, to keep him from blackmailing her. She's put her husband in an untenable position that will ruin his career. Her blackmailer, Eduardo Lucas, is living a double life, and he is murdered by his jealous wife, who flees the scene and goes mad. Lady Hope is guilty of committing several serious crimes in this case, including theft, burglary, lying to Scotland Yard to impede an investigation, concealing evidence, interfering with a crime scene by removing evidence, and treason. Yet Sherlock Holmes does not reveal her involvement or her crimes to the police. Instead he goes so far as to himself commit the crimes of withholding evidence and conspiracy to conceal a crime. Holmes insists, "Do not ring (for the butler), Lady Hilda. If you do, then all my earnest efforts to avoid a scandal will be frustrated. Give up the letter and all will be set right. If you will work with me I can

arrange everything. If you work against me I must expose you." She decides to work with him, and all is forgiven the Lady as Holmes, the wizard and sorcerer, returns the paper and metes out his own justice based upon the need for secrecy and discretion in order to save a European catastrophe and a scandal. Holmes tells Watson, "...the curtain rings up for the last act. You will be relieved to hear that there will be no war, that the Right Honourable Trelawney Hope will suffer no setback in his brilliant career, that the indiscreet Sovereign will receive no punishment for his indiscretion, that the Prime Minister will have no European complication to deal with, and that with a little tact and management upon our part nobody will be a penny the worse for what might have been a very ugly incident." One mitigating factor that allows Holmes to go easy on Lady Hope is that she was in complete ignorance of the importance of the document she passed on to her blackmailer because her husband always kept government secrets strictly to himself, never discussing anything of the nature of his work with her. What a close escape for Lady Hilda, who should have known better.

12. *Silver Blaze* is an early story published in 1892 about the disappearance of a racehorse and contains the famous Sherlock Holmes clue of the dog who did not bark in the night. This case has murder, gambling, a love triangle, and Silver Blaze, "the most remarkable horse in England" who is the favorite for the Wessex Cup. When Silver Blaze goes missing and his trainer, John Straker, is found dead on the moor, Holmes follows the clues of curried mutton, a dove-colored silk dress, the dog that is silent in the night, and some

lame sheep. It doesn't take him long to discover that the horse itself killed Straker in self-defense. Holmes finds that Straker, a married man, was leading an expensive double life involving another woman. He was planning to injure Silver Blaze by cutting his tendon and then to bet against his own horse so he'd win money. Silver Blaze kicked Straker to death and was then found wandering by Silas Brown who took him to his nearby stable. Brown disguised the horse, dying its blaze and keeping it hidden in his stable so that his own horse would win the Wessex Cup. Holmes decides to give Silas Brown amnesty because his crime of disguising and hiding Silver Blaze was not pre-meditated. Silas Brown confessed to Holmes, and we've seen how confession is an important component of forgiveness in Holmesian justice. Brown then goes in league with Holmes and agrees to keep Silver Blaze safe and enter him into the Wessex Cup, which Silver Blaze then wins. Undoubtedly the fact that Brown agreed to keep Silver Blaze hidden until race day contributed to Holmes' decision to give him amnesty. Holmes also had faith in the ability of Silver Blaze to win. Victorians followed the example of the upper classes in their love for horse racing, and this tale emphasizes the Victorian code's importance of making an honorable and not a dishonorable profit from such a situation.

13. *The Adventure of the Sussex Vampire* is one of the later cases, published in 1924 and set in 1901. It's also one of the shortest of the stories at 5, 999 words. The case begins with Gothic overtones and the mention of vampires, a case Watson notes, that is "a mixture of the modern and the mediaeval, of the practical and of

the wildly fanciful." Holmes, however, immediately dismisses anything supernatural, as he did in *The Devil's Foot.* "Rubbish, Watson, rubbish! What have we to do with walking corpses who can only be held in their grave by stakes driven through their hearts? It's pure lunacy." "The world is big enough for us. No ghosts need apply." The case is outlined in a letter from James Ferguson, a rugby three-quarter against whom Watson had played. Ferguson's wife, "a Peruvian lady," began to show alarming behavior "alien to her ordinarily sweet and gentle disposition" when she was seen twice assaulting Jacky, the husband's fifteen year old son from a previous marriage. She was also seen sucking blood from a wound on the neck of her own little baby, and was under suspicion of being a vampire, an accusation more easily made because she was of foreign birth and her temperament was "fiery" and "tropical" rather than English. According to her husband, "The fact of her foreign birth and of her alien religion always caused a separation of interests and of feelings ... there were sides of her character which (I) could never explore or understand." Holmes solves the case immediately and tells Watson, "I had, in fact, reached it before we left Baker Street, and the rest has merely been observation and confirmation." He reveals that the wife is loath to tell the truth about Jacky. The "poor little inoffensive cripple" has tried to poison the baby out of an overwhelming jealousy. Holmes doesn't involve the police in this case, even though young Jacky isn't just teasing his new sibling but is actually attempting to murder the baby. Jacky nearly killed the dog Carlo with the poison, and his stepmother became ill after she sucked the poison from the baby's neck wound. Instead of sending Jacky to jail, Holmes recommends the son spend a year at sea, thinking this will straighten him out. Maybe it is better than a year in jail.

This is the only story in which a child is the villain, and, apart from the Baker Street Irregulars, it is only one of a very few stories in which children are involved – some others being *The Yellow Face* and *The Copper Beeches.* An interesting point to compare is Holmes' recommendation in *The Sussex Vampire* that the boy spend a year at sea with Holmes' comments about the-apple-doesn't-fall-far-from-the-tree cruel natured son in *The Copper Beeches.*

14. *The Problem of Thor Bridge.* In this later story published in 1922, Holmes is confronted with a thorny problem in which the victim is the murderer. Despite this tangle, he saves an innocent girl from being convicted of murder. Holmes meets Neil Gibson, a U.S. Senator and the greatest gold mining magnate in the world. Holmes uncovers a dark love triangle with the Gold King, his wife Maria – a creature of the tropics from Brazil - and her rival, the governess. Holmes uses his method to show how Maria, of a passionate and jealous nature and wanting revenge, commits suicide and plants clues to implicate the English governess in her death. There's a crime scene and a dead body where the victim, Maria, committed suicide but attempted to frame the governess and have her convicted of murder. Holmes finds justice for the governess and saves her by revealing what really happened. Maria's crimes are twofold. One crime is suicide, and the other is the attempted murder of the governess which Holmes thwarted. Technically

Maria's suicide was illegal and considered immoral, but Holmes points out that so were Neil Gibson's physical advances to the governess that caused the unfortunate affair, although these too were not prosecutable.

15. The Adventure of the Three Gables was published in 1926 and has a woman, Isadora Klein, "the most lovely widow upon earth," as a spectacular villainess who works with a gang of bullies. Homes and Watson visit Three Gables in Harrow Weald at the request of a Mrs. Maberley, despite their being threatened by a member of the gang to drop the case. She received a good offer to buy the Three Gables, but wonders about an odd provision connected with the offer that specifies she would be legally unable to remove anything at all from her house. Holmes discovers that her recently deceased son, Douglas, had an affair with Isadora Klein and after his death all his effects were sent to his mother, including a manuscript incriminating Isadora Klein in criminal activities. Mrs. Maberley doesn't take Holmes' advice to have someone stay with her, so the gang breaks in, chloroforms her, and succeeds in stealing all but the last page of the manuscript. In an effort to put an end to the affair, Holmes decides to bargain with Isadora Klein, who is about to marry the young Duke of Lomond. Holmes tells her, "I am not the law, but I represent justice so far as my feeble powers go." She tells him her story and how she tried to get the manuscript legally. He sympathizes with her and notes: "Well I suppose I shall have to confound a felony as usual." With that, he extracts a payment of 5,000 pounds from her for Mrs. Maberley to travel around the world. Barney and Susan Stockdale and Steve Dixie will be arrested for burglary, but Holmes lets Isadora go free, despite her crimes against his own client, cautioning her that she can't play with edged tools forever without cutting her hands. Isadora, the leader of the gang, has been responsible for many criminal acts. Her criminal behavior in this case was not just a lapse in judgement, as in other cases where Holmes lets the villain off the hook. Instead her acts were executed with planning and pre-meditation. But Holmes still treats Isadora, a rare woman villain, with Victorian deference, and this perhaps explains the difference in how he'd treat a male villain under the same circumstances. Another possible reason for the deference is that Holmes blackmails Isadora for the 5,000 pounds, even though he doesn't personally benefit from the money. At the beginning of the story, Holmes is threatened by Steve Dixie, a bruiser with the Spencer John gang. Dixie puts himself on the same footing as Holmes when he says: "You ain't the law, and I ain't the law either ...." Since Holmes does break the law in this case by accepting a pay-off from Isadora, Dixie may have been quite right in his remark. (See also Category 2.) Note: Reference *The Priory School* for another case in which Holmes' judgment involves a reward payment.

16. *The Adventure of the Three Students*, published in 1904, is a story in which the crime is a burglary connected to a "painful" cheating scandal that takes place in a University town. Sherlock Holmes is brought in to "settle the matter quietly and discreetly." This case presents a perfect example of a breach of the unwritten laws in which a student is guilty of behavior

that isn't cricket. It is bad form to have a cheating scandal in your university. It would destroy the school's reputation. Comes the agitated tutor, Mr. Hilton Soames, another acquaintance of Watson, who begs Holmes to find out which of three students broke into his room and copied the Thucydides translation for the examination for the Fortescue Scholarship. "When once the law is invoked it cannot be stayed again, and this is just one of those cases where, for the credit of the college, it is most essential to avoid scandal." Soames believes only Holmes can help because his "discretion is as well known as (his) powers." Holmes investigates the students under suspicion and deduces that the guilty student is young Gilchrist. Despite the fact that he seemed to be an example of clean living and had been excelling at both his athletic activities and his school achievements, Gilchrist suddenly cheated. He stopped Playing by the Rules. Cheating of any kind – at cards, at horses, at scholarships - wasn't Playing Fair. Holmes concurs that discretion is all in this case. He announces, "If this matter is not to become public, we must give ourselves certain powers, and resolve ourselves into a small private court-martial." Gilchrist tells everything, and once again confession is good for the soul in Holmes' eyes, resulting in his decision not to make Gilchrist face the law for trial and punishment. Instead he allows Gilchrist to go forward with his life, but not on the same path. Gilchrist has written to the tutor and had "determined not to go in for the examination," but to leave immediately for South Africa and accept a commission he'd been offered in the Rhodesian Police. Holmes considers Gilchrist's confession, repentance and overall behavior as mitigating factors in his punishment. Gilchrist's life – his oeuvre – is more telling than the one criminal act as a mirror into his character. The Sherlock Holmes view of justice in this case is that even though Gilchrist had a moral lapse in his behavior, it was not one that he had planned out. Holmes tells us Gilchrist wasn't a real criminal – rather his crime was a spur of the moment incident not representative of his overall character. In the end, Gilchrist's character proves to be cricket. His refusal to take advantage of the spoils of his victory after the incident balances out his one criminal lapse, restores his moral balance, and puts him once more on a fair playing field. Holmes encourages Gilchrist, saying, "For once you have fallen low. Let us see, in the future, how high you can rise." Essentially go and sin no more.

17. *The Man With the Twisted Lip* was published in 1891. Although Watson notes this case was free of legal crime, a scarred beggar, Hugh Boone, is arrested under suspicion of being responsible for the death of Neville St. Clair. When Holmes tells St. Clair's wife that he believes St. Clair to be dead, she claims he's not and produces a letter from him. Holmes realizes that disguise is the key to the case, and he handily unmasks Hugh Boone as Neville St. Clair, a nice twist where the victim and the criminal are one and the same. Boone immediately challenges Holmes. "If I am Mr. Neville St. Clair, then it is obvious that no crime has been committed, and that, therefore, I am illegally detained." "No crime, but a very great error has been committed," Holmes tells him. In our analysis, we've included begging as a crime statistic here because it was a crime in Victorian England, and,

importantly, Holmes presents St. Clair with an ultimatum – if St. Clair gives up begging, then Holmes will be discreet and save St. Clair and his family from public scandal. "If you leave it to a court of law to clear the matter up," said Holmes, "of course you can hardly avoid publicity. On the other hand, if you convince the police authorities that there is no possible case against you, I do not know that there is any reason that the details should find their way into the papers. Inspector Bradstreet would, I am sure, make notes upon anything which you might tell us and submit it to the proper authorities. The case would then never go into court at all." St. Clair, desperate to avoid scandal, says, "I would have endured imprisonment, ay, even execution, rather than have left my miserable secret as a family blot to my children." Begging is inconsistent with the behavior of a Victorian gentleman, and St. Clair was able to overcome the criminal aspect using the subterfuge of 'selling' matches. Holmes, himself the master at disguise, was of course the one able to solve the mystery.

18. *The Adventure of the Veiled Lodger*, published in 1927 and set in 1896, is the shortest of the 56 stories. It begins with a landlady summoning Holmes for her tenant, Mrs. Eugenia Ronder, who has only once shown her horribly scarred face in all the years she's lived there. Now, Mrs. Ronder wants to tell Holmes something terrible that's on her mind. Holmes quickly deduces that Mrs. Ronder is one side of a love triangle connected to an old murder that is still casting its horrible shadow. Now that the other two sides of the love triangle are both dead, Eugenia reveals to Holmes that she and strongman Leonardo, who was her lover,

murdered her husband, a bully who owned the circus in which they all performed. She confesses that Leonardo used a club with nails to resemble a lion's paw to make it appear as if their circus lion, Sahara King, had killed her husband. But that same night when Eugenia opened the cage, the lion smelled the blood of her husband and attacked her, destroying her beautiful face. Leonardo, who could have saved her, ran cowardly away. From that day she has lived with her face covered, and only now that she has read that Leonardo has drowned could she come forward and confess. Once again Holmes shows sympathy for the villain or villainess who confesses, especially as he believes Leonardo bore the most guilt. In this case, with Eugenia near death, Holmes also shows forgiveness and compassion: "The ways of fate are indeed hard to understand. If there is not some compensation hereafter, then the world is a cruel jest." Holmes and Watson see her ruined face, and Holmes cautions her against committing suicide, which he suspects she might try. When he receives a small blue bottle of prussic acid in the mail a few days later with a note from Eugenia that reads: "I send you my temptation. I will follow your advice," Holmes calls Eugenia a brave woman. To Sherlock Holmes, this was an old case that had been closed years ago on the theory that Sahara King was the murderer. Now that he knows the truth, Holmes declares that "the case is closed," and he lets Eugenia live out the rest of what may be left of her life without informing Scotland Yard. Since Eugenia has suffered enough for her sins, Holmesian justice allows her to die in peace. *Requiescat in pace.* We can hope that Sahara King was somehow vindicated in the murder charge.

B. Cases wherein the Villain escapes - 11

This is the second of the three sub categories in this chapter, the others being 3 A where Holmes decides justice for the villains and 3 C where justice comes from a higher power. This category, 3 B, covers 11 of the 37 cases (30%), where the wrongdoers escape, eluding both Holmes and the grasp of British justice. The cases are:

The Adventure of the Beryl Coronet – 1892
The Adventure of the Engineer's Thumb - 1892
The Five Orange Pips - 1891
The Gloria Scott - 1893
The Greek Interpreter - 1893
The Disappearance of Lady Frances Carfax - 1911
The Musgrave Ritual – 1893
The Resident Patient – 1903
A Scandal in Bohemia – 1891
The Adventure of the Second Stain – 1904
The Adventure of Wisteria Lodge - 1908

7 of these 11 are early cases published between 1891 and 1893. The other four are later, published from 1903 to 1911. Criminal escapes happen much more frequently in Holmes' early published stories by a ratio of 7 (64%) to 4 (36%).

These escape cases can be divided into 2 types. In one, the escapees get away forever with no further word of their fates. In the second, the escapees face justice from a final and higher power.

3 B 1 – Villain escapes and is never heard from again – 6 cases

In six of these 11 cases where the criminals escape Holmes and British Law, they are never again heard from. 5 of these 6 are early cases published from 1891- 1893, with only *Lady Frances Carfax* being later in 1911.

The Adventure of the Beryl Coronet – 1892
The Adventure of the Engineer's Thumb - 1892
The Gloria Scott - 1893
The Disappearance of Lady Frances Carfax - 1911
The Musgrave Ritual - 1893
A Scandal in Bohemia – 1891

1. *The Adventure of the Beryl Coronet* is an exciting tale involving the theft of stones from a valuable jeweled coronet, misplaced trust, a wrongly accused son, a dark love triangle, and a possible compromise of one of the highest and noblest men in England. Banker Alexander Holder, referred by the police, tells Holmes he needs help because "one of the most precious public possessions of the empire," owned by "one of the most exalted names in England," has been stolen from Holder's personal safekeeping. Worse yet, Holder believes his son is responsible. By analyzing the features of the theft, the members of Holder's household, and the many footprints in the snow surrounding the house from which the coronet had been stolen, Holmes correctly deduces that Holder's son is innocent. He disguises himself to test his theory, and then informs Holder that his niece Mary is to blame, along with her confederate and lover, Sir

George Burnwell, “one of the most dangerous men in England -- a ruined gambler, an absolutely desperate villain, a man without heart or conscience.” Holmes fends off an attack on his life by Burnwell and is able to buy back the missing stones. Burnwell and Mary escape, and Holmes is content to let them go in order to save England from a great public scandal. Holder’s niece Mary has forsaken her family for Burnwell, and Holmes confidently predicts that “whatever her sins are, they will soon receive a more than sufficient punishment."

2. *The Adventure of the Engineer’s Thumb*, published in 1892, is a case that Watson himself brings to Holmes’ attention. The story includes crimes galore, such as counterfeiting, assault and attempted murder, not to mention old crimes of the past such as murder. It begins with Watson having to treat Victor Hatherley, whose thumb had just been hacked off in a murderous attack with a cleaver. Hatherley was hired by the German, Colonel Lysander Stark, to perform some light repair work on an hydraulic stamping machine for a munificent sum, but Hatherley had to agree to a pledge of secrecy about the job. He is taken to an unknown location at midnight where he soon realizes that he has been misled about the true purpose of the machine. He barely escapes being killed by Stark and his confederate, an Englishman named Ferguson. Holmes deduces that the machine is used for counterfeiting coins. He further deduces the location of the house and attempts to have the gang arrested by the police he brings along. However, the property is in flames and the gang of three - “the beautiful woman, the sinister German and the morose

Englishman" escape before Holmes, Watson and the law arrive. They are never brought to criminal justice or heard from again. It's one of the few such criminal escapes in the Canon.

3. *The 'Gloria Scott'*, published in 1893, has Holmes telling Watson about his first case - a rough and sad tale about the past sins of the father of one of his only friends at college, Victor Trevor. Holmes is able to deduce many things about Trevor senior when they first meet, and when he mentions the initials "JA," Trevor senior faints. He later encourages Holmes, telling him that being a detective is surely his profession in life. Old Trevor dies from a stroke after reading a coded message saying, "The game is up. Hudson has told all. Fly for your life." The truth is revealed in a letter in which Victor learns his father's real name - James Armitage - and the dark family secrets involving fraud and mutiny and blackmail. Old Trevor had been convicted of theft and transported to Australia aboard the Gloria Scott, on which he participated in a mutiny. But not wanting to murder in cold blood, he and another man, Evans, were set adrift. Then the Gloria Scott exploded, and he and Evans went back but could only save one sailor named Hudson. They were picked up by a ship headed to Australia, and once there, they changed their names to Trevor and Beddoes, made their fortunes digging gold, and returned to England where Trevor senior became a justice of the peace and led a blameless life for 30 years. "He had a reputation for kindness and charity on the countryside, and was noted for the leniency of his sentences from the bench." But Hudson, the lone survivor, appears 30 years later in

England to blackmail both men, threatening to reveal the secret of the mutiny that they both had kept for so long. After Trevor senior's death, neither Hudson nor Beddoes is ever heard from again. Sherlock Holmes suspects that Beddoes has fled from England after murdering the blackmailer Hudson. Victor Trevor, Holmes' university friend, is so heartbroken over his father's story that he leaves England and goes to a Terai tea plantation where he does well.

4. *The Disappearance of Lady Frances Carfax*, a later story published in 1911, is a case in which Holmes tumbles nearly too late to the answer to save Lady Frances Carfax from death. Holmes breaks the law to find her, and discovers that the villain, Henry 'Holy' Peters is passing himself off as the Rev. Dr. Schlessinger and is guilty of fraud and attempted murder. Holmes calls Peters "one of the most unscrupulous rascals that Australia has ever evolved." When Peters and his wife manage a daring escape from Holmes, Holmes notes that, "If our ex-missionary friends escape the clutches of Lestrade, I shall expect to hear of some brilliant incidents in their future career."

5. *The Musgrave Ritual* is a fascinating story in which Holmes solves two mysteries – one the disappearance of two servants, and two, a secret ritual performed by every successive generation of Musgraves. Both these mysteries are overlaid by a love triangle involving the butler, Brunton; Rachel Howells, the second housemaid; and Janet Tregellis, the daughter of the head game keeper. When both Brunton and Rachel go missing, Holmes uses the Musgrave Ritual and follows

Brunton's clever path of reasoning to a hidden treasure. Unfortunately for Brunton, he finds what he seeks but dies in the quest. Holmes suspects that Rachel, the Welsh housemaid, was involved in the treasure hunt and may well have murdered Brunton. But she escapes and evades both Holmesian and British justice. From that day, "nothing was ever heard, and the probability is that she got away out of England and carried herself and the memory of her crime to some land beyond the seas." Whether Rachel murdered Brunton shall never be known for sure, but her black brooding combined with her eventual disappearance point to the act of a vengeful jilted lover and suggest her guilt rather than her innocence.

6. *A Scandal in Bohemia* features Irene Adler, referred to by Holmes as "The Woman" because she is able to outsmart him and make a clean escape. In this, the first Sherlock Holmes short story published in 1891, Holmes helps prevent the crime of blackmail. He immediately deduces that the six foot six man wearing a mask and dressed in "barbaric opulence" who comes to consult him is "Wilhelm Gottsreich Sigismond von Ormstein, Grand Duke of Cassel-Felstein, and hereditary King of Bohemia." The case is an interesting love triangle involving the King and his former mistress, Irene Adler, and the King's fiancée. Irene Adler is threatening to send a compromising photograph of the two of them to the King's fiancée, thereby hoping to thwart the forthcoming marriage. Five attempts to steal the photo have failed, and Irene won't take any money. Holmes to the rescue! He's hired to uncover the hiding place of the compromising photo and retrieve it, effectively ending the blackmail

attempt. Holmes disguises himself twice in this case -- first as an out of work groom where he witnesses Irene Adler's marriage, and then as an elderly clergyman who tricks Irene Adler into revealing where she's hidden the photograph. But before Holmes can get his hands on it, Irene Adler outflanks him. She seems to recognize suddenly that her lover, formerly the Crown Prince, now the King, has changed, just as Shakespeare's Prince Hal changed when he became King. They were in love, but she finally realizes he will never marry her because of class differences – strict class distinctions that are so important to Victorians. Thus Irene decides on the spur of the moment to immediately wed Godfrey Norton. He races to her side, no doubt to confirm in person that she's firm in her decision to marry and to agree on the particulars. So hastily arranged is the marriage that Godfrey must first rush to Gross & Hankey's in Regent Street for a wedding ring. He doesn't even have a best man, and in a serendipitous event, Holmes - coincidently disguised as a groom - stands in to witness the marriage. Irene, thereafter realizing that Holmes is on the case, outflanks Holmes and the King by fleeing the country with her new husband, escaping the law and promising to drop her blackmail attempt. Holmes, using his invaluable discretion, helps to avoid "a great scandal" that threatened to affect the Kingdom of Bohemia. Holmes holds Irene Adler in such high regard for her ability to out-maneuver him that he chooses her photo instead of a valuable emerald snake ring as a token from the King.

<u>3 B 2 – Villain Escapes but later faces justice from on high - 5</u>

Category 3B 1 listed the 11 cases where criminals escape Holmes and the law. This Category 3B2 is a subset of that category. It covers 5 of the 11 escape cases in which, by a turn of fate, the villains are rendered a higher justice from above. In two cases wrongdoers are murdered; in another two they die in shipwrecks; and in one a murderess goes mad. The five cases are:

The Five Orange Pips - 1891
The Greek Interpreter - 1893
The Resident Patient - 1903
The Adventure of the Second Stain - 1904
The Adventure of Wisteria Lodge - 1908

1. *The Five Orange Pips.* This case centers on the "terrible secret society" of the American Ku Klux Klan which has previously murdered John Openshaw's grandfather and father in an effort to reclaim incriminating documents taken from the KKK by the grandfather. Unbeknownst to the clan, these papers have already been destroyed. Now Captain Calhoun and his two confederates from the KKK have sent their warning of five orange pips to John. Holmes grasps the problem immediately and advises John to go home and communicate to the KKK that the papers they want have been destroyed. Unfortunately Holmes' advice comes too late, and John is murdered on his way home. Holmes admits his error and symbolically is later seen eating bread and water, the food of atonement, as if he were a prisoner in jail. Holmes wants his revenge on the three murderers, but they escape aboard the Lone Star of Savannah and are never captured and brought to the law. Instead we are

told that "somewhere far out in the Atlantic a shattered stern-post of the boat was seen swinging in the trough of a wave, with the letters "L. S." carved upon it, and that is all which we shall ever know of the fate of the Lone Star." The justice they receive is from a higher power.

2. The Greek Interpreter is a case with a problem brought to Sherlock by his elder and possibly smarter brother, Mycroft. It's a dark tale of kidnapping, torture, and murder revealed to Holmes by Mr. Melas, the Greek Interpreter. Melas was transported blindfolded to a secret location in which a brother, Paul Kratides, who was trying to prevent his sister Sophy's marriage to a Harold Latimer, is being held captive. Melas must translate as Paul Kratides can speak only Greek. Melas finds out that Latimer has kidnapped Paul and is torturing him to force Paul to sign away his control over Sophy's money. When Paul refuses, Latimer kills him and nearly kills Melas. Dr. Watson revives Melas, and they try to save Sophy, who has been abducted by Latimer and a confederate, Wilson Kemp. When they know their fraudulent swindle has been discovered, Latimer and Kemp manage to escape with Sophy, eluding both Holmesian and British justice. But later Watson reads us a news report about "two Englishmen who had been travelling with a woman had met with a tragic end. They had each been stabbed, it seems, and the Hungarian police were of opinion that they had quarrelled and had inflicted mortal injuries upon each other." Holmes believes that Sophy herself, as the avenging angel, righted the wrongs done to her and her brother.

3. *The Resident Patient*, published in 1893, is a tale in which three villains hold their own mock trial and render a verdict, much like the mock trials held by Sherlock Holmes and Watson. It's also a case in which the villains escape the law, as well as a case that undoubtedly reflects on Conan Doyle's time in the medical profession. A gang of bank robbers, released early from prison, disguise themselves as Russians to enter the house of their former gang member, Sutton, now living under the name Blessington. Sutton had betrayed the rest of the gang to the police, and now the gang wants their revenge. Blessington wants Sherlock Holmes to solve the mystery of who got into his room, but he refuses to tell Holmes what's frightening him. Holmes knows Blessington is lying and says, "I can read in a man's eye when it is his own skin that he is frightened for. It is inconceivable that this fellow could have made two such vindictive enemies as these appear to be without knowing of it. I hold it, therefore, to be certain that he does know who these men are, and that for reasons of his own he suppresses it." Unable to assist Blessington because he's refused to confess his past sin, Holmes leaves with thoughts of returning the next day when Blessington may be at last willing to talk. However, Blessington's past sin finally catches up with him, and he's found hanged in his bedroom the next day, a possible suicide. Holmes unravels Blessington's past and his connection with the Worthington Bank gang he'd double-crossed years ago. He determines that the gang, newly released from prison, tracked down Blessington and took their revenge. Holmes notes, "However, wretch as (Blessington) was, he was still

living under the shield of British Law, and I have no doubt, Inspector, that you will see that, though that shield may fail to guard, the sword of justice is still there to avenge." Using clues including cigars, footprints, a screwdriver and some screws, and scratches on the door lock, Holmes deduces how the three gained entry with the help of the house pageboy, how they held a mock trial, and how they then hanged Blessington and left. The three murderers - Hayward, Biddle and Moffat - escape the grasp of both Holmes and the law. Later they are called to a higher justice as Scotland Yard surmises they were passengers of the ill-fated steamer Norah Creina, lost with all hands off the Portuguese coast.
The page who was complicit in their crime of murder is captured and brought to the law, but the proceedings against him brake down "for want of evidence," so he is not included as a villain.

4. In <u>*The Adventure of the Second Stain*</u>, published in 1904, Holmes forgives Lady Hilda Trelawney Hope her treasonous act of stealing a top secret government letter and handing it over to a blackmailer. Lady Hope was blackmailed by Eduardo Lucas over a letter written by her before her marriage. Lucas was living a double life as a bachelor in London and as a married man, Henri Fournaye, in Paris. His wife, Mme. Henri Fournaye, of Creole origin and highly jealous, traveled to London where she shadowed her husband for several days. Upon seeing another woman - in this case Lady Hope - enter her husband's flat, she rushed in, argued with him, grabbed an Indian knife from a display on the wall and attacked him. She stabbed him in the heart, killing him instantly. She escaped

the scene and traveled back to Paris. However, her servants reported to the authorities that she was insane, and she was diagnosed with a "mania of a dangerous and permanent form." Mme. Fournaye escapes legal justice for her deed, but her punishment is permanent madness. Sherlock Holmes himself never gets involved with the murderess in this case; instead he leaves her to heaven.

5. *The Adventure of Wisteria Lodge.* Published in 1908 and set in 1892, this case is about past sins in Central America, and it has "two sets of foreigners – one at Wisteria Lodge and one at High Gable." John Scott Eccles tells Holmes an odd story about a man named Garcia, his host at Wisteria Lodge, who, it transpires, has been murdered in the night. Holmes and Watson visit the site with Inspector Baynes, and they find a dead white cock, a pail of blood and the bones from a kid or a lamb - all signs of Voodoo sacrificial rituals. Based on this evidence, Inspector Baynes arrests the mulatto cook for the Garcia's murder. Holmes however dismisses Voodoo and instead pulls the threads of the case together and finds that Garcia, one of the group of collaborators at Wisteria Lodge, had attempted to murder someone at High Gable, but he failed. In turn, Garcia is murdered by his intended victim, Don Murillo, the Tiger of San Pedro, "the most lewd and bloodthirsty tyrant that had ever governed any country with a pretence to civilization" who "sold his soul to the Devil in exchange for money." Murillo has been posing nearby under the name of Henderson. Another confederate in Garcia's group was Miss Burnet, an Englishwoman who, posing as governess, had infiltrated Don

Murillo's camp to spy on them. When her involvement is uncovered, she's held prisoner. Miss Burnet, who is really Signora Victor Durando, justifies her actions and those of her confederates who want revenge and justice by eliminating Don Murillo, saying: "What does the law of England care for the rivers of blood shed years ago in San Pedro, or for the ship-load of treasure which this man has stolen? To you they are like crimes committed in some other planet. But *we* know. ... To us there is no fiend in hell like Juan Murillo, and no peace in life while his victims still cry for vengeance." Holmes and Baynes work independently to help her break away from Murillo at the train station. Murillo and his party flee, escaping Holmes and English justice. But six months later, he and his confederate Lucas are found murdered in Madrid – another case of justice rendered from on high.

C. Cases where justice comes from on high – 13

In addition to the five cases in Category 3B 2 (above) where escapees eventually meet a higher form a justice, there are 13 other cases with a variety of crimes and villains in which one or more of the wrongdoers also receives justice from an even higher power. The 13 cases in this Category 3C plus the previous 5 in Category 3B2 amount to a total of 18 cases where justice comes from on high, accounting for 32% of the 56 stories. Unlike the cases where most of the wrongdoers repent and are forgiven or have their punishments mitigated, in these cases where justice comes from a higher power, the wrongdoers do not repent. Repentance is a central factor in Holmesian justice, and without it, the villains are subject to harsh punishment, often death, madness, maiming or suicide.

The Cardboard Box - 1893
The Adventure of Charles Augustus Milverton - 1904
The Adventure of the Copper Beeches - 1892
The Adventure of the Creeping Man - 1923
The Devil's Foot - 1910
The Final Problem - 1893
The Adventure of the Golden Pince-Nez - 1904
The Adventure of the Illustrious Client - 1924
The Musgrave Ritual - 1893
The Adventure of the Red Circle - 1911
Silver Blaze - 1892
The Adventure of the Six Napoleons - 1904
The Adventure of the Speckled Band - 1892

1. In *The Adventure of the Cardboard Box*, published in 1893, one villain, James Browner, the husband in a love triangle and the murderer of his wife and her lover, is given over to the law for punishment. (Under Category 2). However, another wrongdoer, Miss Sarah Cushing, whose jealousy incited the crime, never faces the law. Browner insisted that Sarah Cushing, his wife's sister, "... had some hand in bringing about the events which led to the tragedy." Although Holmes cannot extract legal justice or his own brand of justice from Sarah, she does pay a price. Holmes finds her "extremely ill ... suffering since yesterday from brain symptoms of great severity." When Sarah viewed the horrible contents of the cardboard box, she knew what

it meant, who sent it, and why it had been sent to her. She knew immediately who had murdered her sister and her sister's lover, and she knew she was an accessory, morally if not legally, to the double murder. James Browner, her brother in law, blamed Sarah in his confession and cursed her, claiming, "It was Sarah's fault, and may the curse of a broken man put a blight on her and set the blood rotting in her veins." We don't know whether Holmes visits Sarah again or whether she recovers from her brain fever. Although Holmes cannot extract justice from Sarah, her illness is her punishment and the direct result of her crime - and possibly a direct result of James Browner's curse.

2. *The Adventure of Charles Augustus Milverton,* published in 1904, features Milverton, the "king of all blackmailers" and "the worst man in London," trying to extort a large sum of money from Lady Eva Brackwell, a beautiful debutante soon to be married to the Earl of Dovercourt. Lady Brackwell begs Holmes to help her because Milverton threatens to deliver several of her "imprudent" letters to her fiancé - letters that would halt the marriage. Milverton's blackmail schemes have ruined many lives, but his victims hope to avoid scandal and don't go to the police, so Milverton knows he will never be arrested. Sherlock Holmes, asked to retrieve these sensitive letters, disguises himself as Escott the plumber and woos Milverton's housemaid Agatha, quickly becoming engaged to her to obtain information about the Milverton household. Holmes tells Watson that "it's a sporting duel between this fellow Milverton" and himself. Contradictions abound in this case. Sherlock Holmes admits his caddish behavior with his

fiancée Agatha. In fact he knows he's set up a love triangle with another admirer of Agatha, yet he's working chivalrously to save Lady Eva's honor. Holmes loathes Milverton: "I've had to do with fifty murderers in my career, but the worst of them never gave me the repulsion which I have for this fellow." Milverton is murdered, but when asked by Lestrade to look into the case, Holmes refuses, saying that in this matter his "sympathies are with the criminals rather than with the victim." Holmes would have liked to be able to hand Milverton over to the law, but he could not. Instead, Milverton gets his just deserts from a former female victim, a noblewoman whose life he ruined, who shoots him dead, imposing a punishment swifter and harsher than the laws of England. Holmes says, "I think that there are certain crimes which the law cannot touch, and which therefore, to some extent, justify private revenge." Although legally the crime of murder is considered worse than the crime of blackmail, in this instance Holmes morally equates Milverton with the worst murderer, and he and Watson let the murderess escape (under Category 3-A). They both feel in Milverton's case "that justice had overtaken a villain."

3. The Adventure of the Copper Beeches, published in 1892 and set in 1889, is a curious case in which no police are called in and the crime may not be a crime in the legal sense. Holmes advises his client, Violet Hunter, that no sister of his should accept a situation as governess for the Jephro Rucastle household because the extremely high pay and unusual conditions are abnormal and predictors of trouble. Violet takes the situation anyway, and as required by the Rucastles, has her hair cut and performs various odd duties in addition to governess. After she discovers a hidden wing in a deserted part of the house and a fearsome mastiff roaming the country estate, Holmes deduces that she's been hired not as a governess but to impersonate someone, namely Alice, Rucastle's daughter, who is not in Philadelphia but is a prisoner in the locked wing. Holmes, alarmed by the destructive behavior of the younger Rucastle child under Violet's care, posits social learning theory that children reflect the behavior of the parents, parents who, in this case, may be devising some harmful scheme involving Alice. Holmes, Watson and Violet enter the sinister house to rescue Alice, but find she has fled with her fiancé. Rucastle arrives home unexpectedly and catches them in the locked wing. Furious, he releases Carlo, his mastiff, on them, but the starved dog attacks him instead. Watson shoots the dog, and Rucastle survives, "living but horribly mangled" and "a broken man." Although, according to Holmes, Rucastle could not be punished by the laws of England, he's disfigured and ruined physically for the rest of his life by his own dog through his own actions, becoming the objective correlative of his own character. When his daughter Alice runs away with her lover, Rucastle does indeed lose access and control over Alice's money. This closes the circle, as it was his greed for Alice's money that brought on his flagrant breach of the Unwritten Code.

We have pointed out that Holmes sought no police involvement because in his estimation Rucastle committed no legal crime in holding his daughter in the house until she would sign a paper giving him complete control over her money. However, in this,

Holmes may have been in error. Alice could not sign any paper for Rucastle giving him control of her monies unless she had attained her majority, otherwise her signature would have been challenged. We also might infer she was of age because she elopes with her fiancé and marries him without any formal consent from her father. Thus, assuming she was of age, Holmes was wrong, and Rucastle could have been charged with both false imprisonment and embezzlement as part of a fraudulent attempt to cheat Alice of her monies.

It is interesting to note that in *The Creeping Man*, published 31 years later, Holmes reminds Watson of his remarks about the social behavior learning theory he propounded: "You may recollect that in the case which you, in your sensational way, coupled with the *Copper Beeches*, I was able, by watching the mind of the child, to form a deduction as to the criminal habits of the very smug and respectable father."

4. The Adventure of the Creeping Man, published in 1923 and set in 1903, is a dark tale with overtones of Stevenson's *Dr. Jekyll and Mr. Hyde*. It has the same basic theme of "When one tries to rise above Nature one is liable to fall below it. The highest type of man may revert to the animal if he leaves the straight road of destiny." Both stories focus on the dual nature of man, changes in physical appearance, and the importance of reputation. Like *Jekyll and Hyde*, it is also filled with a mood of impending disaster and sexual tension. The central question for Holmes is "Why does Professor Presbury's wolfhound, Roy, endeavour to bite him?" The Professor, a Camford

University physiologist, has begun to manifest certain sinister character changes. Following his recent engagement to a much younger woman and a trip to Prague, he has turned secretive and furtive, and his daughter and his laboratory assistant fear some tragedy is imminent. Holmes is alarmed by reports that one night the Professor was seen creeping along a corridor in a strange manner, and another night was seen peering in at his daughter's second floor bedroom window. With these strong overtones of possible sexual ravishment or violation of the Professor's daughter, Holmes sends the daughter to London "till we can assure her that all danger is past." He then focuses on the dates and the 9-day intervals in which these incidents took place, on the dog's strange behavior, and on the professor's visit to Prague, and he deduces that Presbury is taking some sort of drug. Holmes predicts the next episode of bizarre behavior and watches as the Professor torments his pet wolfhound, Roy, who slips his collar, attacks and badly mauls the Professor. Holmes finds that Presbury has been injecting himself with Langur monkey gland serum supplied by Lowenstein, who was working on the taboo secret of rejuvenescence, popular on the Continent. Holmes promises to stop these unholy scientific experiments that are in opposition to all Victorian mores. The problem is blamed on mad European scientists and not on the English gentleman who might, for various reasons, undertake them. Holmes says, "We cannot arrest the professor because he has done no crime, nor can we place him under constraint, for he cannot be proved to be mad." The Professor's assistant begs Holmes to be discreet, and Holmes agrees, saying, "I think it may be quite possible to keep the matter to ourselves, and also to prevent its recurrence now that we have a free hand." Clearly Presbury exhibits sociopathic behavior toward his daughter and his pet dog. His outlandish acts, committed under the influence of the drug, endanger everyone and everything in his sphere. Presbury commits the crime of reckless endangerment, but this is one of the cases in which Holmes takes it upon himself to decide if the crime might be prosecutable. He keeps silent about the affair to avoid scandal because Presbury pays for his awful behavior when his pet dog mauls him and Watson is forced to shoot the beast. Also Presbury's sociopathic behavior was brought on by the drug, and when the drug is no longer taken, Presbury will revert back once again to being a respectable member of society, which wouldn't be possible if the scandal were made public.

5. *The Adventure of the Devil's Foot.* Published in 1910, this macabre tale with supernatural overtones has Mortimer Tregennis suspected of trying to kill his entire family with a little known poison from the Devil's foot root. His sister Brenda dies and his two brothers are taken so ill that they are removed, both in fits, to a sanitarium. Although Mortimer proclaims his innocence, Holmes suspects him of murder and attempted murder. In the end, Tregennis faces neither Holmesian nor British justice. Instead, he is murdered by Dr. Leon Sterndale, his sister's lover, who poisons him to death with the same Devil's foot root that killed his sister. Tregennis, if guilty, received justice from the heavens via Sterndale. Holmes, although he calls Dr. Sterndale a "lawless lion-hunter," sympathizes with his revenge killing and allows him to return to Africa. I

have always wondered if Holmes was so exhausted during this case he might have missed another solution - one in which Mortimer Tregennis was indeed telling the truth.

6. _The Final Problem_ is an exciting case in which the Heavens end up solving the question of whether Moriarty will kill Sherlock Holmes or Sherlock Holmes will kill Moriarty. When published in 1893, it caused an uproar throughout the world as Sherlock Holmes went over the Reichenbach Falls locked in a deadly embrace with the Napoleon of crime, Professor Moriarty. The Strand Magazine lost 20,000 subscriptions and referred to this story as "The Dreadful Event." Hundreds of letters were written to protest the "death" of the beloved consulting detective, Sherlock Holmes. The story takes place not in London, but "on the continent" and is a tale in which Moriarty wants revenge on Holmes for thwarting him, and Holmes is determined to safeguard the public by ending the criminal network of his deadly enemy, even if it means he must forfeit his own life. Holmes and Moriarty meet, a foreshadowing of their deadly meeting to come at Reichenbach:

"It has been a duel between you and me, Mr. Holmes. You hope to place me in the dock. I tell you that I will never stand in the dock. You hope to beat me. I tell you that you will never beat me. If you are clever enough to bring destruction upon me, rest assured that I shall do as much to you.'

"'You have paid me several compliments, Mr. Moriarty,' said I. 'Let me pay you one in return when I say that if I were assured of the former eventuality I would, in the interests of the public, cheerfully accept the latter.'"

Holmes, having foiled a number of deadly attacks already, knows Moriarty intends to kill him. He knows he is in a life and death struggle in which one of them will perish. At the Reichenbach Falls, Holmes gets rid of Watson by a ruse and leaves a "farewell-suicide" note for him. When Watson returns, he concludes both men went over the Falls together in mortal combat, one on one, each attempting to best the other. Watson regrets the demise of "him whom I shall ever regard as the best and the wisest man whom I have ever known." Holmes had to take the law into his own hands because the proper authorities were unable to lay their hands on Moriarty. But it is the heavens which make the final judgment here and extract final justice. Moriarty falls to his death and Holmes is saved from death, he tells Watson, by the grace of God.

7. *The Adventure of the Golden Pince-Nez*, published in 1904 and set in 1894, contains a new murder, an old murder and a suicide. The tale unfolds as both a lover's triangle and a tale of past sins. Detective Stanley Hopkins tells Holmes that the Yard has no motive and no suspect in connection with the murder of Professor Coram's secretary, Willoughby Smith. Holmes investigates both the exterior and interior of the Professor's house and is most interested in Willoughby Smith's last words - 'The professor — it was she.' Two other clues are the golden pince-nez Hopkins found near the body and a scratch on the face of the bureau. Holmes sets a trap using the ash from

the Professor's Alexandria cigarettes, and he catches the murderess – Anna, the Professor's wife. Holmes accepts that the murder was not premeditated but committed on the spur of the moment when Anna was surprised as she attempted to get some papers from the Professor that would prove the innocence of her former lover, Alexis. Many years ago Professor Coram had betrayed Anna, Alexis and other members of the Russian Brotherhood. Since the Professor is a Russian, Holmes may feel that as a foreigner he's not expected to follow the Unwritten Law like a true Englishman. Since coming to England, the Professor has lived a blameless life and is writing an important manuscript. Perhaps Holmes feels this good behavior mitigates in favor of his past crimes. Perhaps too many years have gone by to bring him to bear for his past crimes, or Holmes may believe that the Russian Brotherhood gang will eventually find the Professor and take their retribution. Anna was trying to redress the Professor's old sins when she committed accidental murder. She determines not to face either British or Holmesian justice, and she poisons herself. Before dying, she begs Holmes to take the papers she came to steal from her husband to the Russian Embassy so they can be used to save her lover Alexis, still in a Russian prison. "Here is the packet which will save Alexis. I confide it to your honour and to your love of justice." Anna, a foreigner, recognizes and acknowledges Holmes' love of justice before she dies by her own hand – a crime itself in Victorian England.

8. The Adventure of the Illustrious Client. In this later story published in 1924, we see that the vile Baron Adelbert Gruner has broken a ton of rules in the

Unwritten Laws with his dastardly treatment of women, including the unprovable murder of his wife, the Baroness. From the beginning we see that the Baron is no gentleman, a view that is confirmed when the Baron sets his thugs on Holmes, another unprovable crime. Baron Gruner is possibly the most "dangerous man in Europe," and he is breaking the rules of Victorian society by courting young Violet de Merville, an innocent he has completely hoodwinked. Holmes does have a measure of success against the Baron by thwarting his impending marriage to Violet, a marriage that most likely would have proven fatal for her. Even though Holmes successfully discharges his duty to his unknown illustrious client – probably King Edward VII, the Baron eludes the law. However, his sins catch up with him when Kitty Winter, one of his former victims, revenges herself by permanently disfiguring him with vitriol. "The wages of sin, Watson—the wages of sin!" said Holmes. "Sooner or later it will always come. God knows, there was sin enough."

Kitty Winter is brought to the law. (See Category 2.) Two other wrongdoers in this case - Holmes and Watson – don't have to face the law. (See Category 4.) Watson tells us that, "Sherlock Holmes was threatened with a prosecution for burglary, but when an object is good and a client is sufficiently illustrious, even the rigid British law becomes human and elastic. My friend has not yet stood in the dock." And Watson never has to pay for entering the Baron's house under false pretenses, posing as an expert in Oriental pottery.

9. <u>*The Musgrave Ritual*</u>, published in 1893, begins with Watson relating that "Holmes in one of his queer humours would sit in an arm- chair, with his hair-trigger and a hundred Boxer cartridges, and proceed to adorn the opposite wall with a patriotic V.R. done in bullet-pocks." Watson here not only confirms Holmes' royalist tendencies, but also he presages the involvement of the Crown in this story. From a box containing his older cases, Holmes shows Watson "...a crumpled piece of paper, an old- fashioned brass key, a peg of wood with a ball of string attached to it, and three rusty old discs of metal," all connected to this tale of a dark love triangle and a mystery from the past. Holmes tells Watson about his visit to Reginald Musgrave, a friend from college, who lives at the Manor House of Hurlstone, an estate with 13 servants, including Brunton, the famous Hurlstone butler who is remembered by all who visit. Brunton, a former schoolmaster, can speak several languages and play nearly every musical instrument, but he's also a Don Juan. Once engaged to the second housemaid, Rachel Howells, he threw her over for Janet Tregellis, the head gamekeeper's daughter, making things tense at Hurlstone. Not only that, but Brunton was caught rummaging through some family papers in the library and was given a week's notice. Musgrave announces that both Brunton and Rachel have disappeared with no trace. All they were able to find in the lake was "a linen bag which contained within it a mass of old rusted, and discoloured metal and several dull-coloured pieces of pebble or glass." Musgrave asks Holmes to help solve the mystery. Holmes first examines the paper Brunton was holding in the library, and he finds it contains a series of questions

and answers from the 17th century. Ten generations of Musgraves have read the catechism but its meaning has been lost in the mists of time. Holmes, knowing that Brunton was investigating this riddle, pursues it, uncovers its meaning, and finds the opening to a deep hole in the cellar of the Manor House. Once the heavy stone over the hole is removed, they find the dead body of Brunton, but no treasure. Holmes connects the bag of metal and glass to the crown of Charles II, left with the Cavalier Sir Ralph Musgrave for safekeeping when the Roundheads were pursuing the Stuart kings. Holmes speculates whether Rachel Howells made the stone drop on purpose to cover the hole before Brunton could climb out of it or whether the stone fell by accident and suffocated Brunton. Yes, the butler did it in this story, and he paid for his deception with his life. Brunton's justice was served from above whether at the hands of Rachel or by accident. One way or the other, she took no pains to try to save him from suffocating to death. (See Rachel Howell's fate under Category 3-B-1)

10. *The Adventure of the Red Circle*, published in 1911, has two wrongdoers, one much worse than the other. The true villain is Giuseppe Gorgiano, a member of a Neopolitan criminal society who has followed fellow countryman Gennaro Lucca and his wife Emilia to London. Gorgiano wants to kill Lucca, who earlier had refused an order from the Red Circle to kill his benefactor. He also lusts after Lucca's wife, Emilia, and wants to possess her. Gorgiano roughs up a landlord where Emilia is lodging, and then in his attempt to murder Gennaro, he himself is stabbed to death by Gennaro. The real criminal, Gorgiano, never

faces Holmesian or British justice, but meets his maker and justice from a higher power through the instrument of Gennaro. Scotland Yard promises to go lightly on Gennaro, recognizing he murdered Gorgiano in self defense.

11. In *Silver Blaze*, the true villain is the racehorse's trainer, John Straker, a retired jockey. He wanted to play the odds in the Wessex Cup and fix the race by nicking Silver Blaze's tendon to guarantee that he wouldn't win. Straker planned to bet heavily against Silver Blaze to fund the expensive double life he was leading with a girlfriend. When Silver Blaze sensed (horse sense?) what Straker was going to do, it felt threatened, reared up in self protection and kicked Straker in the head, killing him. The horse was the murderer here, an instrument of on high, just as the snake was the murderer in *The Speckled Band.* In both cases, the animal was trying to protect itself from harm. In *Silver Blaze*, the horse imposed justice from above on Straker for the crime he was about to commit. The heavens forgive Silver Blaze, who goes on to win the Wessex Cup. Holmes decides an interesting fate for the second villain in *Silver Blaze* under Category 3-A.

12. In *The Adventure of the Six Napoleons*, a man identified as Pietro Venucci, is found murdered at the scene of a break in. He's known as being "from Naples, and...one of the greatest cut-throats in London. He is connected with the Mafia, ... a secret political society, enforcing its decrees by murder." Lestrade concentrates his investigation on this murder and the victim's ties to the Mafia, whilst Holmes concentrates

on the stolen Napoleon busts. Holmes unearths Pietro's connection to the theft of the Borgia Pearl as being his sister, Lucretia, who was a maid to the pearl's owner, the Princess of Colona. Pietro ends up being knifed to death in the same manner he used on his victims, a fitting sword of justice from above. Holmes does catch Pietro's murderer, a one-time sculptor named Beppo who was also involved in the theft, and he sends Beppo to jail. (See Category 2.)

13. The Adventure of the Speckled Band is another early story, published in 1892, and it was Conan Doyle's favorite. The villain in this story is Dr. Grimesby Roylott, who is struggling to maintain his estate, Stoke Moran, and its grounds. He's a wild, vile tempered man who keeps a cheetah and a baboon and a snake on the property, and he doesn't make a good impression on Holmes and Watson when he storms into 221B. He's a genuine villain and the stepfather from hell. Holmes investigates and deduces that Roylott has been coaxing a snake through a ventilator from his room to his step daughter's, hoping its bite will be fatal to her, thus allowing him to keep her money. He's already murdered one step daughter and is trying to kill the other so he can have access to her fortune as well. Holmes could have turned Roylott over to the law, but Holmes thrashes the snake, forcing it back through the ventilator to Roylott's room. The snake he intended to bite his step daughter instead bites him, catching Roylott in his own death trap. Roylott makes a "horrible cry," and Holmes admits that by hitting the snake, he was "no doubt indirectly responsible for Dr. Grimesby Roylott's death, and I cannot say that it is likely to weigh very heavily upon my conscience." The official inquiry disagreed and "came to the conclusion that the doctor met his fate while indiscreetly playing with a dangerous pet."

This is one of three short stories in the Canon where an animal is a killer, the others being *The Lion's Mane* and *Silver Blaze.*

Statistical Analysis

Crimes involved

61 crimes take place in these 37 cases. Some stories have more than one crime, including *Charles Augustus Milverton, The Devil's Foot, The Dying Detective, The Engineer's Thumb, The Golden Pince-Nez, The Greek Interpreter, The Illustrious Client, The Musgrave Ritual, The Naval Treaty, The Six Napoleons, The Speckled Band* and *Thor Bridge* with two crimes each; and *The Abbey Grange, The Copper Beeches, Lady Frances Carfax, The Naval Treaty, The Priory School* and *The Second Stain* with three.

By far the most common crimes are murder (18), attempted murder (12), and accessory to murder (2) with a total of 32 incidents comprising 52% of all crimes. Burglary/Theft/Robbery comes in second with 8 or 14%; and Blackmail is next with 4 or 7%.

Accessory to murder – 2
The Abbey Grange
The Cardboard Box

Aiding in the escape of a felon – 1
The Priory School

Begging – 1
The Man with the Twisted Lip

Bigamy - 1
The Noble Bachelor

Blackmail – 4
Charles Augustus Milverton
The Gloria Scott
A Scandal in Bohemia
The Second Stain

Burglary/Theft /Robbery – 8
The Beryl Coronet
The Blue Carbuncle
The Musgrave Ritual
The Naval Treaty
Silver Blaze
The Six Napoleons
The Three Gables
The Three Students

Condoning a felony – 1
The Priory School

Counterfeiting – 1
The Engineer's Thumb

Disorderly Conduct – Reckless Endangerment – 1

The Creeping Man

False Imprisonment – 1

The Copper Beeches

Fraud – 3

A Case of Identity - Embezzlement
The Cooper Beeches - Embezzlement
Lady Frances Carfax - Swindling

Kidnapping – 2

Lady Frances Carfax
The Priory School

Murder - 18

The Abbey Grange
The Boscombe Valley Mystery
Charles Augustus Milverton
The Crooked Man
The Devil's Foot
The Dying Detective
The Five Orange Pips
The Golden Pince-Nez
The Greek Interpreter
The Illustrious Client
The Musgrave Ritual
The Red Circle
The Resident Patient
The Second Stain
The Six Napoleons
The Speckled Band
The Veiled Lodger
Wisteria Lodge

Attempted Murder – 12
- The Copper Beeches
- The Devil's Foot
- The Dying Detective
- The Engineer's Thumb
- The Final Problem
- The Greek Interpreter
- The Disappearance of Lady Frances Carfax
- The Naval Treaty
- The Red Circle
- The Speckled Band
- The Sussex Vampire
- Thor Bridge

Treason/espionage –2
- The Naval Treaty
- The Second Stain

Suicide – 2
- The Golden Pince-Nez
- Thor Bridge

Withholding evidence – 1
- The Abbey Grange

Criminals

54 criminals are involved in these 37 stories - 17 females and 37 males, one of whom is a child. Males outweigh females 69% to 31%. And more of these wrongdoers are British – 34 (63%) than are Non-British – 20 (37%).

Female – 17 (31% of the 54 criminals)

The Abbey Grange (Lady Brackenstall)
The Abbey Grange (Theresa Wright, Maid)
The Beryl Coronet
The Cardboard Box
Charles Augustus Milverton
The Engineer's Thumb
The Golden Pince-Nez
A Case of Identity (Mrs. Windibank)
The Lady Frances Carfax
The Musgrave Ritual
The Noble Bachelor
A Scandal in Bohemia
The Second Stain – (Lady Hope)
The Second Stain – (Mme. Fournaye)
The Three Gables
Thor Bridge
The Veiled Lodger

Male – 37 (69% of the 54 criminals)

The Abbey Grange
The Beryl Coronet
The Blue Carbuncle
The Boscombe Valley Mystery
Charles Augustus Milverton
The Copper Beeches
The Creeping Man
The Crooked Man
The Devil's Foot – Mortimer Tregennis
The Devil's Foot – Dr. Sterndale
The Engineer's Thumb – Col. Stark
The Engineer's Thumb – Dr. Becher
The Final Problem
The Five Orange Pips

The Gloria Scott
The Greek Interpreter – Latimer
The Greek Interpreter - Kemp
A Case of Identity
The Illustrious Client
The Disappearance of Lady Frances Carfax
The Musgrave Ritual
The Naval Treaty
The Priory School – James Wilder
The Priory School – Duke of Holderness
The Red Circle – Gorgiano
The Red Circle - Lucca
The Resident Patient – Biddle
The Resident Patient – Moffat
The Resident Patient – Hayward
The Second Stain
Silver Blaze – Straker
Silver Blaze – Silas Brown
The Six Napoleons
The Speckled Band
The Sussex Vampire
The Three Students
Wisteria Lodge

British – 34– (63%)
The Abbey Grange
The Beryl Coronet - 2
The Blue Carbuncle
The Cardboard Box
Charles Augustus Milverton - 2
The Copper Beeches
The Creeping Man
The Crooked Man
The Devil's Foot - 2

The Final Problem
The Gloria Scott
The Greek Interpreter -2
A Case of Identity - 2
The Musgrave Ritual -2
The Naval Treaty
The Priory School -2
The Resident Patient - 3
A Scandal in Bohemia
The Second Stain (Lady Hope)
Silver Blaze -2
The Speckled Band
The Sussex Vampire
The Three Students
The Veiled Lodger

Non-British - 20 – (37%)
The Abbey Grange (Australian) - 2
The Boscombe Valley Mystery (Australian)
The Engineer's Thumb (German) - 3
The Five Orange Pips (American)
The Golden Pince-Nez (Russian)
The Illustrious Client – (Austrian)
The Disappearance of Lady Frances Carfax (Australian) - 2
The Noble Bachelor (American)
The Red Circle (Italian) - 2
The Second Stain (French – M. & Mme. Fournaye) - 2
The Six Napoleons (Italian)
Thor Bridge (Brazilian)
The Three Gables (Spanish)
Wisteria Lodge (Central American)

2 - American
5 - Australian
1 - Austrian
1 - Brazilian
1 - Central American
2 - French
3 - German
3 - Italian
1 - Russian
1 - Spanish

The misdeeds in at least 22 of these cases involve potential public scandal or injurious publicity, and Holmes handles these cases with discretion and his own brand of justice in order to avoid the scandal:

The Abbey Grange (Murder, Accessory to murder and Withholding evidence)
The Boscombe Valley Mystery (Blackmail and Murder)
The Beryl Coronet (Theft)
The Blue Carbuncle (Burglary)
Charles Augustus Milverton (Blackmail)
The Copper Beeches (Fraud)
The Creeping Man (Aberrant behavior & Sexual escapades)
The Crooked Man (Attempted Murder and Betrayal)
A Case of Identity (Fraud and Improper, Predatory Sexual Behavior)
The Illustrious Client (Murder and Improper sexual behavior)
The Naval Treaty (Burglary & Espionage & Attempted murder)
The Noble Bachelor (Bigamy)

The Priory School (Kidnapping, Condoning a felony and Aiding in the escape of a felon)
A Scandal in Bohemia (Blackmail)
The Second Stain (Blackmail and Burglary/Theft and treason)
The Speckled Band (Murder & Attempted Murder)
The Sussex Vampire (Attempted Murder)
Thor Bridge (Suicide & Attempted Murder)
The Three Gables (Burglary and Attempted Murder)
The Three Students (Burglary and Cheating)
The Man with the Twisted Lip (Begging)
The Veiled Lodger (Murder)

<u>Reasons Sherlock Holmes forgives crimes:</u>

1.Revenge/Avenge/Retribution to right a wrong-1 (4%)

The Devil's Foot – Murder

2. Save Monarch & country (British or other) - 3 (12%)

The Naval Treaty – Burglary & Treason
A Scandal in Bohemia - Blackmail
The Second Stain – Blackmail and Theft

3. Right an infraction of the Unwritten Laws/Code of Honor –12 (48%)

Charles Augustus Milverton - Murder
The Copper Beeches - False Imprisonment and Fraud (Embezzlement)
The Creeping Man – Scandal & Aberrant behavior: Sexual escapades
The Crooked Man – Attempted Murder & Betrayal
A Case of Identity - Aberrant behavior

The Noble Bachelor – Bigamy
The Priory School – Kidnapping, Condoning a felony and Aiding in the escape of a felon
Silver Blaze – Concealing a stolen horse
The Sussex Vampire –Attempted child Murder by child
The Three Gables – Burglary – Accessory to murder
The Three Students – Burglary
The Man with the Twisted Lip – Begging and leading a double life

4. Perpetrator is ill/ near Death /Suicide– 5 (20%)
    Boscombe Valley – Blackmail
    The Cardboard Box - Accessory to murder
    The Golden Pince Nez – Murder
    Thor Bridge – Suicide and Attempted murder
    The Veiled Lodger – Murder

5. Perpetrator dies –2 - (8%)
    The Final Problem
    The Speckled Band

6. Self Defense – 1 – (4%)
    The Abbey Grange – Murder, Accessory to murder & Withholding evidence

7. Christmas Cheer-Forgiveness of Jewel theft–1 - (4%)
    The Blue Carbuncle

Following is a listing of the dispositions of the 37 cases where the wrongdoer is not given over to the law. Note that 5 cases appear twice as there are two villains in each of those cases, namely CHAS, DEVI, MUSG, SECO, and SILV. There are 2 wrongdoers in *A Case of Identity*, but they both commit the same crime and thus the story appears under only one heading.

Cases where Holmes decides justice for the villain - 18
The Adventure of the Abbey Grange (ABBE)
The Adventure of the Blue Carbuncle (BLUE)
The Boscombe Valley Mystery (BOSC)
The Adventure of Charles Augustus Milverton (CHAS)
The Crooked Man (CROO)
The Devil's Foot (DEVI)
A Case of Identity (IDEN)
The Naval Treaty (NAVA)
The Adventure of the Noble Bachelor (NOBL)
The Adventure of the Priory School (PRIO)
The Adventure of the Second Stain (SECO)
Silver Blaze (SILV)
The Adventure of the Sussex Vampire (SUSS)
The Problem of Thor Bridge (THOR)
The Adventure of the Three Gables (3GAB)
The Adventure of the Three Students (3STU)
The Man with the Twisted Lip (TWIS)
The Adventure of the Veiled Lodger (VEIL)

Wrongdoers escape and are never captured – 6
The Adventure of the Beryl Coronet (BERY)
The Adventure of the Engineer's Thumb (ENGR)
The Gloria Scott (GLOR)
The Disappearance of Lady Frances Carfax (LADY)
The Musgrave Ritual (MUSG)
A Scandal in Bohemia (SCAN)

Wrongdoers escape but later get justice from above- 5

The Five Orange Pips (FIVE)
The Greek Interpreter (GREE)
The Resident Patient (RESI)
The Adventure of the Second Stain (SECO)
The Adventure of Wisteria Lodge (WIST)

Cases where wrongdoers get justice from above - 13
The Cardboard Box (CARD)
The Adventure of Charles Augustus Milverton (CHAS)
The Adventure of the Copper Beeches (COPP)
The Adventure of the Creeping Man (CREE)
The Devil's Foot (DEVI)
The Final Problem (FINA)
The Adventure of the Golden Pince-Nez (GOLD)
The Adventure of the Illustrious Client (ILLU)
The Musgrave Ritual (MUSG)
The Adventure of the Red Circle (REDC)
Silver Blaze (SILV)
The Adventure of the Six Napoleons (SIXN)
The Adventure of the Speckled Band (SPEC)

Statistical Analysis:

Wrongdoers meet their death in the tale – 11
- Charles Augustus Milverton
- The Devil's Foot – (Mortimer Tregennis)
- The Final Problem
- The Adventure of the Golden Pince-Nez
- The Adventure of the Greek Interpreter
- The Adventure of the Musgrave Ritual
- The Adventure of the Red Circle - (Gorgiano)
- Silver Blaze- (John Straker)
- The Adventure of the Second Stain - (Henri Fournaye)

The Adventure of the Speckled Band
The Problem of Thor Bridge

Death or Disfigurement by Animals – 4
The Adventure of the Copper Beeches- Carlo the mastiff - disfiguration
The Adventure of the Creeping Man–Roy the Wolfhound-disfiguration
Silver Blaze – Silver Blaze the horse - death
The Adventure of the Speckled Band – a pet snake - death

Die Natural Death – 2
The Boscombe Valley Mystery
The Adventure of the Veiled Lodger

Brain Fever/Madness – 2
The Cardboard Box
The Adventure of the Second Stain

Suicide – 2
The Adventure of the Golden Pince-Nez
The Problem of Thor Bridge

Disfigured by Vitriol – 1
The Adventure of the Illustrious Client

Of these 37 cases, 20 are published before 1901. 17 cases are published later - 7 between 1903 and 1904, and 10 between 1908 and 1927. More than half the cases (54%) in which the villain is not taken to the law for one reason or another are early cases.

Early Cases – 20 – 54%

The Beryl Coronet - 1892
The Blue Carbuncle – 1892
The Boscombe Valley Mystery – 1891
The Cardboard Box – 1893
The Copper Beeches – 1892
The Crooked Man - 1893
The Engineer's Thumb – 1892
The Final Problem - 1893
The Five Orange Pips - 1891
The Gloria Scott - 1893
The Greek Interpreter – 1893
A Case of Identity – 1891
The Musgrave Ritual - 1893
The Naval Treaty – 1893
The Noble Bachelor - 1892
The Resident Patient - 1893
A Scandal in Bohemia – 1891
Silver Blaze – 1892
The Speckled Band – 1892
The Man with the Twisted Lip - 1891

Cases between 1903 – 1904– 7 - 19%

Abbey Grange – 1904
Charles Augustus Milverton - 1904
The Golden Pince-Nez - 1904
The Priory School –1904
The Second Stain – 1904
The Six Napoleons - 1904
The Three Students – 1904

Later cases published between 1908 - 1927 – 10 – 27%

The Creeping Man - 1923
The Devil's Foot – 1910
The Illustrious Client – 1924

The Disappearance of Lady Frances Carfax-1911
The Sussex Vampire – 1924
The Problem of Thor Bridge – 1922
The Red Circle - 1911
The Three Gables - 1926
The Veiled Lodger – 1927
Wisteria Lodge –1908

Chapter 8

Category 4 - Cases in which Sherlock Holmes and/or Dr. Watson Take the Law into Their Own Hands

"Legally, we are putting ourselves hopelessly in the wrong, but I think that it is worth it."
--Sherlock Holmes, The Yellow Face.

"'Thrice is he armed who hath his quarrel just.' We simply can't afford to wait for the police or to keep within the four corners of the law." – Sherlock Holmes, The Disappearance of Lady Frances Carfax

In the very first Sherlock Holmes short story, *A Scandal in Bohemia*, Sherlock Holmes asks Watson, "You don't mind breaking the law? ... Nor running a chance of arrest?" "Not in a good cause," Watson replies. "Oh, the cause is excellent!" Holmes assures him. When Holmes says the cause is excellent, readers believe him. We perceive Holmes as an honorable Victorian gentleman who follows the Code. But Holmes is a detective, and detectives don't always act as Victorian gentleman. Dr. Leslie Armstrong notes in *The Missing Three-Quarter*: "I have heard your name, Mr. Sherlock Holmes, and I am aware of your profession, one of which I by no means approve." As a detective, Holmes frequently must act outside the law in order to accomplish his given task. "Maybe I am committing a felony, but I am saving a soul," he says in *The Blue Carbuncle*. A frustrated Lestrade chides Holmes that as a private detective, he can get away with things that Scotland Yard cannot. In one of the last cases, *The Retired Colourman*, Holmes fully admits he is not always law-abiding, and he tells Watson: "There being no fear of interruption I proceeded to burgle the house. Burglary has always been an alternative profession had I cared to adopt it, and I have little doubt that I should have come to the front." In *Charles Augustus Milverton*, Holmes says, "I have always had an idea that I would have made a highly efficient criminal."

In those cases where Holmes acts outside the law, he's often at his detective best. Sometimes he removes evidence from a crime scene, though he's always careful to leave enough behind so as not to deprive the regular forces of law and order their chance to solve the case, as in *The Devil's Foot*. Sometimes he tricks the villains by using disguises, surprises and even forceful measures to accomplish his purpose, all done with Holmesian gusto. His eyes twinkle and his lips curl in a smile as he undertakes a burglary, no matter that Inspector Lestrade would surely disapprove. But Holmes, not being of the official police, can sometimes act outside the law as long as he believes it is in a good and just cause. It's important to note that in none of the instances where Holmes breaks the law is he arrested. The closest he comes is in *The Illustrious Client* when Baron Gruner threatens to take him before the law. However that fails to happen because, as Watson tells us, "Sherlock Holmes was threatened with a prosecution for burglary, but when an object is good and a client is sufficiently illustrious, even the rigid British law becomes human and elastic. My friend has not yet stood in the dock." In *The Disappearance of Lady Frances Carfax*, Holmes has a close call after he forces his way into Holy Peters' house with a gun and the police are summoned. They tell him to leave the premises because he doesn't have a warrant, and when Holmes complies, no action is taken against him.

Once more in *Charles Augustus Milverton*, both Holmes and Watson would surely have been arrested if they had been caught when they are pursued fleeing the scene of Milverton's murder.

Significantly, Holmes and Watson never repent their crimes. In the cases in this category, they both firmly believe that their actions – however illegal - are done with the highest of motives. Holmes uses his legal lapses as a means to an end – that end being solving a case and bringing a criminal or villain to justice – either to the law or to Holmesian justice. And he always believes that his means justify the desirable end they seek. Watson acts as Holmes' moral compass and occasionally calls some of the shots, as in Charles Augustus Milverton:

"I give you my word of honour -- and I never broke it in my life -- that I will take a cab straight to the police-station and give you away unless you let me share this adventure with you."

"You can't help me."

"How do you know that? You can't tell what may happen. Anyway, my resolution is taken. Other people beside you have self-respect and even reputations."

Under Category 4, there are 23 cases in which Holmes and/or Watson commit crimes and turn the tables on various villains. These 23 cases amount to 41% of the 56 stories in the canon. In each case, the incidents will be analyzed in terms of the illegal action itself, how Holmes justifies it, whether the ends justify the means, and whether we agree or disagree with his decisions to act outside the law. Since any crimes Holmes committed would have been categorized under Victorian legal terms, I asked two experts for assistance. Mr. Simon Hetherington, Publisher of *Halsbury's Laws of England from 2002–13*, and a Member of the Sherlock Holmes Society of London, was kind enough to review this chapter for correct legal terminology. His interesting comments went beyond that, and I thank him enormously for his suggestions. I have incorporated his definitions and put others in end-notes to the chapter. I also wish to credit and thank Sheriff Valerie Johnston, member of the Scottish Judiciary, for all her valuable definitions and interpretations on theft and property crimes and legal terminology in both English and Scottish law. Any mistakes are mine alone.

The 23 cases in this category are:

The Adventure of the Abbey Grange
The Adventure of the Blue Carbuncle
The Boscombe Valley Mystery
The Adventure of the Bruce-Partington Plans
The Adventure of Charles Augustus Milverton
The Adventure of the Copper Beeches
The Devil's Foot
The Final Problem

The Adventure of the Illustrious Client
The Disappearance of Lady Frances Carfax
His Last Bow
The Adventure of the Missing Three-Quarter
The Naval Treaty
The Adventure of the Noble Bachelor
The Adventure of the Norwood Builder
The Adventure of the Retired Colourman
A Scandal in Bohemia
The Second Stain
Silver Blaze
The Adventure of the Solitary Cyclist
The Adventure of the Three Gables
The Veiled Lodger
The Yellow Face

1. *The Adventure of the Abbey Grange*. After a brilliant investigation of the murder site at Abbey Grange, Holmes deduces the identity of the murderer. But Holmes only gives Inspector Hopkins a hint about his deductions. His rationale, he informs Watson, is that: "What I know is unofficial, what he knows is official. I have the right to private judgement, but he has none. He must disclose all, or he is a traitor to his service. In a doubtful case I would not put him in so painful a position, and so I reserve my information until my own mind is clear upon the matter." Then Holmes lures Captain Croker to Baker Street, and urges him to tell all. "Give ... a true account, mind you, with nothing added and nothing taken off. I know so much already that if you go one inch off the straight, I'll blow this police whistle from my window and the affair goes out of my hands forever." Croker tells Holmes that it was a fair fight between him and

Sir Eustace Brackenstall, and that Sir Eustace landed the first blow. But he admits he killed Brackenstall and asks: “Do you think I was sorry? Not I! It was his life or mine, but far more than that, it was his life or hers, for how could I leave her in the power of this madman? That was how I killed him. Was I wrong? Well, then, what would either of you gentlemen have done, if you had been in my position?" Holmes wrestles with the dilemma and tells him, “This is a very serious matter, though I am willing to admit that you acted under the most extreme provocation to which any man could be subjected. I am not sure that in defence of your own life your action will not be pronounced legitimate. However, that is for a British jury to decide. Meanwhile I have so much sympathy for you that, if you choose to disappear in the next twenty-four hours, I will promise you that no one will hinder you." Holmes recognizes that self-defense is a defense to a charge of murder that removes any criminality, but he also recognizes that only a British jury can decide Croker’s claim of self-defense. Holmes resolves to hold such a trial for Captain Croker on the spot, and says, “It is a great responsibility that I take upon myself.”

“... See here, Captain Croker, we'll do this in due form of law. You are the prisoner. Watson, you are a British jury, and I never met a man who was more eminently fitted to represent one. I am the judge.

Now, gentleman of the jury, you have heard the evidence. Do you find the prisoner guilty or not guilty?"

"Not guilty, my lord," said I.

"*Vox populi, vox dei.* You are acquitted, Captain Croker. So long as the law does not find some other victim you are safe from me. Come back to this lady in a year, and may her future and yours justify us in the judgment which we have pronounced this night!"

Holmes and Watson speak for the justice system in this unique case. Holmes uses the Latin, *Vox Populi, vox Dei*, the voice of the people is the voice of God, to acquit Captain Croker. Holmes overlooks the crimes of Accessory and Withholding Evidence committed by Lady Brackenstall and her maid, Theresa Wright. He then puts Captain Croker on parole for a year. "Come back to this lady in a year, and may her future and yours justify us in the judgement which we have pronounced this night!" In Holmes' eyes, he is committing no crime in letting Croker go free, and we trust Holmes so much we agree with his decision, even though Croker admits he killed Sir Eustace. One wonders what Inspector Hopkins would say about Holmes' role as judge and Watson's role as jury, even if Hopkins himself personally agreed with their verdict. Clearly Croker and Lady Brackenstall and her maid as well would have been charged and their cases gone to trial. We would hope they would have been acquitted. The crimes that Holmes and Watson committed here were Aiding and Abetting, Compounding a Felony/Misprision of a Felony, and Withholding Evidence.

2. <u>*The Adventure of the Blue Carbuncle*</u>. In this case, Holmes admits he is "compounding a felony" by letting the jewel thief James Ryder go free. Ryder stole the Countess of Morcar's blue carbuncle, which ended up in the crop of a goose. Holmes already has possession of the jewel before Ryder confesses and

repents his deed, and Holmes decides not to tell Scotland Yard what he's uncovered. Instead, he takes the view that he is "not retained by the police to supply their deficiencies." "Compounding a felony was itself a crime – a misdemeanor – at this time. It amounted to reaching an agreement to let a felon go free in exchange for the return of the goods or some other reward. Thus Holmes is not strictly accurate describing this as compounding a felony, since he does not 'compound with' – i.e. reach an agreement with, the thief, because he already has the jewel in his possession." [xiv] Since Holmes failed to notify the authorities and took steps to conceal James Ryder's crime, he "may be guilty of 'misprision of a felony' – another misdemeanor at the time, which essentially meant keeping a felony secret." [xv] Had Scotland Yard known of Holmes' deception, they might have been able to charge him with perverting the course of justice, [xvi] and aiding, abetting, counselling or procuring as a secondary party to a crime. [xvii] Holmes ends up with not only the jewel – which we are certain he will return to the Countess – but also possibly with the £1,000 reward offered for the blue carbuncle. What about Peterson, the Commissionaire? His wife found the jewel in the goose, and he turned it over to Holmes instead of to Scotland Yard. Peterson, as a Commissionaire, was probably a retired military man and could have used the reward money. Did he and his wife ever get anything except the goose, which was not strictly Holmes' to give? We are left hanging. Holmes usually doesn't operate for financial gain, so we assume the best of him. This is a case in which Holmes has a burst of Christmas spirit, forgives the thief and gives him the gift of freedom. Many would say there's no crime in that.

3. *The Boscombe Valley Mystery*. Holmes displays both humanity and empathy in this tale of old and new sins. Turner confesses to Holmes that he's killed fellow Australian McCarthy over long-term blackmail demands. But Turner is dying and asks for mercy. He wants to die at home and keep his sins from his daughter Alice, who, along with Lestrade, is Holmes' client. Holmes pities Turner and says to Watson, "There, but for the grace of God, goes Sherlock Holmes." Holmes agrees to keep Turner's secret unless he has to reveal it to save McCarthy's son, who's in the dock for the crime. Turner dies shortly after, and Holmes and Watson keep the secret. Their crimes are withholding evidence and perverting the cause of justice. Holmes, in his *Weltanschauung*, believes his illegal acts were worth it to keep Turner's secret. As in *The Priory School*, Holmes felt that there is a debt owed to the future, and this was his way of paying that debt in order for Turner's daughter and McCarthy's son to be able to marry without the burden of their fathers' pasts to taint their future.

4. *The Bruce Partington Plans*. Holmes is entreated by his brother Mycroft, the Prime Minister, the Admiralty and even Lestrade to use his powers to tackle an important case involving stolen submarine plans. Mycroft pleads, "In all your career you have never had so great a chance of serving your country." They even offer to put his name on the next Honors list, but Holmes says, "I play the game for the game's own sake." Part of playing the game is to win the

game, and to win, Holmes has to get proof that the spy, Hugo Oberstein, is involved in the theft of the plans. So he decides to burgle Oberstein's house in a search for evidence. Watson is skeptical, but Holmes convinces him to be a co-conspirator.

"Could we not get a warrant and legalize it?"

"Hardly on the evidence."

"What can we hope to do?"

"We cannot tell what correspondence may be there."

"I don't like it, Holmes."

"My dear fellow, you shall keep watch in the street. I'll do the criminal part. It's not a time to stick at trifles. Think of Mycroft's note, of the Admiralty, the Cabinet, the exalted person who waits for news. We are bound to go."

My answer was to rise from the table. "You are right, Holmes. We are bound to go."

He sprang up and shook me by the hand. "I knew you would not shrink at the last," said he, and for a moment I saw something in his eyes which was nearer to tenderness than I had ever seen."

As for Holmes doing the criminal part as he promises Watson, even if Watson had stayed outside he would still be aiding and abetting or even be considered a full participant in the burglary. But Holmes and Watson break into the place together, search it, and uncover some newspaper slips from the Daily Telegraph agony column that offer a way to trap Oberstein and his confederate. When Lestrade learns of the burglary, shakes his head and warns Holmes: "We can't do these things in the force, Mr. Holmes.

No wonder you get results that are beyond us. But some of these days you'll go too far, and you'll find yourself and your friend in trouble." Holmes replies, "For England, home and beauty - eh, Watson? Martyrs on the altar of our country." And after Oberstein is caught in the trap, Holmes is presented with a "remarkably fine emerald tie-pin" on a visit to Windsor Castle. Breaking and entering does pay - or it did for Holmes in this case of "great national importance," in which Holmes felt the end justified the means.

5. *Charles Augustus Milverton.* – Holmes and Watson are real heroes in this case as they strike a blow against a fiendish blackmailer who's ruined many lives, mostly women. But Holmes is very clear about his intention to break the law on behalf of justice because the law can't touch the blackmailer. Holmes tells Watson:

"I intend to burgle the Milverton house. My dear fellow, I have given it every consideration. I am never precipitate in my actions, nor would I adopt so energetic and, indeed, so dangerous a course, if any other were possible. Let us look at the matter clearly and fairly. I suppose that you will admit that the action is morally justifiable, though technically criminal. To burgle his house is no more than to forcibly take his pocketbook -- an action in which you were prepared to aid me."

Watson, attempting to tread the legal line that provides there must be criminal intent, replies, "It is morally justifiable so long as our object is to take no articles save those which are used for an illegal purpose." Holmes agrees: "Exactly. Since it is morally justifiable, I have only to consider the question of personal risk. Surely a gentleman should not lay much stress upon this, when a lady is in most desperate need of his help?" Holmes jokes with Watson and tells him "it would be amusing if we ended by sharing the same cell." Heroes and defenders of justice though they are, Holmes and Watson break more than one law when they put on masks and silent shoes and break into Milverton's house. They are going equipped to steal – another crime in its own right - carrying "a first-class, up-to-date burgling kit." Holmes, the consulting detective, becomes a felon in the eyes of the law and uses the burglary as a chance to prove he can be a master criminal. Watson gives us a suspenseful account of how Holmes works for half an hour breaking open a safe. Watson, excited by the danger, says, "My first feeling of fear had passed away, and I thrilled now with a keener zest than I had ever enjoyed when we were the defenders of the law instead of its defiers. The high object of our mission, the consciousness that it was unselfish and chivalrous, the villainous character of our opponent all added to the sporting interest of the adventure. Far from feeling guilty, I rejoiced and exulted in our dangers." They take Milverton's blackmail papers and burn them, and then they witness a murder, which they fail to stop. Watson explains: "No interference upon our part could have saved the man from his fate, but, as the woman poured bullet after bullet into Milverton's shrinking body I was about to spring out, when I felt Holmes's cold, strong grasp upon my wrist. I understood the whole argument of that firm, restraining grip -- that it was no affair of ours, that justice had overtaken a villain, that we had our own duties and our own objects, which were not to be lost sight of." A murder did happen concurrent with them committing burglary, but it was not committed as part of their criminal enterprise and they were not actively involved in it, so they are not legally accessories to the murder. Further, they had no legal duty to stop the murder, even if they could do so. Holmes and Watson watch the murderess depart and do not report what they know to the police, thus perverting the cause of justice. Sherlock Holmes knows that the noblewoman who murders Milverton does so to avenge what Milverton did to her family, and he justifies it saying, "I think that there are certain crimes which the law cannot touch, and which therefore, to some extent, justify private revenge." Holmes gets himself in hot water in another aspect of this tale when he disguises himself as Escott the plumber and gets engaged to Agatha, the Milverton housemaid, to obtain information on the household routine. He adopts a cavalier attitude when he drops her, telling Watson, "You must play your cards as best you can when such a stake is on the table." As to his fiancée Agatha, we never hear whether she sues Holmes for breach of promise, a civil action that is a tort and not criminal. It would be highly entertaining to see Watson testifying on the witness stand not for Holmes but for Agatha, the plaintiff. (Yes, Mr. Sherlock Holmes did tell me that he had become engaged to the plaintiff. Yes, he told me he got engaged to her so he could worm out the details of Milverton's house and routines. Yes, he did tell me he had no intention of following up on the engagement once he got the information he wanted.) Under this scenario, one wonders what amount in damages Holmes would have to pay. In the final scene of this case, Holmes suggests to Lestrade that the description of one of the two robbers/murderers who were nearly caught at the Milverton murder scene could fit Watson. This is Holmes himself doing his own confession-is-good-for-the-soul, a definite part of the Weltanschauung of Holmesian justice. Good thing that Lestrade, as usual, lacks the insight to follow up on the lead.

6. *The Adventure of the Copper Beeches*. Miss Violet Hunter, the Rucastle governess, lets Holmes and Watson into the Rucastle house to investigate a locked room in which Holmes suspects Rucastle is holding his daughter prisoner to force her to turn over her money to him. Because she lets them in, they are not technically committing the crime of breaking and entering. However, they do trespass into the upstairs locked room where Miss Hunter leads them. "The centre door was closed, and across the outside of it had been fastened one of the broad bars of an iron bed, padlocked at one end to a ring in the wall, and fastened at the other with stout cord. The door itself was locked as well, and the key was not there. This barricaded door corresponded clearly with the shuttered window outside." Holmes cuts the cord and he and Watson forcibly remove the barricade and break down the door. They find the room empty, and Rucastle, returning early, finds them, accuses them of being thieves and spies, and sets free his giant mastiff, Carlo. Carlo attack Rucastle instead and badly mangles him. Watson shoots the dog. Holmes and Watson could have been charged with trespass and possibly with causing damage to property. No charges at all are filed, and Holmes and Watson leave

unimpeded after they establish that the daughter has safely escaped. Watson, who shot the dog to save Rucastle's life, committed no crime as he acted to save a life.

7. *The Adventure of the Devil's Foot*. In this interesting and complex case, Holmes is taking a rest cure in isolated Cornwall. He allows Dr. Leon Sterndale, the explorer and lawless lion hunter, to return to Africa after Sterndale admits that he has murdered his fiancée's brother, Mortimer Tregennis. Sherlock Holmes is guilty of withholding evidence, compounding a felony, and perverting the cause of justice when he lets Sterndale - a confessed murderer - escape. His rationale is that in similar circumstances he believes that he himself might have killed to avenge his loved one's death.

In this story, do we trust Holmes' judgement? He nearly kills himself and Watson with his Devil's Foot experiment. Could Mortimer Tregennis have been telling the truth when he claimed not to know who murdered his sister? Could Holmes have followed more leads in the murder case, including finding out who benefited from Brenda's will? Was Sterndale's wife somehow involved? With all these unanswered questions, we have to wonder whether Holmes' decision to let Sterndale go was a good one. Or was Holmes' decision based on envy? Perhaps Holmes envied Sterndale's life of exploration and lawless lion hunting in Africa. Maybe Holmes saw something of himself in the independent, intelligent, quick-to-act Sterndale.

8. *The Final Problem*. Holmes commits the ultimate crime here by killing Moriarty at the Reichenbach Falls. Because of the recent attempts on his life, he knows that Moriarty is out to murder him. He tells Watson, "There cannot be the least doubt that he would have made a murderous attack upon me. It is, however, a game at which two may play." Holmes knows it is a struggle to the death between him and Moriarty – a struggle in which both may die or one may live. Holmes lives, and his act is a justified act because he exercised his right to self-defense. He was backed into a corner by someone trying to murder him, and he had no chance of escape - nowhere to go - so he acted in self-preservation, not sure if he himself would also be killed. Given this, he technically commits a justifiable homicide in self-defense, rendering him blameless. The note Holmes wrote to Watson indicates that he did conceive his own death to be a real possibility. "I am pleased to think that I shall be able to free society from any further effects of his presence, though I fear that it is at a cost which will give pain to my friends, and especially, my dear Watson, to you." But Holmes not only conceived his own death to be a possibility, he also in the note indicates that he had an intention to take Moriarty down with him. With the note and with his earlier remark to Watson indicating pre-meditation, Holmes could be charged with murder. [xviii] If he were charged and if there were a rigorous application of the law, he might not have been able to claim homicide in self-defense. However, the circumstances were mutual combat in a fair fight where Holmes faced his own death in the situation. It would have been difficult for a jury to affix blame for Moriarty's death onto Holmes.

One other point in this case is “the added dimension that the incident takes place in Switzerland. English law may well have claimed jurisdiction in theory, but extradition is a modern invention, and so in practical terms if Holmes had been apprehended it would have been to face a Swiss legal process.” [xix] Holmes might have had this jurisdictional problem in mind when he chose Reichenbach Falls as the place to confront Moriarty. He certainly was aware of a similar circumstance in *The Illustrious Client* when Baroness Gruner was found dead, her body in the Splugen Pass between the jurisdictions of two countries, Italy and Switzerland.

9. *The Adventure of the Illustrious Client.* This is a case in which Holmes commits more than one crime in the course of saving Violet de Merville from the wicked Baron Gruner. He breaks the law to prevent Violet from a ruinous marriage, and, though unintended, he also aids and abets Kitty Winter, former mistress of Baron Gruner, in getting her revenge. In their first meeting, Colonel Damery, representing the eponymous Illustrious Client (whom we assume to be Edward VII), presents Holmes with a quandary that forecasts trouble when he says, “To revenge crime is important, but to prevent it is more so. It is a terrible thing, Mr. Holmes, to see a dreadful event, an atrocious situation, preparing itself before your eyes, to clearly understand whither it will lead and yet to be utterly unable to avert it. Can a human being be placed in a more trying position?” Holmes is unsuccessful in getting Miss de Merville to dump the Baron, no matter what he tells her. On top of that, the Baron sends two of his well-dressed henchmen to

severely beat Holmes. Sherlock Holmes feels he must burgle Vernon Lodge, Baron Gruner's house, in a good cause. He has to steal the Baron's "brown leather book with a lock, and his arms in gold on the outside," for it contains a record of the Baron's lustful adventures. Only with this evidence will Holmes be able to convince brainwashed Violet de Merville that Baron Gruner is not suitable husband material. Watson enters Gruner's house under false pretenses in the guise of Dr. Hill Barton, an expert in Chinese porcelain, while Holmes trespasses through an open garden window. Holmes steals the book of Gruner's conquests, so we believe it is only bluff when the Baron threatens Holmes with prosecution for burglary – the Baron would certainly not want his book as evidence in a trial. Watson also could be charged with the crime of conspiracy to commit burglary because he was in on the theft. However, Holmes is never prosecuted because, according to Watson, "when an object is good and a client is sufficiently illustrious, even the rigid British law becomes human and elastic. My friend has not yet stood in the dock." Holmes needn't have worried about prosecution. He'd been hired by an illustrious client to whom the system would bow, so he knew he was immune from any legal consequences.

10. *The Disappearance of Lady Frances Carfax*. Holmes is sure that Holy Peters has kidnapped Lady Frances Carfax, but he can't prove it. So he decides to force his way into Holy Peters' house. "There's nothing for it now but a direct frontal attack. Are you armed? We shall be strong enough. 'Thrice is he armed who hath his quarrel just.' We simply can't afford to wait

for the police or to keep within the four corners of the law." Once in the house, Holmes tells Peters: "I mean to find her... I'm going through this house till I do find her." Peters demands a warrant. In response, Holmes half-draws a revolver from his pocket. "This will have to serve till a better one comes." Peters calls Holmes a "common burglar," and Holmes wonderfully responds, "So you might describe me. My companion is also a dangerous ruffian. And together we are going through your house." Holmes then threatens Peters: "If you try to stop us, Peters, you will most certainly get hurt." Peters calls in the police who arrive and tell Holmes he must leave: "Sorry, Mr. Holmes, but that's the law." "Exactly, Sergeant, you could not do otherwise," Holmes replies, and he isn't arrested because he leaves. The next morning, Holmes reappears at Peters' house, where with Watson and the pallbearers, they force the lid from a coffin to reveal a chloroformed but still alive Lady Frances Carfax. In this case, Holmes firmly believes that the end - saving Lady Frances Carfax, justifies the means – trespassing in Peters' house, holding a gun on him, and wrenching the lid from the coffin. Holmes doesn't get charged with any crimes in this tale because his actions were taken based on the premise that a life was at stake, and thus his defense of immediate action and interference to save that life removes any criminality from Holmes' acts. [xx] Even though Holy Peters and his wife escape, the police know their identities and will perhaps one day locate and arrest them.

11. *His Last Bow*. In solving a case of espionage, Sherlock Holmes and Dr. Watson commit crimes in

the name of Queen and Country. They administer chloroform [xxi] to Von Bork, a German citizen and an agent for the Kaiser. Then they ransack his safe and steal all Von Bork's private papers. Von Bork protests: "You are a private individual. You have no warrant for my arrest. The whole proceeding is absolutely illegal and outrageous." Holmes admits: "Absolutely." Then they kidnap Von Bork, and Holmes threatens that if he tries anything foolish, he'll be hanged and "would probably enlarge the too limited titles of our village inns by giving us 'The Dangling Prussian' as a signpost." Holmes, sporting a goatee, is disguised as Mr. Altamont of Chicago, an Irish-born double agent, while Watson plays the role of chauffeur; and the British government on the eve of war sanctions their crimes. The tale is one of patriotism and sacrifice for honor and country. Holmes has spent two years in America to infiltrate Von Bork's network of German spies, and he's taken many of Van Bork's agents down. He's even planted a spy in Von Bork's own house – Martha, the servant, who pets a large black cat that may be hers or may be Von Bork's. She is described by Baron Von Herling, the chief secretary of the legation and Von Bork's colleague, as someone who "might almost personify Britannia." Of course they mean a weak and helpless Britannia, with docile, simple folk who "... are not very hard to deceive." But Martha turns out to be the very antithesis. She's been, in fact, Holmes' personally picked spy and highly successful in turning over many of Von Bork's secrets. England and its honor are themes throughout this tale. The two German spies suspect that England will not honor her treaties not only because they perceive it as weak but also because it's "a utilitarian age.

Honour is a mediaeval conception." But Holmes and Watson refute that perception with their courage and patriotism in the face of war and their hope for the future. Instead of getting arrested for their crimes, we suspect they may get a medal for them. Martha, too.

12. The Adventure of the Missing Three Quarter. Sherlock Holmes and Dr. Watson commit the crime of unlawful entry in this case. They break into an isolated cottage in hopes of finding Godfrey Staunton, who they believe is being held prisoner to prevent him from playing in an important rugby game. Throughout this case, Holmes' profession as private detective is questioned by Staunton's uncle, Lord Mount-James, as well as by Dr. Armstrong. They are enemies, but both agree that Holmes' profession is "open to criticism ... when you pry into the secrets of private individuals, when you rake up family matters which are better hidden..." As Victorians, they demand discretion. They fear scandal, and they both – for different reasons – want Holmes to stop interfering. Holmes explains that "we are doing the reverse of what you very justly blame, and that we are endeavouring to prevent anything like public exposure of private matters which must necessarily follow when once the case is fairly in the hands of the official police." He casts his profession as one of "an irregular pioneer, who goes in front of the regular forces of the country." Once again we find Holmes ready to hush things up: "So long as there is nothing criminal I am much more anxious to hush up private scandals than to give them publicity." Holmes and Watson commit the crime of unlawful entry to help solve the mystery of Godfrey's disappearance. It doesn't matter that they have no criminal motives, it is still a crime. However, Godfrey Staunton would not file charges. And Dr. Armstrong – who has tried to keep Godfrey's secret from Lord Mount-James – finally realizes that Holmes is not an enemy but a friend. He says: "You are a good fellow... I had misjudged you." This case is a mystery without a crime (see Category 1), and had Holmes solved it earlier so that Godfrey Staunton was able to play the match, perhaps Cambridge would have defeated Oxford.

13. *The Naval Treaty.* In this case, Holmes compounds a felony [xxii] by letting a villain, Joseph Harrison, go free. He's committed theft, lied to the police and concealed evidence in connection with a secret treaty between England and Italy that he stole from the offices of Percy Phelps, his sister Annie's fiancé. Holmes fends off a knife attack and traps Joseph Harrison to recover the treaty papers. Then he lets Joseph Harrison go, saying: "Having got them I let my man go, but I wired full particulars to Forbes this morning. If he is quick enough to catch his bird, well and good. But if, as I shrewdly suspect, he finds the nest empty before he gets there, why, all the better for the government. I fancy that Lord Holdhurst for one, and Mr. Percy Phelps for another, would very much rather that the affair never got as far as a police-court." Once again, Holmes acts outside the law and hushes things up, but he is doing so for reasons of Queen and Country, not self-gain. And once again, Scotland Yard knows the facts, even though they have to chase after and will probably never catch Harrison. This is another example of Holmes' using discretion on behalf of the government. He keeps the caper

secret to avoid any negative consequences should the public hear about it.

14. *The Adventure of the Noble Bachelor.* This case revolves around differences between Britain and America, and it centers on the trend at the time for wealthy American girls to be married to titled Englishmen with property and lineage but no money. Lord Robert St. Simon, second son of the Duke of Balmoral, is the noble bachelor who is to be married to Miss Hatty Doran, only daughter of wealthy Aloysius Doran, Esq., of San Francisco, Cal., U.S.A. This sounds a lot like the introduction to the American radio soap opera, "Our Gal Sunday," which posits the question: "Can this girl from a little mining town in the West find happiness as the wife of the wealthy and titled Lord Henry Brenthrup?" In this instance, however, the American girl is wealthier than the British bridegroom. America intrudes on more than just the theme of this story when a presumed dead previous husband from America shows up at the church wedding. The bride spots him as she walks to the altar. She could have halted the ceremony, but she didn't. She commits bigamy by going through with the ceremony. This problem would undoubtedly be handled quickly by her father with an annulment of the second marriage, but Holmes' crime is withholding evidence. Holmes doesn't tell Scotland Yard about the bigamy, and certainly neither Lord St. Simon nor Hatty Doran is going to report what happened. Of course we expect Holmes to exercise discretion, and considering the Duke of Balmoral is involved, he is bound to be circumspect. It is in all their interests to keep it quiet to avoid further public

gossip, scandal and embarrassment to Lord St. Simon and his family. Holmes ends up bringing the parties together to help solve the problem. He even hosts a bridal supper with Hattie and her first husband, Mr. Frank Moulton. I wasn't surprised that Lord St. Simon skipped the festivities.

15. The Adventure of the Norwood Builder. Holmes figures out that the malignant Jonas Oldacre must be hiding in his own house while an innocent young man has been arrested for murdering him. Holmes literally smokes Oldacre out by setting a fire in the middle of a corridor in the top landing of Oldacre's house. He gets Lestrade and three other police constables to carry up two big bundles of straw. Then Watson lights the straw with a match and opens a window, all at Holmes' direction. "A coil of gray smoke swirled down the corridor, while the dry straw crackled and flamed." The flaming straw made a smoldering fire when water was thrown onto it. Even though the fire was set only to smoke out Oldacre and was doused immediately, nonetheless Holmes and Watson probably caused some fire, smoke and water damage, albeit minimal. For their actions, they could be charged with criminal damage to property. The fact that Lestrade and other constables were present would not prevent the action committed from being a crime. Lestrade and the constables and even Watson didn't know exactly what Holmes intended to do, and even if they had known and had assented to it, it would still be considered a crime because the police are not the arbiters of what is criminal. Police powers were exercised for law enforcement, not for interpretation of the law. If Lestrade chose not to prosecute, that is a matter for his discretion, and it would not change the technical legal position. Anyway, Lestrade is so overwhelmed by the display of Holmes' magic when Oldacre appears out of the wood work, there is no chance of a prosecution. Lestrade tells Holmes, "You have saved an innocent man's life, and you have prevented a very grave scandal, which would have ruined my reputation in the Force." One interesting aspect of this crime is that Holmes uses the police constables and Watson as cat's paws to carry the straw, light the fire, open the window and douse the flames. He himself has clean hands – in a literal sense; and so even if there was a prosecution, Holmes would have little chance of being convicted. Nor would (Norwood) the police.

16. *The Adventure of the Retired Colourman*. Scotland Yard couldn't solve this case of Josiah Amberley's disappearing wife so they send it to Holmes, who likens their actions to medical men who "occasionally send their incurables to a quack. They argue that they can do nothing more, and that whatever happens the patient can be no worse than he is." Holmes tells Watson that Amberley's wife and his best friend, Dr. Ray Ernest, "went off together last week–destination untraced. What is more, the faithless spouse carried off the old man's deed-box as her personal luggage with a good part of his life's savings within." Holmes commits his first crime when he forges a telegram from a J. C. Elman, M. A., the vicar in Little Purlington, to decoy Amberley from his home. The real Reverend Elman is outraged and threatens a police investigation, saying: "There is only one vicarage, sir, and only one vicar, and this wire is a scandalous forgery, the origin of which shall certainly

be investigated by the police." This investigation undoubtedly never happens because Inspector MacKinnon is in awe of how the decoy was handled and tells Holmes: "It is masterly." Holmes then openly admits his second crime to MacKinnon: "There being no fear of interruption I proceeded to burgle the house. Burglary has always been an alternative profession had I cared to adopt it, and I have little doubt that I should have come to the front." Holmes is forgiven this bit of lawlessness because it was done in a just cause, but Inspector MacKinnon warns Holmes about his use of irregular methods and insists that "we get there all the same, Mr. Holmes. Don't imagine that we had not formed our own views of this case, and that we would not have laid our hands on our man. You will excuse us for feeling sore when you jump in with methods which we cannot use, and so rob us of the credit."

17. A Scandal in Bohemia. In this very first of the Sherlock Holmes stories we find Holmes and Watson plotting to commit, by their own admission, a criminal deed:

> "You don't mind breaking the law?"
> "Not in the least."
> "Nor running a chance of arrest?"
> "Not in a good cause."
> "Oh, the cause is excellent!"
> "Then I am your man."
> "I was sure that I might rely on you."

Holmes disguises himself as an amiable clergyman and plots to gain entry to Adler's house by the crime of deception. On top of this, Holmes and

Watson cause damage to Adler's private property when, at Holmes' signal, Watson tosses a plumber's smoke rocket through Adler's window and yells fire. The next crime would have been the theft of a photograph, but Irene Adler leaves England, taking it with her and preventing the crime. Two more crimes Holmes commits are connected to his witnessing the marriage of Irene Adler, spinster, to Godfrey Norton, bachelor. Holmes says that he was verbally "vouching for things of which I knew nothing" during the marriage ceremony, and thus he was making a false declaration in order to procure a marriage. The same crime would apply if he had to sign a written instrument. If he did, what name did he use? He was disguised as a "drunken-looking groom, ill-kempt and side-whiskered with an inflamed face and disreputable clothes...." If he signed the famous name of Sherlock Holmes, surely there would have been a flap. Someone would have noticed and remarked, thus ruining his chance to steal the incriminating photo he'd promised to get for the King. If he signed another name, he would have made a false entry in the register, thus committing a crime falling under the general heading of Deception. Holmes doesn't reveal the name he used, and we are left to wonder whether this signed affidavit still resides somewhere in the annals of the Church of St. Monica in the Edgware Road. Holmes uses the rationale of an "excellent cause" to justify the actions he takes that are outside the law in this case. His personal moral benchmark is to always be on the side of justice, even if that means breaking the law to achieve it. Justice means justice as he deems it to be, and that is not necessarily the same thing as the justice of a British court of law.

18. *The Adventure of the Second Stain.* In this case, Holmes has to deal with not only the theft of an important top secret letter, but also with a wife's betrayal of her husband. Lady Hilda Trelawney Hope removed a document from her husband's locked dispatch box and turned it over to a blackmailer. She does not know the document is a highly sensitive letter and could cause irreparable damage to the government. The only way Holmes can reclaim the letter is to get Lady Hope to trust him and admit she took it. The only way Holmes can get her husband back into the good graces of the Foreign Office is to cover up the incident. Once again Holmes has to juggle things as he acts to keep secrets – this time secrets of both a family and the government. To keep the secrets of the government and return her husband to his position in the foreign office, Holmes compounds a felony by hiding Lady Hope's secret in exchange for the letter. He is able to maneuver the safe return of the letter, and he withholds evidence about the crime and covers up Lady Hope's misdeeds – in this case so grave she possibly could have been charged with treason. If her actions did amount to treason, then Holmes might have committed Misprision of Treason, which is a lesser form of treason. [xxiii] Since Holmes is working on behalf of the government, his illegal actions are sanctioned by the urgent need to find the document and keep the whole affair secret. The end justifies the means. Holmes is once again discreet, and he never personally gains from these illegalities – all is done in the name of fair play and justice for the good of England.

19. *Silver Blaze*. In Silver Blaze, Holmes gives Colonel Ross a bit of a comeuppance for his cavalier attitude toward the great detective. Holmes has located the stolen horse at the Mapleton stables of Silas Brown, who disguised the horse by dying the white blaze black and hiding him until the Wessex Cup race was over. Holmes says of Brown, "A more perfect compound of the bully, coward, and sneak than Master Silas Brown I have seldom met with." Holmes however, doesn't have Brown arrested for horse theft. He believes Brown did it on the spur of the moment, seeing a chance for his own financial gain. So after Silas Brown confesses and repents, Holmes lets him off the hook. Then Holmes co-opts Brown and uses him in a scheme to get the better of Colonel Ross. Holmes isn't worried about not turning Brown in to the police, although in not doing so his crimes are compounding a felony and withholding evidence. Holmes says, "I follow my own methods and tell as much or as little as I choose. That is the advantage of being unofficial. I don't know whether you observed it, Watson, but the colonel's manner has been just a trifle cavalier to me. I am inclined now to have a little amusement at his expense. Say nothing to him about the horse." Brown does Holmes' bidding and keeps Silver Blaze at his stable until race day when Holmes dramatically surprises the Colonel with the horse. Silver Blaze, of course, wins the cup – and probably Holmes wins a nice wager. Holmes doesn't shake Silas Brown's hand. He doesn't like him, but he believes that Brown's crime was one of opportunity and was not premeditated. Because Brown confessed and repented, Holmes agrees not to turn him over to the law – especially since Brown's cooperation was

necessary to carry out Holmes' scheme to best the Colonel.

20. *The Adventure of the Solitary Cyclist*. Holmes and Jack Woodley, also known as "Roaring Jack," engage in a boxing brawl at a country pub in this tale. It is true that Woodley, "the greatest brute and bully in South Africa," starts the bar fight with "a vicious backhander." Holmes retaliates and hits Woodley with "a straight left." And the fight goes on. Holmes ends up "with a cut lip and a discoloured lump" on his forehead, while "Mr. Woodley went home in a cart." Holmes could be charged with Affray, "the offence with which people are and were charged with when they fight. A bar-room brawl or street fight falls into this category." [xxiv]

21. *The Adventure of the Three Gables*. In an interesting twist that clearly exemplifies the Holmesian brand of justice, Holmes tells the villainess, Isadora Klein, "I am not the law, but I represent justice so far as my feeble powers go. I am ready to listen, and then I will tell you how I will act." Isadora then confesses and repents, and she agrees with Holmes that "the original sin" was hers, not her victim's. Then Holmes admits he's going to "compound a felony as usual." He agrees not to report Klein's involvement in the burglary at Three Gables to the authorities in exchange for five thousand pounds from her. Holmes calls his crime compounding a felony, but it might also be called blackmail. Holmes is using Klein's fear of revealing her involvement in a criminal ring to extract money from her, even though the money is not for him but to make reparations to

his client, the victim's mother, who'd been roughed up during the burglary. In law, the blackmailer does not have to benefit personally for the offence to be committed. [xxv] Although the police are involved in the case, they are unlikely to uncover Isadora Klein's part, and Holmes isn't going to inform them. As he has in other cases, Holmes lets Isadora Klein off the hook because she confesses and repents - both necessary elements in Holmesian justice. What role her being female plays in Holmes' decision is unclear. Watson says: "So roguish and exquisite did she look as she stood before us with a challenging smile that I felt of all Holmes's criminals this was the one whom he would find it hardest to face." Holmes does give deference to women such as Irene Adler and Violet Smith and Lady Hope, and maybe Holmes fell for Isadora's blaming Italy and her too-enthusiastic friends for what happened with Douglas Maberley. We do know that he not only forgives her, but he also offers her advice: "Have a care! Have a care! You can't play with edged tools forever without cutting those dainty hands." She escapes by giving him a payoff, but the members of the Spencer John gang who worked for her aren't so lucky. Holmes gives them over to the law to pay for all their misdeeds.

22. *The Adventure of the Veiled Lodger* concerns itself with a love triangle and an old crime. Eugenia Ronder and her lover, Leonardo, the circus strongman, planned to murder her cruel husband who ran Ronder's wild beast show. They succeeded, but things went wrong when Eugenia herself was mauled by Sahara King, the circus lion. Leonardo deserted her, and she lived her life in seclusion, wearing a veil to

hide her terrible scars. Eugenia heard that Leonardo had recently drowned, and she wants to ease her mind about the crime. She sends for Sherlock Holmes and confesses everything to him and Watson. Holmes, believing that her husband had been a drunk and a bully, is sympathetic. He believes she has suffered enough, and he stops her from thinking of suicide, saying: "The example of patient suffering is in itself the most precious of all lessons." Holmes then puts himself in the role of the prosecutor to decide whether this case of murder, even though it is an old murder, should be tried in the British justice system. Eugenia has confessed and she has suffered - both important elements when Holmes believes that the justice system may not render true justice in a case. Holmes announces, "The case is closed," and he lets Eugenia go free. Holmes thus commits the crime of withholding information on the murder from Scotland Yard. On the side of justice, Holmes does stop her from committing suicide, which would have added another crime to her slate.

23. The Yellow Face. In this story Holmes and Watson aid and abet their client, Mr. Grant Munro, as he forces his way into a house that he doesn't own. Munro had seen his wife at this cottage with another figure in the window that he cannot identify. Eaten up by mistrust of his wife, who has refused to say what she knows of the figure, he determines to enter the cottage. Holmes, who suspects that Mrs. Munro's first husband is in the cottage, realizes that what they are doing is illegal and admits, "Of course, legally, we are putting ourselves hopelessly in the wrong, but I think that it is worth it." "Now follow me," Grant Munro

said, “and we shall soon know all.” “... We followed closely after him. ... and an instant afterwards we were all upon the stairs. Grant Munro rushed into the lighted room at the top, and we entered at his heels.” They trespass, but what they find in the room has nothing to do with any criminal endeavor or a rival lover. Instead they find Munro’s wife, who is hiding a black daughter – an issue from her earlier marriage to an American black man now deceased. She believed that Munro would not accept the daughter, and she required the child to wear a yellow mask to cover her face and disguise her color. Munro agrees to accept the child, while Holmes realizes he failed to solve the mystery. He says: “Watson, if I should ever strike you that I am getting a little overconfident in my powers, or giving less pains to a case than it deserves, kindly whisper ‘Norbury’ in my ear and I shall be infinitely obliged to you.”

Statistical overview

Holmes and Watson troop through the Canon committing some 50 criminal acts in 19 different types of crimes. Of course, as we have seen, in many of the cases the ‘crimes’ turn out to be not crimes at all, because there is a valid defense to them. The 19 categories of crimes are listed below along with the stories in which the crimes are committed. In some stories, more than one crime is committed.

A Case of Identity is not included in this section. I have omitted it because it is not a crime for

Holmes to withhold information from his client, Mary Sutherland, although it may be morally questionable. A word of clarification concerning the terminology of the crime of compounding a felony – a crime Holmes says he is going to commit in several of the stories. "Compounding a felony was itself a crime – a misdemeanor - in Victorian times. The distinction between felony and misdemeanor was present at the time of the Holmes stories, and abolished in the second half of the 20th century." [xxvi]

CRIMES COMMITTED

Accessory/Aiding, Abetting, Counseling or Procuring– 3 – 6%

The Adventure of the Abbey Grange (Murder)
The Adventure of the Blue Carbuncle (Theft)
Charles Augustus Milverton (Murder)

Administering a Stupefying or overpowering Drug – 1 – 2%

His Last Bow

Affray – 1 – 2%

The Adventure of the Solitary Cyclist

Blackmail – 1 – 2%

The Adventure of the Three Gables

Breach of Promise (Civil tort action not criminal) – 1 – 2%

Charles Augustus Milverton

Burglary-Breaking & Entering w/ intent to commit crime – 7 – 14%

The Adventure of the Bruce Partington Plans
Charles Augustus Milverton
The Adventure of the Copper Beeches
His Last Bow
The Adventure of the Illustrious Client
The Adventure of the Retired Colourman
The Yellow Face

Compounding a Felony/ Misprision of a Felony – 8 – 16%

The Adventure of the Abbey Grange (Murder, Accessory)
The Adventure of the Blue Carbuncle (Jewel Theft)
The Boscombe Valley Mystery (Murder)
The Adventure of the Devil's Foot (Murder)
The Naval Treaty (Burglary/Espionage)
The Adventure of the Second Stain (Burglary/Espionage)
Silver Blaze (Theft)
The Adventure of the Three Gables (Burglary and assault)

Conspiracy (to commit Burglary) – 1 – 2%

The Adventure of the Illustrious Client (Watson)

Damages to Property - 3 – 6%

The Adventure of the Copper Beeches
The Norwood Builder
A Scandal in Bohemia

Deception – 2 – 4%
Making a False Declaration in order to procure a marriage
A Scandal in Bohemia

Making False Entries in a register – 1 – 2%
A Scandal in Bohemia

Forgery – 1 – 2%
The Adventure of the Retired Colourman

Homicide (in self defense) – 1 – 2%
The Final Problem

Kidnapping – 1 – 2%
His Last Bow

Larceny -2 – 4%
Charles Augustus Milverton
His Last Bow

Misprision of Treason -1 – 2%
The Adventure of the Second Stain

Perverting the Cause of Justice – 4 - 8%
The Adventure of the Blue Carbuncle
The Boscombe Valley Mystery
Charles Augustus Milverton
The Adventure of the Devil's Foot

Trespass – 2 – 4%
The Disappearance of Lady Frances Carfax
The Yellow Face

Unlawful Entry – 1 – 2%

The Adventure of the Missing Three-Quarter

Withholding Evidence – 9 – 18%

The Adventure of the Abbey Grange
The Boscombe Valley Mystery
The Adventure of the Devil's Foot
The Naval Treaty
The Adventure of the Noble Bachelor
The Adventure of the Second Stain
Silver Blaze
The Adventure of the Three Gables
The Adventure of the Veiled Lodger

50 CRIMES COMMITTED BY HOLMES & WATSON
0
1
2
3
4
5
6
7
8
9
Accessory/Aiding or Abetting 3
Administer Drug 1
Affray 1
Blackmail 1
Breach of Promise 1
Burglary 7
Compounding/Misprison of a Felony 8
Conspiracy 1
Damage to Property 3
Deception 2
Forgery 1
Homicide 1
Kidnapping 1
Larceny 2
Misprison/Treason 1
Perverting Justice 4
Trespass 2
Unlawful Entry 1
Withholding evidence 9

The crimes/misdeeds committed by Holmes and Watson involve 13 women and 24 Men. Note that in *Charles Augustus Milverton*, Holmes' crimes involve not only Milverton himself (Burglary), but also involve Milverton's housemaid Agatha (Breach of Promise), and the murderess (Perverting the Cause of Justice). Similarly in *The Abbey Grange,* his crimes involve Lady Brackenstall and her maid as well as Captain Croker.

57% of the persons involved in these stories are British and 43% are non-British.

<u>Females – 13 – 35%</u>

The Adventure of the Abbey Grange – 2
    Lady Mary Brackenstall
    Theresa Wright, Personal Maid
Charles Augustus Milverton - 2
    Agatha the Housemaid (Breach of Promise)
    Noblewoman (murderess)
The Disappearance of Lady Frances Carfax
The Noble Bachelor
A Scandal in Bohemia
The Adventure of the Second Stain – 2
    Lady Hope
    Mrs. Henri Fournaye
The Adventure of the Three Gables – 2
    Isadora Klein
    Susan Stockdale
The Adventure of the Veiled Lodger
The Yellow Face

Males - 24 - 65%

The Adventure of the Abbey Grange
The Adventure of the Blue Carbuncle
The Boscombe Valley Mystery
The Adventure of the Bruce Partington Plans – 2
    Hugo Oberstein
    Colonel Walter
Charles Augustus Milverton
The Adventure of the Copper Beeches
The Adventure of the Devil's Foot – 2
    Mortimer Tregennis
    Dr. Leon Sterndale
The Final Problem
The Adventure of the Illustrious Client
The Disappearance of Lady Frances Carfax
His Last Bow
The Adventure of the Missing Three-Quarter
The Norwood Builder
The Naval Treaty
The Adventure of the Retired Colourman
Silver Blaze –2
    John Straker
    Silas Brown
The Adventure of the Solitary Cyclist – 3
    Carruthers
    Woodley
    Williamson
The Adventure of the Three Gables – 2
    Barney Stockdale
    Steve Dixie

British – 21 - 57 %

The Adventure of the Abbey Grange
The Adventure of the Blue Carbuncle
Charles Augustus Milverton -3
The Adventure of the Copper Beeches
The Adventure of the Devil's Foot - 2
The Final Problem
The Adventure of the Missing Three Quarter
The Naval Treaty
The Norwood Builder
The Adventure of the Retired Colourman
A Scandal in Bohemia
The Adventure of the Second Stain
Silver Blaze – 2
The Adventure of the Solitary Cyclist – 1
The Adventure of the Three Gables – 2
The Adventure of the Veiled Lodger

Non-British – 16 - 43%

The Abbey Grange (Australian) - 2
The Boscombe Valley Mystery (Australian)
The Bruce Partington Plans (German) - 2
The Illustrious Client (Austrian)
The Disappearance of Lady Frances Carfax (Australian) - 2
His Last Bow (German)
The Noble Bachelor (American)
The Second Stain (French/Creole) - 2
The Solitary Cyclist (South African) - 2
The Adventure of the Three Gables (Spanish)
The Yellow Face (American)

American - 2
Austrian - 3
Australian - 3
French/Creole - 2
German - 3
South African - 2
Spanish - 1

Of these 23 cases, 9 are cases published before 1901 (40%); 6 were published between 1903 and 1904 (26%); and 8 were published after 1908 and through 1927 (34%). Holmes and Watson, it seems, committed crimes on a fairly regular basis throughout the Canon, beginning with the first – property damage and deceptions in *A Scandal in Bohemia*, to breaking and entering and forgery in the last, *The Adventure of the Retired Colourman.*

Early Published Cases – 9 – 40%
The Adventure of the Blue Carbuncle
The Boscombe Valley Mystery
The Adventure of the Copper Beeches
The Final Problem
The Naval Treaty
The Noble Bachelor
A Scandal in Bohemia
Silver Blaze
The Yellow Face

Cases between 1903 & 1904 – 6 – 26%
The Adventure of the Abbey Grange
Charles Augustus Milverton
The Adventure of the Missing Three-Quarter
The Norwood Builder

The Adventure of the Second Stain
The Adventure of the Solitary Cyclist

Later Cases after 1908 through 1927 – 8 – 34%
The Adventure of the Bruce-Partington Plans
The Adventure of the Devil's Foot
The Adventure of the Illustrious Client
The Disappearance of Lady Frances Carfax
His Last Bow
The Adventure of the Retired Colourman
The Adventure of the Three Gables
The Adventure of the Veiled Lodger

There are some particulars relating to various crimes/misdeeds Holmes commits. [xxvii] Although we have listed the crimes, certainly some of them would not have got through the prosecutor to make a formal charge against Holmes. For example, in *The Boscombe Valley Mystery,* if there was no duty on Holmes to disclose what he had discovered, then he would not be charged with any crime. Watson, who shoots the mastiff dog, Carlo, in *The Copper Beeches,* and Roy the Wolfhound in *The Creeping Man,* does so in self-defense as the dogs are attacking and human lives are at stake. Watson would never have been charged for these deeds. And in *The Abbey Grange,* Captain Croker kills Sir Eustace in self-defense. Self-defense is a defense to a charge of murder and removes any criminality, so if Croker committed no crime, then technically Holmes committed no felony, which means no compounding or misprision on Holmes' part.

Chapter 9

Category 5 - Cases in Which Sherlock Holmes Was Wrong

"In publishing these short sketches based upon the numerous cases in which my companion's singular gifts have made me the listener to, and eventually the actor in, some strange drama, it is only natural that I should dwell rather upon his successes than upon his failures. And this not so much for the sake of his reputation--for, indeed, it was when he was at his wits' end that his energy and his versatility were most admirable--but because where he failed it happened too often that no one else succeeded, and that the tale was left forever without a conclusion. Now and again, however, it chanced that even when he erred, the truth was still discovered.

- Watson, The Yellow Face

"From the years 1894 to 1901 inclusive, Mr. Sherlock Holmes was a very busy man. ... Many startling successes and a few unavoidable failures were the outcome of this long period of continuous work."

– Watson, *Solitary Cyclist*

Sherlock Holmes wrong? Failures? Impossible. Readers do not conceive of him making mistakes or failing. Yet Holmes says in *The Five Orange Pips,* published in 1891, that "I have been beaten four times--three times by men, and once by a woman."

I suggest these are the four cases, all of them early published cases, to which Holmes was referring:

1. A Scandal in Bohemia - 1891
2. The Five Orange Pips – 1891
3. The Yellow Face - 1893
4. The Man with the Twisted Lip - 1891

1. A Scandal in Bohemia. We can be certain that the one case in which a woman beat Sherlock Holmes is *A Scandal in Bohemia,* the first of the short stories in the Canon. We know that beautiful Irene Adler, adventuress and former mistress of the King of Bohemia, hoodwinks Holmes and escapes with a compromising photograph of her and the King before Holmes has a chance to steal it and return it to the King. Holmes uses two brilliant disguises to trick Adler to reveal where she had hidden the photo, but he never is able to get his hands on it. However, Holmes does win the contest of wits, and he secures Irene Adler's promise never to use the photo to blackmail the King - exactly what Holmes had been hired to accomplish. And she made that promise only because she knew the great detective was on the case. But she definitely bests him by seeing through his subterfuge and escaping.

The only other formidable female criminal Holmes deals with in the short stories is Isadora Klein in *The Three Gables*, and while he lets her get away with her crimes, she pays him a substantial forfeit.

2. The Five Orange Pips. We can state with some confidence that *The Five Orange Pips* is one of the three cases Holmes mentions in which he was beaten by men. This case also is one of the early cases,

published in 1891, the same year as A *Scandal in Bohemia*. Holmes, in trying to prevent a crime, failed to protect his client, John Openshaw from being murdered after leaving 221B on his way home. Holmes allowed Openshaw to travel alone, despite the fact that he knew there were men from the American Ku Klux Kan who had sent Openshaw the five orange pips, symbols that they were going to kill him if they didn't get the papers they wanted. Holmes realized the deadly urgency of the case, and he did urge Openshaw to be cautious, but his mistake was to let him go home unaccompanied so he could be waylaid and murdered. Later, Watson is appalled when he hears Openshaw has been murdered. He says, "Holmes, you are too late." Watson notes that Holmes was "more depressed and shaken than I had ever seen him." Holmes tells Watson, "It becomes a personal matter with me now, and, if God sends me health, I shall set my hand upon this gang. That he should come to me for help, and that I should send him away to his death --!" "They must be cunning devils," he exclaimed at last. "How could they have decoyed him down there? The Embankment is not on the direct line to the station. The bridge, no doubt, was too crowded, even on such a night, for their purpose. Well, Watson, we shall see who will win in the long run. I am going out now!"

In the next scene with Watson, Holmes eats bread and water as a symbolic atonement, punishing himself for his mistake. Holmes personally vows to avenge Openshaw's murder, and he successfully traces the gang's whereabouts. This is one of the few cases in which the villains escape, but Holmes follows up and arranges for their capture when the ship docks. Again making this murder personal, Holmes then sends the leader of the gang five orange pips with a note: "S. H. for J. O." Then he sealed it and addressed it to "Captain James Calhoun, Bark Lone Star, Savannah, Georgia." But Calhoun and his two mates were fated to never receive the orange pips and to never see Holmesian or British justice. Instead they met their fate from the heavens when the Lone Star went down in a bad storm and the crew was lost at sea. Holmes' plan to avenge Openshaw's murder is taken over by a higher power, and thus is the crime justly avenged.

3. *The Yellow Face.* This story is another early one, published in 1893 and set in the mid-1881's. There is a mystery here, but no crime; and Holmes completely fails to deduce the real facts in this mystery because his analysis of the situation is incorrect. His deductions, based on his observations and analysis are incorrect. Holmes infers that the problem brought to him by his client, Grant Munro, must be either a love triangle or blackmail taking place with the first husband at clandestine meetings with Munro's wife. Watson, talking about Holmes' many cases, says, "Now and again, however, it chanced that even when he erred, the truth was still discovered." So it was in this case. Holmes only discovered the truth when he and Watson and his client trespass into a house. Holmes admits, "Legally, we are putting ourselves hopelessly in the wrong, but I think that it is worth it." After they push their way into a room, they uncover Munro's wife's secret -- a Negro daughter she was hiding. Her daughter was the product of her first marriage to a black American from Atlanta, now dead. It is interesting to watch Holmes react once they are in

the house. He removes the child's mask, and both he and Watson laugh because it is not only an unexpected conclusion, it is also trivial and a failure of deductive reasoning. Holmes has broken the principles of his own method and, as he says in *A Scandal in Bohemia*, he makes "a capital mistake to theorize before one has data." Holmes is so upset by his failure that later that night he tells Watson, "...if it should ever strike you that I am getting a little overconfident in my powers, or giving less pains to a case than it deserves, kindly whisper 'Norbury' in my ear and I shall be infinitely obliged to you." It must be remembered that Holmes got his facts from Munro, who was unaware that his wife's first husband was black and that his wife had a daughter. Without these facts, Holmes could not make the bricks. Some might say Holmes was bested by a woman and a child in this case, but I think he put the blame on Grant Munro for creating the mystery by not knowing the truth about his new wife.

4. *The Man with the Twisted Lip*. Published in 1891 and set in 1889, this is a case in which Sherlock Holmes is completely wrong in his deductions when he takes Watson to see Mrs. Neville St. Clair and tells her that he thinks her husband is dead, perhaps murdered on the Monday last. Holmes roars when Mrs. St. Clair produces a letter she's certain was written by her husband and is postmarked later than Monday. Holmes lights his pipe, sits on a bunch of pillows and contemplates the threads of his facts. Next morning he has the solution and says, "I think, Watson, that you are now standing in the presence of one of the most absolute fools in Europe. I deserve to be kicked from here to Charing Cross." Holmes solves

the mystery when he reveals that beggar man Hugh Boone, in prison for murdering Neville St. Clair, is himself none other than Neville St. Clair. St. Clair reveals all and repents, agreeing to never beg again. In return Holmes and the police agree to hush up the affair, in part to avoid scandal but also probably because they look so foolish having claimed St. Clair was murdered while all the time he was languishing in their jail cell.

A Few Other Cases where Holmes admits mistakes

There are a few other notable cases in the Canon in which Holmes makes some blunders in his deductions and admits he was following the wrong path, but in the end, he solves the case. Watson makes reference in *The Solitary Cyclist* to the fact that Holmes had many successes but also some failures as well: “"From the years 1894 to 1901 inclusive Mr. Sherlock Holmes was a very busy man. It is safe to say that there was no public case of any difficulty in which he was not consulted during those eight years, and there were hundreds of private cases, some of them of the most intricate and extraordinary character, in which he played a prominent part. Many startling successes and a few unavoidable failures were the outcome of this long period of continuous work." And Watson informs us in *Thor Bridge* that: "Somewhere in the vaults of the bank of Cox and Co., at Charing Cross, there is a travel-worn and battered tin dispatch box with my name, John H. Watson, M. D., Late Indian Army, painted upon the lid. It is crammed with papers, nearly all of which are records of cases to illustrate the curious problems which Mr. Sherlock

Holmes had at various times to examine. Some, and not the least interesting, were complete failures, and as such will hardly bear narrating, since no final explanation is forthcoming. A problem without a solution may interest the student, but can hardly fail to annoy the casual reader." In *The Musgrave Ritual*, Holmes talks a bit about his early cases before his partnership with Watson: "Yes, my boy, these were all done prematurely before my biographer had come to glorify me." He lifted bundle after bundle in a tender, caressing sort of way. "They are not all successes, Watson," said he. "But there are some pretty little problems among them. "

In *The Lion's Mane*, Holmes calls himself "dull-witted" before he reaches the truth. Here are six more tales in which Holmes is either too slow or admits he was on the wrong track before bringing the threads together to solve the cases.

5. *The Adventure of the Dancing Men*, published in 1903 and set in 1888, is a case in which Hilton Cubitt, a client of Sherlock Holmes, is murdered. It really doesn't get any worse than this for a consulting detective. This case is similar *to The Five Orange Pips*. In both, a male client of Holmes is murdered, and Sherlock Holmes admits he failed to prevent it. Holmes did understand the grave danger for his client, and he tried to prevent a crime. But he and Watson do not make it back to Ridling Thorpe Manor in time to save Cubitt from a confrontation with one of his wife's former suitors. Cubitt is shot dead, and Elsie, his wife, tries to commit suicide. Holmes is utterly despondent, and "his sudden realisation of his worst fears left him in a blank melancholy. He leaned back

in his seat, lost in gloomy speculation." "I anticipated it. I came in the hope of preventing it," he says. Nonetheless he cracks the dancing men cipher and sets a trap to catch the real murderer, Abe Slaney. He redeems himself by solving the crime and saving Elsie from being tried for her husband's murder. In spite of losing Cubitt, Inspector Martin tells Holmes, "I only hope that if ever again I have an important case I shall have the good fortune to have you by my side."

6. *Silver Blaze*. In this tale, Holmes admits: "I made a blunder, my dear Watson, which is, I'm afraid, a more common occurrence than anyone would think who only knew me through your memoirs." Holmes tells Watson he miscalculated: "It is one of those cases where the art of the reasoner should be used rather for the sifting of details than for the acquiring of fresh evidence. The tragedy has been so uncommon, so complete, and of such personal importance to so many people that we are suffering from a plethora of surmise, conjecture, and hypothesis. The difficulty is to detach the framework of fact -- of absolute undeniable fact -- from the embellishments of theorists and reporters. Then, having established ourselves upon this sound basis, it is our duty to see what inferences may be drawn and what are the special points upon which the whole mystery turns." Watson asks Holmes why he didn't go earlier to Exeter, and Holmes admits, "The fact is that I could not believe it possible that the most remarkable horse in England could long remain concealed, especially in so sparsely inhabited a place as the north of Dartmoor. From hour to hour yesterday I expected to hear that he had been found, and that his abductor

was the murderer of John Straker. When, however, another morning had come and I found that beyond the arrest of young Fitzroy Simpson nothing had been done, I felt that it was time for me to take action." Holmes, now on the right path, handily solves the complex case after investigating the scene.

7. *The Disappearance of Lady Frances Carfax*. "Good heavens, Watson, what has become of any brains that God has given me? Quick, man, quick! It's life or death – a hundred chances on death to one on life. I'll never forgive myself, never, if we are too late!" At the last minute, Holmes remembered the essential clue, and he explained to Watson that: "My night was haunted by the thought that somewhere a clue, a strange sentence, a curious observation, had come under my notice and had been too easily dismissed. Then, suddenly, in the gray of the morning, the words came back to me. It was the remark of the undertaker's wife, as reported by Philip Green. She had said, 'It should be there before now. It took longer, being out of the ordinary.' It was the coffin of which she spoke. It had been out of the ordinary. That could only mean that it had been made to some special measurement. But why? Why? Then in an instant I remembered the deep sides, and the little wasted figure at the bottom. Why so large a coffin for so small a body? To leave room for another body. Both would be buried under the one certificate. It had all been so clear, if only my own sight had not been dimmed." After he and Watson save Lady Frances, Holmes tells Watson: "Should you care to add the case to your annals, my dear Watson, ... it can only be as an example of that temporary eclipse to which even the best-balanced mind may be

exposed. Such slips are common to all mortals, and the greatest is he who can recognize and repair them. To this modified credit I may, perhaps, make some claim." Once again, Holmes may have slipped badly, but he recovers, saves Lady Carfax, and solves the crime even though the two criminals, Holy Peters and his wife, escape.

8. *The Adventure of the Three Gables.* Holmes takes a case from a woman who is worried about matters concerning her house, Three Gables. She lives all alone, and Holmes advises her to have her attorney stay overnight. She doesn't follow up, and the house is burgled, and she's assaulted. Holmes admits to Watson, "I made a mistake, I fear, in not asking you to spend the night on guard." Holmes makes up for his mistake in full measure. He not only gets the Spencer John gang of burglars jailed, but he also extracts money from Isadora Klein, the woman who hired the gang, for a round-the-world trip for his client, Mrs. Maberley.

9. *The Adventure of the Abbey Grange.* Holmes jumps off the train with Watson to ponder this case. He thinks he's on the wrong track, and he admits his analytical judgement has been affected by Lady Brackenstall's charming personality – something he never allows. Not only can't he get the truth from anyone at Abbey Grange about the murder of Lord Brackenstall, he admits he had pre-conceived ideas when he began the investigation. "Watson, I simply can't leave that case in this condition. Every instinct that I possess cries out against it. It's wrong—it's all wrong—I'll swear that it's wrong. And yet the lady's

story was complete, the maid's corroboration was sufficient, the detail was fairly exact. What have I to put up against that? Three wine-glasses, that is all. But if I had not taken things for granted, if I had examined everything with care which I should have shown had we approached the case *de novo* and had no cut-and-dried story to warp my mind, should I not then have found something more definite to go upon? Of course I should. Sit down on this bench, Watson, until a train for Chiselhurst arrives, and allow me to lay the evidence before you, imploring you in the first instance to dismiss from your mind the idea that anything which the maid or her mistress may have said must necessarily be true. The lady's charming personality must not be permitted to warp our judgement." They go back to Abbey Grange and Holmes figures out the case handily, without any help from Lady Brackenstall or her maid, both of whom are covering up and lying. Later he tells Watson: "We have got our case—one of the most remarkable in our collection. But, dear me, how slow-witted I have been, and how nearly I have committed the blunder of my lifetime! Now, I think that, with a few missing links, my chain is almost complete." He keeps his solution from Inspector Hopkins. "What I know is unofficial, what he knows is official. I have the right to private judgement, but he has none," and he lets the killer, Captain Croker, go free based on his allegation of self-defense as well as his good character versus the bad character of the victim, Sir Eustace Brackenstall.

10. The Adventure of the Creeping Man. Published in 1923, this tale reflects the promises of a youth drug popularized in the 1920's by the Russian physician,

Serge Voronoff and by Swiss Professor Paul Niehans. They both offered monkey gland transplant therapy using monkey testicles, and the rich and famous flocked to Paris and Lake Geneva to get on the list for this miracle cell therapy. Holmes deduces that some drug from the Continent is being administered to Professor Presbury, but he doesn't know what. Then he has a revelation. "Oh, Watson, Watson, what a fool I have been! It seems incredible, and yet it must be true. All points in one direction. How could I miss seeing the connection of ideas? Those knuckles--how could I have passed those knuckles? And the dog! And the ivy! It's surely time that I disappeared into that little farm of my dreams." He makes up for his lapse and solves the mystery, where Dr. Watson's standard and reliable medical services are needed in the end to keep Presbury alive after being attacked by his own pet dog.

Statistical Overview

Ten categories of misdeeds/crimes are involved in these ten stories where Holmes was wrong or was proceeding on the wrong track. Note that *The Disappearance of Lady Frances Carfax* has two crimes - attempted murder and fraud - and *The Three Gables* has two crimes - assault and burglary, and The Abbey Grange has 3 crimes – murder, accessory to murder and withholding evidence. Other wrongs include Blackmail, Breach of the unwritten laws, and Kidnapping. There are 14 wrongdoers/criminals in this category. Six of the criminals are female; eight are male, and one is an animal, that being the horse, Silver Blaze. Five of the criminals are British and 8 are non-British - with three of the non-British being American. Women and Americans seem to be good at outwitting Holmes.

Misdeeds/Crimes

Accessory to Murder – 1
The Adventure of the Abbey Grange

Assault – 1
The Adventure of the Three Gables

Attempted Murder –1
The Disappearance of Lady Frances Carfax

Blackmail – 1
A Scandal in Bohemia

Breach of the Unwritten Laws – 2
The Adventure of the Creeping Man
The Yellow Face

Burglary – 1
The Adventure of the Three Gables

Fraud – 1
The Disappearance of Lady Frances Carfax

Kidnapping – 1
The Disappearance of Lady Frances Carfax

Murder – 4
The Adventure of the Abbey Grange
The Adventure of the Dancing Men

The Five Orange Pips
Silver Blaze

Withholding Evidence – 1
The Adventure of the Abbey Grange

<u>Breakdown of Miscreants/Villains involved in these cases:</u>

Female – 6 – 40%
The Adventure of the Abbey Grange - 2
The Disappearance of Lady Frances Carfax
A Scandal in Bohemia
The Adventure of the Three Gables
The Yellow Face

Male – 8 – 53%
The Adventure of the Abbey Grange
The Adventure of the Creeping Man
The Adventure of the Dancing Men
The Five Orange Pips
The Disappearance of Lady Frances Carfax
The Adventure of the Three Gables - 2
The Man with the Twisted Lip

Animal – 1 – 7%
Silver Blaze (Horse)

British – 6 – 40%
The Adventure of the Abbey Grange
The Adventure of the Creeping Man
The Man with the Twisted Lip

A Scandal in Bohemia
The Adventure of the Three Gables -2

Non British – 8 – 53%
The Adventure of the Abbey Grange - (Australian) - 2
The Adventure of the Dancing Men – (American)
The Five Orange Pips (American)
The Disappearance of Lady Frances Carfax (Australian) - 2
The Adventure of the Three Gables (Spanish)
The Yellow Face (American)

Horse – 1 – 7%
Silver Blaze

Five of the ten cases cited are early published cases; two are middle and three are later cases. It seems Holmes was more likely to admit he was wrong early in his career, although he did continue having cases throughout his career where he admits he was on the wrong track but had revelations that brought him to the solution.

Early Published Cases – 5 – 50%

A Scandal in Bohemia – 1891
The Five Orange Pips – 1891
Silver Blaze – 1892
The Man with the Twisted Lip - 1891
The Yellow Face – 1893

Middle Cases – 2 - 20%

The Adventure of the Abbey Grange - 1904
The Adventure of the Dancing Men - 1903

Later Published Cases – 3 – 30%

The Disappearance of Lady Frances Carfax – 1911
The Adventure of the Creeping Man - 1923
The Adventure of the Three Gables – 1926

Chapter 10

Villainies and Victims in the Canon

A detailed analysis of the villainies committed and of the victims in the 56 short stories in the Canon will offer an insight into the world of Victorian criminology. It reveals the categories of misdeeds and crimes that Holmes and Watson dealt with as well as the methods of murder, how successful Holmes was at solving various types of crimes, and it also looks at the victims.

In the 56 stories, 104 crimes are committed by 84 villains in a total of 23 categories. This excludes any crimes committed by Holmes and Watson that are detailed in Chapter Eight during their quest for answers to the mysteries in the tales. This also excludes the many occasions, such as in *The Beryl Coronet, The Speckled Band,* and *The Three Gables* wherein Holmes is threatened with violence. Although the threat of violence itself could constitute assault, these threatening instances have not been included as crimes.

If a story has more than one villain committing the same crime, the crime is counted only once. This manifests a difference in the number of crimes committed in total (104) versus the number of crimes committed by males (85) and by females (28) totaling 113. 7 crimes committed by women are done so in collusion with males, so these 7 counts of crime overlap but are counted under both male and female counts, as are 2 of the same crimes committed by 2 women where each crime is counted separately under each woman. Overlapping crimes occur in *The Abbey Grange*; *The Beryl Coronet; The Engineer's Thumb; A Case of Identity, The Disappearance of Lady Frances Carfax;* and *The Three Gables.*

Miscreants commit a wide variety of crimes ranging from the minor crime of concealing a death to the most serious crimes of murder and treason. The following is a compendium categorized by story and sub categorized by the villain. Note that some stories contain more than one crime and more than one villain. Miscreants are listed individually to account for each crime, as in *Charles Augustus Milverton,* which is listed twice. If two or more villains are guilty of the same crime, there is only one entry for the story, counting the one crime, as *in The Beryl Coronet,* but each one of the criminals involved in the crime is listed.

Finally, crimes are included only if they occur within the story itself, so earlier crimes have not been included, such as the probable earlier murder of another engineer by Stark and Ferguson in *The Engineer's Thumb.* However, Eugenia Ronder's old crime of spousal homicide in *The Veiled Lodger* is included because she confesses her guilt, and the incident forms the subject of the story. Also *The Three Gables* includes the crimes of murder by the Spencer John gang and Accessory to Murder by Isadora Klein because Isadora herself confesses her involvement in Douglas Maberley's murder. We have included the murder of Baroness Gruner because it reflects the darkness of the Baron's character and the imminent threat he poses to his fiancée. *The Red*

Circle includes the crimes of both murder and attempted murder because the victim of the murder was also attempting murder.

Since there were no legally defined crimes in four stories, namely *The Blanched Soldier, The Lion's Mane, The Missing Three-Quarter* and *The Yellow Face,* these four stories are not included.

<u>Compendium of types of crimes/misdeeds committed by all 84 villains</u>

Abbey Grange - Captain Jack Croker – Murder
Abbey Grange – Lady Brackenstall and Theresa Wright – Accessory to murder and Withholding evidence
Beryl Coronet - Sir George Burnwell and Mary Holder – Burglary (Jewel Theft)
Black Peter - Patrick Cairns - Murder
Blue Carbuncle - James Ryder – Burglary (Jewel Theft)
Boscombe Valley Mystery - John Turner/Black Jack of Ballarat - Murder
Bruce Partington Plans -Hugo Oberstein – Murder and Treason
Bruce Partington Plans - Colonel Valentine Walter – Treason
Cardboard Box - James Browner – Murder (Double)
Cardboard Box - Miss Sarah Cushing – Accessory to Murder
Charles Augustus Milverton - Charles Augustus Milverton – Blackmail
Charles Augustus Milverton - Noblewoman unnamed - Murder

Copper Beeches - Jephro Rucastle – Fraud/Embezzlement and False Imprisonment
Creeping Man -Professor Presbury – Disorderly Conduct and Endangerment
Crooked Man - Henry Wood - Murder
Dancing Men - Abe Slaney - Murder
Devil's Foot - Mortimer Tregennis – Murder and Attempted Murder
Devil's Foot - Dr. Leon Sterndale – Murder
Dying Detective - Culverton Smith – Murder and Attempted Murder
Empty House - Colonel Sebastian Moran – Murder and Attempted Murder
Engineer's Thumb - Colonel Lysander Stark and Dr. Becher and Elsie – Counterfeiting and Attempted Murder
Final Problem -Professor Moriarty - Attempted Murder
Five Orange Pips - James Calhoun – Murder
Gloria Scott - Hudson – Blackmail
Golden Pince-Nez - Anna 'Coram' - Murder and Burglary and Suicide
Greek Interpreter - Harold Latimer and Wilson Kemp – Murder, Attempted Murder and Fraud/ Embezzlement
Case of Identity - James Windibank and wife – Fraud/Embezzlement
Illustrious Client - Baron Adelbert Gruner – Murder and Assault
Illustrious Client - Miss Kitty Winter – Vitriol Throwing
Lady Frances Carfax - 'Holy' Peters and Annie Fraser – Attempted Murder, Kidnapping and Fraud/Swindle
His Last Bow - Von Bork – Espionage/Treason

Mazarin Stone - Count Negretto Sylvius and Sam Merton – Burglary/Jewel Theft
Musgrave Ritual - Richard Brunton – Theft
Musgrave Ritual - Rachel Howells - Murder
Naval Treaty - Joseph Harrison – Burglary, Espionage and Attempted Murder
Noble Bachelor - Hatty Doran/Mrs. Francis H. Moulton - Bigamy
Norwood Builder - Jonas Oldacre and Mrs. Lexington – Attempted Murder
Priory School - Reuben Hayes – Murder and Kidnapping
Priory School - James Wilder – Accessory to Murder and Kidnapping
Priory School – Duke of Holdernesse – Condoning a felony & Aiding in the escape of a felon
Red Circle - Giuseppe Gorgiano - Attempted murder
Red Circle – Gennaro Lucca - Murder
Red Headed League - John Clay and Duncan Ross - Burglary (Bank Robbery) and Assault
Reigate Squires - Alec Cunningham and Cunningham Sr. – Murder, Attempted Murder and Burglary
Resident Patient - Worthington Bank gang - Biddle, Hayward & Moffat - Murder
Retired Colourman - Josiah Amberley – Double Murder & Attempted Suicide
Scandal in Bohemia - Miss Irene Adler – Blackmail
Second Stain -Lady Hilda Trelawney Hope – Theft & Burglary & Treason
Second Stain - Eduardo Lucas / Henri Fournaye - Blackmail
Second Stain - Madame Fournaye - Murder
Shoscombe Old Place -Sir Robert Norberton – Concealing a death

Silver Blaze - John Straker - Fraud
Silver Blaze - Silas Brown - Theft
Six Napoleons - Beppo – Murder and Jewel Theft and Burglary
Solitary Cyclist – Bob Carruthers – Fraud and Attempted Murder
Solitary Cyclist - Jack Woodley – Fraud and Affray
Solitary Cyclist - Williamson – Fraud and Forced Marriage
Speckled Band - Dr. Grimesby Roylott – Murder and Attempted Murder
Stock-Broker's Clerk - Beddington /Arthur Pinner and Harry Pinner – Burglary/Stock Robbery and Attempted Suicide
Stock Broker's Clerk - Beddington /Hall Pycroft – Murder and Burglary/Stock Robbery
Sussex Vampire - Jack 'Jacky' Ferguson - Attempted Murder
Thor Bridge - Maria Pinto Gibson – Attempted Murder & Suicide
Three Gables - Isadora Klein – Burglary and Accessory to Murder
Three Gables - Spencer John gang (Stockdales and Dixie) – Burglary and Murder
Three Garridebs - John Garrideb – Attempted Murder, Fraud and Counterfeiting
Three Students - Gilchrist – Burglary
Twisted Lip - Neville St. Clair / Hugh Boone – Begging
Veiled Lodger - Mrs. Eugenia Ronder – Murder
Wisteria Lodge - Don Juan Murillo /Tiger of San Pedro – Murder and Kidnapping

Types of Crimes
in the 56 stories
0
5
10
15
20
25
30
35
Accessory Murder
Affray
Aiding Escape of Felon
Assault
Attempted Murder
Attempted Suicide
Begging
Bigamy
Blackmail
Burglary
Concealing a Death
Condoning a Felony
Counterfeiting
Disorderly Conduct
False Imprisonment
Fraud
Kidnapping
Murder
Suicide
Theft
Treason
Vitriol Throwing
Withholding Evidence

Of the 104 crimes committed in the 56 stories, the largest category of crimes is murder. There are 31 murders that constitute 30% of the crimes. Taking into account 4 crimes of Accessory to Murder and 17 Attempted Murders, there are a total of 52 crimes related to murder, or 50%. Burglary at 12% and Fraud at 7% constitute the two next largest categories, followed by Blackmail and Treason/Espionage at 4% each.

Statistical Analysis

Crimes Committed in the 56 Stories by both Males & Females - 104

Accessory to Murder – 4 –4%

The Adventure of the Abbey Grange
The Adventure of the Cardboard Box
The Adventure of the Priory School
The Adventure of the Three Gables

Affray – 1 – 1%

The Adventure of the Solitary Cyclist

Aiding in the Escape of a Felon – 1 – 1%

The Adventure of the Priory School

Assault – 2 – 2%

The Adventure of the Illustrious Client
The Red-Headed League

Attempted Murder – 17 – 16 %

The Adventure of the Devil's Foot -2

The Adventure of the Dying Detective
The Adventure of the Empty House
The Adventure of the Engineer's Thumb
The Final Problem
The Greek Interpreter
The Disappearance of Lady Frances Carfax
The Naval Treaty
The Norwood Builder
The Adventure of the Red Circle
The Reigate Squires
The Adventure of the Solitary Cyclist
The Adventure of the Speckled Band
The Adventure of the Sussex Vampire
The Problem of Thor Bridge
The Adventure of the Three Garridebs

Attempted Suicide – 2 – 2%
The Adventure of the Retired Colourman
The Stock-Broker's Clerk

Begging – 1 – 1%
The Man with the Twisted Lip

Bigamy – 1 – 1%
The Adventure of the Noble Bachelor

Blackmail – 4 - 4%
Charles Augustus Milverton
The Gloria Scott
A Scandal in Bohemia
The Adventure of the Second Stain

Burglary – 13 – 13%
The Adventure of the Beryl Coronet

The Adventure of the Blue Carbuncle
The Adventure of the Golden Pince-Nez
The Mazarin Stone
The Musgrave Ritual
The Naval Treaty
The Red-Headed League
The Reigate Squires
The Adventure of the Second Stain
The Adventure of the Six Napoleons
The Stock Broker's Clerk
The Adventure of the Three Gables
The Adventure of the Three Students

Concealing a Death/Moving a Body – 1 – 1%
The Adventure of Shoscombe Old Place

Condoning a Felony – 1 – 1%
The Adventure of the Priory School

Counterfeiting – 2 – 2%
The Adventure of the Engineer's Thumb
The Adventure of the Three Garridebs

Disorderly Conduct – Endangerment – 1 – 1%
The Adventure of the Creeping Man

False Imprisonment – 1 - 1%
The Adventure of the Copper Beeches

Fraud – 8 – 7%
The Adventure of the Copper Beeches - Embezzlement
A Case of Identity- Embezzlement
The Greek Interpreter – Embezzlement

The Disappearance of Lady Frances Carfax - Swindling
Silver Blaze
The Adventure of the Solitary Cyclist – Fraud (Embezzlement) and Fraud (False Document and Forced Marriage)
The Adventure of the Speckled Band – Fraud/Embezzlement
The Adventure of the Three Garridebs

Kidnapping – 3 – 3%
The Disappearance of Lady Frances Carfax
The Adventure of the Priory School
The Adventure of the Wisteria Lodge

Murder – 31 – 30%
The Adventure of the Abbey Grange
The Adventure of Black Peter
The Boscombe Valley Mystery
The Bruce-Partington Plans
The Adventure of the Cardboard Box – 2 Double Murders
Charles Augustus Milverton
The Crooked Man
The Adventure of the Dancing Men
The Adventure of the Devil's Foot – Mortimer Tregennis
The Adventure of the Devil's Foot - Leon Sterndale
The Adventure of the Dying Detective
The Adventure of the Empty House
The Five Orange Pips
The Adventure of the Golden Pince-Nez
The Greek Interpreter

The Adventure of the Illustrious Client
The Musgrave Ritual
The Adventure of the Priory School
The Adventure of the Red Circle
The Reigate Squires
The Resident Patient
The Adventure of the Retired Colourman –2
The Adventure of the Second Stain
The Adventure of the Six Napoleons
The Adventure of the Speckled Band
The Stock-Broker's Clerk
The Adventure of the Three Gables
The Adventure of the Veiled Lodger
The Adventure of the Wisteria Lodge

Suicide – 2 – 2%
The Adventure of the Golden Pince-Nez
The Problem of Thor Bridge

Theft – 2 - 2%
The Adventure of the Second Stain
Silver Blaze

Treason/Espionage/Spying – 4 – 4%
The Adventure of the Bruce Partington Plans
His Last Bow
The Naval Treaty
The Adventure of the Second Stain

Vitriol (corrosive substance) Throwing – 1 – 1%
The Adventure of the Illustrious Client

Withholding Evidence – 1 – 1%
The Adventure of the Abbey Grange

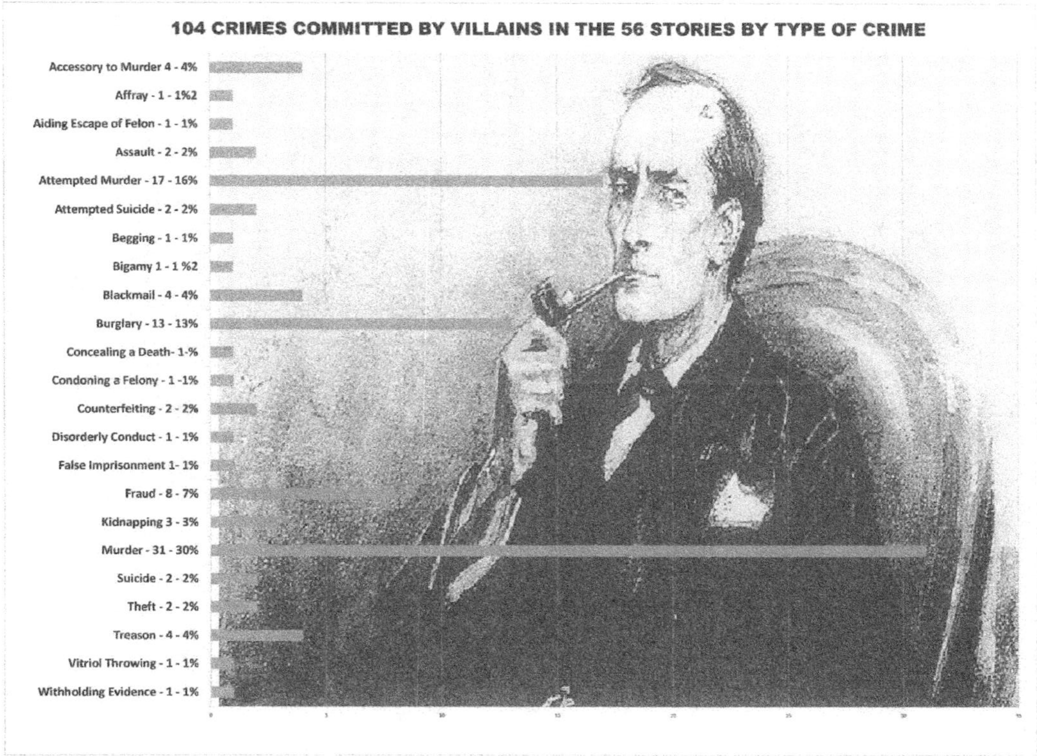
104 CRIMES COMMITTED BY VILLAINS IN THE 56 STORIES BY TYPE OF CRIME
Accessory to Murder 4 - 4%
Affray - 1 - 1%2
Aiding Escape of Felon - 1 - 1%
Assault - 2 - 2%
Attempted Murder - 17 - 16%
Attempted Suicide - 2 - 2%
Begging - 1 - 1%
Bigamy 1 - 1 %2
Blackmail - 4 - 4%
Burglary - 13 - 13%
Concealing a Death- 1-%
Condoning a Felony - 1 -1%
Counterfeiting - 2 - 2%
Disorderly Conduct - 1 - 1%
False Imprisonment 1- 1%
Fraud - 8 - 7%
Kidnapping 3 - 3%
Murder - 31 - 30%
Suicide - 2 - 2%
Theft - 2 - 2%
Treason - 4 - 4%
Vitriol Throwing - 1 - 1%
Withholding Evidence - 1 - 1%

Crimes committed by Males

Following is a compendium by story of the misdeeds/crimes committed by males in the 56 stories in the Canon. There are 64 Male criminals amounting to 76% of the total 84 criminals. Males commit 85 crimes amounting to 82% of the 104 crimes in the Canon. Male crimes/misdeeds fall into 19 criminal categories. Males commit 26 Murders (31% of the 85 male crimes), and 16 Attempted Murders (19%), with 1 Accessory to Murder (1%), for a total of 43 murder-related crimes that amount to 51% of all the male crimes and 41% of the 102 total crimes. After murder, the next most common crime males commit is Burglary (13%), followed by Fraud (9%). These two categories account for 23% of male crimes.

Compendium of 85 Crimes committed by Males

Accessory to Murder – 1 – 1 %
The Priory School – James Wilder

Affray – 1 – 1%
The Solitary Cyclist – Jack Woodley

Aiding in the Escape of a Felon – 1 - 1 %
The Priory School – Duke of Holdernesse

Assault – 2 - 2%
The Illustrious Client – Baron Gruner
The Red-Headed League – John Clay

Attempted Murder –16 – 19%

The Devil's Foot – Mortimer Tregennis - 2
The Dying Detective – Culverton Smith
The Empty House – Colonel Moran
The Engineer's Thumb – Colonel Stark and Dr. Becher
The Final Problem - Moriarty
The Greek Interpreter – Kemp and Latimer
The Disappearance of Lady Frances Carfax – Holy Peters
The Naval Treaty – Joseph Harrison
The Norwood Builder – Jonas Oldacre
The Red Circle - Giuseppe Gorgiano
The Reigate Squires – Cunningham Sr. and Alec
The Solitary Cyclist - Carruthers
The Speckled Band – Grimesby Roylott
The Sussex Vampire – Jacky Ferguson
The Three Garridebs – John Garrideb

Attempted Suicide – 2 – 2%

The Retired Colourman - Josiah Amberley
The Stock-Broker's Clerk – Arthur/Harry Pinner

Begging – 1 – 1%

The Man with the Twisted Lip – Neville St. Clair

Blackmail – 3 - 4%

Charles Augustus Milverton - Milverton
The Gloria Scott - Hudson
The Second Stain – Lucas/ Fournaye

Burglary – 11 – 13%

The Beryl Coronet – Sir George Burnwell
The Blue Carbuncle – James Ryder
The Mazarin Stone – Count Sylvius and Sam Merton
The Musgrave Ritual - Brunton
The Naval Treaty – Joseph Harrison
The Red-Headed League – Clay and Ross
The Reigate Squires – Cunningham, Sr. and Alec
The Adventure of the Six Napoleons - Beppo
The Stock Broker's Clerk – Pinner and Pycroft
The Adventure of the Three Gables – Barney Stockdale and Steve Dixie
The Adventure of the Three Students - Gilchrist

Concealing a Death – 1 – 1%

The Adventure of Shoscombe Old Place – Sir Robert Norbertson

Condoning a Felony – 1 – 1%

The Priory School – Duke of Holdernesse

Counterfeiting – 2 – 2%

The Adventure of the Engineer's Thumb – Col. Stark and Dr. Becher
The Three Garridebs – John Garrideb

Disorderly Conduct – Endangerment – 1 – 1%

The Creeping Man – Professor Presbury

False Imprisonment – 1 - 1%

The Copper Beeches – Jephro Rucastle

Fraud – 8 – 9%

The Copper Beeches – Embezzlement – Rucastle

A Case of Identity – Embezzlement - Windibank

The Greek Interpreter – Embezzlement – Kemp and Latimer

The Disappearance of Lady Frances Carfax – Swindling – Holy Peters

Silver Blaze – John Straker

The Solitary Cyclist–Fraud-Embezzlement & False Marriage – Woodley and Williamson

The Speckled Band – Embezzlement – Grimesby Roylott

The Three Garridebs – John Garrideb

Kidnapping – 3- 4%

Lady Frances Carfax – Holy Peters

Priory School – Wilder & Hayes

Wisteria Lodge – Don Murillo

Murder – 26 – 31%

The Abbey Grange – Captain Croker

The Adventure of Black Peter – Patrick Cairns

The Boscombe Valley Mystery – John Turner

The Adventure of the Bruce-Partington Plans - Hugo Oberstein

The Adventure of the Cardboard Box – Double Murder – James Browner

The Crooked Man – Henry Wood

The Dancing Men – Abe Slaney

The Devil's Foot – 2 murders, 1 ea-Tregennis and Dr. Sterndale

The he Dying Detective – Culverton Smith

The Empty House – Colonel Moran
The Five Orange Pips – James Calhoun
The Greek Interpreter – Kemp and Latimer
The Illustrious Client – Baron Gruner
The Priory School - Reuben Hayes
The Red Circle - Gennaro Lucca
The Reigate Squires – Cunningham, Sr. & Alec
The Resident Patient – Biddle, Hayward & Moffat
The Adventure of the Retired Colourman – Double Murder – Josiah Amberley
The Adventure of the Six Napoleons - Beppo
The Speckled Band - Dr. Grimesby Roylott
The Stock-Broker's Clerk - Beddington /Hall Pycroft
The Adventure of the Three Gables – Barney Stockdale and Steve Dixie
The Adventure of the Wisteria Lodge – Don Murillo

Theft – 1 – 1%
Silver Blaze – Silas Brown

Treason/Espionage/Spying – 3 – 4%
The Adventure of the Bruce Partington Plans - Oberstein and Walter
His Last Bow – Von Bork
The Naval Treaty - Joseph Harrison

No males commit suicide in the 56 stories, but two male criminals attempt it. One, Josiah Amberley in *The Retired Colourman,* tries to swallow a white pellet, but Holmes springs at his throat and stops him, saying "No short cuts, Josiah Amberley. Things must be done decently and in order." The other is one of the British Beddington brothers (alias Arthur Pinner and Harry Pinner) in *The Stock-Broker's Clerk*, but Holmes and Watson thwart his attempt to hang himself. Both men must face British justice for their crimes.

85 Crimes Committed by Male Villains
0
5
10
15
20
25
30
Accessory Murder 1
Affray 1
Aiding Escape of Felon 1
Assault 2
Attempted Murder 16
Attempted Suicide 2
Begging 1
Blackmail 3
Burglary 11
Concealing a Death 1
Condoning a Felony 1
Counterfeiting 2
Disorderly Conduct 1
False Imprisonment 1
Fraud 8
Kidnapping 3
Murder 26
Theft 1
Treason 3

Crimes committed by Females in the Canon

20 women commit 28 crimes amounting to 27% of the 104 crimes in the stories. Women in some stories commit more than one crime, as in *The Abbey Grange* and *The Golden Pince-Nez*. They also commit crimes in concert with men. The 28 crimes are committed in 13 criminal categories. Accessory to Murder – 4 ; Attempted Murder – 3; Bigamy – 1 ; Blackmail – 1; Burglary – 4; Counterfeiting – 1; Fraud – 2; Murder – 5; Suicide – 2; Theft – 1; Treason – 1; Vitriol (corrosive substance) Throwing – 1; and Withholding evidence – 2. It should be noted that 6 of the crimes that women commit are done so in collusion with males, so 6 counts of crime done by females overlap 6 men's crimes, but they are all counted separately for the purposes of this compendium. The overlapping crimes are in *The Beryl Coronet; The Engineer's Thumb; A Case of Identity, Lady Frances Carfax;* and *The Three Gables*. Although it is unlikely that Sarah Cushing in *The Cardboard Box* would be legally indicted as an accessory to the murders committed by James Browner, I have included her in this compendium because James Browner accuses her of being the root cause. If not legally, she is morally culpable in the eyes of Sherlock Holmes who sees her as a criminal getting away with her sin in halls of British justice but paying for it according to the laws of heaven with her descent into madness.

There are 12 crimes relating to murder committed by women, or 43% of the 28 total female crimes. This is in contrast to the 43 murder-related crimes committed by men which amount to 51% of all 85 male crimes.

Murder is the most common women's crime in the Canon. Women commit 5 murders (19% of female crimes) in five tales (9% of the 56 stories). Three women commit attempted murder (11%); and 4 women are accessories to murder (14%). These 12 murder-related crimes comprise only 12% of the 104 crimes in the stories, a percentage far below the 51% of murder-related crimes that men commit. Men are four times more likely to commit murder in the stories.

<u>20 Female Wrongdoers & their 28 Crimes</u>

The Abbey Grange – Lady Brackenstall – Accessory to murder and Withholding evidence (with Theresa Wright)
The Abbey Grange – Theresa Wright, Maid – Accessory to murder and Withholding evidence
The Beryl Coronet - Mary Holder – Burglary/Jewel Theft (with Burnwell)
The Cardboard Box - Miss Sarah Cushing – Accessory to Murder
Charles Augustus Milverton - Noblewoman unnamed – Murder
The Engineer's Thumb - Elsie – Counterfeiting (with Col. Stark)
The Golden Pince-Nez - Anna 'Coram' - Murder and Burglary and Suicide
A Case of Identity – Mrs. Windibank – Fraud (Embezzlement)
The Illustrious Client - Miss Kitty Winter – Vitriol Throwing

The Disappearance of Lady Frances Carfax - Annie Fraser – Attempted Murder, Kidnapping and Fraud
The Musgrave Ritual - Rachel Howells – Murder
The Norwood Builder – Housekeeper Mrs. Lexington– Attempted Murder
The Adventure of the Noble Bachelor - Hatty Doran/Mrs. Francis H. Moulton - Bigamy
A Scandal in Bohemia - Miss Irene Adler – Blackmail
The Adventure of the Second Stain -Lady Hilda Hope – Theft and Burglary and Treason
The Adventure of the Second Stain - Madame Fournaye - Murder
The Problem of Thor Bridge - Maria Pinto Gibson – Attempted Murder and Suicide
The Adventure of the Three Gables - Isadora Klein – Burglary and Accessory to Murder (with Barney Stockdale and Steve Dixie of the Spencer John gang)
The Three Gables - Susan Stockdale – Burglary (with Barney Stockdale and Steve Dixie)
The Adventure of the Veiled Lodger - Mrs. Eugenia Ronder – Murder

<u>Compendium of 28 Crimes in 13 categories Committed by Females</u>

Accessory to Murder – 4 –14%

- The Adventure of the Abbey Grange – Lady Brackenstall
- The Adventure of the Abbey Grange – Theresa Wright, Maid
- The Adventure of the Cardboard Box - Miss Sarah Cushing
- The Three Gables – Isadora Klein

Attempted Murder – 3 – 11%

Lady Frances Carfax – Annie Fraser
The Norwood Builder – Mrs. Lexington
The Problem of Thor Bridge – Maria Pinto Gibson

Burglary – 4 – 14%

The Beryl Coronet – Mary Holder
The Golden Pince-Nez – Anna Coram
The Second Stain – Lady Hope
The Three Gables – Susan Stockdale and Isadora Klein

Murder – 5 – 19%

The Golden Pince-Nez – Anna Coram
Charles Augustus Milverton – unnamed Noblewoman
The Musgrave Ritual – Rachel Howells
The Second Stain – Mme. Fournaye
The Veiled Lodger – Eugenia Ronder

Fraud – 2 – 7%

A Case of Identity – Mrs. Windibank
The Disappearance of Lady Frances Carfax – Annie Fraser

Suicide – 2 – 7%

The Golden Pince-Nez – Annie Coram
The Problem of Thor Bridge – Maria Pinto Gibson

Withholding evidence – 2 – 7%

The Abbey Grange – Lady Brackenstall
The Abbey Grange – Theresa Wright, Maid

Other – 6 – 21%

Bigamy – 1
The Noble Bachelor – Hattie Doran

Blackmail – 1
A Scandal in Bohemia – Irene Adler

Counterfeiting – 1
The Engineer's Thumb - Elsie

Theft – 1
The Second Stain – Lady Hope

Treason – 1
The Second Stain – Lady Hope

Vitriol (corrosive substance) Throwing – 1
The Illustrious Client – Kitty Winter

SUICIDE

Two females commit suicide in the 56 stories as noted above, accounting for 7% of the 28 crimes committed by women. Another female, Elsie Cubitt in *The Dancing Men,* attempts suicide but recovers. In Victorian times, suicide was considered a crime. According to Carolyn A. Conley in *The Unwritten Law*: "Technically suicide was illegal, and persons who attempted it were liable to imprisonment. Those who aided and abetted a suicide were guilty of murder." [xxviii] This may be one reason why Sherlock Holmes succeeds in preventing Mrs. Eugenia Ronder from committing suicide with Prussic Acid in *The Veiled Lodger*. The two women criminals who commit suicide, one in *The Golden Pince-Nez*, and one in *Thor Bridge,* do so for very different reasons. In *The Golden Pince-Nez*, Anna Coram has just killed someone while trying to keep her presence a secret. She did not plan the murder, she's remorseful, and she takes poison to spare her from facing the law. Furthermore, she has entrusted Sherlock Holmes with carrying out her final goal of freeing her lover in Russia. There was no way Holmes and Watson could have prevented her act. The motives of Maria Pinto Gibson in *Thor Bridge* are very different. She kills herself in a mad revenge attempt to frame the governess for her murder. She believes the governess is her husband's lover, and she plants clues that lead the police to suspect the governess, whom she wants to suffer the ultimate penalty. Both these women who commit suicide are foreign, not British. Anna Coram is Russian and Maria Pinto Gibson is Brazilian.

We do not count Elsie Cubitt's suicide attempt in *The Dancing Men* because she is not a criminal, though her attempt was a violation of the law.

28 Crimes Committed by Female Villains
0
0.5
1
1.5
2
2.5
3
3.5
4
4.5
5
Accessory Murder 4
Attempted Murder 3
Bigamy 1
Blackmail 1
Burglary 4
Counterfeiting 1
Fraud 2
Murder 5
Suicide 2
Theft 1
Treason 1
Vitriol Throwing 1
Withholding Evidence 2

CRIME OF MURDER

As reviewed earlier, crimes related to murder are the largest percentage of the 104 crimes committed in the 56 stories. There are 34 murderers, 29 male and 5 female who commit 31 murders, accounting for 30% of all crimes. With 17 Attempted Murders (17%), and 3 Accessory to Murder (3%), there are a total of 51 murder-related crimes (49% of 104 crimes) in the 56 stories

Here is a compendium of the methods of murder used by the villains detailing how the victims died. We have omitted Silver Blaze from this list of human murderers. We have included the snake as a method of murder used by the murderer in *The Speckled Band.*

Methods of Murder – How the victims died
The name in each case is the murderer

Captain Jack Croker (The Abbey Grange) – Victim beaten to death with poker
Patrick Cairns (Black Peter) – Victim harpooned
John Turner/Black Jack of Ballarat (The Boscombe Valley Mystery) – Victim shot
Hugo Oberstein (The Bruce Partington Plans) – Victim head crushed possibly in fall from a train
James Browner (The Cardboard Box) – Victims beaten to death with stick
Noblewoman unnamed (Charles Augustus Milverton) – Victim shot
Henry Wood (The Crooked Man) – Victim dies of apoplexy
Abe Slaney (The Dancing Men) – Victim shot

Mortimer Tregennis (The Devil's Foot) – Victims poisoned
Dr. Leon Sterndale (The Devil's Foot) – Victim Poisoned
Culverton Smith (The Dying Detective) – Victims Poisoned
Colonel Sebastian Moran (The Empty House) – Victim shot with air gun
James Calhoun (The Five Orange Pips) – Victim drowned
Anna 'Coram' (The Golden Pince-Nez) - Victim stabbed
Harold Latimer (The Greek Interpreter) – Victims poisoned by charcoal fumes
Wilson Kemp (The Greek Interpreter) – Victims poisoned by charcoal fumes
Baron Gruner (The Illustrious Client) - Victim pushed over cliff
Rachel Howells (The Musgrave Ritual) – Victim suffocated
Reuben Hayes (The Priory School) – Victim beaten on the head
Gennaro Lucca (The Red Circle) – Victim stabbed
Alec Cunningham (The Reigate Squires) – Victim Shot
Cunningham, Sr. (The Reigate Squires) – Victim Shot
Biddle of the Worthington Bank gang -(The Resident Patient) – Victim hanged
Hayward of the Worthington Bank gang -(The Resident Patient) – Victim hanged
Moffat of the Worthington Bank gang -(The Resident Patient) – Victim hanged
Josiah Amberley (The Retired Colourman) – Double Murder - Victims gassed

Madame Fournaye (The Second Stain) – Victim stabbed to the heart with an Indian dagger
Beppo (The Six Napoleons) – Victim stabbed a confederate
Dr. Grimesby Roylott (The Speckled Band) – Snakebite
Beddington/Hal Pycroft (The Stock-Broker's Clerk) – Murder Victim beaten
Barney Stockdale - Spencer John Gang (The Three Gables) – Victim beaten to death
Steve Dixie - Spencer John Gang (The Three Gables) – Victim beaten to death
Mrs. Eugenia Ronder (The Veiled Lodger) – Victim Beaten and Mauled
Don Juan Murillo /Tiger of San Pedro (Wisteria Lodge) – Victim beaten – head smashed to a pulp

<u>Compendium of Methods of Murder used by Villains</u>

Beaten to death/Mauled - 8 – 26%

The Adventure of the Abbey Grange – Victim beaten to death with poker

The Adventure of the Cardboard Box –2 Victims beaten to death with stick

The Adventure of the Priory School - Victim beaten on the head

The Stock-Broker's Clerk – Victim beaten- blow on the head

The Adventure of the Three Gables – Victim beaten

The Adventure of the Veiled Lodger – Victim beaten and mauled by special lion's foot club

The Adventure of Wisteria Lodge – Victim beaten – head smashed to a pulp

Poisoned – 4 – 13%

The Adventure of the Devil's Foot – Tregennis - Victim poisoned by fumes derived from devil's foot root

The Adventure of the Devil's Foot – Leon. Sterndale – Victim poisoned by fumes derived from devil's foot root

The Adventure of the Dying Detective – Victim poisoned by infection from tropical disease

The Greek Interpreter - Charcoal poisoning

Shot – 5 – 16%

The Boscombe Valley Mystery

Charles Augustus Milverton

The Adventure of the Dancing Men

The Adventure of the Empty House

The Reigate Squires

Stabbed – 4 - 13%

The Adventure of the Golden Pince-Nez

The Adventure of the Red Circle

The Adventure of the Second Stain

The Adventure of the Six Napoleons

Gassed – 2 - 6%

The Adventure of the Retired Colourman – 2 Victims Gassed

Fall – 2 – 6%

The Adventure of the Bruce Partington Plans – Fall from a train

The Adventure of the Illustrious Client – Fall from a cliff

Other – 6 – 20%

Fear/Shock/Apoplexy – 1

The Crooked Man - Victim dies of apoplexy

Drowned – 1

The Five Orange Pips - Victim pushed into water and drowned

Harpooned – 1

The Adventure of Black Peter – Victim harpooned

Hanged – 1

The Resident Patient – Victim hanged

Snakebite – 1

The Adventure of the Speckled Band – Snakebite

Suffocation – 1

The Musgrave Ritual – Victim suffocated

Murderers used 12 different methods to eliminate their victims. The most common method was beating a victim to death (8 victims - 26%). Next was shooting with 5 victims at 16%, followed by poisoning and stabbing with 4 victims each at 13%.

12 METHODS OF MURDER
USED BY 34 KILLERS
ON 31 VICTIMS
0
1
2
3
4
5
6
7
8
9
Beaten/Mauled 8
Drowned 1
Fall 2
Fear/Shock 1
Gassed 2
Hanged 1
Harpooned 1
Poisoned 4
Shot 5
Snakebite 1
Stabbbed 4
Suffocation 1

Methods of Murder used by Male Killers

Of the 34 killers, 29 are male (85%), and they commit 26 of the 31 murders (84%). 2 male killers, namely James Browner in *The Cardboard Box,* and Josiah Amberley in *Retired Colourman*, each commit a double murder. One other story, *The Devil's Foot*, has 2 murderers who each kill a different victim. In *The Resident Patient*, 3 killers hang one victim, and in *The Greek Interpreter*, 2 killers conspire and kill one victim. In *The Reigate Squires*, 2 killers conspire and shoot one victim. In *The Five Orange Pips*, over a period of some time the KKK's agents kill at least 3 people in the Openshaw family, the closest to serial killers in the stories. I have included only the one murder that happens within the story.

In comparison to 29 male killers committing 26 murders, there are only 5 female killers in the 56 stories who commit a total of 5 murders. No female murderess kills more than one victim. Men in the short stories commit five times as many murders as do women.

Male killers use 11 methods of murder, versus females who use 4. The first preference for male killers is beating at 26%, followed by shooting and poisoning at 15% each, then stabbing at 8%.

Motives for male killers vary, but money is more prominent than love. Money is the underlying motive in 15 stories: *Black Peter, The Boscombe Valley Mystery, The Devil's Foot, The Dying Detective, The Empty House, The Final Problem, The Five Orange Pips, The Greek Interpreter, The Priory School, The Reigate Squires, The Resident Patient,*

The Six Napoleons, The Speckled Band, The Stock-Broker's Clerk, and *Wisteria Lodge.*

Love is the motive for murder in only five stories, namely *The Abbey Grange, The Cardboard Box, The Crooked Man, The Dancing Men, and The Red Circle.* Love is the ostensible motive for the murder of Mortimer Tregennis by Dr. Sterndale in *The Devil's Foot.* Money and a love triangle are the motives in *The Retired Colourman.* Espionage/Spying is the reason in *The Bruce Partington Plans.*

11 Methods of 26 Murders used by 29 Male Killers

Beaten to death/Mauled – 7 – 27%

The Adventure of the Abbey Grange – Victim beaten to death with poker

The Adventure of the Cardboard Box – 2 victims beaten to death with stick

The Adventure of the Priory School - Victim beaten on the head

The Stock-Broker's Clerk – Victim beaten- blow on the head

The Adventure of the Three Gables – Victim beaten resulting in pneumonia and death

The Adventure of the Wisteria Lodge – Victim beaten – head smashed to a pulp

Poisoned – 4 – 15%

The Adventure of the Devil's Foot – Mortimer Tregennis – Victims poisoned with devil's foot root

The Adventure of the Devil's Foot – Dr. Sterndale – Victim poisoned with devil's foot root

The Adventure of the Dying Detective – Victim injected with tropical disease
The Greek Interpreter - Charcoal poisoning

Shot – 4 – 15%
The Boscombe Valley Mystery
The Adventure of the Dancing Men
The Adventure of the Empty House
The Reigate Squires

Stabbed – 2 – 8%
The Adventure of the Six Napoleons
The Adventure of the Red Circle

Gassed – 2 – 8%
The Adventure of the Retired Colourman – 2 victims

Falls – 2 – 8%
The Adventure of the Bruce Partington Plans – Victim's head crushed in fall from train
The Adventure of the Illustrious Client - Victim falls from a cliff

Other –5- 19%
Fear/Shock– The Crooked Man - Victim dies of apoplexy
Drowned –The Five Orange Pips - Victim pushed into water and drowned
Harpooned - Black Peter – Victim Harpooned
Hanged – The Resident Patient – Victim hanged
Snakebite- The Speckled Band – Victim bitten by snake

Methods of Murder by 29 Male Killers in 26 Murders
0
1
2
3
4
5
6
7
8
Beaten/Mauled 7
Drowned 1
Fall 2
Fear/Shock 1
Gassed 2
Hanged 1
Harpooned 1
Poisoned 4
Shot 4
Snakebite 1
Stabbbed 2

Methods of Murder used by Female Killers

There are only five murderesses in the short stories, and they comprise only 16% of the total 31 murderers. Women use four methods of murder, with stabbing as the preferred method at 40%. Perhaps surprisingly no women use poison to kill. Poison and shooting for male murderers rank at 15% each, but those methods are outranked by beatings at 23% as the preferred method of murder by men. Women have only one beating as a method of murder in *The Veiled Lodger,* and in this case, the woman involved did not perform the act alone but colluded in the murder with her male lover.

None of these five murderesses faces the law. Holmes lets Eugenia Ronder go free in *The Veiled Lodger.* The unnamed noblewoman who shoots Charles Augustus Milverton escapes, as does Rachel Howell in *The Musgrave Ritual.* In *The Second Stain,* Mme. Fournaye goes insane, and her crime of spousal homicide does not come to trial. The fifth murderess, Anna Coram in *Golden Pince-Nez,* commits suicide.

Unlike most male killers, the motives of female killers are entangled with love and love triangles that have gone against them in every case.

Isadora Klein in *The Three Gables* is not included as a murderess because in her confession, she claims she never intended for the Spencer John gang to kill Douglas, her former lover, and Holmes believes her. It is arguable, though, that as the instigator of the beating she is equally culpable, and a strict application of the law could well have seen her convicted of Douglas' murder. Her confession, however, confirms that the gang did beat Douglas severely, resulting in his death, so he is included as a victim of male killers.

4 Methods of Murder of 5 Female Killers

Beaten and Mauled with fake Lion paw tool – 1 – 20%
The Adventure of the Veiled Lodger

Shot – 1 – 20%
Charles Augustus Milverton

Stabbed – 2 – 40%
The Adventure of the Golden Pince-Nez
The Adventure of the Second Stain

Suffocated – 1 – 20%
The Musgrave Ritual

Methods of Murder by 5 Female Killers
2.5
2
1.5
1
0.5
0
Beaten/Mauled 1
Shooting 1
Stabbing 2
Suffocation 1

Nationality of 34 Killers

Of the 29 male and 5 female killers, 68% are British versus 32% non-British. 3 women are British (9% of the 34), and 2 are non-British. 20 male killers are British (59%), and 9 are not.

<u>British - 23 – 68%</u>

Captain Jack Croker (The Abbey Grange)
Patrick Cairns (Black Peter)
James Browner (The Cardboard Box)
Noblewoman unnamed (Charles Augustus Milverton)
Henry Wood (The Crooked Man)
Mortimer Tregennis (The Devil's Foot)
Dr. Leon Sterndale (The Devil's Foot)
Colonel Sebastian Moran (The Empty House)
Harold Latimer (The Greek Interpreter)
Wilson Kemp (The Greek Interpreter)
Rachel Howells (Musgrave Ritual)
Reuben Hayes (The Priory School)
Alec Cunningham (The Reigate Squires)
Cunningham, Sr. (The Reigate Squires)
Biddle - Worthington Bank gang - (Resident Patient)
Hayward – Worthington Bank gang (Resident Patient)
Moffat – Worthington Bank gang (Resident Patient)
Josiah Amberley (The Retired Colourman)
Dr. Grimesby Roylott (The Speckled Band)
Beddington/Hal Pycroft (The Stock-Broker's Clerk)
Barney Stockdale – Spencer John Gang (The Three Gables)
Steve Dixie - Spencer John Gang (The Three Gables)
Mrs. Eugenia Ronder (The Veiled Lodger)

Non-British – 11 – 32%

John Turner/Black Jack of Ballarat (The Boscombe Valley Mystery) – Australian
Hugo Oberstein (The Bruce Partington Plans) – German
Abe Slaney (The Dancing Men) – American
Culverton Smith (The Dying Detective) – Sumatran
James Calhoun (Five Orange Pips) – American
Anna 'Coram' (Golden Pince-Nez) – Russian
Baron Gruner (Illustrious Client) - Austrian
Gennaro Lucca (Red Circle) – Italian
Madame Fournaye (Second Stain) – French Creole
Beppo (Six Napoleons) - Italian
Don Juan Murillo /Tiger of San Pedro (Wisteria Lodge) – Central American

American - 2
Australian –1
Austrian - 1
Central American - 1
French Creole - 1
German - 1
Italian - 2
Russian – 1
Sumatran - 1

34 KILLERS BY SEX & NATIONALITY
29
5
23
11
Male Killers 29 - 85%
Female Killers 5 - 15%
British Killers 23- 68%
Non-British Killers 11 - 32%

31 murders occur in 28 of the stories, making a murder the central mystery in 50% of the 56 stories. Double murders occur in 3 stories, namely *The Cardboard Box, The Devil's Foot* and *The Retired Colourman*, amounting to 11% of the 28 murder stories, or 5% of the 56 stories.

Murder Stories 28 of 56 (50%)

Murders - Early Published Stories – 10 – 36%

Boscombe Valley Mystery - 1891
Cardboard Box – 1893
Crooked Man – 1893
Five Orange Pips – 1891
Greek Interpreter – 1893
Musgrave Ritual - 1893
Reigate Squires - 1893
Resident Patient – 1893
Speckled Band - 1892
Stock-Broker's Clerk - 1893

Murders - Middle Stories - 9 - 32%

Abbey Grange – 1904
Black Peter - 1904
Charles Augustus Milverton – 1904
Dancing Men - 1903
Empty House – 1903
Golden Pince-Nez – 1904
Priory School - 1904
Second Stain – 1904
Six Napoleons - 1904

Murders - Later Published Stories –9 – 32%

Bruce Partington Plans – 1908
Devil's Foot - 1910
Dying Detective – 1913
The Adventure of the Illustrious Client - 1924
Red Circle – 1911
Retired Colourman - 1926
Three Gables - 1926
Veiled Lodger – 1927
Wisteria Lodge – 1908

Attempted Murder

Attempted murder is committed 16 times by 18 villains in 13 of the stories. Various attempts on Holmes' life are included here, including the attempt by Colonel Moran to shoot him, even though Holmes tells Lestrade not to charge him on that count. I have also included the two Tregennis brothers as an attempted murder by Mortimer Tregennis in *The Devil's Foot.*

Methods of 16 Attempted Murders – 10 Methods by 18 villains

Mortimer Tregennis (The Devil's Foot) – Poison- 2 Tregennis brothers
Culverton Smith (The Dying Detective) – Poison
Colonel Moran (The Empty House) –Attempted shooting of Holmes
Colonel Lysander Stark /Fritz (The Engineer's Thumb) –Attempted Murder with butcher's cleaver
Mr. Ferguson / Dr. Becher (The Engineer's Thumb) – Attempted Murder
Professor James Moriarty (The Final Problem) - Attempted Murder-3 methods
Harold Latimer (The Greek Interpreter) – Charcoal poisoning
Wilson Kemp (The Greek Interpreter) – Charcoal poisoning
Henry 'Holy' Peters /Dr. Schlessinger (Lady Frances Carfax) – Attempted Murder - suffocation & chloroform poisoning
Annie Fraser /Mrs. Schlessinger (Lady Frances Carfax) – Attempted Murder

Joseph Harrison (The Naval Treaty) – Attempted murder of Holmes
Jonas Oldacre/Mr. Cornelius (The Norwood Builder) – Attempted Murder – Frame innocent person for murder
Mrs. Lexington (The Norwood Builder) – Attempted Murder – Frame innocent person for murder
Giuseppe Gorgiano (The Red Circle) –Attempted Murder – Stabbing
Cunningham Sr. (The Reigate Squires) – Attempted Murder of Holmes- Strangling
Alec Cunningham (The Reigate Squires) - Attempted Murder of Holmes – Strangling
Dr. Roylott – (The Speckled Band)- Attempted Murder - Snakebite
Maria Pinto Gibson (Thor Bridge) – Attempted Murder – Frame innocent person for murder

The 10 methods used by 18 villains in these 16 attempted murders are:

Framing an Innocent Person for Murder – 2 – 13%
The Norwood Builder
The Problem of Thor Bridge

Stabbing – 3 - 19%
The Adventure of the Engineer's Thumb
The Naval Treaty
The Adventure of the Red Circle

Poisoning – 4 – 25%
The Adventure of the Devil's Foot -2
The Adventure of the Dying Detective
The Greek Interpreter

Other – 7 – 43%

Shooting – 1
The Adventure of the Empty House

Strangling – 1
The Reigate Squires

Suffocation & Chloroform Poisoning – 1
The Disappearance of Lady Frances Carfax

Assault with a bludgeon – 1
The Final Problem

Attempt to run over with horse van – 1
The Final Problem

Hurling a brick from a roof – 1
The Final Problem

Snakebite – 1
The Adventure of the Speckled Band

Chapter 11 contains a detailed analysis of the 84 villains and whether they operated alone or in concert with an accomplice or a gang. It also looks at how Holmes deals with the villains and their final outcomes.

Chapter 11

A Profile of the Holmesian Villain

"I love to come to close grips with my man. I like to meet him eye to eye and read for myself the stuff that he is made of."

- Sherlock Holmes, The Illustrious Client

What is the stuff that makes up a villain in the Canon? What does a Holmesian villain look like? The 56 short stories contain 84 human villains and 3 animals, and there is no typical villain.

The Sherlockian tales reflect the Victorian love of sports and fair play. They saw the world as a large game, and they attempted to impose rules upon the playing of this game. Indeed, Holmes' logic and his Method can be seen as a superior understanding of the rules in play that govern both nature and human society. These rules not only formed the basis of the Victorian Code, they also form the basis on which Holmes judges the criminals in the Canon. Again and again we see a villain being judged in terms of the fair playing field.

Victorian values had very clear distinctions between good and bad and innocent and guilty. Sometimes those terms need to be redefined within the context of Holmesian justice in the stories. These clear distinctions blur when Holmes sets free a murderer, as he does in *The Boscombe Valley Mystery* and *The Abbey Grange*. Holmes has his reasons for letting villains go, and his reasons are personal, not legal. His reasons stem from his direct relationship with both the villain and the victim. In *The Boscombe Valley Mystery*, Holmes is sympathetic because the murderer is about to die, and furthermore the murderer's beautiful, violet-eyed daughter is his client. Holmes makes his decision in this case not only based on those factors but also because the murderer has confessed and repented, and Holmes has conviction that he will never kill again. In *The Abbey Grange* Holmes forgives not only a murder, but overlooks the crimes of accessory to murder and withholding evidence. He lets the murderer go, telling him to return in one year to marry the wife of the man he's just slain. It sounds like a soap opera, but it is serious stuff. Holmes as judge gives the murderer a year of self-enforced probation because the murder was not pre-meditated - it was an act of self-defense. Holmes makes his decision about justice in this case by looking to the characters of those involved and by looking to secure the future.

Victorian literate classes viewed most crime as taking place outside their own social circles in the unfortunate world peopled with criminals who made their living as pickpockets, petty thieves, forgers, vagrants, prostitutes and burglars. These criminals were considered outsiders who operated in their own sphere for the most part. However, while there are some members of the criminal community who appear in the Canon, notably the Spencer John gang in *The Three Gables*, most of the criminals Holmes deals with are very British, Victorian upper and middle class, and certainly not part of the unfortunate class who live in a criminal community.

Often the villain, the crime and its punishment must be judged within the Holmesian context of good and evil rather than the judicial context of legal and illegal. Holmes is the one who ultimately determines whether a criminal is or is not a good Victorian gentleman or lady.

Before any statistical analysis of villainy, I would like to take a look at some of the Canon's exceptional villains.

Super Villains

When considering the Holmesian villain it is interesting to compare the quality of various villains. Super villains such as Professor Moriarty, Baron Gruner and Irene Adler are all respected by Holmes – respected not as good people but as worthy adversaries. They are people who are brilliant and play the game with Sherlock Holmes with both élan and intelligence. They test him, and they occasionally best him. And because they test his mental abilities, he respects them. When confronted by no activity, Holmes resorts to cocaine. When confronted by an exceptional villain, Holmes is at his best.

These exceptional villains live as Victorian ladies and gentlemen. Holmes loves to have them praise him and tell him what a great detective he is. These are the people he lives to beat.

Each of these particular criminals has individual, exceptional characteristics which might include beauty, brains, breeding and accomplishments. Holmes loves a challenge, and these exceptional criminals present him with his greatest challenges. The cases Holmes tackles with these criminals are the most stimulating and memorable cases to him, and in some of these particular cases, Holmes keeps memorabilia to remind him of his successes.

These exceptional villains have something in common. They always elude the law. They never commit crimes that are legally ascribable to them. In some cases the law knows about them, but can do nothing legally. In other instances, they are so successful that the police don't even know they exist.

Professor Moriarty

The *uber* criminal in the Canon is of course Professor James Moriarty, the Napoleon of Crime. At least one larger-than-life villain is necessary to pit against Sherlock Holmes who is a larger-than-life hero. Professor Moriarty is a man who "pervades London, and no one has heard of him." Moriarty is a very British arch-villain, and his success puts him on a level playing field with Sherlock Holmes. When they struggle in one-on-one combat – both mental and physical - in *The Final Problem*, it's a fair fight between two equal opponents. Perhaps Holmes is even a bit more capable than Moriarty because Holmes has to fend off not just Moriarty himself but also all his underlings who try to kill him. Holmes operates either alone or with Watson, sometimes availing the services of the rag-tag Baker Street Irregulars. Scotland Yard is no help to Holmes - they don't credit Moriarty's existence, *a la* J. Edgar Hoover and the American Mafia. Even Watson wonders if Moriarty really exists. That's how clever Moriarty has been in his criminal career.

Physical descriptions of villains in the Canon are very important and worthy of close scrutiny because Holmes can invariably deduce a wealth of information from a person's physical characteristics. Holmes describes Moriarty as "extremely tall and thin, his forehead domes out in a white curve, and his two eyes are deeply sunken in this head. He is clean-shaven, pale, and ascetic-looking, retaining something of the professor in his features. His shoulders are rounded from much study, and his face protrudes forward, and is forever slowly oscillating from side to side in a curiously reptilian fashion. He peered at me with great curiosity in his puckered eyes." This description of Moriarty does not lead us to immediately assume that he's a criminal. Then we learn further from Holmes that Moriarty is "a man of good birth and excellent education, endowed by nature with a phenomenal mathematical faculty. At the age of twenty-one he wrote a treatise upon the Binomial Theorem, which has had a European vogue. On the strength of it he won the Mathematical Chair at one of our smaller universities, and had, to all appearance, a most brilliant career before him." All these added facts put Moriarty in a positive light, and we view him as a brilliant professor. But then Holmes reveals that, "The man had hereditary tendencies of the most diabolical kind. A criminal strain ran in his blood, which, instead of being modified, was increased and rendered infinitely more dangerous by his extraordinary mental powers. Dark rumours gathered round him in the university town, and eventually he was compelled to resign his chair and to come down to London, where he set up as an army coach. So much is known to the world, but what I am telling you now is what I have myself discovered." So Holmes takes us to Moriarty's dark side, his inherited criminal strain made darker by his great intellect. Atavism is referred to in several other stories in the Canon, including *The Copper Beeches, The Greek Interpreter*, The Speckled Band, and *The Sussex Vampire*, where Holmes alludes to hereditary throwbacks, original sin, and social learning techniques.

Holmes tells Watson how he finally identified "ex-Professor Moriarty of mathematical celebrity" as "a power behind the malefactor, some deep organising power which forever stands in the way of the law, and throws its shield over the wrongdoer. ... He is the organiser of half that is evil and of nearly all that is undetected in this great city. He is a genius, a philosopher, an abstract thinker. He has a brain of the first order. He sits motionless, like a spider in the centre of its web, but that web has a thousand radiations, and he knows well every quiver of each of them. He does little himself. He only plans. But his agents are numerous and splendidly organised. Is there a crime to be done, a paper to be abstracted, we will say, a house to be rifled, a man to be removed--the word is passed to the Professor, the matter is organised and carried out. The agent may be caught. In that case money is found for his bail or his defence. But the central power which uses the agent is never caught--never so much as suspected. This was the organisation which I deduced, Watson, and which I devoted my whole energy to exposing and breaking up." This description of Moriarty sets him up as Holmes' nemesis, his arch adversary. It also elevates Moriarty into a category similar to Mycroft Holmes, who sits like a spider in the middle of the web of British government.

Moriarty is one of a few criminals in the Canon who does operate in a criminal community – a community Holmes calls the "higher criminal world of London." He is not a usual Holmesian villain in the sense that he commits one crime that Holmes investigates and solves. Rather he's the power behind a crime wave in London, and only Holmes is aware of his far-reaching criminal sway.

A crucial characteristic of Moriarty is that he will never confess or repent his criminal activities. To the contrary, he's proud of being a worthy opponent of Sherlock Holmes, and he intends to beat Holmes, even if he has to kill him. Holmes lets us know that Moriarty is evil, and this sets up the ultimate conflict between super hero and arch foe at Reichenbach Falls. Because we know about the pervasive and far reaching influence of Moriarty and his criminal gang, we realize how dangerous this encounter is for Holmes. One of them or both of them have to go. In *The Empty House*, when we discover that Holmes lives, we are not only glad that Holmes is back with us, we are also satisfied that good triumphed over evil.

Holmes uses his Method to evaluate Moriarty as he does with all criminals. First he observes the individual carefully. He makes deductions based on what he sees. Secondly, Holmes assesses the individual's background. Then he assesses character and the ambition, the incentives, the desires that motivate the individual. Holmes finds Moriarty dressed like a gentleman, living like a gentleman, but not acting like one. Moriarty's double life revolves around his criminal empire. Then at the last, Holmes assesses an individual's willingness to confess and repent of any crimes. Moriarty lacks this willingness, and Holmes concludes that Moriarty's overall character poses a threat not only to him personally but to mankind, setting up the good versus evil Palaestrian battleground from which only one of the two can emerge. Truly a legendary conflict.

Colonel Moran

Another exceptional criminal in the Canon is Colonel Sebastian Moran, "the second most dangerous man in London" according to Holmes. Moran is part of Moriarty's gang, and in *The Empty House,* Holmes captures him and has him arrested for the murder of Ronald Adair.

As with Moriarty, we are given a look at Moran's physical characteristics, his background and his character, all of which Holmes uses to understand the criminal and the crime or crimes.

Moran is a handsome and compelling figure. We get a detailed description of him with his "tremendously virile and yet sinister face... the brow of a philosopher above and the jaw of a sensualist below, the man must have started with great capacities for good or for evil. But one could not look upon his cruel blue eyes, with their drooping, cynical lids, or upon the fierce, aggressive nose and the threatening, deep-lined brow, without reading Nature's plainest danger-signals." "His two eyes shone like stars. ...He was an elderly man, with a thin, projecting nose, a high, bald forehead, and a huge grizzled moustache. An opera hat was pushed to the back of his head, and an evening dress shirt-front gleamed out through his open overcoat. His face was gaunt and swarthy, scored with deep, savage lines." His background is not that of a usual criminal either. "Moran, Sebastian, Colonel. Unemployed. Formerly 1st Bengalore Pioneers. Born London, 1840. Son of Sir Augustus Moran, C.B., once British Minister to Persia. Educated Eton and Oxford. Served in Jowaki Campaign, Afghan Campaign, Charasiab (despatches), Sherpur, and Cabul. Author of `Heavy Game of the Western Himalayas,' 1881; `Three Months in the Jungle,' 1884. Address: Conduit Street. Clubs: The Anglo-Indian, the Tankerville, the Bagatelle Card Club." Watson remarks that Moran's career is that of an honorable soldier, but Holmes replies: "There are some trees, Watson, which grow to a certain height and then suddenly develop some unsightly eccentricity. You will see it often in humans. I have a theory that the individual represents in his development the whole procession of his ancestors, and that such a sudden turn to good or evil stands for some strong influence which came into the line of his pedigree. The person becomes, as it were, the epitome of the history of his own family." Watson refers to the theory as "rather fanciful," and although Holmes doesn't insist upon it, his observations here on heredity are similar to the ones he made about Professor Moriarty.

Colonel Moran lives in two spheres. In one, he is a member of Moriarty's criminal gang. In the other, he's a part of respectable society. Unfortunately, Moran cheats at cards, and cheating is against the Victorian code. When Ronald Adair played with Moran, he discovered Moran cheated and threatened to expose him. This would have been ruinous for Moran in several ways. First of all, Moran would have to resign his Club membership and promise to never play cards again, so it would be a great financial loss. Secondly, Moran would be disgraced because cheating was a fraud and a breach of the Unwritten Laws as well, so he would be ostracized from society. Holmes knows Moran would never confess or repent his crimes. When they meet on equal footing, Holmes wins the match because he is able to successfully deduce all but one of Colonel Moran's actions based upon knowledge he's derived from Moran's physical description, background and character analysis. First Holmes taunts Moran about falling into the trap he's set: "I wonder that my very simple stratagem could deceive so old a Shikari." Then Holmes brags: "I did not anticipate that you would yourself make use of this empty house and this convenient front window. I had imagined you as operating from the street, where my friend Lestrade and his merry men were awaiting you. With that exception all has gone as I expected." And Moran gives Holmes his due, muttering: "You fiend! You clever, clever fiend!"

John Clay

A third villain in the Canon with exceptional qualities is John Clay, alias Vincent Spaulding. In *The Red-Headed League*, Holmes calls him "the fourth smartest man in London, and for daring I am not sure that he has not a claim to be third." Clay attended Eton and Oxford and his grandfather was a Royal Duke. He is "a bright-looking, clean-shaven young fellow" with "a clean-cut, boyish face." Clay doesn't physically resemble a stereotypical criminal – quite the opposite. Even when he's caught red handed robbing the bank and handcuffed, Clay asserts his rank and upbraids the constables: "I beg that you will not touch me with your filthy hands ... You may not be aware that I have royal blood in my veins. Have the goodness, also, when you address me always to say 'sir' and 'please.' " This case stimulates Holmes, and at the end he undoubtedly enjoys hearing Clay say to him, "You seem to have done the thing very completely. I must compliment you." Holmes answers: "And I you ... Your red-headed idea was very new and effective."

Baron Gruner

Baron Adelbert Gruner, another extraordinary villain, is described as having breeding: "a real aristocrat of crime with a superficial suggestion of afternoon tea and all the cruelty of the grave behind it. He is an excellent antagonist, cool as ice, silky voiced and soothing as one of your fashionable consultants, and poisonous as a cobra." Physically Gruner is "extraordinarily handsome, with a most fascinating manner, a gentle voice and that air of romance and mystery which means so much to a woman. He is said to have the whole sex at his mercy and to have made ample use of the fact." Like the other top criminals in the Canon, the Baron comes to his criminal life by choice. His villainous *modus operandi* is to dominate and take advantage of women. We are told in this case that the Baron murdered his wife and that he has had a string of mistresses whom he has used and humiliated and sometimes injured physically. On top of all that, he's a heel, a cad and an arrogant bully who keeps a locked book that records all his female conquests. Yet, he's acted cleverly and left no evidence. So far the Baron has escaped legal justice. Now Holmes accepts the challenge of preventing the Baron's next conquest. To do it, Holmes resorts to burglary and steals the Baron's book, using it as evidence to convince the Baron's fiancée of his real character. Even though Holmes is successful at preventing the marriage, the Baron is never brought to legal justice for any of his past or his contemplated future crimes.

These four exceptional villains with all their background and education and family ties live like gentlemen. They have not been forced by poverty to become criminals. They have chosen to become criminals. They have cast their criminal nets and involved others in their cold blooded villainy. In this respect they also differ from many of the other villains in the Canon who commit acts in hot blood to avenge or revenge or prevent crimes.

Three of these super villains are British, and one - Baron Gruner - is Austrian. Each is dealt with harshly in the Canon. Moriarty is killed. Game over. Later we find that Holmes misses the challenge that Moriarty presented. Moran and Clay are both captured and turned over to British law. Baron Gruner is never arrested, but he is scarred for life when Kitty Winter throws vitriol at him, and his exposure as a shameless immoralist ruins forever his social status.

Exceptional Female Villainesses

As with male villains, there are also some remarkable villainesses in the Canon. Although they are similar in some ways to their male counterparts, Holmes has very different dealings with them. The few women wrongdoers in the Canon reinforce the Victorian view that women were weak and helpless creatures who needed protection. Only 21% of the stories have women as villains, compared to 75% with male villains. Examining Holmes' female villains further supports these statistics. These villainesses were women who were unique as opposed to ordinary.

Irene Adler

Irene Adler is the ultimate villainess in the stories. She is both beautiful and smart. She attempts to blackmail the King of Bohemia, but she escapes legal justice, retains her freedom, and keeps the incriminating document. She matches wits with Holmes, and she wins. What a coup.

Holmes perhaps underestimates Irene Adler. He puts a great deal of effort and time and uses at least two disguises to figure out where Irene has hidden the photograph she threatens to use to blackmail the King of Bohemia. Holmes himself plans to commit a crime and burgle her house to get it, but she foils him and flees before he can get his hands on it. Holmes has a truly unique relationship with this clever villainess. First he is a sworn witness to her wedding while he's disguised as an out of work groom – a bit of marvelous symbolism. Then he receives her kindly attentions when he pretends to be injured while disguised as a clergyman. She smartly tumbles to his scheme and adroitly outwits him, but knowing that Holmes is on the case undoubtedly contributes to her promise to end her attempt at blackmail. This is a great plot for the first Sherlock Holmes story. It has royalty, love triangles, disguises, a wedding, and a truly beautiful and memorable female villainess who actually bests the great detective. And all this without a completed crime because Holmes successfully ends the blackmail threat. Holmes, like the rest of the world, always remembers Irene Adler as The Woman. No wonder this first short story was immensely popular and readers couldn't wait for the next one.

Isadora Klein

Isadora Klein appears in *The Three Gables*, one of the later stories published in 1926. She is, like Irene Adler, exceptionally beautiful. Watson describes her as "tall, queenly, a perfect figure, a lovely mask-like face, with two wonderful Spanish eyes which looked murder at us both." Holmes tells us she's *la belle dame sans merci*. She's a rare female Holmesian villain who lives on the fringe of the criminal community. According to Holmes, "She married the aged German sugar king, Klein, and presently found herself the richest as well as the most lovely widow upon earth." She consorts with a gang of bullies – the Spencer John gang - who carry out her orders. Holmes tells her that he knows she ordered her henchmen to beat him up, and he warns her that she has put herself "in the power of a band of rascals who may blackmail or give you away." Holmes has to get the truth out of Isadora, and Watson tells us that, "So roguish and exquisite did she look as she stood before us with a challenging smile that I felt of all Holmes's criminals this was the one whom he would find it hardest to face. However, he was immune from sentiment." Holmes does report the gang members to the police for burgling the Maberley house, but he never reports Isadora. Why not? What motivates Holmes in this case to let Isadora go free? She has certainly crossed the line into a criminal sphere and committed planned criminal acts, not spur of the moment crimes of hot blood. She even admits she was complicit in Douglas Maberley's beating and eventual death, but she denies she wanted him dead. Even though Isadora has such a criminal background, she admits to Holmes - the confessor- that she sinned. She also says she's sorry, and she asks him to give her a second chance. Sherlock Holmes believes in forgiveness if the sinner confesses and is sorry, and in this case Holmes also believes in redemption. Isadora will be shortly marrying the Duke of Lomond and will take her place as a respected member of upper class society. Victorian readers, like today's readers, probably did not think of Isadora Klein as a good Victorian gentlewoman. She has involved herself in a host of crimes with the Spencer John gang. Yet Holmes lets her go free – even though the gang members she deals with will face the law. She tells Holmes that she didn't know the gang would be so rough on Douglas Maberley, and Holmes bases his judgement on her statements, despite the fact that the gang also burgled and roughed up Douglas' mother. It also seems that Holmes takes into account Isadora's wealth and beauty – she was "the richest as well as the most lovely widow upon earth.' These give her social standing, as does her plan to marry the young Duke of Lomond. Holmes may also be considering her Spanish heritage – she has "the real blood of the masterful Conquistador." She's a foreigner, and we hear over and over again from Holmes and Watson how the tropics make the blood run hot, so perhaps her sins are more easily forgiven because she's a Spaniard rather than an Englishwoman.

Holmes uses his discretion to keep the sins of this distinctly interesting villainess a secret. Then he "compounds a felony" and commits one himself by blackmailing her for five thousand pounds to compensate Mrs. Maberley. He treats Isadora as he treats no other villain in the Canon who has committed the crimes that she has. Her motives are not pure, as in the case of Lady Hope. Isadora's crimes are premeditated and her intention was always to impose her wishes and have her own way. In the end, Holmes faces her down, and after getting the money and telling her to go and sin no more, I think he got what he judged was the best justice possible in the circumstances.

Lady Hilda Trelawney Hope

Another interesting villainess is a Lady who doesn't intend to commit any crime at all, unlike Isadora Klein, but in the end she is responsible for at least three serious crimes – theft, treason and burglary. In *The Second Stain*, published in 1904, this villainess doesn't ask Holmes for any help. Instead Holmes has to threaten to expose her to her husband, and he begs her to trust him so he can solve the case. Lady Hope has been a good wife and has led a blameless life. Unlike other villains in the stories, she has not intentionally sinned. But she is being blackmailed, and to satisfy the blackmailer, she does something she bitterly regrets. She puts her husband's career and his honor in jeopardy by using a duplicate key to his dispatch box and stealing a sensitive paper. When she finally comes to understand the gravity of her action, she bravely retrieves the paper and gives it to Holmes. He replaces it in her husband's dispatch box and reveals nothing of her involvement. Throughout most of this story, Lady Hope is clueless about the importance of this paper, even telling Holmes that she "thought of destroying it." Despite Lady Hope's crimes - stealing the paper, committing treason by giving it to a foreign spy, and committing burglary to retrieve the document - Holmes uses his discretion. Holmes keeps her involvement secret in order to avoid not only a government scandal but also a family scandal so that Lord Hope will not be disgraced and lose his position. This is another case in which Holmes commits some crimes himself. He withholds evidence, but he does it for the greater good. He has to forgive a lot of Lady Hope's sins, but he's able to do so precisely because of Lady Hope's ignorance of the content and importance of the paper she stole. Lady Hope is grateful, but so are a few governments, justifying Holmes' actions in forgiving and protecting a woman who had no intent to commit a crime but very nearly toppled a government.

Demi Villains

In the world of Holmesian villains, some villains are worse than others. In the stories, there are a number of demi-villains who are the more common variety run-of-the-mill evil doers who have redeeming qualities. In many cases, Holmes sympathizes with their provocations and even their eye-for-an-eye philosophy. Their crimes are on a smaller scale, and their criminal plans are not as far reaching as Moriarty's. We enjoy watching Holmes investigate these other less remarkable villains and solve their crimes, but Holmes himself admits he is not stimulated as much by these more commonplace cases as he is by the challenge of a superior intellect. He prefers, as do some of his super villains, to hunt big game.

Sir Robert Norberton in *Shoscombe Old Place* is a character who is not really a villain, though he commits a minor crime. He is described as "... being a dangerous man. He is about the most daredevil rider in England -- second in the Grand National a few years back. He is one of those men who have overshot their true generation. He should have been a buck in the days of the Regency -- a boxer, an athlete, a plunger on the turf, a lover of fair ladies, and, by all account, so far down Queer Street that he may never find his way back again." Physically he has a "terrible figure, huge in stature and fierce in manner" with a "strong, heavily moustached face and angry eyes." Despite the negative adjectives (terrible, huge, fierce, strong, angry) that promise a villain, Sir Robert is not. He loved his sister, and after he confesses to Holmes, he receives only a mild censure from the police.

Richard Brunton, the butler in *The Musgrave Ritual*, is another demi-villain. Holmes – like the reader - is impressed with Brunton's intelligence and cunning in figuring out the Musgrave Ritual. But in doing so, Brunton breaks the unwritten rules between himself and Reginald Musgrave, and as such he breaks one of the fundamental rules of society by not knowing his place. He's not portrayed as one of the usual villains, but instead as "a man of great energy and character" who is invaluable in the household. He is "a well-grown, handsome man, with a splendid forehead," "who speaks several languages and plays nearly every musical instrument." It is surprising that he has remained satisfied as butler. Brunton's big fault is that he is a ladies' man, and that ultimately gets him killed. After he drops his fiancée, Rachel Howells, for another woman, Rachel takes out her murderous revenge on him. Brunton is perhaps more a good villain than an evil one.

One of the saddest villains in the stories is Colonel Valentine Walter, younger brother of Sir James Walter. Colonel Walter steals the Bruce Partington plans from his brother's office at the Admiralty. As a consequence, his brother dies from the shame. We know the Colonel felt guilty, as he fainted when Holmes confronted him. The Colonel is no usual criminal. He's from an excellent family, he has "soft, handsome and delicate features," and he has the bearing of a gentleman. Holmes is surprised Valentine is involved in this treasonous crime, and he remarks: "How an English gentleman could behave in such a manner is beyond my comprehension." Holmes then convinces Valentine to cooperate to mitigate his sentence: "Let me advise you to gain at least the small credit for repentance and confession, since there are still some details which we can only learn from your lips." The Colonel agrees to help capture Hugo Oberstein, and his prison term is reduced, but he dies after the second year of his sentence, in disgrace and with his brother's death on his hands.

Another semi villain is Joseph Harrison in *The Naval Treaty*. He is described as "a rather stout man who received us with much hospitality. His age may have been nearer forty than thirty, but his cheeks were so ruddy and his eyes so merry that he still conveyed the impression of a plump and mischievous boy." This is not the usual description of a villain. However, Joseph commits a spur of the moment burglary with terrible consequences, and he also attacks Sherlock with a knife. Holmes solves the mystery and, despite the attack, lets Harrison get away for the good of the country and the good of his family. Holmes has told us that Harrison is like a mischievous boy, so obviously Holmes hopes Harrison has learned a lesson and will stay out of trouble, reminiscent of Gilchrist in *The Three Students*.

Crimes where Men take Advantage of Women

One of the touchstones of the Victorian code and of the Canon as well is that women needed to be protected. This conviction carried through into the Sherlock Holmes stories, where in 17 or 30% of the 56 adventures, men take advantage of women, thus reinforcing the necessity that society must do everything possible to protect women lest they become victims. Holmes, on the whole, treats his women clients well, defending them and helping them solve their problems – the one exception being *A Case of Identity*. In this case Holmes discovers his female client is being duped by her stepfather and her mother, but he declines to reveal what he's discovered, so at the end of the story, she's at the same point as she was at the beginning – no wiser and no better off.

In these 17 stories, there is a theme of character, and the villain in each of these stories shares an unfortunate character trait - a criminal penchant for taking advantage of women.

Sir Eustace Brackenstall, the real villain in *The Abbey Grange*, is a jealous alcoholic who physically abuses his wife, Mary Fraser, as well as her maid and her pet dog. He is a brutal bully who makes her life miserable.

Sir George Burnwell holds such sway over Mary Holder that she betrays her uncle and steals the Beryl coronet for him.

Charles Augustus Milverton maintains his power over many women by means of blackmail, threatening to reveal secrets that would cause them to lose not just their homes but their places in society. He bleeds them dry.

Jephro Rucastle in *The Copper Beeches* runs a tight household with a vicious dog. He keeps his younger second wife subdued and apparently agreeable while he holds Alice, his daughter from a previous marriage, a prisoner in an upper story room in an effort to secure her fortune for himself.

Abe Slaney in *The Dancing Men* would probably today be called a stalker. In a trans-Atlantic love triangle, he follows Elsie from America to England and kills her husband Hilton. Elsie attempts suicide, and Holmes cleverly captures Abe, who fails in his quest to win back Elsie.

In *The Greek Interpreter,* Harold Latimer romances Sophy Katrides and then he and his partner, Wilson Kemp, kidnap her brother Paul and eventually murder him in order to gain control over Sophy's inheritance.

James Windibank disguises himself as Hosmer Angel and courts his stepdaughter in a bizarre, aberrant scheme to maintain control of her money in *A Case of Identity*. Windibank also completely controls his older wife, who is complicit in this bizarre love triangle.

aron Gruner in *The Illustrious Client* poses as a gentleman, but in reality is a dangerous criminal, out to trap his fiancée into a marriage in which she will become a pawn of his lascivious and murderous character.

Henry 'Holy' Peters with his wife in tow disguises himself as a religious figure, commits fraud and attempts murder on the "drifting and friendless" Lady Frances Carfax.

In *The Musgrave Ritual*, Brunton the butler is a ladies' man involved in a fiery love triangle. After he rejects Rachel Howells for another woman, he is so sure of his powers over her that he asks her to help him in his scheme to uncover some lost treasure. But Rachel takes her revenge, and he dies because of it.

Jonas Oldacre in *The Norwood Builder* is a twisted and revengeful rejected lover. He devises a dark plot against his former fiancée, now Mrs. McFarlane, whom he has never forgiven for long ago rejecting him. He fakes his own death, and with the aid of his housekeeper Mrs. Lexington, he hides in a secret room and places false clues to incriminate her son, John McFarlane, who is arrested for his murder. He resembles a male Agatha Christie, who disappeared and watched quietly under an assumed identity while her first husband Archie was suspected of murdering her.

Giuseppe Gorgiano in *The Red Circle* is another stalker. He follows Emilia and Gennaro Lucca from Italy to London, plotting to kill the husband in order to possess the wife as his own. In this dark love triangle, things take a bad turn for Gorgiano when Scotland Yard, Pinkertons and Sherlock Holmes track him down. They find him dead, stabbed in the throat by the husband in self-defense.

Josiah Amberley has made life miserable for his young wife. He is a miser who controls her daily life. He covers up the double murder of his wife and her lover so well in *The Retired Colourman* that he nearly commits the perfect crime were it not for his poor character and other clues that help Holmes expose him.

In *The Second Stain*, Henri Fournaye, alias Eduardo Lucas, leaves his wife in Paris to lead a double life in London where he blackmails women. His wife catches up with him and kills him, letting all his other female victims – including Lady Hilda Trelawney Hope - off the hook.

Jack Woodley, Bob Carruthers and Mr. Williamson stalk Miss Violet Smith, perpetrate fraud, and force her into a false marriage in order to secure her inheritance in *The Solitary Cyclist*. Luckily Violet asks Sherlock Holmes to help her. First Holmes wins a boxing match with Woodley, and then he is able to wrest her from the entanglement.

In *The Speckled Band,* Dr. Grimesby Roylott dominates his two step daughters - an easy task in Victorian and Edwardian times. They obey him fully. He murders one of them for financial gain and gets away with it, and when he attempts to murder the other, Sherlock Holmes intervenes, saves her, and puts a stop to his evil designs. Roylott in turn dies by his own devices.

In *The Man with the Twisted Lip*, Neville St. Clair fools his wife everyday by pretending to go to work in the City when instead he disguises himself as Hugh Boone and begs on the streets for the money to run his household. He keeps his wife in the dark because not only is begging illegal, but this ruse is against all the Victorian unwritten laws. He knows well that he, his wife, and his family would be disgraced if his secret life was discovered. He is not a classic abuser, but he is leading a double life, taking advantage of his wife's belief in his good character. Holmes unmasks him, and he confesses and repents and promises to never do it again, something that sets him apart from all the other abusers of women in the Canon.

Physical Characteristics of Villains

Watson and Holmes take great pains to describe the villains they encounter in the stories with wonderful word pictures of eyes, faces, noses, mouths, ears, hair, complexion, voices, size, age, manner and dress in which the use of negative or unsavory adjectives or adverbs in the description gives readers a big clue to the villainous nature of the character being introduced. Sometimes it is in the coloring of the face or the shape of the nose or the ear. Sometimes it is in the size of the face or the hands. It might be the voice itself, or even the general manner. Certain features lend themselves to the criminal bent, and because of the similarity in the description of these features, we are able to immediately spot most of the villains throughout the Canon.

One feature Watson and Holmes particularly notice are the eyes of the villains, many of which are gray, keen and deep set. Culverton Smith in *The Dying Detective* has "two sullen, menacing grey eyes." Jonas Oldacre in *Norwood Builder* is described by McFarlane as having has "keen grey eyes," and later by Watson as having "shifty light-grey eyes and white eyelashes" Charles Augustus Milverton also has "two keen grey eyes," that have "hard glitter" and are "restless and penetrating." We are told about Wilson Kemp in *The Greek Interpreter* that "the terror of (his) face lay in his eyes, ... steel grey, and glistening coldly with a malignant, inexorable cruelty in their depths." Dr. Grimesby Roylott in *The Speckled Band* has "deep-set, bile-shot eyes." Don Murillo in *Wisteria Lodge* has "dark, deep-set, brooding eyes." In *The Creeping Man*, Professor Presbury's "eyes were his most remarkable feature, keen, observant, and clever to the verge of cunning." Colonel Moran in *The Empty House* has savage, "cruel blue eyes, with their drooping, cynical lids." Patrick Cairns in *Black Peter* has "two bold, dark eyes (that) gleamed behind the cover of thick, tufted, overhung eyebrows." In *The Veiled Lodger*, Mrs. Rodner says her husband had "small, vicious eyes darting pure malignancy." Baron Gruner has "large, dark, languorous eyes which might easily hold an irresistible fascination for women."

Count Sylvius in *The Mazarin Stone* has fierce, "dark murderous eyes." Sir Robert Norberton in *Shoscombe Old Place* has "angry eyes." Compare these descriptions to the "clear eyes" of Hilton Cubitt, the victim in *The Dancing Men*. Holmes says he is a man far from the fogs of Baker Street, and "he seemed to bring a whiff of strong, fresh, bracing, east-coast air with him."

Another important facial feature used to help describe a villain is the nose. Abe Slaney in *The Dancing Men* sports "a great, aggressive hooked nose." Count Sylvius in *The Mazarin Stone* has the "long curved beak of an eagle." Dr. Grimesby Roylott in *The Speckled Band*, has a "high, thin, fleshless nose, (giving him)... somewhat the resemblance to a fierce old bird of prey." Josiah Amberley is described as looking "like some horrible bird of prey." And Dr. Leon Sterndale is described in *The Devil's Foot* as having a "hawk-like nose." Baron Gruner has "little waxed tips of hair under his nose, like the short antennae of an insect." Colonel Moran in *The Empty House* has a "fierce, aggressive nose."

The mouth of the villain is particularly telling as well. 'Holy' Peters in *Lady Frances Carfax* has a "cruel, vicious mouth." Count Sylvius in *The Mazarin Stone* sports "a formidable dark moustache shading a cruel, thin-lipped mouth." Colonel Sebastian Moran has a "bristling moustache." And Baron Gruner in *The Illustrious Client* has a "straight, thin-lipped mouth. If ever I saw a murderer's mouth it was there -- a cruel, hard gash in the face, compressed, inexorable, and terrible. It was Nature's danger-signal, set as a warning to his victims."

The color and shape of the face also give us unmistakable clues into the criminal character with descriptions that evoke the abnormal, such as "seared," "burned," "coarse," "greasy," and "yellow." Dr. Roylott in *The Speckled Band* has "a large face, seared with a thousand wrinkles, burned yellow with the sun, and marked with every evil passion." Culverton Smith has a "great yellow face, coarse-grained and greasy." Holy Peters has "a large red face." Patrick Cairns in *Black Peter* has "a fierce bull-dog face ... framed in a tangle of hair and beard." Don Murillo in *Wisteria Lodge* has a "parchment face" that is "yellow and sapless." James Windibank in *A Case of Identity* is "sallow-skinned." John Turner in *The Boscombe Valley Mystery* has a face of "ashen white." Baron Gruner's face is "swarthy, almost Oriental" with "hair and moustache (of) raven black, the latter short, pointed, and carefully waxed." Colonel Moran has a "threatening, deep-lined brow;" a "sinister face" with "the brow of a philosopher above and the jaw of a sensualist below."

Sherlock Holmes always pays particular attention to the ears. "As a medical man, you are aware, Watson, that there is no part of the body which varies so much as the human ear. Each ear is as a rule quite distinctive and differs from all other ones. In last year's Anthropological Journal you will find two short monographs from my pen upon the subject." Holy Peters' ear was a clue in *Lady Frances Carfax*, for he had "a disfigured left ear which had been badly bitten in a saloon-fight."

Quite a number of villains are described as being big, huge or giant. The shoulders and chest of Josiah Amberley in *The Retired Colourman* have "the framework of a giant." Count Sylvius in *The Mazarin Stone* is a "big, swarthy fellow." Eugenia Ronder's husband in *The Veiled Lodger* is a "huge bully of a man." Dr. Sterndale in *The Devil's Foot* has a "huge body." The "enormous limbs" of John Turner in *The Boscombe Valley Mystery* "showed that he was possessed of unusual strength of body and of character." Dr. Grimesby Roylott in *The Speckled Band* is "a huge man." Emilia describes Giuseppe Gorgiano in *The Red Circle* as "a huge man. Not only was his body that of a giant, but everything about him was grotesque, gigantic, and terrifying." Harold Latimer in *The Greek Interpreter* is a "powerful, broad-shouldered young fellow." And Sir Robert Norberton in *Shoscombe Old Place* is a "terrible figure, huge in stature and fierce in manner."

In *Thor Bridge*, Neil Gibson, who is an American Senator and millionaire, is described in the negative terms of a villain. "His tall, gaunt, craggy figure had a suggestion of hunger and rapacity. An Abraham Lincoln keyed to base uses instead of high ones would give some idea of the man. His face might have been chiselled in granite, hard set, craggy, remorseless, with deep lines upon it, the scars of many a crisis. Cold grey eyes, looking shrewdly out from under bristling brows, surveyed us each in turn." We find out he's not a villain but the husband of the victim. However, this description reinforces Holmes' assessment that he is selfish and used to getting what he wants. Holmes berates him for being at the center of the unfortunate love triangle that ended with his wife committing suicide. Holmes blames him for putting the governess into an impossible situation, and he also blames him for relying on his wealth to get him out of the situation. So in this tale, he is the default villain. It was his actions that led to the crisis and to the suicide of his wife. We are able to pick up the clues that he has a bad character in the description we're given, in which so many items match up with the villains, including those grey eyes.

One villain, James Calhoun in *The Five Orange Pips*, is an anomaly because he's never physically described. We are given no details at all about him other than that he and his two mates are "the only native-born Americans in the ship." Holmes wants to personally revenge Openshaw's murder, so he sends Calhoun the five orange pips -"S.H. for J. O." But revenge and justice don't come from Holmes or the law, they come from the heavens for the never-described James Calhoun and his two mates.

Foreign Villains

Although some people think that most of the 84 villains in the Canon are foreign, that is not the case. 58 are British, or 69%, and 26 or 31% are non-British - a nearly 3 to l ratio. Regarding the 34 murderers, a similar proportion follows with 23 or 68% being British and only 11 or 32% being non-British.

When the wrongdoer is a foreigner, such as in *The Illustrious Client*, *Thor Bridge* or *Wisteria Lodge,* these foreigners are people who do not act according to the Victorian Code. Victorians didn't expect foreigners to act like them. Victorians anticipated more emotional and less rational behavior from foreigners, and this presumption is usually reflected in the stories.

Italians, German, Spanish, Central American and Peruvian characters were all easy suspects of crimes because they were foreigners. These characters aren't quite English gentlemen or ladies, and therefore they are automatically suspicious characters whenever anything goes amiss. Mrs. Ferguson in *The Sussex Vampire* is innocent, but she is Peruvian, and her husband actually considers that she might have vampire tendencies. Like her, anyone coming from a hot climate was considered prone to commit hot blooded crimes – crimes Victorians considered so very un-British. This is true for Maria Pinto Gibson in *Thor Bridge*, Don Murillo in *Wisteria Lodge*, Beppo in *The Six Napoleons*, Guiseppe Gorgiano in *The Red Circle, and* Count Sylvius in *The Mazarin Stone.* Holmes says, "It is well they don't have days of fog in the Latin countries - the countries of assassination."

Mme. Fournaye in *The Second Stain* is French Creole. She is considered hot blooded, which is taken into consideration in her behavior and her crime. The Australian and South African villains are also easy suspects, but they are depicted differently. These criminals are rough and tumble, like the reputation of the colonies themselves, as in *The Solitary Cyclist, Lady Frances Carfax,* and *The Boscombe Valley Mystery.* They aren't quite like the English, so they are considered prone to break the conventions of the Victorian Code and commit violent acts due to their restless colonial temperament.

American Connections

Of all foreign villains, Sherlock Holmes has a special feeling for Americans. In *The Noble Bachelor* he says, "It is always a joy to meet an American, Mr. Moulton, for I am one of those who believe that the folly of a monarch and the blundering of a minister in far-gone years will not prevent our children from being some day citizens of the same world-wide country under a flag which shall be a quartering of the Union Jack with the Stars and Stripes."

Nine stories have connections to America. In some the villain is from America, and in others it is the wife or husband of the villain who hails from the U.S.A.

The Copper Beeches – Rucastle's daughter Alice is supposedly in Philadelphia USA
The Dancing Men – Cubitt's wife Elsie comes from the USA. The killer is from the USA and connected to a Chicago gang
The Five Orange Pips –Killers are American. KKK involvement
The Illustrious Client – Baron Gruner was to go to the states for business On the Cunard Line
His Last Bow - Holmes disguises himself as Altamont, an Irish-American spy
The Noble Bachelor –Lord St. Simon's bride is an American from San Francisco
Thor Bridge – Neil Gibson is an American Senator - the Gold King of the USA
The Three Garridebs – John Garrideb and Roger Prescott are from USA – Chicago
The Yellow Face – Munro's wife formerly lived in the USA

<u>Australian Connections</u>

Six stories have connections to Australia. We hear in *The Abbey Grange* that Australia has a "freer, less conventional atmosphere" than the English life, with its proprieties and its primness."

The Abbey Grange – Lady Mary Brackenstall (née Fraser) grew up in Australia
Boscombe Valley – McCarthy and Turner are from Australia
Gloria Scott – Trevor Sr. went to Australia and made his fortune
Lady Frances Carfax – Villains Holy Peters and Annie Fraser are from Australia
The Empty House – Ronald Adair, son of Governor of an Australian colony
The Priory School – James Wilder must emigrate to Australia

<u>Other Foreign Connections</u>

There are 18 additional stories with other foreign villains and connections. In two of these stories a foreigner is quickly suspected of the crime, but later cleared. In *The Naval Treaty*, a young Frenchman named Gorot is initially suspected of the theft because he is French. In *The Priory School*, Heidegger the German Master is initially suspected of the kidnapping. Noteworthy is that Inspector Bardle in *The Lion's Mane* considers the jellyfish to not be English.

The Dying Detective – Culverton Smith comes from Sumatra.

His Last Bow – Germans Von Bork and Baron Von Herling
The Engineer's Thumb – Colonel Lysander Stark & Elsie are from Germany
The Illustrious Client - Baron Adelbert Gruner – Austrian
The Creeping Man –Dorak is Slavonic, and Lowenstein is from Prague.
The Golden Pince-Nez - Professor Coram and his wife Anna are Russian
The Mazarin Stone – Count Negretto Sylvius is half Italian
The Naval Treaty – Gorot, a French Huguenot, is suspected of the theft
The Priory School – Heidegger the German master is suspected of the kidnapping
The Red Circle –Villain Giuseppe Gorgiano, an Italian criminal, leader of the Red Circle, a Neapolitan society which was allied to the old Carbonari, an organization of Italian criminals.
The Resident Patient – Gang members impersonate Russian and son who Consult w/ Trevelyan
The Second Stain - Blackmailer Lucas, aka M. Henri Fournay and his Creole wife from Paris, Mme. Fournaye
The Six Napoleons – Beppo is Italian
The Solitary Cyclist – Carruthers and Woodley are from South Africa
The Sussex Vampire – Mrs. Ferguson is from Peru, South America
Thor Bridge – Neil Gibson's deceased wife is Brazilian
The Three Gables – Isadora Klein is Spanish, pure Conquistador

Wisteria Lodge - Don Murillo, Tiger of San Pedro, is from Central America

Statistics on the Holmesian Villains

As we've seen in Chapter 11, there are 84 villains in the short stories – 64 males and 20 females. Males comprise 76% of the 84 wrongdoers, a 3 to 1 ratio to 24% of females. 58 are British (69%), and 26 are non-British (31%). Four of the 26 non-British are American (16%).

These 84 villains commit 104 crimes in 23 categories. 64 Male criminals commit 85 crimes in 19 criminal categories. 20 women commit 28 crimes in 13 criminal categories. Males commit three times as many crimes as women.

Of the 104 crimes committed in the short stories, the largest category of crimes is Murder. There are 31 murders that constitute 30% of the crimes done by 34 murderers, 29 male and 5 female. Taking into account 4 crimes of Accessory to Murder and 17 Attempted Murders, there are a total of 52 crimes related to murder, or 50%. Burglary at 12% and Fraud at 7% constitute the two next largest categories, followed by Blackmail and Treason/Espionage at 4% each. (See Chapter 10 for a more detailed breakdown on the crime statistics.)

64 Male Villains - 76 % of the 84 villains

Abbey Grange - Captain Jack Croker - Murder
Beryl Coronet - Sir George Burnwell – Jewel Theft
Black Peter - Patrick Cairns - Murder
Blue Carbuncle - James Ryder – Jewel Theft

Boscombe Valley Mystery -John Turner/Black Jack of Ballarat - Murder
Bruce Partington Plans -Hugo Oberstein – Murder and Treason
Bruce Partington Plans - Colonel Valentine Walter – Treason
Cardboard Box - James Browner – Murder - Double
Charles Augustus Milverton - Charles Augustus Milverton – Blackmail
Copper Beeches - Jephro Rucastle – Fraud (Embezzlement) and False imprisonment
Creeping Man -Professor Presbury – Disorderly Conduct - Endangerment
Crooked Man - Henry Wood - Murder
Dancing Men - Abe Slaney - Murder
Devil's Foot - Mortimer Tregennis – Murder and Attempted Murder
Devil's Foot - Dr. Leon Sterndale - Murder
Dying Detective - Culverton Smith – Murder and Attempted Murder
Empty House - Colonel Sebastian Moran – Murder and Attempted murder
Engineer's Thumb - Colonel Lysander Stark – Counterfeiting and Attempted Murder
Engineer's Thumb - Dr. Becher – Counterfeiting and Attempted Murder
Final Problem - Professor Moriarty - Attempted Murder
Five Orange Pips - James Calhoun – Murder
Gloria Scott - Hudson – Blackmail
Greek Interpreter - Harold Latimer - Murder and Fraud/Embezzlement
Greek Interpreter - Wilson Kemp - Murder and& Fraud/Embezzlement

Case of Identity - James Windibank – Fraud/Embezzlement
Illustrious Client - Baron Adelbert Gruner – Murder and Assault
His Last Bow - Von Bork – Espionage/Treason
Lady Frances Carfax – Henry 'Holy' Peters - Attempted Murder, Kidnapping and Fraud
Mazarin Stone - Count Negretto Sylvius– Jewel Theft
Mazarin Stone - Sam Merton – Jewel Theft
Musgrave Ritual - Richard Brunton – Theft
Naval Treaty - Joseph Harrison – Burglary and Espionage and Attempted murder
Norwood Builder - Jonas Oldacre – Attempted Murder
Priory School - Reuben Hayes – Murder and Kidnapping
Priory School - James Wilder – Accessory to Murder and Kidnapping
Priory School – Duke of Holdernesse – Condoning a felony and Aiding in the escape of a felon
Red Circle - Giuseppe Gorgiano - Murder
Red Circle - Gennaro Lucca - Murder & Attempted murder
Red Headed League - Duncan Ross - Burglary (Bank Robbery)
Red Headed League – John Clay – Assault and Burglary (Bank Robbery)
Reigate Squires - Alec Cunningham – Murder and Burglary
Reigate Squires - Cunningham Sr. – Murder and Burglary
Resident Patient - Worthington Bank gang - Biddle – Murder

Resident Patient - Worthington Bank gang - Hayward - Murder
Resident Patient - Worthington Bank gang - Moffat - Murder
Retired Colourman - Josiah Amberley – Double Murder & Attempted Suicide
Second Stain - Eduardo Lucas / Henri Fournaye - Blackmail
Shoscombe Old Place -Sir Robert Norberton – Concealing a death
Silver Blaze - John Straker - Fraud
Silver Blaze - Silas Brown - Theft
Six Napoleons - Beppo – Murder and Burglary
Solitary Cyclist – Bob Carruthers – Fraud/Embezzlement and Attempted Murder
Solitary Cyclist - Jack Woodley – Fraud/Embezzlement and Forced Marriage and Affray
Solitary Cyclist - Williamson – Fraud / Embezzlement and Forced Marriage
Speckled Band - Dr. Grimesby Roylott – Murder and Attempted Murder
Stock-Broker's Clerk - Beddington posing as Arthur Pinner and Harry Pinner – Burglary (Stock Robbery) and Attempted suicide
Stock-Broker's Clerk – Beddington posing as Hall Pycroft – Murder and Burglary (Stock Robbery)
Sussex Vampire - Jack 'Jacky' Ferguson (CHILD)-Attempted Murder
Three Gables - Spencer John gang –Barney Stockdale – Burglary and Murder
Three Gables - Spencer John gang –Steve Dixie – Burglary and Murder

Three Garridebs - James Winter/'Killer' Evans/John Garrideb/ Morecroft – Attempted Murder, Fraud and Counterfeiting
Three Students - Gilchrist – Burglary
Twisted Lip - Neville St. Clair / Hugh Boone – Begging
Wisteria Lodge - Don Juan Murillo /Tiger of San Pedro – Murder and Kidnapping

<u>20 Female Villains - 24% of the 84 villains</u>

Lady Brackenstall (Abbey Grange)
Theresa Wright (Abbey Grange)
Miss Mary Holder (Beryl Coronet)
Miss Sarah Cushing (Cardboard Box)
Noblewoman unnamed (Charles Augustus Milverton)
Elsie (Engineer's Thumb)
Anna 'Coram' (Golden Pince-Nez)
Mrs. Windibank (A Case of Identity)
Miss Kitty Winter (Illustrious Client)
Annie Fraser (Disappearance of Lady Frances Carfax)
Hatty Doran/Mrs. Francis H. Moulton (Noble Bachelor)
Mrs. Lexington –Housekeeper (Norwood Builder)
Miss Rachel Howells (Musgrave Ritual)
Miss Irene Adler / Mrs. Godfrey Norton (Scandal in Bohemia)
Lady Hilda Hope (Second Stain)
Madame Fournaye (Second Stain)
Maria Pinto Gibson (Thor Bridge)
Isadora Klein (Three Gables)
Susan Stockdale (Three Gables)
Mrs. Eugenia Ronder (Veiled Lodger)

3 Animals commit Murder

Jellyfish (Lion's Mane)
Horse (Silver Blaze)
Snake (Speckled Band)

<u>British – 58 - 69% of the 84villains</u>

Abbey Grange
Beryl Coronet - 2
Black Peter
Blue Carbuncle
Bruce Partington Plans – 1 (Colonel Walter)
Cardboard Box - 2
Charles Augustus Milverton - 2
Copper Beeches
Creeping Man
Crooked Man
Devil's Foot - 2
Empty House
Engineer's Thumb – 1 (Ferguson)
Final Problem
Gloria Scott
Greek Interpreter - 2
Case of Identity - 2
Illustrious Client - 1 (Kitty Winter)
Lady Frances Carfax – Annie Fraser
Mazarin Stone – 1 (Sam Merton)
Musgrave Ritual - 2 (Brunton and Rachel Howells)
Naval Treaty
Norwood Builder – 2
Priory School – 3
Red Headed League - 2

Reigate Squires – 2
Resident Patient – 3
Retired Colourman
Scandal in Bohemia
Second Stain –1 (Lady Hope)
Shoscombe Old Place
Silver Blaze - 2
Solitary Cyclist – 1 (Williamson)
Speckled Band
Stock Broker's Clerk – 2
Sussex Vampire
Three Students
Man with the Twisted Lip
Three Gables – 3 (Barney & Susan Stockdale & Steve Dixie)
Veiled Lodger

Non-British –26 – 31% of the 81 villains

Abbey Grange – Australian -2
Boscombe Valley Mystery – Australian
Bruce Partington Plans – German
Dancing Men – American
Dying Detective - Sumatra
Engineer's Thumb – German (Stark & Elsie) - 2
Five Orange Pips – American
Golden Pince-Nez – Russian
Illustrious Client - Austrian
His Last Bow - German
Lady Frances Carfax – Australian (Peters)
Mazarin Stone - Italian
Noble Bachelor – American
Red Circle – Italian - 2

Second Stain – French/Creole (Mr and Mme Fournaye) - 2
Six Napoleons - Italian
Solitary Cyclist – South African (Woodley & Carruthers) – 2
Thor Bridge – Brazilian
Three Gables - Spanish
Three Garridebs – American
Wisteria Lodge – Central American

American – 4
Australian- 4
Austrian - 1
Brazilian -1
Central American - 1
French/Creole - 2
German - 4
Italian - 4
Russian - 1
South African - 2
Spanish – 1
Sumatra – 1

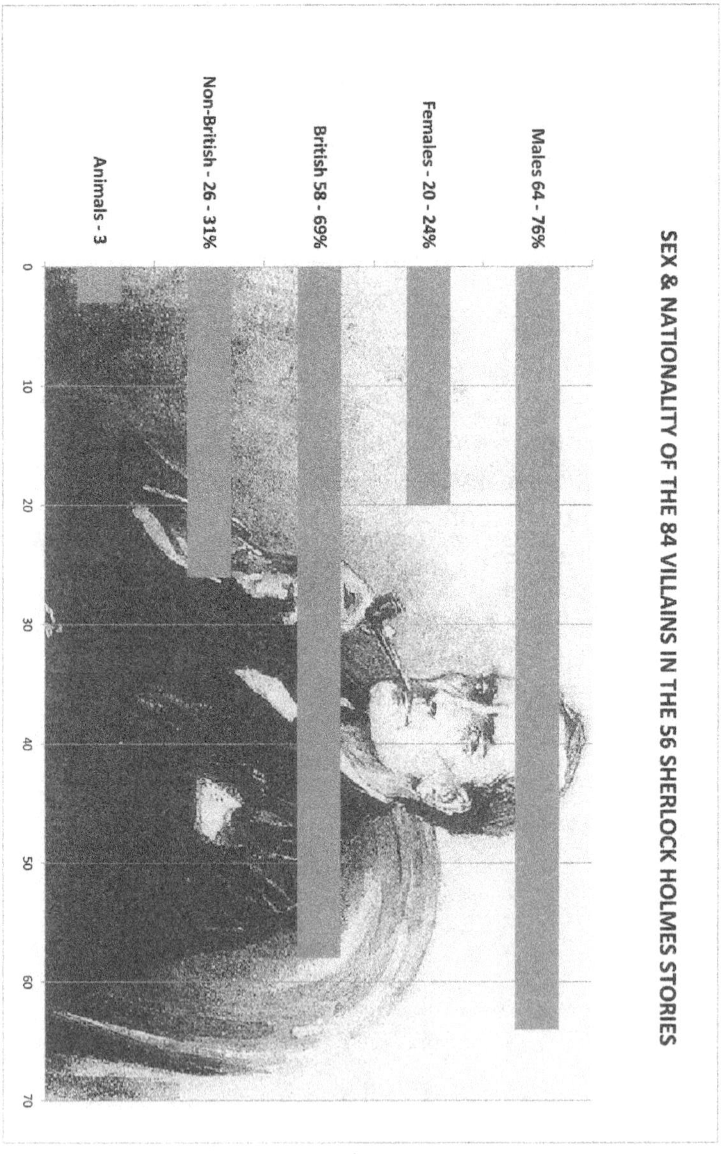
SEX & NATIONALITY OF THE 84 VILLAINS IN THE 56 SHERLOCK HOLMES STORIES
Males 64 - 76%
Females - 20 - 24%
British 58 - 69%
Non-British - 26 - 31%
Animals - 3
0
10
20
30
40
50
60
70

Villains Arrested

Holmes arrests 31 of the 84 villains (37%). He handles these villains in different ways. Of these 31 arrested, 28 (90%) are male, and only 3 are female (10%), a wide margin of males to females. The three women arrested are Kitty Winter, whose crime of vitriol throwing will be handled in the courts with mitigation; and Susan Stockdale, a member with her husband of the Spencer John gang in *The Three Gables*; and Mrs. Lexington, the housekeeper in *The Norwood Builder,* who is complicit with Oldacre in the conspiracy to murder John McFarlane. The fact that so few women in the stories are arrested reflects the Victorian attitude that women are the weaker sex and should be protected. Holmes lets Isadora Klein, who works with the Spencer John gang, go free. However, she does have to pay compensation to Holmes' client, Mrs. Maberley, for the privilege.

Villains Arrested – 31 - 37% of the 84 villains

Patrick Cairns (Black Peter) - Murder
Hugo Oberstein (Bruce Partington Plans) – Murder & Treason
Colonel Valentine Walter (Bruce Partington Plans) – Treason
James Browner (Cardboard Box) – Murder
Abe Slaney (Dancing Men) - Murder
Culverton Smith (Dying Detective) – Murder and Attempted murder
Colonel Sebastian Moran (Empty House) Murder and Attempted murder
Miss Kitty Winter (Illustrious Client) Vitriol throwing

Von Bork (His Last Bow) – Espionage/Treason
Count Negretto Sylvius (Mazarin Stone) – Burglary (Jewel theft)
Sam Merton (Mazarin Stone) – Burglary (Jewel theft)
Jonas Oldacre/Mr. Cornelius (Norwood Builder) – Attempted murder
Mrs. Lexington – Housekeeper (Norwood Builder) – Attempted murder
Reuben Hayes (Priory School) – Murder and Kidnapping
Gennaro Lucca (Red Circle) – Murder
John Clay /Vincent Spaulding (Red-Headed League) – Assault and Burglary (Bank robbery)
Duncan Ross (Red-Headed League) – Burglary (Bank robbery)
Alec Cunningham (Reigate Squires) – Murder
Cunningham, Sr. (Reigate Squires) – Murder
Josiah Amberley (Retired Colourman) – Murder
Sir Robert Norberton (Shoscombe Old Place) – Concealing a death
Beppo (Six Napoleons) – Murder and Theft
Bob Carruthers (Solitary Cyclist) – Fraud and Attempted murder
Jack Woodley (Solitary Cyclist) – Fraud and Affray
Williamson (Solitary Cyclist) – Fraud and Forced marriage
Beddington /Arthur Pinner & Harry Pinner (Stock-Broker's Clerk) – Burglary (Stock Robbery) and Attempted suicide
Beddington /Hall Pycroft – (Stock-Broker's Clerk) Murder and Burglary (Stock Robbery)
Steve Dixie – Spencer John gang (Three Gables) – Burglary and Murder

Barney Stockdale – Spencer John gang (Three Gables) Burglary and Murder
Susan Stockdale – Spencer John gang (Three Gables) Burglary
James Winter/'Killer' Evans/John Garrideb/ Morecroft (Three Garridebs) – Attempted murder and Fraud and Counterfeiting

Of the 31 villains Holmes sends to the law, 21 are British (68%) and 10 are Non-British (32%).

<u>British – 21 – 68%</u>
Patrick Cairns (Black Peter) - Murder
Colonel Valentine Walter (Bruce Partington Plans) – Treason
James Browner (Cardboard Box) – Murder
Colonel Sebastian Moran (Empty House) – Murder and Attempted murder
Miss Kitty Winter (Illustrious Client) Vitriol Throwing
Sam Merton (Mazarin Stone) – Burglary (Jewel theft)
Jonas Oldacre/Mr. Cornelius (Norwood Builder) – Attempted Murder
Mrs. Lexington – Housekeeper (Norwood Builder) – Attempted Murder
Reuben Hayes (Priory School) – Murder & Kidnapping
John Clay /Vincent Spaulding (Red-Headed League) – Burglary (Bank Robbery) and Assault
Duncan Ross (Red-Headed League) – Burglary (Bank Robbery)
Alec Cunningham (Reigate Squires) – Murder, Attempted murder and Burglary
Cunningham, Sr. (Reigate Squires) – Murder, Attempted murder and Burglary

Josiah Amberley (Retired Colourman) – Murder & Attempted suicide
Sir Robert Norberton (Shoscombe Old Place) – Concealing a death
Williamson (Solitary Cyclist) – Fraud & Forced Marriage
Beddington /Arthur Pinner & Harry Pinner (Stock-Broker's Clerk) – Burglary (Stock Robbery) and Attempted suicide
Beddington /Hall Pycroft – (Stock-Broker's Clerk) - Murder and Burglary (Stock Robbery)
Steve Dixie – Spencer John gang (Three Gables) – Burglary & Murder
Barney Stockdale – Spencer John gang (Three Gables) Burglary & Murder
Susan Stockdale – (Three Gables) Burglary

<u>Non-British Other – 10 – 32%</u>
Hugo Oberstein (Bruce Partington Plans) – Murder and Treason
Abe Slaney (Dancing Men) - Murder
Culverton Smith (Dying Detective) – Murder and Attempted Murder
Von Bork (His Last Bow) – Espionage/Treason
Count Negretto Sylvius (Mazarin Stone) – Burglary (Jewel Theft)
Gennaro Lucca (Red Circle) – Murder
Beppo (Six Napoleons) – Murder and Theft
Bob Carruthers (Solitary Cyclist) – Fraud and Attempted Murder
Jack Woodley (Solitary Cyclist) – Fraud (Forced Marriage) and Affray

James Winter/'Killer' Evans/John Garrideb/ Morecroft (Three Garridebs) – Fraud, Counterfeiting, and Attempted Murder

Villains Holmes sets free

Compared to the 31 villains arrested, Holmes lets 25 villains go free – 15 men (60%); 1 male child (4%); and 9 women (36%). Females rate statistically high here, considering there are a total of only 20 female villains. Out of the 84 villains in the Canon, the 25 he sets free or doesn't pursue for criminal charges account for 30%.

Holmes decides to let them go free for a variety of reasons. First and foremost, to Holmes, the wrongdoer must confess. Confession is good for the soul. He expects confession and repentance, and he gets it from most of them. He does make some exceptions to this requirement. Jack Croker in *The Abbey Grange* is a killer who isn't sorry he murdered Sir Eustace Brackenstall, and Lady Brackenstall and her maid withhold evidence and refuse to admit their part in the crime. However, Holmes heavily weighs factors including the characters of the criminals and the victims in his decision to let a wrongdoer go free. Holmes also considers letting someone go free when it is in the best interest of the government if the public does not hear about a crime. Sometimes he lets them go to keep the secrets of a family or a worthy individual. Holmes doesn't like Joseph Harrison in *The Naval Treaty* or James Wilder in *The Priory School*, but he lets them both go – Harrison to keep the government's secrets, and Wilder to keep the family secrets of the Duke of Holdernesse. He lets

Gilchrist go in *The Three Students* and gives him a second chance because his crime was not premeditated.

Wrongdoers Holmes sets free – 25 – 30% of 84 total wrongdoers

Captain Jack Croker (Abbey Grange) - British
Lady Brackenstall (Abbey Grange) – Australian
Theresa Wright (Abbey Grange) - Australian
James Ryder, (Blue Carbuncle) – British
John Turner (Boscombe Valley Mystery) – Australian
Sarah Cushing (Cardboard Box) – Brain fever. Holmes does not pursue - British
Noblewoman Unnamed – (Charles Augustus Milverton) - British
Jephro Rucastle (Copper Beeches) – Mauled by dog - British
Professor Presbury (Creeping Man) – Mauled by dog - British
Henry Wood (Crooked Man) – British
Dr. Leon Sterndale (Devil's Foot) - British
James Windibank/Hosmer Angel (Case of Identity) – British
Mrs. Windibank (Case of Identity) - British
Baron Gruner (Illustrious Client) – Austrian
Joseph Harrison (Naval Treaty) - British
Hatty Doran/Mrs. Francis H. Moulton (Noble Bachelor)- American
James Wilder (Priory School) –British
Duke of Holdernesse (Priory School) – British
Lady Hilda Trelawney Hope (Second Stain) –British
Silas Brown (Silver Blaze) – Theft –British
Jack 'Jacky' Ferguson (Sussex Vampire) – British

Isadora Klein (Three Gables) – Spanish
Gilchrist (Three Students) – British
Neville St. Clair /Hugh Boone (Twisted Lip) - British
Mrs. Eugenia Ronder (Veiled Lodger) – British

Of these 25 set free, 19 or 76% are British and 6 or 24% are Non-British (3 Australians, 1 American, 1 Austrian, and 1 Spanish).

Escapees

In 11 of the 56 cases (20%), there are 18 villains who flee and escape both Holmes and the law. This includes 12 men (67% of the 18) and 6 women (33%). These 18 escapees account for 21% of the 84 villains in the Canon. The 12 men who escape amount to 14% of the 84 human villains, and the 6 women constitute 7%. Some do not live long to enjoy their singular achievement of escaping the great detective. We have not included the unnamed noblewoman in *Charles Augustus Milverton* in this category, but rather in the category of Villains Holmes sets free, since he knows her identity and ultimately decides her fate by refusing the case.

Villains who Escape – 18 – 21% of 84 total villains

BERY - Burnwell –Never heard from
BERY - Mary Holder – Never heard from
ENGR- Col. Stark –Never heard from
ENGR - Dr. Becher - Never heard from
ENGR- Elsie - Never heard from
FIVE - James Calhoun - Later shipwrecked
GLOR – Hudson –Never heard from again

GREE – Harold Latimer –Later murdered (Stabbed)
GREE - Wilson Kemp – Later murdered (Stabbed)
LADY - Holy Peters – Never heard from again
LADY - Annie Fraser – Never heard from again
MUSG - Rachel Howells – Never heard from again
RESI –Biddle (Worthington Bank gang) - Later shipwrecked
RESI -Hayward (Worthington Bank gang) – Later shipwrecked
RESI - Moffat (Worthington Bank gang)- Later Shipwrecked
SCAN - Irene Adler - Fled to the Continent
SECO - Mme. Fournaye - Brain Fever
WIST -Don Juan Murillo – Later murdered (method unknown)

8 of these 11 cases (73%) are early published cases between 1891 and 1893. One case (9%) is a Middle Case published in 1904. Two (18%) are later cases published between 1908 and 1927. By a wide margin, most of the escapes happen in the early cases.

Early published Cases – (1891-3) – 8 cases – 73%

Beryl Coronet – Never heard from again
Engineer's Thumb – Never heard from again
Five Orange Pips – Later die at sea
Gloria Scott – Never heard from again
Greek Interpreter –Later murdered
Musgrave Ritual – Never heard from again
Resident Patient – Never heard from again
Scandal in Bohemia – Escape to the Continent

Middle cases – 1903-4 – 1 – 9%

Second Stain – 1904 – Escape to Paris, mental breakdown

Later cases published between 1908- 1927 – 2 – 18%

Disappearance of Lady Frances Carfax – Never heard from again
Wisteria Lodge – 1908 – Later murdered

Escaped but died sometime later (subset of Escaped) – 7 of 18 – 39%

James Calhoun (Five Orange Pips) - Shipwrecked
Harold Latimer (Greek Interpreter) – Murdered - Stabbed
Wilson Kemp (Greek Interpreter)- Murdered - Stabbed
Biddle - Worthington Bank gang -(Resident Patient) Shipwrecked
Hayward – Worthington Bank gang (Resident Patient) Shipwrecked
Moffat – Worthington Bank gang (Resident Patient) Shipwrecked
Don Juan Murillo (Wisteria Lodge) – Murdered no method mentioned

Villains Killed in the course of the story – 8 –10%

Charles Augustus Milverton - Shot
Mortimer Tregennis (Devil's Foot) - Poisoned
Professor James Moriarty (Final Problem) – Fell to death

Richard Brunton (Musgrave Ritual) - Suffocated
Giuseppe Gorgiano (Red Circle) - Stabbed
Henri Fournaye (Second Stain) - Shot
John Straker (Silver Blaze) – Trampled by horse
Grimesby Roylott (Speckled Band) - Snakebite

Villains who Die in the course of the story /natural death – 1 – 1%

John Turner/Black Jack of Ballarat (Boscombe Valley Mystery)

Villains who Die in the story/ suicide – 2 – 2%

Anna 'Coram' (Golden Pince-Nez) - Poison
Maria Pinto Gibson (Thor Bridge) - Shot

Villains who Attempt Suicide in the story – 3 – 4%

Josiah Amberley (Retired Colourman) poison – white pellet
Beddington /Arthur Pinner & Harry Pinner (Stock-Broker's Clerk) – Theft/Stock Robbery - Hanging
Mrs. Eugenia Ronder (Veiled Lodger) - Poison

Arrested and Die sometime later - 1

Colonel Valentine Walter (Bruce Partington Plans) – Died in prison

Villains Injured in the story – 7 – 9%

In 7 of the stories, Holmes watches as 7 villains end up in purgatory – somewhere between heaven and hell. These 7 individuals are changed physically and emotionally and cannot go back to what they were. Three have brain fever, and we never know whether they recover (Sarah Cushing, Rachel Howells and Mme. Fournaye). One is shot (Woodley); and one has vitriol thrown at him (Baron Gruner). Two are badly mauled by their own pet dogs – Rucastle who was a true villain, and Professor Presbury who was not a criminal but who broke the laws of nature, and Holmes felt he should have known better.

Sarah Cushing (Cardboard Box) – Brain Fever – Never prosecuted
Jephro Rucastle (Copper Beeches)– Mauled by Dog – Never prosecuted
Professor Presbury (Creeping Man)–Mauled by Dog– Never prosecuted
Baron Gruner (Illustrious Client) – Vitriol attack – Never prosecuted
Rachel Howells (Musgrave Ritual) – Brain Fever - escaped
Madame Fournaye (Second Stain) – Brain Fever - escaped
Jack Woodley (Solitary Cyclist) – Gun shot – sent to the law

<u>Summary</u>

In summary, the 84 villains in the 56 stories have these outcomes:

Arrested	-	31	-	37%
Holmes sets free	-	25	-	30%
Escape	-	18	-	21%
Killed in story	-	8	-	10%
Die by Suicide	-	2		2%

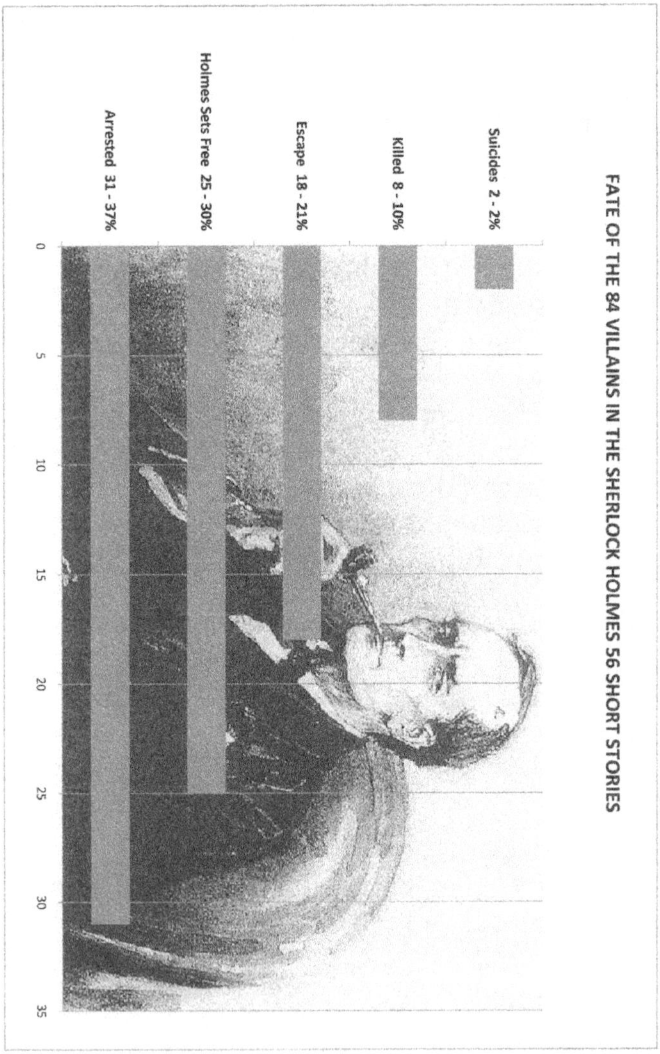
FATE OF THE 84 VILLAINS IN THE SHERLOCK HOLMES 56 SHORT STORIES
Suicides 2 - 2%
Killed 8 - 10%
Escape 18 - 21%
Holmes Sets Free 25 - 30%
Arrested 31 - 37%
0
5
10
15
20
25
30
35

Villains who work Alone

35 villains commit their misdeeds without confederates. I have excluded non-human villains, such as the Lion's Mane. Villains work alone in 30 of the stories compared to the 25 stories in which they have accomplices.

Villains who work alone - 35– 42% of 84 villains - in 30 stories (54% of the stories)

Patrick Cairns (Black Peter)
James Ryder (Blue Carbuncle)
John Turner/Black Jack of Ballarat (Boscombe Valley Mystery)
Charles Augustus Milverton
Noblewoman Unnamed – (Charles Augustus Milverton)
Jephro Rucastle (Copper Beeches)
Professor Presbury (Creeping Man)
Henry Wood (Crooked Man)
Abe Slaney (Dancing Men)
Mortimer Tregennis (Devil's Foot)
Dr. Leon Sterndale (Devil's Foot)
Culverton Smith (Dying Detective)
Hudson (Gloria Scott)
Anna 'Coram' (Golden Pince-Nez)
Baron Adelbert Gruner (Illustrious Client)
Miss Kitty Winter (Illustrious Client)
Rachel Howells (Musgrave Ritual)
Joseph Harrison (Naval Treaty)
Hatty Doran (Noble Bachelor)
Giuseppe Gorgiano (Red Circle)
Gennaro Lucca (Red Circle)

Josiah Amberley (Retired Colourman)
Miss Irene Adler (Scandal in Bohemia)
Lady Hilda Trelawney Hope (Second Stain)
Henri Fournaye (Second Stain) - Blackmail
Madame Fournaye (Second Stain)
Sir Robert Norberton (Shoscombe Old Place)
John Straker (Silver Blaze)
Silas Brown (Silver Blaze)
Dr. Grimesby Roylott (Speckled Band)
Jack 'Jacky' Ferguson (Sussex Vampire)
Maria Pinto Gibson (Thor Bridge)
James Winter/'Killer' Evans/John Garrideb/ Morecroft (Three Garridebs)
Gilchrist (Three Students)
Neville St. Clair / Hugh Boone (Man with the Twisted Lip)

Villains who work with Accomplices

49 villains do not commit their crime alone but work with one or more accomplices. This amounts to 14 more than the 25 villains who work alone, or 58% of the 84 villains in the 56 stories. These 49 villains appear in 25 of the stories (45% of the 56). Some of these 49 wrongdoers work together in the same story, such as in *The Abbey Grange, The Bruce Partington Plans, The Cardboard Box, The Engineer's Thumb, The Greek Interpreter, A Case of Identity, Lady Frances Carfax, The Mazarin Stone, The Norwood Builder, The Priory School, The Red-Headed League, The Reigate Squires, The Resident Patient, The Solitary Cyclist, The Stock-Broker's Clerk*, and *The Three Gables*. In other stories, the accessories to a crime are not counted as criminals, such as in The

Final Problem where there is a gang involved; and in *The Five Orange Pips,* where Captain Calhoun has two American mates, but they are not named; as well as in *The Six Napoleons* where Beppo has an accomplice but murders him; and in *The Veiled Lodger,* where her accomplice in the crime, Leonardo, is dead and doesn't appear in the story.

In some cases there may be only one or two accomplices, as in *The Abbey Grange, The Engineer's Thumb, A Case of Identity, The Norwood Builder, The Priory School, The Reigate Squires* and *The Solitary Cyclist.* In others, a gang may be involved, such as in *The Boscombe Valley Mystery,* John Turner was a member of the Ballarat Gang in Australia. In T*he Golden Pince-Nez,* the Brotherhood, a gang of Russian nihilists, is the root cause for betrayal. In *The Dancing Men,* Abe Slaney belonged to a gang of seven in Chicago where Elsie's father was the boss. And in other stories there are even more formidable gangs, including the Ku Klux Klan, the Mafia, the Spencer John gang, the Worthington Bank gang, and the Moriarty and Moran gang. Holmes understood, more than Scotland Yard, the vast extent of the large-scale organized crime empire run by Professor Moriarty. Holmes kept records of the gang's activities and tried to intervene, and, according to Moriarty, Holmes was very successful at attacking and virtually breaking Moriarty's criminal apparatus.

Holmes and Watson must match wits with a large number of off-scene players, making their successes even more remarkable. Holmes does have what he refers to in *The Sussex Vampire* as his "Agency," a "small but very efficient organization," as he describes it in *Lady Frances Carfax.* With the

Agency, he has access to the Baker Street Irregulars, various dog trackers, and an array of interesting and unusual underground accomplices who frequently assist him, including Shinwell Johnson, an agent Holmes uses in the London criminal underworld; Mercer, his general utility man; Langdale Pike, his reference for social scandal; and Mr. Barker, his hated rival upon the Surrey shore who wears "gray-tinted glasses and a large Masonic pin projecting from his tie." He even occasionally uses Billy the Page Boy and the boy in buttons. Watson tells us in *Black Peter* that Holmes "had at least five small refuges in different parts of London, in which he was able to change his personality." Holmes also makes frequent use of the telegraph, and he never hesitates to use his extensive research files, a library, Scotland Yard's files, or the Agony Column. He is also a master at uncovering information from housemaids, landscapers, disgruntled, discharged employees, and patrons of the local pubs.

<u>Villains who work w/ accomplices</u> – 49 – 58% of 84 wrongdoers

Captain Jack Croker (Abbey Grange)
Lady Brackenstall (Abbey Grange)
Theresa Wright (Abbey Grange)
Miss Mary Holder (Beryl Coronet)
Sir George Burnwell (Beryl Coronet)
Hugo Oberstein (Bruce Partington Plans)
Colonel Valentine Walter (Bruce Partington Plans)
James Browner (Cardboard Box) – Murder
Miss Sarah Cushing (Cardboard Box)
Colonel Sebastian Moran (Empty House)

Colonel Lysander Stark /Fritz (Engineer's Thumb)
Mr. Ferguson / Dr. Becher (Engineer's Thumb)
Elsie (Engineer's Thumb)
James Calhoun (Five Orange Pips)
Professor James Moriarty (Final Problem)
Harold Latimer (Greek Interpreter)
Wilson Kemp (Greek Interpreter)
James Windibank/Hosmer Angel (A Case of Identity)
Mrs. Windibank (A Case of Identity)
Henry 'Holy' Peters (Lady Frances Carfax)
Annie Fraser (Lady Frances Carfax) – Attempted Murder and Fraud
Von Bork (His Last Bow)
Count Negretto Sylvius (Mazarin Stone) – Jewel Theft
Sam Merton (Mazarin Stone)
Richard Brunton (Musgrave Ritual)
Jonas Oldacre (Norwood Builder)
Mrs. Lexington (Norwood Builder)
Reuben Hayes (Priory School) – Murder and Kidnapping
James Wilder (Priory School) – Kidnapping
Duke of Holdernesse (Priory School) – Condoning a felony and Aiding in the escape of a felon
John Clay /Vincent Spaulding (Red-Headed League) – Burglary (Bank Robbery) and Assault
Duncan Ross (Red-Headed League) Burglary (Bank Robbery)
Alec Cunningham (Reigate Squires) – Murder, Burglary & Attempted murder
Cunningham, Sr. (Reigate Squires) – Murder, Burglary and Attempted murder
Biddle - Worthington Bank gang -(Resident Patient)
Hayward – Worthington Bank gang (Resident Patient)
Moffat – Worthington Bank gang (Resident Patient)

Beppo (Six Napoleons) Burglary and Murder and Jewel Theft
Bob Carruthers (Solitary Cyclist) – Fraud and Attempted Murder
Jack Woodley (Solitary Cyclist) – Fraud, False Marriage and Affray
Williamson (Solitary Cyclist) – Fraud and False Marriage
Beddington /Arthur Pinner & Harry Pinner (Stock-Broker's Clerk) – Burglary/Stock Robbery
Beddington /Hall Pycroft) – Murder and Burglary
Isadora Klein (Three Gables) – Burglary and Accessory to Murder
Steve Dixie – Spencer John gang (Three Gables) – Burglary
Barney Stockdale – Spencer John gang (Three Gables) – Burglary
Susan Stockdale – Spencer John gang (Three Gables) - Burglary
Mrs. Eugenia Ronder (Veiled Lodger) - Murder
Don Juan Murillo (Wisteria Lodge) - Murder

Villains who threaten or attack Holmes/Watson

Holmes and or Watson sustain attacks by 18 villains, and these attacks occur in 16 or 29% of the 56 stories. There are additional attacks on them in the course of the stories, but those attacks are made by persons other than the villains, such as in *The Beryl Coronet* when a gem dealer tries to attack Holmes, and Holmes claps a pistol to his head; or when Phillip Green mistakenly attacks Watson in *Lady Frances Carfax* and Holmes saves him. Although Jonas Oldacre does not physically attack Holmes, he is included in this *list (The Norwood Builder*) because of his open and hostile threat to get even with Holmes. Milverton never physically attacks Holmes, but he is included because he threatens Holmes with the gun he has in his pocket during his visit to 221B.

<u>Villains who threaten or attack Holmes /Watson – 18 – 21% of the 84 villains</u>

Patrick Cairns (Black Peter)
Sir George Burnwell (Beryl Coronet)
Jephro Rucastle (Copper Beeches)
Milverton (Charles Augustus Milverton)
Culverton Smith (Dying Detective)
Colonel Moran & gang (Empty House)
Professor Moriarty & gang (Final Problem)
Baron Adelbert Gruner (Illustrious Client)
Joseph Harrison (Naval Treaty)
Jonas Oldacre (Norwood Builder)
John Clay /Vincent Spaulding (Red-Headed League)
Alec Cunningham (Reigate Squires)
Old Mr. Cunningham (Reigate Squires)
Williamson (Solitary Cyclist)
Dr. Grimsby Roylott (Speckled Band)
James Winter/'Killer' Evans/John Garrideb/ Morecroft (Three Garridebs)
Barney Stockdale - Spencer John gang (Three Gables)
Steve Dixie, the Bruiser (Three Gables)

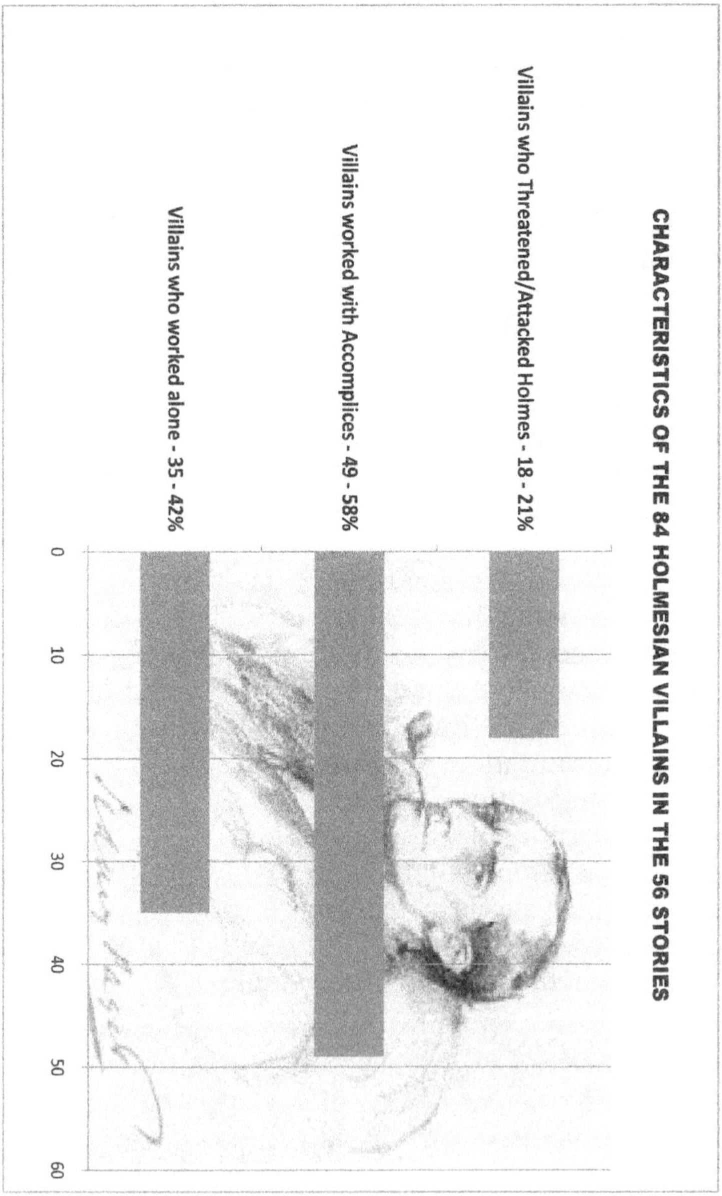
CHARACTERISTICS OF THE 84 HOLMESIAN VILLAINS IN THE 56 STORIES
Villains who Threatened/Attacked Holmes - 18 - 21%
Villains worked with Accomplices - 49 - 58%
Villains who worked alone - 35 - 42%
0
10
20
30
40
50
60

Villains with titles/appellations

Of the 84 villains, Holmes deals with 20 who have titles (24%). There are 17 men and 3 women with titles, including a Duke, 2 Ladies; a noblewoman of uncertain rank; 2 Sirs (a title before the given name of a knight or baronet); 2 squires; an aristocrat whose Grandfather is a Royal Duke; an Austrian Baron; an Italian Count; 3 Colonels; a Captain; 3 Dr.'s and 2 Professors. Of these, 17 are British (85%) and only 3 are non-British (15%).

British – Men - 14
Duke of Holdernesse (Priory School) – Condoning a felony and Aiding in the escape of a criminal- Let go by Holmes
Sir Robert Norberton (Shoscombe Old Place) – Charged w/minor offense
Sir George Burnwell (Beryl Coronet) – Escapes (Jewel Theft)
Squire Alec Cunningham (Reigate Squires) – Arrested for Murder
Squire Cunningham, Sr. (Reigate Squires) - Arrested for Murder
John Clay /Vincent Spaulding (Red-Headed League) – Aristocratic family of Nobility (grandfather was a Royal Duke) – Arrested for Bank Robbery
Colonel Sebastian Moran (Empty House) – Arrested for Murder
Colonel Valentine Walter (Bruce Partington Plans) – Arrested-Treason/Espionage
Captain Jack Croker (Abbey Grange) – Let go by Holmes (Murder)

Dr. Grimesby Roylott (Speckled Band) – Killed by snake (Murder)
Dr. Leon Sterndale (Devil's Foot) – Let go by Holmes (Murder)
Dr. Becher /Mr. Ferguson (Engineer's Thumb) – Escapes (Counterfeiting, Murder)
Professor James Moriarty (Final Problem) – Murder - Killed by Holmes
Professor Presbury (Creeping Man) – Disturbing the Peace – Maimed

Women – British - 3
Lady Brackenstall (The Abbey Grange) Let go (Accessory to murder and Withholding evidence)
Lady Hilda Trelawney Hope (Second Stain) Let go by Holmes (Burglary, Theft & Possible Treason)
Noblewoman unnamed (Charles Augustus Milverton) – Escapes (Murder)

Foreign – Non-British - 3
Colonel Lysander Stark/Fritz (Engineer's Thumb) – Escapes (Counterfeiting & Murder)
Count Negretto Sylvius (Mazarin Stone) – Arrested (Jewel Theft)
Baron Adelbert Gruner (Illustrious Client) – Maimed (Breach of Unwritten Laws)

These 20 criminals commit amongst themselves 26 crimes out of the 104 in the Canon (25%). In four cases, multiple crimes occur. In *The Abbey Grange,* Lady Brackenstall is an Accessory to murder and withholds evidence. In *The Engineer's Thumb*, both murder and counterfeiting are committed. In *The Priory School*, the Duke condones a felony and aids in the escape of a felon; and in *The Second Stain*, Lady Hope commits burglary, theft and treason. These 20 criminals appear in 17 of the 56 stories (30%).

<u>Crimes Committed by 20 Persons w/appellations - 26</u>

Accessory to Murder – 1 – 4%
Lady Brackenstall (The Abbey Grange)

Aiding in the escape of a felon – 1 – 4%
Lord Holdernesse (The Priory School)

Assault – 1 – 4%
Baron Gruner (The Illustrious Client)

Burglary – 2 – 7%
John Clay /Vincent Spaulding (The Red-Headed League)
Lady Hope (The Second Stain)

Concealing a Death (minor offense)– 1 -4%
Sir Robert Norberton (Shoscombe Old Place)

Condoning a Felony – 1 – 4%
Lord Holdernesse (The Priory School)

Counterfeiting – 1 – 4%
Dr. Becher/Mr. Ferguson (Engineer's Thumb)

Disturbing the Peace - 1 - 4%
Professor Presbury (The Creeping Man)

Murder & Attempted Murder – 11 – 42%

Captain Jack Croker (The Abbey Grange)
Noblewoman unnamed (Charles Augustus Milverton)
Dr. Leon Sterndale (The Devil's Foot)
Colonel Moran (The Empty House)
Colonel Lysander Stark/Fritz (The Engineer's Thumb)
Dr. Becher/Mr. Ferguson (The Engineer's Thumb)
Professor James Moriarty (The Final Problem)
Baron Gruner (The Illustrious Client)
Squire Alec Cunningham (The Reigate Squires)
Squire Cunningham, Sr. (The Reigate Squires)
Dr. Grimesby Roylott (The Speckled Band)

Theft – 3 – 12%

Sir George Burnwell (The Beryl Coronet)
Count Negretto Sylvius (The Mazarin Stone)
Lady Hilda Trelawney Hope (The Second Stain)

Treason – 2 - 7%

Colonel Valentine Walter (The Bruce Partington Plans)
Lady Hilda Trelawney Hope (The Second Stain)

Withholding Evidence – 1 – 4%

Lady Brackenstall (The Abbey Grange)

Of the 20, 7 are arrested; 4 escape; 2 die; 2 are maimed; and 5 Holmes lets go with no charges.

Arrested – 7 – 35%

Sir Robert Norberton – Shoscombe Old Place
Alec Cunningham – The Reigate Squires
Old Mr. Cunningham – The Reigate Squires
John Clay/Vincent Spaulding – The Red–Headed League
Colonel Moran – The Empty House
Colonel Valentine Walter – The Bruce Partington Plans
Count Negretto Sylvius – The Mazarin Stone

Escape – 4 – 20%

Sir George Burnwell – The Beryl Coronet
Colonel Lysander Stark – The Engineer's Thumb
Dr. Becher/Mr. Ferguson – The Engineer's Thumb
Noblewoman unnamed – Charles Augustus Milverton

Die – 2 – 10%

Professor Moriarty – The Final Problem
Dr. Grimesby Roylott – The Speckled Band

Maimed –2 – 10%

Professor Presbury – The Creeping Man
Baron Gruner – The Illustrious Client

Not Charged – 5 – 25%

Captain Jack Croker –The Abbey Grange
Lady Brackenstall – The Abbey Grange
Dr. Leon Sterndale – The Devil's Foot
Duke of Holdernesse – The Priory School
Lady Hilda Hope –The Second Stain

The 4 who successfully escape are Sir George Burnwell in *The Beryl Coronet*, the unnamed Noblewoman who shoots Milverton, and both Colonel Lysander Stark and Dr. Becher in *The Engineers Thumb*. The percentage of villains with titles who escape (20%) is almost the same as the percentage of all villains who escape (21%) out of a total of 84 villains. 5 of the 20 or 25% are never charged, and Holmes deals lightly with Sir Robert Norberton in *Shoscombe Old Place* because Sir Robert didn't commit any serious crime. If we add the 4 escapees and the 5 Never Charged, it amounts to 9 out of 20 wrongdoers with appellations or 45% who don't face legal justice. This figure is only slightly lower than the 43 villains or 51% of the total 84 villains who escape or are let go by Holmes. So it seems that Holmes does appear to give these villains with appellations a little extra leeway because of their status.

Others of these involved, such as the two Squires in *The Reigate Squires,* act bad all the way around. Not only do they burgle their neighbor's home to steal documents to commit fraud, but they also murder their coachman and, perhaps even worse, they attempt to strangle Sherlock Holmes. They are both summarily arrested for murder. John Clay alias Vincent Spaulding whose grandfather is a Duke also gets harsh treatment from Holmes, especially because Clay draws a revolver on Sherlock. Colonel Moran is arrested for murder, but Colonel Lysander Stark escapes. Colonel Valentine Walter is arrested and dies in prison, and Captain Croker and Lady Brackenstall are let go by Holmes on the grounds of self-defense, although Croker must serve a year of self-enforced probation. Dr. Roylott of Stoke Moran, the last survivor of what was a wealthy but dissolute and violent tempered aristocratic Anglo-Saxon family of Surrey, is himself killed by his own instrument of murder, his pet snake. Baron Gruner is maimed by vitriol, and Professor Presbury is maimed by his dog.

Motives

The love triangle is a common motive for crime in the Canon, and it figures in at least 25 cases to one degree or another (45% of the 56 stories) as either the motive for the crime or as the reason someone might be suspected of a crime. It is the specific motive in 15 murder and attempted murder cases:

The Abbey Grange
The Boscombe Valley Mystery
The Cardboard Box
The Crooked Man
The Dancing Men
The Golden Pince-Nez
The Greek Interpreter
The Musgrave Ritual
The Norwood Builder
The Retired Colourman
The Second Stain
The Red Circle
Thor Bridge
The Three Gables
The Veiled Lodger

Here are 10 other cases involving love triangles:

The Beryl Coronet

The Creeping Man
The Copper Beeches
A Case of Identity
The Illustrious Client
The Lion's Mane
The Noble Bachelor
A Scandal in Bohemia
The Solitary Cyclist
The Yellow Face

Stories with Multiple Villains

23 of the 56 stories (41%) have multiple wrongdoers (not necessarily acting together).

16 stories have 2 villains – 28% of the 56

The Beryl Coronet (Mary Holder and her lover, Sir George Burnwell)
The Bruce Partington Plans (Colonel Walter and Hugo Oberstein)
The Cardboard Box (James Browner and Sarah Cushing)
Charles Augustus Milverton (Milverton & Noblewoman unnamed)
The Devil's Foot (Mortimer Tregennis and Dr. Leon Sterndale)
The Greek Interpreter (Harold Latimer and Wilson Kemp)
A Case of Identity (James Windibank and Mrs. Windibank)
The Illustrious Client (Baron Gruner and former mistress Kitty Winter)
Lady Frances Carfax (Henry 'Holy' Peters and Annie Fraser)

The Mazarin Stone (Count Sylvius and Sam Merton)
The Musgrave Ritual (Brunton the Butler and Rachel Howells the housemaid)
The Norwood Builder (Jonas Oldacre and Mrs. Lexington the housekeeper)
The Red-Headed League (John Clay and Duncan Ross)
The Reigate Squires (Cunningham, Sr. and Alec Cunningham)
Silver Blaze (John Straker and Silas Brown)
The Stock-Broker's Clerk (the 2 Beddington brothers)

6 stories have three villains – 11% of the 56 stories

The Abbey Grange (Capt. Croker, Lady Brackenwell and Theresa Wright
The Engineer's Thumb (Col. Lysander Stark, Dr. Becher and Elsie)
The Priory School (James Wilder, Reuben Hayes and Lord Holderness)
The Resident Patient (Worthington Bank gang - Biddle, Hayward and Moffat)
The Second Stain (Lady Hope, Mme. Fournaye and Lucas/ Fournaye)
The Solitary Cyclist (Carruthers, Woodley & Williamson)

1 story has 4 villains – 2% of the 56 stories

The Three Gables (Isadora Klein, Barney Stockdale, Susan Stockdale, and Steve Dixie –the Spencer John Gang)

The 23 Stories with multiple villains were published as follows:

Early (1891–1893) – 11 - 48%

- The Beryl Coronet – 1892
- The Cardboard Box - 1893
- The Engineer's Thumb - 1892
- The Greek Interpreter – 1893
- A Case of Identity - 1891
- The Musgrave Ritual - 1893
- The Red-Headed League – 1891
- The Reigate Squires - 1893
- The Resident Patient - 1893
- Silver Blaze - 1892
- The Stock-broker's Clerk - 1893

Middle (1903–1911) – 9 – 39%

- The Abbey Grange - 1904
- The Bruce Partington Plans - 1908
- Charles Augustus Milverton - 1904
- The Devil's Foot – 1910
- Lady Frances Carfax - 1911
- The Norwood Builder - 1903
- The Priory School - 1904
- The Second Stain - 1904
- The Solitary Cyclist – 1903

Later (1921-1926) – 3 – 13%

- The Illustrious Client - 1924
- The Mazarin Stone - 1921
- The Three Gables – 1926

Chapter 12

Victims

To Sherlock Holmes, the character of the victim is one important clue in evaluating a crime. In *The Abbey Grange*, even though Captain Croker admits he killed Sir Eustace Brackenstall, Holmes gives Croker moral credit because of Sir Eustace's stained character. Not only does Sir Eustace abuse his wife, he also abuses her dog. Similarly in *The Adventure of the Second Stain,* Holmes gives Lady Hilda Trelawney Hope some moral credit not only because the crime she commits was not planned, but also because the victim, her husband, has an impeccable character and represents the government. In *Black Peter*, even though the victim, Peter Carey, is a complete scoundrel and hated by almost everyone for his cruelty, Holmes brings his killer, Patrick Cairns, to the law. Holmes uses many different touchstones in his evaluations, but he justifies his judgments in his assessments of the overall characters of both villains and victims.

Physical Appearance of Victims

Holmes often regards the victims as accountable in their own way, and the physical descriptions of the victims categorize them, like the villains, as either good or evil. When Holmes decides that a crime can be forgiven, he often paints the victim of the crime as being killed for a good reason. If the victim is culpable, the reader gets clues from the many negative adjectives that are used in the descriptions.

One example is in *The Veiled Lodger,* in which Eugenia Ronder and Leonardo, her lover, murder her husband. Eugenia gives Holmes and Watson two photographs – tangible proof of the different physical appearances of her husband and her lover, and she says, "Those two pictures will help you, gentlemen, to understand the story." Her husband, says Watson, has "a dreadful face like a wild pig or a wild boar" with a "vile mouth champing and foaming in its rage ..." with "small, vicious eyes darting pure malignancy as they looked forth upon the world. Ruffian, bully, beast it was all written on that heavy-jowled face." Watson then describes Leonardo in completely different terms with no negative adjectives as "a professional acrobat, a man of magnificent physique, taken with his huge arms folded across his swollen chest and a smile breaking from under his heavy moustache – the self-satisfied smile of the man of many conquests." Eugenia tells Holmes, "My husband was not fit to live. We planned that he should die." Even though she confesses this was a pre-meditated crime, Holmes believes that the victim – her husband – contributed to his own death, and he also knows she is dying, so he lets Eugenia go free and discourages her from ending her own life prematurely.

In other stories, this difference between murderer and victim is sometimes less obvious For example, in *The Devil's Foot*, Dr. Leon Sterndale, one murderer, is described as having a huge body with a "craggy and deeply seamed face with fierce eyes and hawk-like nose." Compare this to the description of the other murderer, Mortimer Tregennis, who has "a pale drawn face," with "pale lips" that quivered and "dark eyes" with an anxious gaze." Sterndale's description is consistent with other physical descriptions of true villains in the stories, while the description of Tregennis is closer to that of a victim than a murderer. Yet in this story, when Sterndale murders Mortimer Tregennis, Holmes tacitly approves the revenge killing and lets Sterndale go free. Holmes never believes Tregennis, but he does believe Sterndale.

In *Charles Augustus Milverton,* the unnamed noblewoman who empties her gun into Milverton is described as "a tall, slim, dark woman," having "a dark, handsome, clear-cut face -- a face with a curved nose, strong, dark eyebrows shading hard, glittering eyes, and a straight, thin-lipped mouth set in a dangerous smile." We feel sympathy for her because we've been privy to Milverton's snarky blackmail operations, and we can see ourselves in the trapped position of the victims. Holmes says Milverton is "as cunning as the Evil one," and he can't be brought to the law. He's "the worst man in London, and I would ask you how could one compare the ruffian, who in hot blood bludgeons his mate, with this man, who methodically and at his leisure tortures the soul and wrings the nerves in order to add to his already swollen money-bags?" She confronts Milverton as "the woman whose life you have ruined." We, like Holmes, despise the man and silently cheer when she riddles his body with bullets and then grinds her heel into his face. We believe her when she says she is going to stop him from ruining any other lives and going to "free the world of a poisonous thing." Even though Holmes later identifies the noblewoman, he withholds this information from the police. And we are glad he does. This is definitely a murder that the victim brought on himself.

James Windibank in *A Case of Identity* is a singular villain in many ways. Instead of being described with universally negative adjectives, he's portrayed as somewhat non-descript, "a sturdy, middle-sized fellow, some thirty years of age, clean-shaven, and sallow-skinned, with a bland, insinuating manner, and a pair of wonderfully sharp and penetrating grey eyes." It's the grey eyes that provide the clue that James Windibank may be more bad than good. Indeed we find he is a liar and a con man who assumes a fake identity and courts his own step-daughter to isolate her from other suitors so he can control her money. Holmes uncovers Windibank's duplicity, but then fails to reveal it to the step-daughter. Why? Windibank does not confess or show remorse, things other villains in the Canon do to get Holmes' forgiveness. And Holmes doesn't forgive Windibank; instead he chases him out of 221B. And it is difficult to believe that Windibank and his wife - who is complicit in their scheme - will discontinue this con game.

There are some clues in this case that support Holmes' dismissive treatment of his client Mary Sutherland, the step-daughter. She is described very differently from other female victims in the stories. Mary is "a large woman" who wears "a heavy fur boa and a large curling red feather in a broad-brimmed hat...tilted in a coquettish Duchess of Devonshire fashion over her ear." Our first impression of her is heavy and broad and large. When we contrast this large, heavy, broad figure wearing an outrageous red feather and boa to our mental picture of the exquisitely dainty and fashionable Duchess of Devonshire, Mary emerges like a comic figure in a Regency play. As her description continues, we get an idea of her character. "From under this great panoply she peeped up in a nervous, hesitating fashion at our windows, while her body oscillated backward and forward, and her fingers fidgeted with her glove buttons. Suddenly, with a plunge, as of the swimmer who leaves the bank, she hurried across the road." We don't picture Mary as a charming young woman who needs help, but rather we see her as a bulky, overdressed, silly figure who is nervous, hesitant and fidgety. She's a looming, "full-sailed merchant-man" launching herself ungainly into 221B - certainly not the attractive and sympathetic figure of a stereotypical Victorian lady in distress. When Holmes asks her leading questions, she is thick-headed and unable to fathom his inferences. Holmes depicts her as a stupid, trusting woman with a "preposterous hat and ...vacuous face," who lacks insight into her situation. He immediately tumbles to the facts, and the reader, like Holmes, cannot believe that Mary can be so naïve about her step-father. Holmes knows what is going on, and so do we. Holmes tells her "to let Mr. Hosmer Angel vanish from your memory, as he has done from your life." But even after Holmes repeats this advice, Mary admits, "I cannot do that. I shall be true to Hosmer. He shall find me ready when he comes back." Holmes tells Watson that Mary is delusional, and he decides not to tell her because, "If I tell her she will not believe me." This is a case in which Holmes doesn't fulfill his obligation to his client, but we're given plenty of clues to explain why he doesn't. This case resonates with us today because Holmes gives us a look at the true character of so many people who are victimized in frauds and scams. Through Mary's character, he demonstrates how much the victim's gullibility often makes them complicit in the fraud. The victim desires to actively participate in the fraud because the victim wants to believe the outcome will be what he or she expects it to be, not what is the reality.

There are two other examples of instances in which the victim plays a role in his own downfall, and each is different. One is in *The Norwood Builder* where a supposed victim - Jonas Oldacre – is described as "a little, wizened man," with "an odious face – crafty, vicious, malignant, with shifty, light-gray eyes and white lashes." With the negative adjectives and adverbs, readers immediately suspect that Oldacre is probably up to no good and that he's not a victim. Then we contrast Oldacre's description to that of the suspected murderer, John Hector McFarlane, who "was flaxen-haired and handsome, in a washed-out negative fashion, with frightened blue eyes, and a clean-shaven face, with a weak, sensitive mouth. His age may have been about twenty-seven, his dress and bearing that of a gentleman." The reader suspects that this weak, blue eyed flaxen haired handsome gentleman is not a murderer, and the mystery takes off from there. When at the end we see Oldacre captured, we know he's evil because he was described as such, and his description reflects his own bad character which led to his downfall.

Similarly in *The Three Garridebs*, the victim, Nathan Garrideb, contributes to his own undoing. His characteristics are not those of a villain. Rather he is described as elderly, stooping and somewhat blind - "very tall, loose jointed, round-backed..., gaunt and bald, some sixty-odd years of age," with "a cadaverous face, the dull dead skin of a man to whom exercise was unknown. Large round spectacles and a small projecting goat's beard (were) combined with his stooping attitude." He is a typical doddering professor –a perfect candidate for being hoodwinked. And he wants the promised five million pounds badly to fulfill his dream of a collection named after him. He goes mad when the five million pounds vanish, despite being warned that the chimera windfall was part of a scheme to dupe him. Like Mary Sutherland in *A Case of Identity*, Nathan's character – his desire to believe and participate in the scam - makes him complicit in it.

Statistical Analysis of Murder Victims

31 Victims of Murder in 29 cases

The Adventure of the Abbey Grange
The Adventure of Black Peter
The Boscombe Valley Mystery
The Bruce-Partington Plans
The Adventure of the Cardboard Box – 2 Double Murder
Charles Augustus Milverton
The Crooked Man
The Adventure of the Dancing Men
The Adventure of the Devil's Foot – Mortimer Tregennis
The Adventure of the Devil's Foot - Dr. Sterndale
The Adventure of the Dying Detective

The Adventure of the Empty House
The Five Orange Pips
The Adventure of the Golden Pince-Nez
The Greek Interpreter
The Adventure of the Illustrious Client
The Musgrave Ritual
The Adventure of the Priory School
The Adventure of the Red Circle
The Reigate Squires
The Resident Patient
The Adventure of the Retired Colourman –2 Double Murder
The Adventure of the Second Stain
The Adventure of the Six Napoleons
The Adventure of the Speckled Band
The Stock-Broker's Clerk
The Adventure of the Three Gables
The Adventure of the Veiled Lodger
The Adventure of the Wisteria Lodge

Of the 31 victims in the 29 murder cases, 26 victims are male (84%), and 5 are female (16%). Men are more than 6 times more likely to be killed in a Sherlock Holmes story than are women. This statistic dovetails with the Victorian attitudes about protecting women from violence and harm.

Male Victims of Murder – 26 – 84%

The Abbey Grange – Lord Brackenstall
Black Peter – Black Peter Carey, Retired Sea Captain
The Boscombe Valley Mystery – Charles McCarthy from Australia
The Bruce-Partington Plans - Cadogan West

The Cardboard Box – Double Murder with 1 Male victim - Alec Fairbairn
Charles Augustus Milverton – Charles Augustus Milverton
Crooked Man – James Barclay
Dancing Men – Hilton Cubitt
Devils Foot – Mortimer Tregennis
Dying Detective – Victor Savage
Empty House – Hon. Ronald Adair
Final Problem – Professor Moriarty
Five Orange Pips – John Openshaw
Golden Pince-Nez – Willoughby Smith
Greek Interpreter – Paul Kratides
Musgrave Ritual- Richard Brunton
Priory School –Heidegger, German Master
Reigate Squires – William Kirwan, coachman
Resident Patient – Sutton alias Blessington
Retired Colourman – Double murder with 1 Male victim – Dr. Ray Ernest
Second Stain – Henri Fournaye alias Eduardo Lucas
Stock-Broker's Clerk - Guard
Veiled Lodger – Eugenia's Ronder's husband
Wisteria Lodge – Aloysius Garcia

<u>Female Victims of Murder – 5 – 16%</u>

Cardboard Box – Mary Cushing Browner
Devil's Foot – Brenda Tregennis
The Illustrious Client – Baroness Gruner
Retired Colourman – Mrs. Amberley
Speckled Band - Julia Stoner

Victims according to Male Killers or Female killers

All five female victims are killed by males, with 2 of the 5 female victims murdered as part of double murders committed by men. One female victim in *The Speckled Band* is the victim of what appears to be a serial killer, her step-father.

21 of the 26 male victims are murdered by men (81%). The 5 other male victims (19%) are murdered by females. Female killers murder only male victims – no female kills another female. Of the five male victims killed by females, 4 were killed in connection with love triangles and the other was related to blackmail, with a love triangle probably the basis for the blackmail.

The great disparity in the Canon between the number of male killers versus female killers and the disproportionate number of male victims to female victims might suggest that there is some deterrent operating linked to the Victorian idea that women are more fragile and must be protected. Indeed, Richard Brown in his blogspot article "Murder and assault crimes on the person," indicates that judicial authorities held this view and regarded any crimes of violence against women as utterly unacceptable. http://richardjohnbr.blogspot.co.uk/2011/03/murder-and-assault-crimes-against.html)

In the non-murder crimes in the 56 stories, there were plenty of women who fell victim to con-men, blackmailers and frauds, reference *Charles Augustus Milverton, The Copper Beeches, A Case of Identity, The Illustrious Client, The Disappearance of Lady Frances Carfax, The Second Stain*, and *The Solitary Cyclist*.

Today in comparison, CitizensReportUK.org [xxix] reports that in 2012 London Murders, two thirds of homicide victims or 66% now are male as opposed to the 87% of male victims in the Holmes stories. The same statistics report that female victims have increased from 13% in the Canon to 33% today. The most common method used for homicide today is a knife or sharp instrument which accounts for approximately 40% of homicides for both men and women. The second most common method today for male victims is punching or kicking. For female victims, it is strangulation. Gun and firearm murders represent 6% of victims. Female victims are most likely to be killed by someone they know (approx 78%), with around 47% of female victims being killed by a partner or ex-partner. Male victims know their assailant approximately 57% of the time, being killed by a partner or ex-partner 5% of the time.

<u>Victims of Male Killers – 26 – 84%</u>

The Abbey Grange - male
Black Peter - male
The Boscombe Valley Mystery - male
The Bruce-Partington Plans - male
The Cardboard Box – 2 – 1 female and 1 male
The Crooked Man - male
The Dancing Men - male
The Devil's Foot – 2 – 1 female and 1 male
The Dying Detective - male
The Empty House - male
The Five Orange Pips - male
The Greek Interpreter – male
The Illustrious Client - female

The Priory School - male
The Red Circle - male
The Reigate Squires - male
The Resident Patient - male
The Retired Colourman – 2 – 1 female and 1 male
The Six Napoleons – male
The Speckled Band – 1 female
The Stock Broker's Clerk - male
The Three Gables – male – Douglas Maberley
Wisteria Lodge – male – Aloysius Garcia

Victims of Female Killers – 5 – 16%

Charles Augustus Milverton – male –Blackmailer
The Golden Pince-Nez – male - Husband's assistant
The Musgrave Ritual – male - Lover
The Second Stain – male - Husband
The Veiled Lodger – male - Husband

Victims British – 23 – 74%

The Abbey Grange – male – Sir Eustace Brackenstall
Black Peter – male – Peter Carey
The Bruce-Partington Plans – male – Arthur Cadogan West
The Cardboard Box – 1 female – Mary Cushing
The Cardboard Box - 1 male – Alec Fairbairn
Charles Augustus Milverton – male –Charles Augustus Milverton
The Crooked Man – male – Colonel James Barclay
The Dancing Men – male - Hilton Cubitt
The Devil's Foot – 1 female – Brenda Tregennis
The Devil's Foot - 1 male – Mortimer Tregennis
The Dying Detective – male – Victor Savage

The Empty House – male – Hon. Ronald Adair
The Five Orange Pips – male – John Openshaw
The Golden Pince-Nez – male – Willoughby Smith
The Musgrave Ritual – male – Richard Brunton
Reigate Squires – male – William Kirwin
The Resident Patient – male – Mr. Blessington
The Retired Colourman – 1 female – Mrs. Amberley
The Retired Colourman – 1 male – Dr. Ray Ernest
The Speckled Band – 1 female – Julia Stoner
The Stock Broker's Clerk – male – unnamed armed watchman
The Three Gables – male – Douglas Maberley
The Veiled Lodger – male – Husband – Mr. Ronder

<u>Victims Non-British - 8 – 26%</u>

The Boscombe Valley Mystery – male – Charles McCarthy
The Greek Interpreter – male – Paul Katrides
The Illustrious Client – female – Baroness Gruner
The Priory School – male - Heidegger
The Red Circle – male - Giuseppe Gorgiano
The Second Stain – male – Eduardo Lucas/Henri Fournaye
The Wisteria Lodge – male – Aloysius Garcia

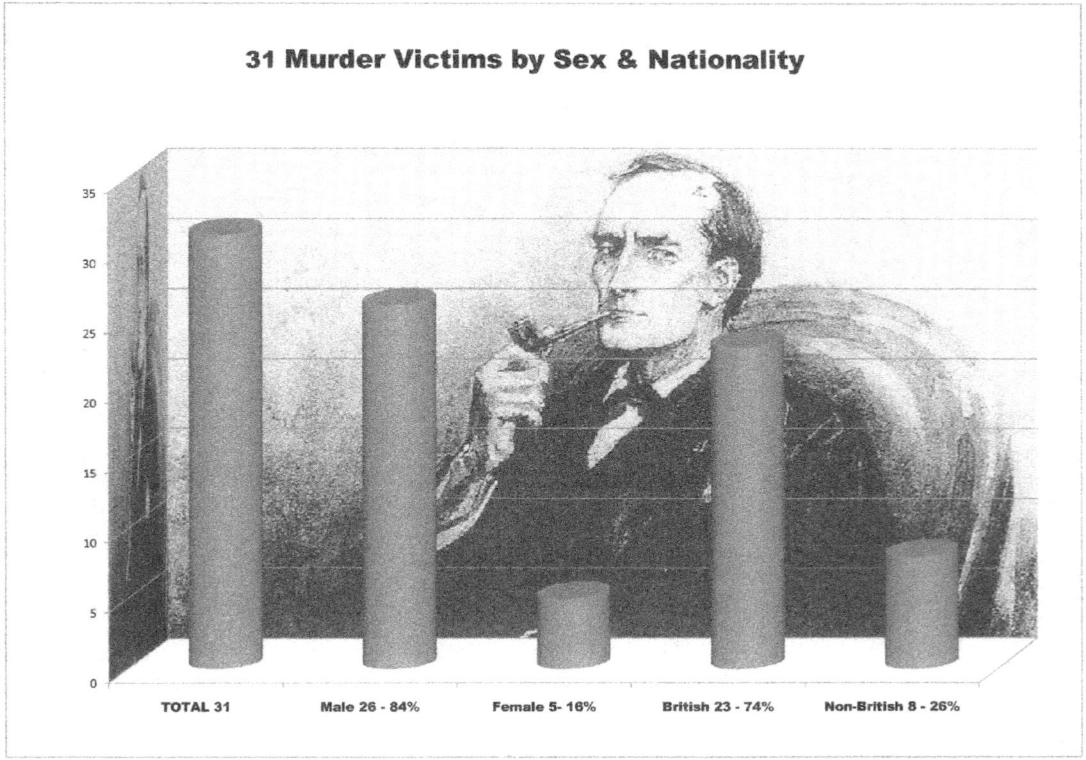
31 Murder Victims by Sex & Nationality
35
30
25
20
15
10
5
0
TOTAL 31
Male 26 - 84%
Female 5- 16%
British 23 - 74%
Non-British 8 - 26%

PROFILE OF SEX OF VICTIMS BY SEX OF KILLERS
0
5
10
15
20
25
30
35
Total Victims 31
Victims of Male Killers 26 - 84%
Victims of Female Killers 5 - 16%
Male Victims of Male Killers 21 - 81%
Female Victims of Male Killers 5 - 19%
Male Victims of Female Killers 5 - 100%
Female Victims of Female Killers 0

Chapter 13

Aliases, Disguises and Impersonations

While Sherlock Holmes is famous for his disguises, interestingly 26 - nearly a third of the 84 villains in the 56 stories - also use aliases, impersonations or disguises. There are 22 males and 4 females who adopt these ruses. Maybe Holmes' own successful use of disguise is one reason why he is able to so successfully ferret out these villains.

These many aliases, disguises and impersonations are linked directly to the strict behavior rules in the Victorian code. A man – or a woman – might be able to change his or her life by changing their name, as in *The Boscombe Valley Mystery, Gloria Scott,* and *A Scandal in Bohemia.* The subterfuges also afford part of the means by which villains commit crimes and hope to escape detection, as in *The Engineer's Thumb, A Case of Identity, Lady Frances Carfax, The Norwood Builder, The Red Headed League, The Resident Patient, The Second Stain, The Stock-Broker's Clerk, The Man with the Twisted Lip,* and *Wisteria Lodge.* By contrast, in *The Copper Beeches,* Violet Hunter, a non-villain who is one of Holmes' clients, is coerced by her employer into disguising herself by cutting her hair and wearing a blue dress. Assuming another identity has been a constant and popular theme in stories from Shakespeare's time, and Holmes comes to grips with a goodly number of clever operators in the short stories.

<u>26 Villains who use aliases/disguises – 31% of the 84 villains</u>

James Ryder/John Robinson (Blue Carbuncle) 1892
John Turner/Black Jack of Ballarat (Boscombe Valley Mystery) – 1891
Colonel Lysander Stark /Fritz (Engineer's Thumb) - 1892
Mr. Ferguson / Dr. Becher (Engineer's Thumb)
James Armitage/Trevor, Sr. (Gloria Scott) – 1893
Anna uses alias of Coram. Real name unknown. (Golden Pince-Nez) - 1904
James Windibank/Hosmer Angel (A Case of Identity) - 1891
Henry 'Holy' Peters /Dr. Schlessinger(Lady Frances Carfax) - 1911
Annie Fraser /Mrs. Schlessinger (Lady Frances Carfax)
Hatty Doran/Mrs. Francis H. Moulton (Noble Bachelor) - 1892
Jonas Oldacre/Mr. Cornelius (Norwood Builder) – 1903
Biddle - Worthington Bank gang -(Resident Patient) Count, Russian Nobleman - 1893
Hayward – Worthington Bank gang (Resident Patient) Son of Russian Nobleman
Moffat – Worthington Bank gang (Resident Patient) Russian Nobleman
Sutton alias Blessington (Resident Patient)
John Clay /Vincent Spaulding (Red-Headed League) – 1891

Duncan Ross / Wm. Morris / Archie (Red-Headed League)
Irene Adler / Slim youth in an ulster disguise (Scandal in Bohemia) - 1891
Eduardo Lucas / Henri Fournaye (Second Stain) – Blackmail – 1904
Jack Carruthers/Black Beard for disguise (Solitary Cyclist) 1903
Williamson/ex-clergyman posing as a cleric (Solitary Cyclist) 1903
Beddington /Arthur Pinner & Harry Pinner (Stock-Broker's Clerk) - 1893
Beddington /Hall Pycroft (Stock-Broker's Clerk)
James Winter/'Killer' Evans/John Garrideb/ Morecroft (Three Garridebs) - 1924
Neville St. Clair / Hugh Boone (Man with the Twisted Lip) - 1891
Mr. Henderson/ Don Murillo/ Tiger of San Pedro (Wisteria Lodge) – 1908

The 26 villains appear in 18 stories. Eleven are early published cases between 1891 and 1893; 4 are published between 1903 and 1904; and 3 are later published cases between 1908 and 1926. Characters who assume other identities is a tactic most frequently used by villains in the earlier stories.

Villains who use disguises/aliases in the 56 stories
30
25
20
15
10
5
0
Villains who use disguises/aliases 25
Female Villains 5 -20%
Male Villains 20 - 80%

Non-Villain Disguises

Sherlock Holmes often turns the tables on a villain with his own successful impersonations, frequently using this ruse as an invaluable tool in his kit bag of investigative techniques.

In the very first short story, *A Scandal in Bohemia,* Watson brags about how good Holmes is at disguise. “It was not merely that Holmes changed his costume. His expression, his manner, his very soul seemed to vary with every fresh part that he assumed. The stage lost a fine actor, even as science lost an acute reasoner, when he became a specialist in crime.” In that story, Holmes proves to us that he is indeed a master of subterfuge when he dons two effective disguises. In a neat parallel, in the same story the villainess, Irene Adler, disguise s herself as well.

There are 22 instances in which assumed identities are used by other than the villain in a story. 13 of these are when Holmes, Watson and/or Mycroft use these options, and 9 are instances in which other non-villain characters adopt them. The 22 instances occur in 21 stories, 9 of which are early published cases from 1891 to 1893; 4 are published between 1903 and 1904; and 8 are later cases published from 1908 through 1924. These deceptions by non-villains were common throughout the Canon.

Disguises adopted by Holmes, Watson and Mycroft

The Beryl Coronet (1892) - Holmes is disguised as a common loafer - an “ill-dressed vagabond”

Black Peter (1904) – Holmes’ alias is Captain Basil.

Charles Augustus Milverton (1904) – (1) Holmes and Watson don dress clothes to appear to be theatre-goers; (2) Holmes & Watson use black silk masks to burgle Milverton's house; and (3) Holmes turns himself into a plumber called Endicott to woo the housemaid Agatha.

The Dying Detective (1913) – Holmes impersonates a dying man so successfully he fools both Watson and Culverton Smith into believing that he has contracted a deadly disease.

The Disappearance of Lady Frances Carfax (1911) – Holmes is disguised as an unshaven French *ouvrier* in a blue blouse.

The Empty House (1903) – Sherlock Holmes impersonates a poor, elderly, deformed bibliophile. He also relates his experiences as an explorer and a scientist studying coal tar derivates.

The Final Problem (1893) – Holmes is disguised as a "venerable Italian priest."

Final Problem (1893) – Mycroft Holmes is disguised as a coachman for a brougham

His Last Bow (1917) – Holmes disguises himself as Altamont, a motor expert and spy from America, and Watson is in disguise as a chauffeur.

The Illustrious Client (1924) - Watson impersonates Dr. Hill Barton, 369 Half Moon Street, Chinese Porcelain expert, in order to divert Baron Gruner.

The Mazarin Stone (1921) - (1) Holmes is disguised as a workman looking for a job. (2) Holmes is disguised as an elderly lady.

A Scandal in Bohemia (1891) – (1) Holmes disguises himself as a groom to obtain information, and he witnesses Irene's wedding. (2) Holmes disguises himself as an elderly clergyman.

The Stock-Broker's Clerk (1893) - Holmes masquerades as Mr. Harris of Bermondsey, and Watson as Mr. Price of Birmingham.

The Man with the Twisted Lip (1891) – Holmes is disguised as an old opium addict who puts on a doddering, loose-lipped senility.

Disguises adopted by other non-villain characters

The Copper Beeches (1892) – Client Violet Hunter is hired to unwittingly impersonate her employer's daughter, Alice.

The Gloria Scott (1893) – Beddoes is also known as Evans, and Mr. Trevor is the new identity of John Armitage.

The Golden Pince-Nez (1904) – Anna's agent from a private detective firm was disguised as Sergius, the second secretary who left hurriedly.

The Red Circle (1911) – Mr. Leverton of Pinkerton's American Agency is disguised as a cabman.

A Scandal in Bohemia (1891) – The King of Bohemia wears a mask when he meets Sherlock Holmes, and he uses the alias of Count von Kramm.

Silver Blaze (1892) – Silver Blaze, the horse, is disguised

The Three Garridebs (1924) – Roger Prescott used the alias of Waldron

Wisteria Lodge (1908) - Miss Burnet is really Signora Victor Durando. Lucas was known as Lopez.

The Yellow Face (1893) – Lucy is disguised with a mask and long white gloves

Aliases and impersonations have become easier in the 20th century than in the Victorian era with the help of copiers, the internet, cars and the road system. Many criminals have been able to lead successful double, even triple, lives. However, as we move through the 21st century, it's becoming much more difficult because of all the video surveillance, forensic science, tracking mechanisms, and identification requirements in most day-to-day transactions. It is much harder today to lead a double life or to commit the perfect crime without leaving any trace.

Disfigured Villains

In addition to Jacky, the child villain in *The Sussex Vampire*, who is deformed due to an accident in childhood and who takes out his frustrations and hatred on his step-mother and step-brother, there are a few other deformed or scarred or otherwise abnormal villains in the stories. Although enlightened in many respects, the Victorian sense of what was proper meant that people did not display their deformities but rather were hidden away out of sight, to live in seclusion. They were sometimes considered warped and twisted and were to be pitied and ignored. Sometimes the physical deformity might be seen as an outward sign of an evil nature. Many of the characters in the Canon bear out this view.

Eugenia Ronder in *The Veiled Lodger* was mauled by a lion and shields her horribly scarred face from sight. Neville St. Clair disguises himself as a disfigured man in *The Man with the Twisted Lip.* In The *Retired Colourman,* Josiah Amberley has an artificial leg. In *Lady Frances Carfax,* Holy Peters has "a disfigured left ear which had been badly bitten in a saloon-fight." Culverton Smith in *The Dying Detective,* is described by Watson as having a deformity with a skull of "enormous capacity," but a figure that is "small and frail, twisted in the shoulders and back like one who has suffered from rickets in his childhood."

In a couple of instances, the physical disfigurement follows the villainy. In *The Illustrious Client,* villain Baron Gruner's former mistress, Kitty Winter, throws vitriol at him, badly scarring him. Mme. Fournaye in *The Second Stain,* stabs her husband to death, goes mad, and is institutionalized – not a deformity, but an abnormality. And Jephro Rucastle in *Copper Beeches* and Professor Presbury in *The Creeping Man,* are both mauled by their pet dogs and will undoubtedly suffer scars and deformities resulting from those attacks.

Other non-villains who are deformed or scarred or considered not normal are crippled Henry Wood in *The Crooked Man,* who leads the vagabond life of an outcast from all communities, reduced to performing tricks with his mongoose for money; and Godfrey Emsworth in *The Blanched Soldier,* who lives in seclusion believing he has leprosy. In *The Devil's Foot*, two of the Tregennis brothers go mad from poison and are institutionalized; and Lucy, the daughter in *The Yellow Face, is* hidden away and forced to wear a mask and long white gloves to disguise her color.

Chapter 14

One Fixed Point

"Good old Watson! You are the one fixed point in a changing age." - *His Last Bow*

Above all, Holmes and Watson are creatures of Victorian and Edwardian London. They live in it, eat, think, sleep, read, travel, work and socialize in it. And most importantly, they are detectives in it. Holmes calls Watson "the one fixed point in a changing age," in a story written in 1917 and set in 1914. Readers see that the world is on the brink of war and will change drastically, never to be the same.

In the stories, all the crimes, the criminals and the victims live in the confines of the Victorian code, and we see Holmes and Watson dealing with the many breaches of the code and applying their own brand of justice. Sometimes we've seen that justice is a dichotomy between the world of legal justice and the world of true justice as they see it to be. Through the eyes of the Canon, throughout this book, we see that Victorian society, too, was a dichotomy. The ideals of the gentlemanly class, honor, loyalty, respect for women, the perceived need of women to be protected, chivalry and honesty were frequently honored in the breach. Many adventures contain the worst sort of behavior, by both men and women, and by aristocrats, the wealthy, and every other class. Most fundamentally, Holmes and Watson feel they can mete out justice. They set themselves up as arbiters of the Victorian code - a code and a way of life and a way of thinking which, according to Holmes, Watson embodies. And even though Holmes and Watson frequently violate the code and rules of British law, they excuse themselves for these violations, fully believing they are acting in a just cause. They believe in some instances that the end justifies the means in order to achieve true justice. Whatever analytical and scientific techniques Holmes employs, he is above all a human being who sees justice through the prism of his own personal code. And he sometimes surprises us when he lets a murderer or a thief go. His personal considerations are weighty, consistent for the most part, and reflect his time. That is why virtually all the stories are set in the Victorian and Edwardian periods, even though sixteen of the 56 Sherlock Holmes stories were published between 1910 and 1927. Had the stories spilled into post WWI and the modern world, Holmes would have been pushed out of his familiar milieu with all the familiar touchstones he relies upon.

Perhaps the best way for moderns to look at the Victorian Code is to see it as a set of ideals to which Victorians aspired, and some could not or did not achieve. Indeed it is probable that the Victorian fetish for privacy and discretion was a result of the difficulty in adhering to the entire Code at all times. Keeping one's lapses private enabled everyone to ignore or excuse any lapse. If no one knew, then it never really happened. This is probably why so many people drifted into leading double lives.

The central theme throughout the Canon is justice. And this is justice as seen through the prism of

Judeo-Christian thought forming the framework of Holmes' convictions. It can be boiled down to "do unto others as you would have them do unto you." People who are not able to fulfill this ideal deserve punishment - punishment being a penalty for wrongdoing and to expiate the sin of their transgression, as well as an example to discourage other weak souls from transgressing. For those who recognize and admit their wrongdoing, the punishment is less severe than for those who do not. Simply put, those who confess their transgression and repent can be used as examples to affirm the wrongness of the deed to society in general. They also can act as a deterrent to others who might consider transgressing in future.

There is tension in Judeo-Christian thought between the Old Testament where justice is an eye for an eye, and the New Testament in which forgiveness is given after repentance and vengeance belongs to the Lord. Equally, there is a tension within the Canon. Sherlock Holmes himself is central in that tension. He lives in and is of the Victorian age, but he is always applying new inventions, new theories and his "method" - a new way of investigation that disturbs the calm surface of that world. He is in many ways the embodiment of the new man, a man whose accomplishments are more important than his lineage. And Holmes' accomplishments are such that he can and does change the world in the sphere of detection.

Holmes handles the tension successfully not only by applying his scientific principles to a case, but also by seeing the case through the perspective of his *Weltanschauung*. He takes the crime, the criminal, the victim, the motive, the circumstances, and the other characters involved who gain or suffer from the crime, and he puts them all into the cauldron of his world-view. The product of that mixture emerges as his unique brand of justice. Holmes may appear to be an individual who suppresses his emotions and is more a machine than a man, but that is not his record in the 56 stories. Upon our examination, we find that his judgments are based not only upon reason but also upon his interaction with people – both physically and emotionally. It is Sherlock Holmes' relationship with the characters and the motives that make up his strong suit. He does not make evaluations of a case in a vacuum, and he's never afraid to admit he was looking in the wrong direction before he came to the correct conclusions. Holmes becomes the operating factor who manages and tames the tensions in the Victorian code and in each of the stories. We see him reaching in and pulling Lady Hope out of the fire. We see him forgiving Eugenia Ronder for her past sins. We see him risking it all to rid the world of Moriarty. And we come to understand the considerable emotional depth as well as the ratiocination involved in the *Weltanschauung* of Sherlock Holmes.

Is Sherlock Holmes a tortured figure? His use of drugs seems to be the outward manifestation of his inward suffering. Holmes, for all his use of logic and reason, is not a Nihilist. I believe that Sherlock Holmes feels more deeply emotionally and not less deeply than other people. His drug use is the objective correlative of his inner tension and torture. He is always considering the eternal question of why are we here – to what purpose do we live. He tells Watson in *The Cardboard Box*, "What object is served by this circle of misery and violence and fear? It must tend to some end, or else our universe is ruled by chance, which is unthinkable. But what end? There is the great standing perennial problem to which human reason is as far from an answer as ever." And in *The Veiled Lodger*, Holmes says to Eugenia Ronder, "The ways of fate are indeed hard to understand. If there is not some compensation hereafter, then the world is a cruel jest." And in *The Boscombe Valley Mystery,* he says: "God help us! Why does fate play such tricks with poor, helpless worms? I never heard of such a case as this that I do not think of Baxter's words, and say, 'There, but for the grace of God, goes Sherlock Holmes.'"

The stories all present sin and justice and retribution through the eyes of a Victorian gentleman. As society totally changed and upended during Victorian times, it became steadily more wealthy, more educated and more anonymous. All these changes led to more opportunities for crime – people who were more educated could see more possibilities for crime, and people who were anonymous felt less constrained by the community to not commit crime. The strict Victorian Code was a response to this. It was an effort to create a new workable code of behavior for a changing society. Since the end of the Victorian era, the same factors – wealth, education and anonymity – have continued to change and expand, and society is still struggling to develop mechanisms to cope with these changes.

Some of the post-Victorian changes have been in the area of race relations, the sexual revolution, technology, the youth culture, and political correctness versus free speech.

Thus, the viewpoints we have and the societal touchstones we have do not correspond to those of the Victorians. This should always be kept in mind when examining any Sherlock Holmes story or any other period literature. We must judge and enjoy each story on its own merits and within the context of the audience for which it was written. To fail to do so will lose much of what the writer was trying to say. It is a tribute to the stories that they remain so popular today, and that Sherlock Holmes has outlived his time yet continues to be the most popular detective the world has ever known.

Remember, it's always 1895!

"Here dwell together still two men of note
Who never lived and so can never die:
How very near they seem, yet how remote
That age before the world went all awry.
But still the game's afoot for those with ears
Attuned to catch the distant view-halloo:
England is England yet, for all our fears—
Only those things the heart believes are true.
A yellow fog swirls past the window-pane
As night descends upon this fabled street:
A lonely hansom splashes through the rain,
The ghostly gas lamps fail at twenty feet.
Here, though the world explode, these two survive,
And it is always eighteen ninety-five."
— "221B", Vincent Starrett

Afterword

Conan Doyle's Favorite Stories

Arthur Ignatius Conan Doyle loved his Queen and country. He followed the code of honor and the rules of sportsmanship, and everything he did in life was cricket. He embodied the essence of a gentleman, as did his finest creation, Sherlock Holmes, who only broke the law when he believed such an action was justified in the code. Doyle may have wanted to be remembered for his other works, but it is Sherlock Holmes who made him famous and keeps him famous.

Here is a listing of Conan Doyle's favorite Sherlock Holmes stories from a 1927 article in The Strand Magazine when Doyle made his selection. [xxx]

How I Made My List by A. Conan Doyle

"When this competition was first mooted I went into it in a most light-hearted way, thinking that it would be the easiest thing in the world to pick out the twelve best of the Holmes stories. In practice I found that I had engaged myself in a serious task. In the first place I had to read the stories myself with some care. "Steep, steep, weary work," as the Scottish landlady remarked. I began by eliminating altogether the last twelve stories, which are scattered through the *Strand* for the last five or six years. They are about to come out in a volume form under the title *The Casebook of Sherlock Holmes,* but the public could not easily get at them. Had they been available I should have put two of them in my team - namely, 'The Lion's Mane' and 'The Illustrious Client'. The first of these is hampered by being told by Holmes himself, a method which I employed only twice, as it certainly cramps the narrative. On the other hand, the actual plot is among the very best of the whole series, and for that it deserves its place. 'The Illustrious Client', on the other hand, is not remarkable for plot, but it has a certain dramatic quality and moves adequately in lofty circles, so I should also have found a place for it.

However, these being ruled out, I am now faced with some forty odd candidates to be weighed against each other. There are certainly some few an echo of which has come to me from all parts of the world, and I think this is the final proof of merit of some sort. There is the grim story ***'The Speckled Band'.*** That I am sure will be on every list. Next to that in popular favour and in my own esteem I would place ***'The Red-Headed League'*** and ***'The Dancing Men',*** on account in each case of the originality of the plot. Then we could hardly leave out the story which deals with the only foe who ever really extended Holmes, and which deceived the public (and Watson) into the erroneous inference of his death. Also, I think the first story of all should go in, as it opened the path for the others, and it has more female interest than is usual. Finally, I think the story which essays the difficult task of explaining away the alleged death of Holmes, and which also introduces such a villain as Colonel Sebastian Moran, should also have a place. This puts ***'The Final Problem', 'A Scandal in Bohemia',*** and ***'The Empty House'*** upon our list, and we have got our first half-dozen.

But now comes the crux. There are a number of stories which really are a little hard to separate. On the whole I think I should find a place for ***'The Five Orange Pips'***, for though it is short it has a certain dramatic quality of its own. So now only five places are left. There are two stories which deal with high diplomacy and intrigue. They are both among the very best of the series. The one is 'The Naval Treaty' and the other ***'The Second Stain'.*** There is no room for both of them in the team, and on the whole I regard the latter as the better story. Therefore we will put it down for the eight place.

And now which? ***'The Devil's Foot'*** has points. It is grim and new. We will give it the ninth place. I think also that ***'The Priory School'*** is worth a place if only for the dramatic moment when Holmes points his finger at the Duke. I have only two places left. I hesitate between 'Silver Blaze', 'The Bruce-Partington Plans', 'The Crooked Man', 'The Man with the Twisted Lip', 'The Gloria Scott', 'The Greek Interpreter', 'The Reigate Squires', 'The Musgrave Ritual', and 'The Resident Patient'. On what principle am I to choose two out of those? The racing detail in 'Silver Blaze' is very faulty, so we must disqualify him. There is little to choose between the others. A small thing would turn the scale. ***'The Musgrave Ritual'*** has a historical touch which gives it a little added distinction. It also has a memory from Holmes' early life. So now we come to the very last. I might as well draw the name out of a bag, for I see no reason to put one before the other. Whatever their merit - and I make no claim for that - they are all as good as I could make them. On the whole, Holmes himself shows perhaps the most ingenuity in ***'The Reigate***

Squires', and therefore this shall be twelfth in my team.

It is proverbially a mistake for a judge to give his reasons, but I have analysed mine if only to show any competitors that I really have taken some trouble in the matter."

Doyle's Top 12 stories

1. The Adventure of the Speckled Band 1892
2. The Redheaded League 1891
3. The Adventure of the Dancing Men 1903
4. The Final Problem 1893
5. A Scandal in Bohemia 1891
6. The Adventure of the Empty House 1903
7. The Five Orange Pips 1891
8. The Adventure of the Second Stain 1904
9. The Adventure of the Devil's Foot 1910
10. The Adventure of the Priory School 1904
11. The Musgrave Ritual 1893
12. The Reigate Squires 1893

Later, considering his short stories about Sherlock Holmes written after 1927, and reconsidering some written before that date, Doyle added seven more favorites.

13. Silver Blaze 1892
14. The Adventure of the Bruce-Partington Plans 1908
15. The Crooked Man 1893
16. The Man with the Twisted Lip 1891
17. The Greek Interpreter 1893
18. The Resident Patient 1893
19. The Naval Treaty 1893

From his own list, it is clear that Doyle's overall favorites were from his early stories published from 1891 to 1893. They amount to 13 of the 19 stories (68%) he eventually listed. His middle stories were published from 1903 to 1910, and they account for the other 6 of his favorites (32%). None of his later stories is on the list, even though when he made his second selection of favorites in 1927, he could easily have included some of them. And Doyle did like a good murder -- note that 15 out of his 19 favorite stories (79%) were ones with murders as the mystery. These are the High Crimes.

Favorite Stories with Murders – 15 of 19 – 79%

The Adventure of the Speckled Band 1892
The Adventure of the Empty House 1903
The Five Orange Pips 1891
The Adventure of the Second Stain 1904
The Adventure of the Dancing Men 1903
The Final Problem 1893
The Adventure of the Devil's Foot 1910
The Adventure of the Priory School 1904
The Musgrave Ritual 1893
The Reigate Squires 1893
The Greek Interpreter 1893
Silver Blaze 1892
The Adventure of the Bruce-Partington Plans 1908
The Crooked Man 1893
The Resident Patient 1893

	CRACKING THE CODE OF THE CANON	
Stories	**Villains**	**Crimes**
The Adventure of the Abbey Grange	Captain Jack Croker	Murder
The Adventure of the Abbey Grange	Lady Brackenwell & Theresa Wright	Accomplices & Withholding evidence
The Adventure of the Beryl Coronet	Sir George Burnwell & Mary Holder	Burglary -Jewel Theft
The Adventure of Black Peter	Patrick Carins	Murder
The Adventure of the Blanched Soldier	NO CRIME	NO CRIME
The Adventure of the Blue Carbuncle	James Ryder	Jewel Theft
The Boscombe Valley Mystery	John Turner/Black Jack of Ballarat	Murder
The Adventure of the Bruce Partington	Hugo Oberstein	Murder & Treason
The Adventure of the Bruce Partington	Colonel Valentine Walter	Treason
The Adventure of the Cardboard Box	James Browner	Double Murder
The Adventure of the Cardboard Box	Miss Sarah Cushing	Accessory to Murder
The Adventure of Charles Augustus	Charles Augustus Milverton	Blackmail
The Adventure of Charles Augustus	Noblewoman unnamed	Murder
The Adventure of the Copper Beeches	Jephro Rucastle	False Imprisonmt & Fraud/Embezzlement
The Adventure of the Creeping Man	Professor Presbury	Disorderly Conduct /Endangerment
The Crooked Man	Henry Wood	Murder
The Adventure of the Dancing Men	Abe Slaney	Murder
The Adventure of the Devil's Foot	Mortimer Tregennis	Murder & Attempted Murder
The Adventure of the Devil's Foot	Dr. Leon Sterndale	Murder & Attempted Murder
The Adventure of the Dying Detective	Culverton Smith	Murder & Attempted Murder
The Adventure of the Empty House	Colonel Sebastian Moran	Murder
The Adventure of the Engineer's Thumb	Colonel Stark, Dr.Becher & Elsie	Counterfeiting & Attempted Murder
The Final Problem	Professor Moriarity	Attempted Murder
The Five Orange Pips	James Calhoun	Murder
The 'Gloria Scott'	Hudson	Blackmail
The Adventure of the Golden Pince-Nez	Anna 'Coram'	Burglary, Murder & Suicide
The Greek Interpreter	Harold Latimer & Wilson Kemp	Murder, Att. Murder & Fraud/Embezzlement
A Case of Identity	James Windibank & Mrs.Windibank	Fraud/Embezzlement
The Adventure of the Illustrious Client	Baron Adelbert Gruner	Murder & Assault
The Adventure of the Illustrious Client	Miss Kitty Winter	Vitriol Throwing
The Disappearance of Lady Frances	Holy Peters & Annie Fraser	Attempt Murder, Kidnap & Fraud/Swindle
His Last Bow	Von Bork	Espionage/Treason
The Adventure of the Lion's Mane	NO CRIME	NO CRIME
The Mazarin Stone	Count Sylvius & Sam Merton	Burglary/Jewel Theft
The Adventure of Missing Three Quarter	NO CRIME	NO CRIME

	CRACKING THE CODE OF THE CANON	
Stories	**Villains**	**Crimes**
The Musgrave Ritual	Richard Brunton	Theft
The Musgrave Ritual	Rachel Howells	Murder
The Naval Treaty	Joseph Harrison	Burglary, Attempt Murder & Espionage
The Adventure of the Noble Bachelor	Hatty Doran/Mrs. Francis H. Moulton	Bigamy
The Norwood Builder	Jonas Oldacre & Mrs. Lexington	Attempted Murder
The Adventure of the Priory School	Reuben Hayes	Murder & Kidnapping
The Adventure of the Priory School	James Wilder	Accessory to Murder & Kidnapping
The Adventure of the Priory School	Duke of Holdernesse	Condoning a felony & Aid escaping felon
The Adventure of the Red Circle	Gennaro Lucca & Giuseppe Gorgiano	Murder & Attempted Murder
The Red-Headed League	John Clay & Duncan Ross	Burglary /Bank Robbery & Assault
The Reigate Squires	Alec Cunningham & Cunningham Sr.	Murder, Attempted Murder & Burglary
The Resident Patient	Worthington Bank gang	Murder
The Adventure of the Retired Colourman	Josiah Amberley	Double Murder & Attempted Suicide
A Scandal in Bohemia	Miss Irene Adler	Blackmail
The Adventure of the Second Stain	Lady Hilda Trelawney Hope	Theft & Burglary & Treason
The Adventure of the Second Stain	Eduardo Lucas / Henri Fournaye	Blackmail
The Adventure of the Second Stain	Madame Fournaye	Murder
The Adventure of Shoscombe Old Place	Sir Robert Norbertson	Concealing a death
Silver Blaze	John Straker	Fraud
Silver Blaze	Silas Brown	Theft
The Adventure of the Six Napoleons	Beppo	Murder & Jewel Theft & Burglary
The Adventure of the Solitary Cyclist	Bob Carruthers	Fraud /Embezzlement & Attempted Murder
The Adventure of the Solitary Cyclist	Jack Woodley	Fraud/Embezzlement & Forced Marriage & Affray
The Adventure of the Solitary Cyclist	Williamson	Fraud /Embezzlement & Forced Marriage
The Adventure of the Speckled Band	Dr. Grimesby Roylott	Murder, Attempted Murder & Fraud/Embezzele
The Stock-Broker's Clerk	Beddington /Arthur & Harry Pinner	Burglary/Stock Robbery & Attempted Suicide
The Adventure of the Sussex Vampire	Jack 'Jacky' Ferguson	Attempted Murder
The Problem of Thor Bridge	Maria Pinto Gibson	Attempted Murder & Suicide
The Adventure of the Three Gables	Isadora Klein	Burglary & Accessory to Murder
The Adventure of the Three Gables	Spencer John gang –Stockdales & Dixie	Burglary & Murder
The Adventure of the Three Garridebs	James Winter/Evans/John Garrideb/ Morecroft	Fraud & Counterfeiting & Attempted Murder
The Adventure of the Three Students	Gilchrist	Burglary
The Man with the Twisted Lip	Neville St. Clair / Hugh Boone	Begging
The Adventure of the Veiled Lodger	Mrs. Eugenia Ronder	Murder
The Adventure of Wisteria Lodge	Don Juan Murillo/Tiger of San Pedro	Murder & Kidnapping
The Yellow Face	NO CRIME	NO CRIME

			CATEGORIES						
Stories	**1**	**2**	**3**	**4**	**5**	**Book**	**Year**	**Words**	**Abbrev**
The Adventure of the Abbey Grange			X	X	X	R	1904	9,233	ABBE
The Adventure of the Beryl Coronet			X			A	1892	9,783	BERY
The Adventure of Black Peter		X				R	1904	8,181	BLAC
The Adventure of the Blanched Soldier	X					C	1926	7,755	BLAN
The Adventure of the Blue Carbuncle			X	X		A	1892	7,879	BLUE
The Boscombe Valley Mystery			X	X		A	1891	9,681	BOSC
The Adventure of the Bruce Partington Plans		X		X		L	1908	10,761	BRUC
The Adventure of the Cardboard Box		X	X			L	1893	8,730	CARD
The Adventure of Charles Augustus Milverton			X	X		R	1904	6,775	CHAS
The Adventure of the Copper Beeches			X	X		A	1892	9,948	COPP
The Adventure of the Creeping Man			X		X	C	1923	7,726	CREE
The Crooked Man			X			M	1893	7,183	CROO
The Adventure of the Dancing Men		X			X	R	1903	9,686	DANC
The Adventure of the Devil's Foot			X	X		L	1911	7,740	DEVI
The Adventure of the Dying Detective		X				L	1913	5,823	DYIN
The Adventure of the Empty House		X				R	1903	8,761	EMPT
The Adventure of the Engineer's Thumb			X			A	1892	8,342	ENGR
The Final Problem			X	X		M	1893	7,203	FINA
The Five Orange Pips			X		X	A	1891	7,378	FIVE
The 'Gloria Scott'			X			M	1893	7,892	GLOR
The Adventure of the Golden Pince-Nez			X			R	1904	8,989	GOLD
The Greek Interpreter			X			M	1893	7,058	GREE
A Case of Identity			X			A	1891	7,030	IDRN
The Adventure of the Illustrious Client		X	X	X		C	1924	9,834	ILLU
The Disappearance of Lady Frances Carfax		X	X	X	X	L	1910	10,055	LADY
His Last Bow		X		X		L	1917	6,126	LAST
The Adventure of the Lion's Mane	X					C	1926	7,234	LION
The Mazarin Stone		X				C	1921	5,716	MAZA
The Adventure of the Missing Three Quarter	X					R	1904	8,076	MISS

	CATEGORIES								
Stories	**1**	**2**	**3**	**4**	**5**	**Book**	**Year**	**Words**	**Abbrev**
The Musgrave Ritual			X			M	1893	7,632	MUSG
The Naval Treaty			X	X		M	1893	12,701	NAVA
The Adventure of the Noble Bachelor			X	X		A	1892	8,157	NOBL
The Norwood Builder		X		X		R	1903	9,286	NORW
The Adventure of the Priory School		X	X			R	1904	11,507	PRIO
The Adventure of the Red Circle		X	X			L	1911		REDC
The Red-Headed League		X				A	1891	8,189	REDH
The Reigate Squires		X				M	1893	7,186	REIG
The Resident Patient			X			M	1893	7,355	RESI
The Adventure of the Retired Colourman		X		X		C	1926	5,559	RETI
A Scandal in Bohemia			X	X	X	A	1891	8,599	SCAN
The Adventure of the Second Stain			X	X		R	1904	9,737	SECO
The Adventure of Shoscombe Old Place		X				C	1927	6,301	SHOS
Silver Blaze			X	X	X	M	1892	9,650	SILV
The Adventure of the Six Napoleons		X	X			R	1904	8,392	SIXN
The Adventure of the Solitary Cyclist		X		X		R	1903	7,908	SOLI
The Adventure of the Speckled Band			X			A	1892	9,880	SPEC
The Stock-Broker's Clerk		X				M	1893	6,832	STOC
The Adventure of the Sussex Vampire			X			C	1924	5,999	SUSS
The Problem of Thor Bridge			X			C	1922	9,666	THOR
The Adventure of the Three Gables		X	X	X	X	C	1926	6,090	3GAB
The Adventure of the Three Garridebs		X				C	1924	6,231	3GAR
The Adventure of the Three Students			X			R	1904	6,508	3STU
The Man with the Twisted Lip			X		X	A	1891	9,271	TWIS
The Adventure of the Veiled Lodger			X	X		C	1927	4,499	VEIL
The Adventure of Wisteria Lodge			X			L	1908	11,591	WIST
The Yellow Face	X			X	X	M	1893	7,540	YELL
	A - ADVENTURES 1891-1892								
	M - MEMORIES 1892-1893								
	R - RETURN - 1903-1904								
	L - LAST 1908-1917 (except Cardboard Box - 1893)								
	C - CASEBOOK 1921-1927								

Stories Alpha by Title with Page Numbers (1)

Stories Alpha by Title with Page Numbers (2)

Also from Diane Gilbert Madsen

The Literati Mysteries with DD McGil

Cadger's Curse, Hunting For Hemingway,
and

The Conan Doyle Notes (The Hunt For Jack The Ripper)

"Holmesians have long speculated on the fact that the Ripper murders aren't mentioned in the canon, though the obvious reason is undoubtedly the correct one: even if Conan Doyle had suspected the killer's identity he'd never have considered mentioning it in the context of a fictional entertainment. Ms Madsen's novel equates his silence with that of the dog in the night-time, assuming that Conan Doyle did know who the Ripper was but chose not to say – which, of course, implies that good old stand-by, the government cover-up. It seems unlikely to me that the Ripper was anyone famous or distinguished, but fiction is not fact, and "The Conan Doyle Notes" is a gripping tale, with an intelligent, courageous and very likable protagonist in DD McGil."

The Sherlock Holmes Society of London

Also from MX Publishing

MX Publishing is the world's largest specialist Sherlock Holmes publisher, with over a hundred titles and fifty authors creating the latest in Sherlock Holmes fiction and non-fiction.

From traditional short stories and novels to travel guides and quiz books, MX Publishing caters for all Holmes fans.

The collection includes leading titles such as Benedict Cumberbatch In Transition and The Norwood Author which won the 2011 Howlett Award (Sherlock Holmes Book of the Year).

MX Publishing also has one of the largest communities of Holmes fans on Facebook with regular contributions from dozens of authors.

www.mxpublishing.com

Also from MX Publishing

Three biographies of Sir Arthur Conan Doyle, from award winning author Alistair Duncan.

The Norwood Author

An Entirely New Country

No Better Place

The Norwood author won The Howlett Award (Sherlock Holmes Book of the Year) in 2011.

Also from MX Publishing

Sherlock Holmes and The Adventure of The Grinning Cat

"Joseph Svec, III is brilliant in entwining two endearing and enduring classics of literature, blending the factual with the fantastical; the playful with the pensive; and the mischievous with the mysterious. We shall, all of us young and old, benefit with a cup of tea, a tranquil afternoon, and a copy of Sherlock Holmes, The Adventure of the Grinning Cat."

Linda Hein, Hein & Co Used Books, and founding officer of the Amador County Holmes Hounds Sherlockian Society

NOTES

Chapter 1

[i] "The Adventure of the Three Garridebs"
[ii] "The Red-Headed League"
[iii] "A Scandal in Bohemia"
[iv] "The Sign of the Four"
[v] "The Adventure of the Mazarin Stone"
[vi] "A Scandal in Bohemia"
[vii] "A Scandal in Bohemia"
[viii] "A Study in Scarlet"

Chapter 3

[ix] McKay, Brett & Kate. "Manly Honor: Part III — The Victorian Era and the Development of the Stoic-Christian Code of Honor." (Essay) http://www.artofmanliness.com/2012/11/06/honor-during-victorian-era/
[x] Ibid.
[xi] "The Second Stain"

Chapter 6

[xii] Conley, Carolyn A. "The Unwritten Law: Criminal Justice in Victorian Kent," 1991, Oxford Univ Press, N.Y, p 68

Chapter 7

[xiii] Camp, Anthony. 'The English church courts and their records.' Family Tree Magazine, vol. 15, no. 9 (July 1999). http://www.family-tree.co.uk)

Chapter 8

[xiv] "Compounding a felony was itself a crime – a misdemeanor - at this time. It amounted to reaching an agreement to let a felon go free in exchange for the return of the goods or some other reward. Thus Holmes is not strictly accurate to describe this as compounding a felony, since he does not "compound with" – i.e. reach an agreement with, the thief, because he already has the jewel in his possession." - Simon Hetherington, Publisher of *Halsbury's Laws of England* 2002–

13, Member of the Sherlock Holmes Society of London, in correspondence with the author Diane Gilbert Madsen dated May 6th 2015.

xv Ibid.

xvi "Perverting the course of justice is usually used in the context of active judicial process, not the detection of crime." Ibid.

xvii "Although the term "accessory" is a familiar term, and not actually inaccurate, the actual terms for being a secondary party to a crime were "aiding, abetting, counselling or procuring." Being an "accomplice" is not a separate English legal term, and not a crime per se. "Aiding and abetting" is a better term, and better expresses the idea of allowing or encouraging the criminals to go free or make their escape. Ibid.

xviii Many crimes of the late 19th and early 20th centuries were common law crimes, created and defined over a long time by the courts. Many, but not all, have since been codified in statute. This makes their development harder to trace. Perhaps surprisingly, murder is a crime at common law, not against statute. The penalty for it, and certain defences to it, are set by statute, but the crime itself is a common law crime, and its definition is a classic of the common law, including the phrase "malice aforethought", which has been the subject of judicial interpretation for hundreds of years." Ibid

xix Ibid.

xx "There is a difference between a defence and an excuse –in that a defence would remove the criminality from an act that would otherwise be a crime. For example, a man who kills in self-defence is not a murderer who has a justification; he has not committed a crime at all. Similarly, an act which at that moment was justified for the protection of life or property would have afforded Holmes a defence in many cases. So threatening Holy Peters with a gun – which would be threatening behaviour in other circumstances – is not a crime because Holmes is acting for the protection of Lady Frances Carfax's life." Ibid.

[xxi] "The correct description of the offence was (and still is) Administering a stupefying or overpowering drug, committed by anyone who: 'shall unlawfully apply or administer to or cause to be taken by, or attempt to apply or administer to or attempt to cause to be administered to or taken by, any person, any chloroform, laudanum, or other stupefying or overpowering drug , matter, or thing, with intent in any of such cases thereby to enable himself or any other person to commit, or with intent in any of such cases thereby to assist any other person in committing, any indictable offence….'" Ibid.

[xxii] "Compounding a felony: Here there is an element of agreement – albeit that Harrison has little choice in the matter – and something is recovered as a result." Ibid.

[xxiii] Ibid

[xxiv] Ibid

[xxv] Ibid

[xxvi] Ibid

[xxvii] *The Case and the Canon: Anomalies, Discontinuities, Metaphors Between Science & Literature*, ed. Alessandra Calanchi et al 2011, Vandenhoeck & Ruprecht pages 125-6.

[xxviii] Conley, Carolyn A. *The Unwritten Law.* Oxford U Press, 1991, p. 62.

Chapter 12

[xxix] http://www.citizensreportuk.org/news/2012/01/12/british-murders-2012-victims-of-murder-homicides-and-fatal-violence-mapped/

Afterword

[xxix] Taken from http://www.sherlock-holmes.co.uk/library/doyle.html

www.ingramcontent.com/pod-product-compliance
Lightning Source LLC
Chambersburg PA
CBHW070307040726
47501CB00018B/367
* 9 7 8 1 7 8 0 9 2 9 7 1 2 *